INCARNATE

BOOK ONE OF THE INCARNATE ACCOUNTS

JUSTIN SCHUELKE

COPYRIGHT

For James.

You are always there for me, encouraging me to make my dreams come true.
Thanks for sharing them with me.

I love you.

PROLOGUE

*D*ying is the worst. Unfortunately, that's pretty much how my day started out. And ended, of course.

To add insult to injury, I was in the middle of nowhere. The Empty Quarter, it was called: a desert extending for hundreds of miles in Saudi Arabia. I leaned against a rock and dropped my pack, digging out my canteen and taking a quick swig. I checked my watch: ten a.m. How was it so damn hot at ten a.m.?

Keep moving, Emery, I told myself. I needed to push forward, to outrun the guilt. To stay ahead of the accusing eyes and the mocking laughter that pursued me whenever I stopped to think too long.

Baked and barren earth crisscrossed with the occasional swish of sand stretched out in all directions, broken only by these sandstone formations jutting out like nightmarish, jagged teeth. I had started early to avoid being caught in the harshest heat, but the sun had risen a few hours ago. Gentle warmth had quickly intensified, becoming an ever-present weight pressing against my veiled face and lightweight clothes. Sweat and sunblock dampened my face and occasionally stung my eyes. I was a *literal* hot mess.

None of this was right, either. I was hunting the Yeti—that's right, not *a* yeti, *the* Yeti. Don't worry, I'll explain later. Suffice it to say I was hunting "yeti." It had been causing a bit of a commotion in Saudi Arabia lately, leaving three locals dead. It had to be stopped. And when a mythical creature begins to hurt or kill people, I'm called in. I'm like 007—if James Bond exclusively hunted down dangerous mythical creatures that were only real because people spread the myth around in the first place.

Maybe I'm not like 007 at all. I'm more badass.

You might be wondering what the Yeti was doing in the desert. If so, you are way ahead of the curve. I was asking myself the same thing. The Yeti's domain should have been in the Himalayas. Icy, cold, snowy—basically the exact opposite of this desert. So what the hell happened?

That's what I was investigating.

With a sigh, I hefted my pack over my shoulder and left the dubious shade of the sandstone pillar to wilt beneath the sun in the open expanse of the desert. My limbs felt heavy despite my light attire, as if my sweat were anchoring me to the ground. A breeze should be the perfect respite to a hot, sunny day, but the "breezes" here were worse than the dead heat: they blew in like the breath of the Dragon, flurrying up bits of sand that stung my eyes, even with the cloth protecting my face. I raised my hand to shield myself against a sudden billow of sand and grit.

The flurry was just as it should be, if I were on the Yeti's home turf. Well, that wasn't quite right, since the flurry should be snow, but otherwise it matched perfectly. Which meant if I looked down...

There it was. Perfectly imprinted in the cracked brown earth like it was cut from a cookie mold: a giant footprint. Massive, really. Tipped with claw indentations, it looked like the track of a human-bear hybrid, but bigger.

I was close. Just to make sure, I fished my phone out of my pocket and snapped a quick pic. Looking at the result, I nodded, satisfied. The image was distorted, the camera refusing to focus on the footprint. I covered my face as another gust whipped sand up all around me. Sure enough, when I examined the ground again, the print had all but vanished. Typical of the Yeti.

Now the hard part. I secured thick goggles over my eyes and reknotted the cloth snug against my face, enveloping my nose and mouth. I oriented myself in a direction perpendicular to the print and started walking. I tried to pay attention to everything at once; the Yeti should be nearby. The frustrating thing about hunting a Predator incarnate outside of its Territory is the unknown. They're stronger in their Territory, of course, but at least they're consistent.

Seriously. Yeti in the desert—what was *with* that?

The sand kicked up again, and I plunged forward without hesitation, my heart pounding with anticipation and danger. I lived for this: monsters and the hunt. It kept me from thinking about the dead eyes that haunted my quiet moments. My failure.

Maybe next time I would be young, able to forget. Until then, I would keep fighting monsters. Try to balance the scales with some good deeds. And if I died on a hunt, that was just another way of escaping.

The wind and sand flicked against my clothes and face, but I could only feel their pressure against my protection. I resisted the urge to turn away from the fiercest gales, instead steeling myself and pushing into them. The last time I hunted the Yeti flashed through my mind, the parallels surreal. Unyielding, freezing winds instead of unrelenting heat. Snow flurries versus sand. Frozen and baked footprints. A silhouette in the freezing blizzard abruptly towering over me, a shadow suddenly looming over me in the sandstorm—

Oh shit.

I flung myself backward, a heavy paw swiping through the air where my head was a moment before. I landed hard—the ground was more packed earth than sand, despite the bits billowing around me—and rolled, throwing my bag down against the ground and ripping my dart gun free from its holster at my calf. That paw had easily been twice the size of my head, and the muscles behind it were... well, let's just say that swipe could have crushed a car. My skull would have caved as easily as squishing a pea between your fingers.

The howling of the wind and sand seemed to amplify, and I realized the Yeti was roaring its rage at me. Without thinking, I raised the gun and fired at the creature's menacing silhouette. It loomed before me, filling most of my vision. I could hardly...

Miss.

The thing about tranquilizer darts is that they're propelled by compressed gas. They're essentially fired from a modern-day blowgun; any sort of crosswind and the dart might as well be a badminton shuttlecock in a tornado. And there was plenty of crosswind in that sandstorm.

You also might be wondering why I'd be using a *tranquilizer gun* against something the size of the Yeti. After all, unlike on TV shows, in real life it can take the better part of an hour for a tranq to take full effect. Hold that thought.

I was still scrambling to my feet when the Yeti's next strike hammered down. It only winged me, but it still carried enough force to slam me into the ground and drive the breath from my lungs. I expertly rolled (flopped) onto my back and scooted backward, trying to create some space between me and the homicidal beast. I dragged in huge lungfuls of air, the cloth covering my face sucking into my mouth with each gasp.

The Yeti bellowed again, and between the whips of sand I fully saw it for the first time. Its shaggy white fur was matted a brownish-tan from who-knows-how-much desert dirt. Beady red eyes glowed like embers above a wolfish muzzle that was out of place in otherwise gorilla-like features. And it. Was. Huge. It stood 14 feet tall, its head between twice and three times the size of a human's, so the collar around its neck must be the size of a normal human belt.

Wait. Collar? Everything seemed to slow as I took in some other odd details: the fresh welts across its face, the harness it wore with— was that a bandolier? The runny, muddied brown striations in its fur, like the brown coloring was melting. Was it dye? Even if the purpose was to dye the Yeti's fur tan for camouflage in the desert, that was something far too sophisticated for the Yeti to do alone. Something was seriously amiss.

I didn't have time to dwell, though. As the Yeti came for me once again, I ignored the burning in my side and scrambled to my feet, fumbling to load another dart—but I was never going to make it. The Yeti was on me in an instant, heavy paws pulling and shredding at my clothes. I released a shout—it was *not* a scream—and slammed the butt of the handgun into the Yeti's muzzle, briefly stunning it. I tore out of its grasp, cloth and a little skin ripping as I escaped its sharp claws.

I had a moment's respite. Enough time for the sand and sweat to sting my fresh wounds, for my lungs to remind me they were burning. But not nearly enough time to load a dart gun.

Screw this.

I flung myself yet again... but this time, I did so *at* the Yeti. Teeth gritted, jaw clenched, eyes squinted. I hurled the empty dart gun at its face, then I launched myself forward as the Yeti flinched from the ineffective missile. I followed the thrown weapon, covering the distance between the Yeti and me in one leap, and plunged the tranquilizer dart I'd been gripping in my left hand into the creature's shoulder. The effect was instantaneous. Every impressive muscle beneath me went taut before spasming, and then the Yeti toppled.

I fell on top of it, riding it down to the ground. I'd say "wrestled it down to the ground," but I was too exhausted to do much more than cling on as it collapsed. The Yeti looked up at me with eyes softened by the tranquilizer, and I glimpsed an almost human expression on its face.

"Easy, big guy," I said, my voice too dry to achieve the soothing tone I was going for. But the Yeti seemed to relax, its body shuddering under me as it succumbed to death. Yes, that's right, death by tranquilizer—or, more accurately, by capture. Don't worry, I'll explain fatal flaws later. As with most incarnate things, there's a lot to learn. "It's almost over." I said it quietly, but the howling sandstorm had all but ceased, so it came out louder than I expected. "You'll be home before you know it."

"Funny," a muffled voice said behind me, as I felt something hard and metallic against the back of my head. "I was just about to say the same thing to you, Emery Luple."

There was the sharp report of a gunshot, and then, like the Yeti, I unceremoniously died.

PART I

Loophole

1

*My name is Emery Luple, and I am an incarnate. I am the protagonist of
this story. The worst part about being an incarnate is the death. Multiple
deaths. I've had quite a few of them, at this point. Sometimes when myths
and legends come to life, it falls to me to take care of them. So who am I?
What am I? Let's see if you can figure it out for yourself.*

This is my story.

◠

Two years, eight months, three weeks, and six days later...

I was lying on something comfortable, and as I sat up, I
realized it was a couch. A cozy one, worn and invitingly
familiar. I had never seen this couch before, of course, but at the

same time, the memory of Mom giving it to me when I moved to college was crisp in my mind. It was unsettling to remember something that didn't happen, but it was entirely expected—and in a way, it felt like it *did* happen, with the memory so sharp.

As my senses awakened, information flooded in. A torrent of memories, too fast, too much to parse through. Family, self-awareness, friends, my social circle, height, emotions, preferences, physical shapes—*stop*. Compartmentalize. Focus on one thing at a time.

Who was I this time? My physical attributes tended to change more than my mental and emotional ones, but there were always changes. I usually felt somewhat genderless at first, which happens when you've spent lifetimes in different bodies. Hell, it can happen when you haven't. That feeling usually diminished as my new sense of self manifested, but not always. Was I young or mature? Did I have all of my hair? Was I fit, nerdy, both? I felt tall, but not the tallest I'd ever been.

A mirror. I needed a mirror.

My feet carried me through the small apartment—no, it was an office—with familiarity, my body and mind comfortable with this place even though I'd never been here before. That happens. Every reincarnation.

As I passed knickknacks and décor, my mind automatically adjusted, filling me in: I bought that vase over there to spruce up the place; that refrigerator was here when I moved in, and I was surprised it was still working; that desk I found online for practically nothing; that comb on the bathroom sink—*yes!* I had hair!—was from a drugstore two blocks away. My reincarnation always provided me with a backstory, and for some reason, it was never the same one. It was certainly convenient: waking up as a brand-new person in an unfamiliar place, it was nice to have an established life. And I definitely wouldn't want to reincarnate as a newborn. The amount of time I'd lost already stung; can you imagine if I lost several more years just growing up or going through puberty again? I could hardly hunt down the Vampire incarnate as a toddler.

But this new life that overlaid mine was problematic, too. It felt oddly hollow. After all, I didn't truly know anyone in my life. That knowledge haunted me, sometimes, when I felt especially lonely or vulnerable. But the illusion was a complete one: not only did I have memories of friends and family I'd never met, I had feelings for them, too. For example, Mom lived a half hour away and supported my blog channel even though she secretly hoped I would finish college. My best friend, Rachelle, graduated high school with me last year and helped me run my business— and did not put up with any of my attitude. I was faintly annoyed with my cousin for some reason that was totally my fault. Dammit, and I liked Nicole, too; I'd have to make it up to her. Even though that immortal corner of my mind reminded me that *I* had not wronged her.

You see? Being an incarnate is complicated. Reincarnation is probably the most convoluted part: a new body, a fresh identity, fabricated memories, a few new personality quirks, and a hell of a lot of baggage from prior lives... *if* I remembered it all. I'll get to that in a moment. I'd done it enough, though, to have an idea of how to navigate it. And it always started with a mirror. With a deep breath, bracing myself, I examined my reflection.

Dark hair, all legs, and an oh-so-familiar grin. There was a slight cockiness to it that... well, I didn't hate it. Below that, a smooth, masculine jawline underlined a rather small nose—and small ears, I realized, even sticking out as they were from my short haircut. I ran my hand over my head, feeling the close-shaven stubble and then the thick hair on top. My hand came away with the residue of some gel that kept my style swept up and forward. I was White, at least in part, with some Latino thrown in. My skin was smooth and nearly hairless, and a sudden memory of a summer spent on the beach with my family informed me I tended not to burn. A nice contrast to my desert-hating former life.

A summer spent on the beach? Was I finally wealthy? My very affordable clothing—jeans and a tee, nothing exciting, though I did appreciate how the shirt showed off my shoulders and toned arms— and the worn couch I woke up on quickly quashed my excitement.

Nope, I would need to start from scratch, financially. But that was nothing new.

Then it hit me: Emery Luple was a nineteen-year-old guy.

I was pleased. But I knew I would have been happy no matter what. After so many incarnations and countless lives as all genders and ethnicities, I had found I was equally capable regardless of the body I was in. And that notion transcended gender and race, too; I'd spent lifetimes facing physical, mental, and societal challenges... but for the most part it was the way I was treated by others that changed, that obstructed my abilities, and I could navigate around that. I'd been doing it a long time. Don't get me wrong, it was never easy. But over the course of decades, it was becoming easier. The march of progress seemed, more often than not, to follow the idea of "two steps forward, one step back." At least I could convince myself it was a net gain—most days.

Of course, there was more to gender than the physical body. My identity did not wholly change upon reincarnation, but aspects of it did. Usually my sense of identity and my new physical form matched, but every once in a while, they didn't. That made sense to me; I was no different from anyone else in that regard. When that happened, I made whatever changes I could to reconcile the two. In the end, I just wanted to feel like *me,* even if my sense of "me" changed from time to time. Even mortals could relate to that.

I was fairly young. This was good and bad. I'd be able to push my body further, recover faster, and eat more junk food. I'd have a harder time being taken seriously by people older than me, and I'd have to prove my maturity. Which might be difficult if I didn't stow that cocky grin. I pulled a few faces in the mirror, trying to see which expressions rang true and which looked forced. Ooh, I had great puppy-dog eyes and a scathing look of disappointment. Nice. My smile always seemed to have that slight smugness to it, though. I'd need to work on it. In my experience, people did not respond well to a self-satisfied teen. Confident, yes. Arrogant, not so much.

As I watched myself in the mirror, words suddenly bubbled out of me. "Hello, you beamish boy." Whoa, was that my voice? It was deeper than I thought it would be. "Don't just stand there in uffish thought. Get a move on!" I said the words with a strange compulsion, as though someone were telling me what to say rather than me just saying it. It felt natural, but was there anything natural about calling yourself a "beamish boy"? I shrugged, feeling silly. I *had* been wondering what my voice sounded like, and hearing myself speak had a sudden effect on me, reminding me that I was *alive* again.

Oh, right. The other problem with being young: reincarnation played havoc with my ability to recall my past lives' experiences. I use that word instead of "memories" because I didn't have amnesia, exactly. If someone brought up an event from my past—my real past, I mean; not the backstory from this new life—I could usually remember it. But the younger I was in a new life, the fewer experiences I remembered on my own. I always associated it with the concept of "with age comes wisdom," which isn't entirely fair: I've known plenty of wise youths and a handful of foolish elders. Still, the older I was when I reincarnated, the easier it was to immediately access my experiences. At nineteen, I would need to earn many of my experiences again. The loss was not as world-shattering as you might expect—removing some of those experiences helped me to adjust to my new life more easily, to throw myself into *this* Emery without the burden of a different life, another past.

I'd dwelled long enough. With a last lingering look at my new reflection, I left the mirror.

"Emery?" a voice called from the front office. I paused. That sounded like Rachelle.

"I'm in the back," I hollered. Good timbre, this voice. Bet I could sing.

She came around the corner, toting a large box that clanked as she walked. I reached out and plucked it from her, holding it easily. Damn. Rachelle wasn't weak, so I must be *buff*. How awesome was that?

"What's with the smirk?"

"Nothing," I replied quickly, dropping my grin. "What are these for?"

The look of exasperation she sent my way was familiar and friendly. She was a tiny girl, no more than 5'2"—but do not *ever* call her petite. She will hit you. Hard. Long hair highlighted varying shades of brown and tucked behind her ears framed eyes that usually sparkled with humor but could turn flat and annoyed in a flash. She was about my age, which made sense; we'd been good friends through high school. And, just to be clear: yes, this was *technically* my first time meeting her.

"Congratulations, Emery!" She gave me a hug that became awkward with the bulky box, but it still felt good. She had an effortless cheer to her that made me want to smile and be excited for no reason at all. Wait... congratulations? I searched my memories, and it jumped out at me. As of midnight last night, my website and corresponding ad campaign had gone live.

"Now that you're customer facing, you should really brighten up the place," she was saying. "I was going to get you flowers, but I was worried they wouldn't set the right tone." She eyed my outfit critically, but she didn't say anything about it. I got the feeling she thought it didn't quite fit the tone, either.

I grinned, letting the memories of this incarnation flow into me. "You just thought I wouldn't be able to keep them alive."

"Which is also why I didn't get you a goldfish. Have you seen the website yet?" she asked. When I didn't respond quickly enough, she rolled her eyes. "Come on. We'll look at it together."

We made our way to the front office. The building consisted of three rooms, all packed together like the segments of an ant. The back was functionally my apartment, with the couch where I'd woken up. That part wasn't completely furnished yet—just my luck, I reincarnated *before* moving all my things from Mom's house. Still, a small corner of my mind thrilled: I had a mom this time around! I was an orphan in a shocking number of incarnations.

The middle room was set up for filming, my equipment stacked in one corner: an expensive camera, a boom microphone, heavy curtains to separate the filming area from the rest of the room, and a very nice monitor. I was impressed. I didn't usually reincarnate with so much technology at my fingertips. The only other feature in the room was a half bathroom cut into the opposite corner. Not even a shower, so I wondered how I was planning on living here full time.

The front room was the office proper. It had the wooden desk I'd procured online, hardwood floors, and a single fake plant in one of the curtain-less windows. Rachelle was right; I would certainly need to spruce the office space up. I noticed a tall pot of flowers on the desk's corner, and I didn't remember receiving them. I frowned and gestured to them. "I thought you said no flowers."

"I did," Rachelle answered, leaning forward and examining the tag. "Aw, Emery, they're from your mom. She has *way* more faith in you than I do."

I popped open my silver laptop. There were two chairs on the business side of the desk and a computer chair behind it. I walked around the desk and took one of the two chairs on that side, spinning the laptop to face me. Rachelle took the other chair and then began fussing with the vase I'd seen, turning it this way and that until she was satisfied.

"*There's Always a Loophole: Finding the 'Normal' in Paranormal,*" I read aloud. The website was flashy, with moving font for the title and an old-timey feel to the black-and-white photos that slowly revolved on the page. As I watched the animation, more artificial memories bubbled to life in my mind, filling in the gaps. "I'm some sort of ghost hunter?" I asked in disbelief.

Rachelle scrunched up her nose. "What? Very funny." She searched my face for a moment, clearly expecting me to say something more. "Do you not like it?" She suddenly seemed worried.

I recovered quickly. "No, sorry, just thought there would be more color."

She sniffed and went back to adjusting the vase. "Oh sure, *now* you want color. After you finally convinced me black-and-white would appeal to your viewers."

"*Our* viewers," I corrected, knowing it would make her happy and smooth over my blunder. Sure enough, I saw her pleased smile even as she turned to hide it from me. I scrolled down on the website and clicked on the "About Me" link.

My name is Emery "Loophole" Luple, and I am a born skeptic. All my life I've been solving the unsolved, searching for truths behind myths, and even tackling the dangerously cliched and overindulged world of the super-natural. I've been making video blogs for almost three years to debunk the mysteries of the world (please follow me on my channel, There's Always a Loophole) *right before your very eyes. With over a hundred videos, I've yet to be stumped, and I'm challenging you to help me find all of the mysteries of Earth. I'm hoping the next big adventure is one all of you will go on with me!*

Huh.

I had to admit, it was a pretty clever and convenient way for me to track incarnates. Actually, damn. It let me capitalize on, even *monetize* tracking incarnates. And while it lacked a certain... subtlety... was that going to upset me?

My phone buzzed on the table. Rachelle snatched it before I could and, holding it out of reach, said matter-of-factly, "It sounds more official when you have an assistant." She answered the phone. "Hello, you've reached the office of Emery Luple; how may I help you?"

I snorted, but I could feel myself smiling. I looked back at the laptop while she talked with the caller. News articles competed for my attention like a rotating billboard: one about an impending economic downturn, another about the rising price of oil, one about a decapitation in New York, and a local story about a shooting in Seattle. All typical doom-and-gloom articles. Although decapitations were rare in the 21st century.

"All right, Caden, I have your information, and I will be sure Emery gets in contact with you as soon as possible. Thanks for call-ing, and remember: 'There's always a Loophole!'" Rachelle quoted my oh-my-god-it's-so-cheesy signature video sign-off. Still, I felt a surge of pride. She handed me one of my own business cards, where she'd written the caller's information. Caden Malek.

"Thanks."

The front door opened before I could say anything else, and an uncomfortable-looking man stepped in. For a moment, he just stared around the room and at us as if unsure how to proceed. He had Middle Eastern features, which jolted my mind back to my death in the desert, but I brushed that aside. He was middle-aged, with a black goatee that matched his black hair and eyes. His hair was bound back into a tail, revealing pierced ears: the right with a dangling earring and the left with studs. He wore an odd turtleneck, white and loose-fitting, tucked into black slacks adorned with a weighty copper belt buckle. Boat shoes completed his ensemble.

The silence stretched as we looked him over and he awkwardly returned our scrutiny. His eyes kept roving back and forth between us, as if seeking something he wasn't able to find. "Hello there!" Rachelle to the rescue. "How can we help you?"

He plastered on a smile and walked forward, and I realized he was younger than I'd first guessed. Maybe early thirties. "I seek Emery Luple," he said in a lightly accented voice.

Rachelle and I looked at each other, and then I raised my hand in a weak half wave. "I'm Emery," I said.

Although his smile didn't alter, it suddenly looked more predatory. I resisted the urge to step back as he came forward, saying, "I wasn't sure I was in the right place. I've been a fan for a long time."

Rachelle responded like a human being: she smiled welcomingly. I responded like an incarnate: I dove to the ground and pulled her down to the hardwood floor.

Mine was the correct reaction.

A sizzling bolt of white-blue fire sheared over our heads and exploded in an intense *crack* against my newly acquired desk, followed by a dull roar as the desk went up in flames like dry kindling. Actually, scratch that. It went up in flames so spectacularly that it was more like a firework than any wood. My shoulder hit the hardwood floor, my arms wrenching as I dragged Rachelle down with me. Taken completely off guard, she released a squeal and landed heavily on top of me, her elbow connecting with my face. As the noise and heat of the explosion washed over us, she panicked and began thrashing at me in her attempt to regain her feet.

This body was new to me, but lifetimes confronting incarnates had instilled in me instincts completely foreign to mortal nineteen-year-olds. Every new body is different, and I'd hardly had time to figure out mine; this was going to be a crash course. I rolled away from Rachelle and toward our attacker. I sprang to my feet and full-body tackled him at waist height—and man oh man, was this body designed for tackling! I was pretty tall to begin with, and my wide shoulder span was backed up by lean muscles and long arms that extended my reach. I swear I could feel my muscles bunching, coiling, then springing into action as I executed a tackle any football player would envy...

And passed right through the incarnate.

As I connected, or *should* have connected, the man disintegrated into thick, bright-red smoke. My perfect tackle carried me too far, and I crashed to the floor for the second time in less than a minute. Floor two, Emery zero. As my momentum carried me through the red mist, my nostrils filled with a surprisingly pleasant cinnamon smell.

I'm not sure if it was adrenaline or my newfound youth, but I was back on my feet a blink later. I *liked* this body. No way was I giving it up without a fight. Besides, if I died here, it would be my shortest reincarnation ever, by at least a day. And that would hurt my pride.

My heart was pounding. The red mist was drifting unnaturally, like a cloud of blood, to the other side of the room, behind my desk-turned-inferno. Embers spiraled through the air. Rachelle was on her feet, her back pressed against one of my curtain-less windows. Our eyes met, and she began to inch her way over to me. She was pale, and I could see the whites all the way around her irises. But she was alive.

As I saw her fear, something hot and protective flashed through me. She was a mortal, unprepared for this, simply collateral damage in a fight between two entities she wasn't even aware existed. I was immortal, and this was *my* world. I would keep her safe. To do that, I needed to think. What could I do to defeat this incarnate? In my instinct to move first and ask questions later, I hadn't had any time to think about which incarnate I was facing. Oh sure, maybe *you've* guessed by now, but you've had the luxury of me telling you exactly how it played out. If I had explained this to you in the way I'd experienced it so far, it would go something like this:

Why is he smiling like that? Oh no. An incarnate. Get down. Down, Emery! Oh crap, don't forget about Rachelle. Ow! Ack. Whoa, explosion! Noise. Hot. Hot-hot-hot! Gotta get up. Move, Emery! Dang, check out this body, it was made *for tackling. C'mon, Emery, admire later, tackle now. Red mist. Mmm, cinnamon. I miss food. Focus, Emery. Which incarnate is this?*

Tough to get in much reflection during all that.

My attention alighted on an object rolling on the floor, clearly thrown from the desk when it exploded. I looked back at my desk-slash-bonfire. The laptop was nowhere to be seen, but I was certain it would be a lifeless black lump somewhere in the heart of that flame. The flowers, though, the ones that had ornamented the corner of my desk... petals and dirt were smeared across the hardwood like a trail of blood, but the pot was miraculously intact.

No, not "miraculously."

The red mist swirled, forming the vague shape of the man, then coalesced *into* him, his teeth bared, body poised as though ready to pitch a fastball. I dove for the flowerpot as he threw his arm forward. A ball of fire the size of my head went careening above me and roared into the front wall. The resulting crash was immense. It sounded like the whole neighborhood was being bombed. This second explosion rocked the building, timber and plaster cracking and splintering, and the wall caved outward violently. A whoosh of air pulled at me and sent the pot spinning toward me on the floor. Splinters, fire, smoke, and debris were hurled out into the street. If anyone had been standing near the main entrance...

My fingers closed on the flowerpot, and I snatched it up. "Hey!" I screamed over the cacophony, trying to get the incarnate's attention, and I pointed the mouth of the pot toward him.

The man was in the process of lobbing another fireball at me, but he froze as though I held something far deadlier in my hands. In the aftermath of the explosions, I could hear pieces of the wreckage still pattering on the pavement and ravaged porch, the crackle of fire, the roof groaning in protest at the abrupt absence of one of its supporting walls.

The man watched me like a cornered cat, unmoving even as I climbed slowly to my feet, my eyes never leaving his black, beady ones, the flowerpot held out before me like a loaded gun.

Then he bobbed his head in a gracious acknowledgment of defeat—undercut, somewhat, by the ruinous remains of my office all around us—and dissolved into bright scarlet smoke that soon wafted away. The conflagration formerly known as my desk subsided into a much more reasonable campfire, confirming the incarnate's departure.

As keenly as I wanted to take a deep breath, there was still a lot of smoke in the small room. I approached Rachelle (who, impressively, was not curled into the fetal position), snaked my arm around her tiny shoulders, and led her out of the hellish office space.

3

"*What* the hell was that?" Rachelle burst out as I finished my call with 9-1-1. She was staring at my office, features slack with disbelief.

I followed her gaze. The office looked like the face of a demon, its gaping maw surrounded by a corona of flames, its face scorched black. "The Genie," I answered absently, my mind already racing ahead. I would need to salvage what I could from the office, of course, but what next? Mom lived only a few miles away. I could crash there for a bit. But... an attack only minutes after being reincarnated. Whoever had attacked me must have been counting the days, but how did they know *where*... oh. My website. Of cou—

"A *genie*?" Rachelle screeched, incredulity stretching her voice into a range generally achieved only by bats.

Pulled out of my reverie, I responded automatically. "*The* Genie," I said, then gave her an abashed half smile as I saw her blank look. "Blank" with a whole lot of "panicked" thrown in, and a pinch of "murderous." "Sorry, I'm just guessing," I lied, hoping it would comfort her. Mortals don't like it when you know more than them. True fact.

People had begun to congregate around the burning wreckage and accompanying plume of black smoke. A tallish woman with stark white hair that looked like a cross between a sheep and a cloud hurried toward us. "Are you two all right?" she called out.

"Just bruised, I think," I replied with what I hoped was a reassuring smile. "Rachelle, are you okay?" I said it for this woman's sake, but I found myself assessing my friend as I spoke. She looked spooked. Anger was rising to cover up her vulnerability; she was scared, and she didn't know how to deal with it. She was also... well, a bit *smudged*. Soot had been smeared over her right cheekbone and caught in her hair where she'd clearly run her fingers through it.

Her eyes met mine, and her anger softened. She turned to the approaching woman. "I'm fine, too. Could be a lot worse." If my smile looked anything like the feeble attempt she shared with the woman, it wasn't reassuring at all.

"I'll call the fire department," the woman offered, taking out her phone.

"Already done," I assured her. So she did what any mortal would do once they'd established that everyone was okay: she started taking pictures of the wreckage on her phone.

"Do you know what happened?" she asked.

Rachelle let out a sound that could have been a laugh, a sob, or both. I quickly answered, "Not sure. The way that wall blew out, though—I think I saw something like that on the news once. Maybe it was some sort of... gas leak?"

The woman nodded as if that made all the sense in the world. At this point, a crowd was forming. Sirens could be heard in the distance.

"Emery Luple?" a gruff voice called. I turned to see a familiar man striding toward us. He was Black, with salt-and-pepper hair; middling height, crooked nose, slight hitch to his gait. Mid-to-late fifties. He carried himself with the commanding air of an officer, and the civilian clothes he wore were like dressing up Barbie as a doctor: that is to say, a costume more than an outfit. He looked like a career military man, perhaps a retired one. "I'm Captain—"

"Gregory Gregorius!" I greeted him, taking his proffered hand and shaking it firmly. It was rough and calloused, warm, dry, and firm. If anyone was identifiable by nothing more than their handshake, it was the Watchman incarnate. Dozens of handshakes, phone calls, and case files flickered through my memories. Whether I was investigating monsters or hunting them, I was always safer with Gregory Gregorius watching my back.

All of this went through my mind in a blink, and the captain stepped back and regarded me with an unreadable expression. He was always guarded, his face rarely betraying any emotion.

"Rachelle," I said, "this is a very old and dear friend of the family." Mostly true. "Gregory, this is my friend Rachelle. She was with me when my office exploded."

He nodded at Rachelle in greeting, then turned back to me, somber. "We should speak. Alone."

"Oh *hell* no." Rachelle's look could have been incarnated as Daggers. "You aren't leaving me here." The heat in her expression was fueled in part by the thinly veiled alarm threatening to overtake her. "Besides, you need to give a report to the police."

I vacillated. She was a mortal, and this was incarnate business. But she had just survived something she couldn't explain, and she needed to know enough to not talk. "She's right about the report," I acknowledged.

Gregory reached into the pocket of his dark gray jacket and withdrew a badge. "I am the police. I'll take your statement."

My reply was drowned out by the staccato honking of the approaching fire trucks' horns. There were two trucks, as well as an ambulance—even though I had told them no one was injured—and I could see the flashing lights of two more approaching police SUVs. Within heartbeats of their arrival, geared-out firefighters were teeming around the area, unspooling a flat gray fire hose. Others cordoned off the area, establishing room to work while guiding the crowd back and away. Gregory's badge kept them from pushing me aside, and I protectively grabbed Rachelle's hand. I didn't really want her involved, but I couldn't leave her like this. Even though we'd only met less than an hour ago, I *felt* like we were best friends, like I'd known her my entire life. Illusion or not, the emotions were real.

Gregory's lips thinned at my action, but he didn't argue. He escorted us off to one side to allow the firefighters room to work. It was no accident that the move also provided us with some privacy, making it much easier to avoid being overheard.

"What happened?" he asked, concise as always.

I licked my lips and glanced sideways at Rachelle, but I'd brought this on myself. No half measures now. "We were attacked by the Genie."

My words drew a curse from him. "Any idea who's controlling him?"

I threw up my hands. "I've been back for less than an hour!" He nodded, as though he expected that response, then waited expectantly. I sighed. "I'm really not sure," I said slowly, thinking it out, "but I suppose it's probably the same person who killed me in the desert. They're the most likely person to have my reincarnation timed so perfectly."

"Do you know their identity?" the Watchman asked.

I shook my head ruefully. "No, they got the drop on me."

"*What?*" Rachelle had heard enough. "Emery, what are you talking about?" She bit off each word, her confusion manifesting as frustration. "Reincarnation? *Killed?* You say a *genie* attacked us? That's ridiculous. Beyond ridiculous. I know what happened back there, but..." She fell silent, breathing heavily. Uh-oh. She was hyperventilating. I opened my mouth to speak, but she raised her own hand sharply to cut me off. She closed her eyes. Took a few deep breaths. I found myself fighting a grin despite the situation. Damn, she was tough. "Where is the loophole?" she asked, after a moment. There was a quiet desperation in her voice. "You've spent the last few years devoted to finding things exactly like this. *And explaining them.* So make me understand. Tell me what I'm missing. Tell me the loophole."

Where to start? I saw her battle her own fear and force calmness into her features, and as I watched, I allowed my memories from this incarnation to flow into me. I valued our friendship and wouldn't have been able to make *There's Always a Loophole* without her. I wasn't romantically interested in her, but I was loath to lose her as a friend. And I could. Our friendship might hinge on what I told her next. But *should* I salvage it? If I pushed her away, wouldn't she be safer? People were always safer when they weren't involved with me. A shadow fell over my thoughts, but I shook it off.

"Rachelle," I began, my decision made. I said it gently but firmly, capturing her attention and holding it. "Do you know the myth of the genie?" She nodded sharply, silently. "Do you know the myth of bigfoot?" Nod. "The myth of the unicorn?" I received a third nod, this one complete with get-on-with-it eyes. "Do you know the myth of Galliogook?" Her eyebrows furrowed, and she shook her head. Not surprising. I'd just made that up. "The first three are real. The last is not. Do you know why?"

Her mouth popped open, but she snapped it closed again. She inhaled sharply through her nose, then shook her head.

"Because people believe in them. Think about them. Mold them in clay and doodle them in art books. Tell stories about them, write about them in novels. When that happens, when enough people think about them, all of those collective thoughts and beliefs are pooled together to create the very entity, the very *thing* that those people think is nothing more than legend." I tried to evaluate her expression, but it was guarded. "By sustaining the myth, people contribute to its very existence. The result is people, places, and things called incarnates."

Rachelle calmly raised her hand as though to say she had a question. "Where's the loophole?" she asked pointedly.

"What? Rachelle, I'm telling you..." I trailed off. Tried again. "The loophole, this time, is that it's all *true.*"

She rolled her eyes and glanced at Gregory to gauge his reaction. Gregory, as usual, could have been carved from stone for all the emotion he showed. His stoicism seemed to rattle her.

"Okay," she said. Her voice was a little too loud. "Say I believe you. Genies are real. Bigfoot is real. Why are they attacking you?"

I held up a finger. "Actually, only half of that is correct. Bigfoot is real. And *the* Genie is real. But not *Genies,* not plural. You see, there is only ever one incarnation of a myth. So 'genies' don't exist. One Genie. The Genie incarnate. The one Genie to represent the dozens of myths and legends out there. That's how it works."

"Who makes up all these rules?" she asked irritably.

I shrugged. "Who makes up *any* rules? Who makes up the rules of gravity? Is it science? God? Politicians? This is just the way it is."

She looked at me with more than a hint of disbelief. However, her skepticism was slowly being eroded by her interest. I felt a surge of guilt, though. A significant portion of her trust in me was fabricated; she *thought* she'd known me for years, but it was a lie. We'd only met an hour ago, no matter what our memories said, and I was divulging knowledge that invited her to enter my dangerous world. As an immortal, I could handle it. I was unable to confidently say the same for Rachelle, and that worry wiggled its way into my mind. I watched her face as she bit her lip in thought. I could almost see the cogs of her mind clicking together, using what I'd told her and applying it to what we'd seen.

Gregory looked ready to interrupt our discussion, but he held back. I couldn't tell if he disapproved of me sharing this with a mortal.

"So," she prompted, "I believe you mentioned you being killed? How does that factor into this?"

"Well, I suppose that's another loophole, of sorts. You see, I'm an incarnate, too."

Her eyebrows threatened to lift out of her head. "Oh?" she asked archly. "And have you always been? Were you going to tell me? What kind of incarnate are you, exactly? The Boy-Next-Door incarnate?"

I found myself smiling, which elicited a dangerous flash in her eyes. "That's pretty clever," I told her defensively. "I did die, in my previous life. It happens now and again. But since I'm an incarnate, I... well, I *re*incarnated." I gestured at my body.

Rachelle's face screwed up. "Wait. Reincarnation? Oh my god, are you..." her voice went hushed, "*Jesus*?"

"What? No!"

"Then what *are* you?" she pressed.

Memories of my past lives flooded my mind. Wrestling the Nemean Lion. Staking Dracula. Taking down the Yeti in the unforgiving desert. I hesitated for a moment, then cleared my throat. "I'm the Monster Hunter incarnate," I announced with pride. "You know: Van Helsing? Theseus? Buffy the Vampire Slayer?"

"I don't remember any of them being able to reincarnate," Rachelle said dubiously.

"Then you haven't seen all the episodes of *Buffy*," I quipped. She wasn't amused, so I sobered up my tone. "All incarnates can reincarnate, Rachelle. As long as the myth survives, so too does the incarnate."

She worked through this information in her head. I kept quiet, giving her space to think. Nearby, but out of earshot, the firefighters had quickly gotten the upper hand on the fiery remains of my office. The property had been roped off with yellow caution tape, and the crowd on the other side of the police line was thinning. A news van had also arrived while we'd been talking, and it looked like a reporter was speaking with some of the remaining members of the crowd.

Another flash of memory assailed me: I had been an investigative journalist once, in a not-so-distant previous life. I'd been a gorgeous Black woman at the time, all soft curves and sharp tongue. I'd fallen for a mortal man, Huntington, and our short-lived romance was a warm velvet memory. *No, wait.* I knew this memory. Thinking of Huntington always led to the same place: blank, lifeless eyes staring through me, beyond me, empty. Sobs wracking me as I held his body. Morrigan's mocking laugh, gloating over me, followed by the impact of the only bullet I'd ever welcomed. When I reincarnated, I made a vow: I'd never fall in love with a mortal again.

Blinking the memory away, I focused on Rachelle struggling with the enormity of what I'd told her. I wasn't worried about falling in love with her, but I *did* just involve her in my world. I suddenly wasn't sure if my decision to preserve our friendship was the better choice.

Hi. It's me, Emery. I must apologize for lying to you. It isn't anything
personal. In my defense, at the time, I didn't know I was lying. The
incarnate info that I shared with Rachelle? All true. Like, seriously *true. So*
be careful next time you go poking around in the woods looking for your
local fabled monster. Curiosity killed the cat, and all that. So which part
was a lie? ___, __ ____ __ ____ __ __ __ _____ _____.
Huh. Would you look at that. Spoilers.
Only one way to find out.
Happy sleuthing.

~

T he Watchman drove. He needed my help with a haunting
        in a town nearby. He'd come searching for me when he'd
seen my website go live, which was exactly what the site was designed
for. It was a call to the incarnates of the world. A summons for my
friends and a warning to my enemies: the Monster Hunter incarnate
was reborn.

It was quiet in the SUV. Rachelle was deep in thought. Gregory
was... well, Gregory. He didn't talk much. Never had. I sat in the back,

in the middle seat, while Rachelle rode shotgun. Letting her have the front seat was the least I could do after the mess I'd dragged her into.

We'd cleaned up as best we could and were heading to a house off an out-of-the-way highway in a small suburb called Maple Valley. Quaint-sounding, right? But apparently some *thing* had been terrorizing the family that lived there. Rachelle had insisted on tagging along, of course, and it seemed too good of an opportunity to pass up; I could show her the reality of my claims while I worked. I shelved the nagging worry for her safety in a corner of my mind, something my last two incarnations would have been unable to do. This Emery was different: he longed to trust again. Which was terrifying in its own right—so I stowed that along with my worry. Besides, hauntings were rarely dangerous, for all that they could be frightening. They were also, all too often, fake. But Gregory would not have sought me out on mere rumor.

"I get why the Genie attacked you," Rachelle said abruptly, turning in her seat to regard me, "but I don't understand why he stopped."

I assumed an offended expression. "Because I vanquished him."

"Yes, but *how*?"

I hesitated. "Incarnates always have a fatal flaw... a sort of Achilles' heel, I guess you could say. A kryptonite. A weakness that, if you can find it, you can exploit. Some are well known: a silver bullet for the Werewolf incarnate, Rumpelstiltskin's own name, sugar cookies for the Santa Claus—"

"You're joking."

I broke into a grin. "Obviously. Like I'd go around announcing Santa's weakness." She opened her mouth, but I barreled on. "The Genie's got a bit of a rough life. His fatal flaw is—"

"His lamp," she said. My eyebrows shot up, and she gave me a smug smile. "I'm right, aren't I?"

"You're a quick learner," I replied. "More importantly, the Genie can be bound to *any* container. So I used—"

"The flowerpot! Of course!"

"Stop doing that," I grumbled. "Takes all the fun out of it." The

SUV took an off-ramp that made a tight spiral, and I had to grab the seats in front of me to keep my balance. "Most of the time, incarnates can try to conceal their fatal flaw, but they cannot harm it. The Genie had no problem frying my laptop—or, hell, my entire office—but the pot was untouched. I realized what that meant and threatened him with it."

She was quiet for a few moments, pondering that. The road noise was a comfortable drone dampened by the SUV's quality construction. We passed neighborhoods and apartment complexes on our right, while on our left were trees and a river, with a trail for joggers and bikers. There weren't many people out this late in the afternoon in mid-March. It was overcast but dry, and sunset was less than a couple hours away. With the gray sky, it felt like it was already getting darker.

"Why would the Genie not want to serve you?" Rachelle asked. "I mean, other than you're *you*."

"Wow. That hurts. Truly."

"Seriously, though, why? If you captured him, then you would be his new master, right? Would you be a worse master than his current one?"

"Those are good questions," I told her. "There are a couple of possible reasons." I began to tick them off on my fingers. "First, the Genie cannot work directly against his master's wishes. If the wish was worded carefully, the Genie would be perfectly bound to try to continue serving the person who made the wish. Second, the Genie is freed upon completion of his third wish. If I captured him, it would have started his wishes over, and he'd be further from freedom. Third, the only method I know of to slay the Genie is to capture him first. Incarnates are immortal, after a fashion, but reincarnation requires a set amount of time. And the reincarnation process... sucks. It's not painful or anything, but you never reincarnate exactly as you were. You miss out on precious time, and you also lose your current form. It can make you feel a lot less... *you*. At least for a while." *Sometimes forever.* I tried another angle. "If I told you that you could go to sleep tonight and wake up three years from now in another body and another life, would you take me up on it?"

Rachelle gave me a sad little smile. "Some days, yeah."

"Dark." I grinned. "But in general you wouldn't, right? You feel, I don't know, *attached* to who you are. There are certain aspects you might like to change, but you'd lose everything—friends, family, loved ones—and gain all new ones. And you don't get to decide how you reincarnate. You could wake up as anyone, Rachelle." I pitched my voice low and dramatic. "*Anyone.*"

She rolled her eyes, then sighed. "Okay, I get your point."

The SUV pulled off the road and onto a long, bumpy drive. The area was sparsely developed, and we passed only a few driveways, leading to modest houses that looked forlorn in the waning light.

"Emery?" Rachelle asked in a small voice. "You told Gregory you just reincarnated. But I've known you since middle school." She left the question unasked. It hung there, like a big black spider dangling from a thread of web, demanding attention. I considered. Opened my mouth—

"We're here." Gregory's words cut off whatever I might have said, and I saw a flicker of relief in Rachelle's eyes. She didn't want to know. But it was clear she already suspected.

Turning off the engine, Gregory exited the vehicle and strode toward the house. Rachelle and I hurried after him. The residence was a single story with a few rooms stuck on like afterthoughts—probably additions to the original structure. And it was clearly old, the blue paint faded to gray. A family of three waited outside the front door, anxiously watching us approach. The porch stairs creaked as we ascended, the wood giving slightly beneath our weight.

The two adults stood protectively over their little boy, who was maybe four years old. The father, a Black man with close-cropped dark hair and a stylized goatee, sported a Seattle Seahawks jersey that matched the baseball cap the little boy wore. The mother, dressed in jeans and a tailored shirt, had much lighter skin, perhaps a mixed background, and brown hair braided to one side. If I had to guess, they were in their early forties. There were the first traces of gray in the father's hair, and the mother's outfit had the look of being chosen for comfort and durability rather than fashion. There was nothing too noteworthy about their son, though his coloring favored his father's side, and his chubby cheeks were downright cherubic.

"Mr. and Ms. Conrad, my name is Captain Gregory Gregorius. We spoke on the phone."

"I'm Skye, and this is my husband, Hank," the woman said. "And this is our son, Kolby."

I introduced myself and Rachelle as colleagues of Gregory's— people ask surprisingly few questions in these situations—then asked what was wrong.

"It sounds ridiculous," Hank said, "but our house is home to a... a guest. Been there for years; probably longer than us."

"There's a ghost story around these parts," Skye chimed in, "about a shadow man and his bird. All the neighbors know about him. And every once in a while, drivers on the highway claim to see him. Usually late at night."

"We've known for some time that it—or he—lives with us. In our crawl space, we think. But unlike everyone else in the area, we know the truth: he's harmless. In fact, we think of him as kind of a protector." As Hank spoke, Skye hugged her son closer. "We occasionally leave leftovers from our supper for him. We'll hear him every now and again: creaks on the floorboards or the flapping of wings. We always leave the laundry room window open. We try to be thoughtful. After all, it's probably more his house than ours."

"He likes to hide things," Skye said. "Things of no consequence. But he helps us find things, too. Can't find my keys, or Kolby's toys, or lose an earring—you're all but guaranteed to find them in a spot you had already checked, as if they'd been there all along. But we know."

Rachelle cast a sidelong glance at me. "Did something change?" I asked them gently.

Skye spoke. "Yes. Last night he did something to Kolby. We aren't sure what. We heard the flapping of wings—his bird, we're sure—and Kolby was playing near the laundry room. I ran in to make sure he was okay. I mean, we trust... but what kind of mom would I be if I didn't make sure? Anyway, I ran to Kolby, and he suddenly started spouting gibberish, like, like—" She sputtered and faltered, tears spilling down her cheeks.

Hank hung his head. "Like he was cursed. Or something. And now he won't speak at all." He lowered himself down on his haunches, eye level with Kolby, and said, "It's okay, kiddo, you aren't in any trouble." Kolby stared back with overly large eyes but didn't reply.

Skye swallowed a few times, and when she spoke again, she was calmer but sounded desolate. "I'm not sure what to do. We don't have the money to move, especially not right away. But how can we stay here now?"

I nodded in understanding. "Allow me to take a look around. May we go inside?"

They gave their approval, and I entered, Rachelle on my heels. Gregory stayed out front with the family.

Stepping over the threshold was eerie, as though cobwebs brushed against my soul. The inside of the small house smelled like old lavender. Outside, the sky had begun to darken in earnest, and the interior was even darker. I could make out silhouettes and shadows in the living room—a skeletal chair, a spidery plant—all punctuated by the dimly lit eyeholes that were the windows. I groped across the rough plaster until my fingers found the light switch. When I flicked it on, the living room lit up, innocuous and inviting with the dark banished. A small sign just above the light switch read, "A House Becomes a Home When Love Is Inside."

The house was still and quiet, like I'd entered a great beast that was holding its breath. I took another step in. It was a tidy home, especially given they had a small child. There were a few toys in a low-hanging hammock topped with a tower of stuffed animals. Their eyes seemed to follow me as I slowly creaked my way across the linoleum and past the dark kitchen off to my left. Ahead was a stunted hallway. I sidled up to its mouth, eyeing the three doorways beyond. The first led to a bathroom, which carved into the kitchen's space, and then there were two closed doors, one on either side of the corridor. If I had to guess, I'd say I'd found the bedrooms. Not yet ready to explore those silent, empty—*please be empty*—rooms, I turned on my heel to retreat...

And nearly leapt out of my skin when Rachelle was *right the freak behind me.*

"Which came first?" she asked, unfazed by my startled jump.

"What?" I screeched, my heart hammering in my chest.

She was watching me with unconcealed amusement. "Sorry." She neither looked nor sounded apologetic. In fact, I think she was covering a snicker. I bit back a retort, willing my frantic pulse to settle down. Great. I was in the best shape of multiple lifetimes, and I was scared of the dark. Go figure. I rationalized that my immortal mind simply knew the *real* terrors and dangers that called the dark their home. Yeah, that was definitely it.

Rachelle, oblivious to my distracted thoughts, was talking. "I was just thinking: does the myth always have to come before the incarnate? I mean, take Bigfoot. Lots of local legends from hunters claiming to see him. But how did the first one happen? Was Bigfoot incarnate there and a hunter saw him, and it..." she gestured, groping for words, "immortalized him? Or did some hiker make up the story to scare his Boy Scouts and it stuck, then Bigfoot materialized into being?"

My heart had finally sunk back to its usual place in my chest, and I felt in control of my voice again. "Age-old question. Which came first, the chicken or the egg?"

"Is that evasive Emery-speak for 'I don't know?'"

The kitchen. I walked there with purpose this time, refusing to give Rachelle the satisfaction of seeing me rattled. "Of course I know," I replied. "The myth comes first. But the Philosopher incarnate disagrees." She puzzled over that for a moment while I turned on the lights. A small, neat kitchen greeted us. "Here's an example: someone sees something completely innocent in the woods, but their mind plays tricks on them and they begin to spread tales of a creature they saw. The story grows into a legend until it lodges itself in local folklore, and then *bam!* After hundreds of retellings and who knows how many years, we have ourselves an incarnate. But the thing they saw in the woods—was it real? Hence the question: chicken in the woods, or egg in the retelling?" Looking around, I saw nothing out of the ordinary: a stovetop, a dinner table with wooden chairs, pots and pans hanging from a rack, the pattering of small footsteps running through the living room and down the hallway behind me, a refrigerator that hummed quietly, a number of white-painted drawers, and—

A chill went down my spine.

"Did you hear that?" Rachelle whispered. She didn't look afraid. If anything, she looked excited. Awesome. My mortal friend was far braver than I. *I don't think so.*

I was about to bravely deny hearing anything when the soft click of a door being closed came from down the dark hallway.

A suspicion bloomed in my mind. I recalled an ancient memory, walking through a dark village at night, holding an oil lantern before me. Baiting a trap with a shard of mirror. Boggarts could never resist the allure of a shiny object...

"Do you have a penny?" I asked quietly.

"What?"

"A penny. Or any change?" She shook her head. I looked around, then walked over to the drawers and began hunting for what I'd need. I found a rather polished spoon, but I was worried it would be too big. I kept rooting around until I finally found a small key—probably a spare housekey—and then I began to rummage through the pantry. I found olive oil. It would have to do.

"Emery, what are you doing?" When I didn't immediately respond, instead taking the two objects to the kitchen sink, she grabbed my arm. "You know what it is?"

I hesitated. "I think so. Probably."

She crossed her arms. "And?" I began to pour the olive oil over the key, making it gleam as much as possible.

"I think it's a boggart of some sort. They're attracted to shiny things." I walked back to the mouth of the hallway, looking down the short, dark corridor. "And the dark, unfortunately."

"Wait, don't you mean 'the Boggart incarnate?'" Rachelle asked.

"Congrats. You've just graduated to Incarnates 201. That's how it works, yes. But I don't know which exact incarnate it is. Boogeyman, Goblin, Slenderman, Gremlin... there are quite a few possibilities. I just meant 'boggart' as an umbrella term, because all those have a lot of similarities. But each is unique, so each gets its own incarnation."

All three doors had been open when we'd entered, but now only the master bedroom's was ajar. I took a deep breath, steeling myself, then walked forward. I placed my hand on the laundry room door. Nothing. I frowned and looked at the other closed door. Placed my hand on it.

If I had been a cat or dog, my hackles would have spiked straight up. As it was, I could feel the little hairs on the nape of my neck. An incarnate's domain. Depending on the classification of the incarnate, it would either be a Sanctum (like mine), a Safe Haven, a Territory, or a Lair. I *really* hoped it wasn't a Lair. If my suspicions were correct, it was not.

I pushed open the door.

The hinges protested, groaning. Inside the room were a child's bed, a few toys scattered on the floor, and a nightstand with a lamp on it. A small window let in the only light, completely inadequate to brighten the room. I motioned for Rachelle to stay put, then crossed the threshold slowly. Did the bedspread's lower ruffles just move, or was that my imagination? A closet against the far wall was mostly closed, but an inch of darkness at one side seemed almost to call to me. Did I hear... breathing?

Yeah, I did. But it was Rachelle. She'd followed me into the room —of course.

I cautiously placed the shiny key on the bed, careful to let it catch the dying light and sparkle. Well, it would have sparkled in the sunlight. In the final light of day, it glimmered. It would have to do.

I grabbed Rachelle's hand and tugged her toward the small window, deliberately turning our backs to the room as we looked outside. I held my breath.

There was a creak from behind us, and then the sound of the bedroom door clicking closed again. I tensed. If my hunch about the incarnate was correct, this would all be resolved quickly, without harm to anyone. My hunches tended to be right. Usually.

The muscles in my back were rigid, uncomfortable, but I didn't turn around. Rachelle, thankfully, took my lead, her jaw clenched tight as she stared unblinking out the window.

I felt something brush against the back of my leg, then heard weight settle on the bed.

I turned.

A figure sat on the bed, turning the key over and over in its hands covetously. I couldn't see its face from this angle, hidden as it was by the baseball cap's visor. I crouched down so we were on the same level. The incarnate glanced at me before turning his attention back to the key. His complexion in the darkness was tinged a greenish-black, and his overly large eyes caught the light in the room and gleamed.

"Hi, Kolby," I said.

5

The incarnate turned the key around in his hands, fascinated as it caught the light of the lamp we'd switched on.

"Maybe I should have given him the shiny object *after* we talked to him," I remarked.

"What is he?" Rachelle breathed. She was watching him with a mixture of fascination, horror, and adoration.

"The Kobold incarnate," I informed her. "He's harmless, by the way." In German folklore, kobolds were house sprites. They were mischievous and occasionally malicious if ignored, but typically they coexisted with the homeowners with little to no fuss. To top it off, they were also shape-shifters. Their favorite form? A crow. Kolby fit seamlessly with the story the Conrads had told us. I wondered if the shadow man was another of his forms... or if there might be another incarnate hidden around these parts.

"Ohh, 'Kolby,' I get it."

I paused, vaguely annoyed. "I didn't catch that. How obvious."

Rachelle patted me on the head. "At least you're pretty." She sat down on the bed next to Kolby, utterly unafraid. The incarnate's glamour was already distracting her. "Can he talk?"

I glanced at the closed bedroom door. "Gregory will keep Mr. and Ms. Conrad occupied," I told the Kobold, "so you may speak freely."

Kolby looked up at me, considering. Then his eyes were pulled back down to the object in his hands. "Sorry for the deception," he piped. His voice was that of the quintessential child, high and clear, almost songlike.

I gave him an encouraging smile, but since he wasn't looking at me, it hardly mattered. "You had no reason to trust any of us. No need to apologize. How long have you been masquerading as their child?"

Kolby hopped off the bed and stowed his shiny new treasure in the closet. I saw a handful of glittering objects in there before he shut the door again. Then he rejoined us on the bed. "Almost sixteen years. The glamour keeps them from suspecting, of course, and they've provided me with a good life." His big eyes misted. "I've tried to give back, where I can. They were unable to have kids..."

I understood immediately. Symbiotic relationships between incarnates and mortals were not all that uncommon, especially for Prey incarnates. *Prey* being the less-than-scientific classification encompassing the incarnates who live alone or alongside humans without threatening mortal lives or society. Between you and me, I think Prey banded together many years ago and coined the term to exaggerate their harmlessness. It is, unfortunately, not entirely accurate. Prey can, in fact, cause harm. But what rule doesn't have its exception?

Prey incarnates dwell in Safe Havens, nooks or refuges often hidden from mortals and other incarnates alike, little enclaves where they can live peacefully. Unlike Predators, their built-in defense mechanisms are—usually—nonlethal. Hence the glamour. For those of you unfamiliar with the fairy-tale word, *glamour* is a sort of illusionary spell that obfuscates the true world, enchanting those under its sway. Kind of like hypnosis, it often induces docility and compliance in mortals. Which explains Kolby's "parents" not becoming suspicious about having a four-year-old son for sixteen years. We incarnates are susceptible, too, which is why I didn't see the greenish cast to Kolby's skin until his identity was known to me. But once I identified glamour, it was well within my power to resist it.

I looked at Kolby and his big, glistening eyes and refrained from pulling him into my lap and comforting him. Well. I could *mostly* resist the glamour.

"What happened last night?" I asked him. "Did something change?"

The little creature looked miserable, his face scrunching inward at the memory. "I found something shiny in the laundry room. It was a clear night, and the moonlight was shining off of something reflective."

"Ooh, what was it?" Rachelle asked dreamily, the glamour making it harder for her to concentrate.

Kolby gave a half shrug. "Something shiny," he repeated helpfully. It was hard to hold it against the little guy. He was just so cute. It made me want to snuggle with him, maybe take him home with me like a stray puppy and...

I shook my head to clear it. "Could you turn down the charm a little?" I grumbled. His glamour was extra potent, here in his Safe Haven. "So. You found a shiny. What happened then?"

"I did what I always do. I snatched it up and inspected it thoroughly, then rushed back to show Mommy Skye what I'd found." The image made me think of a cat presenting a dead rat to its owner. "But when I showed it to her, I began to babble incoherently. All the words were *wrong.* Not what I was trying to say at all." He shuddered, and Rachelle put a comforting arm around his shoulders. The Kobold incarnate snuggled into the embrace, looking up at me with wide eyes. "It confuddled the glamour, too. As I was spewing nonsense, Mommy Skye was looking at me in horror. I stopped talking and have been too afraid to try since."

I considered. "Do you remember what you said?"

The little guy shook his head, burrowing into Rachelle's arm. "No. Not really. I think I said something about my tummy and a tree, but I don't really remember."

Scratching my head, I asked, "Do you have the object still? Can I see it?"

With a resigned sigh, Kolby clambered off the bed and moved to his stash in the closet. Rachelle looked appalled. "After what it did to you, you *kept* it?"

"It's still shiny," the Kobold muttered defensively into the closet.

After a few moments of rummaging through his collection, he produced a small disk. A compact mirror, I realized. It was closed now, a smooth peach color. I held my hand out, palm up, and Kolby begrudgingly handed it over to me, his small hand lingering on its smooth surface before relinquishing it entirely. I turned the object over in my hands, trying to see if I sensed anything *off* about the item.

I should clarify: I don't have any sort of secret superpower to sense these things. The effects from earlier—hair standing on edge, sensations as I crossed the threshold—those are more or less ordinary phenomena. What I *do* possess is an immortal mind, years of experience honing my innate talents, and the oft-underestimated power of knowledge. I'd encountered many of these incarnates before. I knew what to look for, what senses to attune. Mortals are just as capable of this: like when you feel eyes at your back, or when you recognize patterns subconsciously and guess the next action that someone, or something, will take. The only advantage I had was practice and time. Unfortunately, some of that was negated by my youth in this incarnation, which made accessing those memories challenging. But I'd regain it all eventually.

So as I examined the object with my senses, I tried to open myself up to the possibility of any sensation, hoping I would gain some clue or insight into why the object had affected Kolby so profoundly.

Nothing.

I very carefully popped the compact mirror open, just a crack. Smelled it. Peeked in. Nada. Hmm. I opened it the rest of the way and looked at my reflection. For a moment, I didn't recognize the image that looked back at me. I still was unaccustomed to this body, this face. *My* face, I told myself. I flashed a smile at my reflection, admiring my unfamiliar features. I wasn't Adonis incarnated, but I was attractive in my own, self-satisfied way. For whatever reason, I usually reincarnated as a rather attractive individual. Maybe because the Monster Hunter incarnate is stereotypically sexy. I'm sure that's it.

"Hello, you beamish boy," I said to my reflection. The words came unbidden again. Was that a habit this version of Emery had whenever he looked at himself in the mirror? Just a quirk in my backstory? I mean, people do weird things when they're alone in front of a mirror. Don't deny it. You do, too.

"Are you quite done admiring yourself?" Rachelle asked.

I felt my face heat and snapped the mirror shut. "There doesn't seem to be anything odd about it," I concluded. "Unless what I said was gibberish to the two of you?"

Rachelle snorted. "Not gibberish. A tad conceited, perhaps, but the words made sense." Still stung, I didn't meet her gaze.

"Well, whatever it was that affected you, Kolby, it's gone now. It could have been a bunch of different things, like the phase of the moon's light reflecting off of the mirror, or the time of night." I looked down at the compact in my hand. "I know this is your shiny, but I'm going to take it with me. We don't want a relapse."

Kolby nodded reluctantly, his eyes following the mirror until I slipped it into my pocket.

"Come on, let's inform Mr. and Ms. Conrad that the house is safe again."

IT TOOK SOME CONVINCING, but we eventually cajoled Skye and Hank back into the house. Kolby's glamour soothed them, and their relief at seeing their "son" talking again smoothed over the rest. I crafted a tall tale about the compact mirror being a cursed object and that once I removed it from their house, they'd be safe. And I promised their guest was still around and would protect little Kolby.

Mr. and Ms. Conrad were by no means gullible people, but Kolby's glamour worked like, well, magic. I probably could have told them anything, and their proximity to—and love for—Kolby would have made them immune to logic. It concerned me, but ultimately they were a happy family. No reason to disrupt that, and I didn't consider Kolby a monster.

We stayed for a meal—Skye insisted—and Hank turned out to be quite the cook. The hour was growing late when we finally pulled out of that dirt drive and headed back to the city.

"So," Rachelle said with a yawn, stretching the word out, "what's your fatal flaw, Emery?"

"Inquisitive friends," I returned. I cracked a yawn, too. Contagious things.

She reclined her chair a bit, sinking into it. "Cute," she complained, without venom.

"Our weakness is not something we innately know," I said. "And it's certainly not something we like to share."

She nodded sleepily. "Makes sense," she muttered.

Gregory turned on the radio, letting the noise fill the silence. We hadn't even hit the freeway before Rachelle began snoring. I gave Gregory Rachelle's address and then sat back, letting him focus on driving. I dozed for a while, too, but I came awake when I heard a newscaster updating a familiar story.

"—headless body found in Larchmont, just outside New York City," a woman's voice announced. "That makes three this week. Authorities have not yet released the identities of the three individuals. The FBI has confirmed it is now involved in the case but declined to provide further comment to the press. However, it is rumored none of the victims' heads have been recovered at this time."

"What do you think of that?" I asked Gregory quietly.

He grunted. "Good time not to be in New York," he replied.

That... that *almost* sounded like a joke. I grinned. "Can't say I disagree." I let it drop. "So, back there. You owe the Conrads a favor or something?"

From where I sat, I couldn't read his expression. Then again, he rarely had them. "You want to know why I sought you out for something so easily resolved." It wasn't quite a question, so I shrugged. "I needed to make sure you were really *you*, Emery."

"What's that supposed to mean?"

"I thought you were in New York," he said. At my confused silence, he grunted. "We've worked pretty closely together for quite a number of incarnations, now. I lost you for a bit when you took off to the Middle East. Feared the worst. But for the last year, someone has been hunting monsters in New York, so I figured you must just be busy—until I saw your website pop up here in Seattle and I realized it wasn't you who'd been busy."

I felt a sinking sensation in the pit of my stomach. "Someone else hunting monsters? You sure your information wasn't wrong?" I knew the answer before he shook his head, though. The Watchman didn't make that kind of mistake.

Someone was impersonating me.

Formal Incarnate Lesson One: Classification of Incarnates
By Emery Luple

*H*ello, class. Today we are going to learn the four classifications experts have coined for incarnates. Now, I use the term "experts," but I really just mean "me and some people I know." Perhaps I should say "sources familiar with incarnates."

Ahem. The four classifications (in escalating order of threat level) are as follows: Benign, Prey, Predator, and Malevolent. The system is useful, but sadly not foolproof. For example, the Vampire incarnate is a Malevolent because it feeds on people. But a few dozen years ago, it went vegetarian. Turns out plants high in glucose and chlorophyll provide nourishment to it. At any rate, this reduced its threat level from Malevolent to Predator. One could even argue that it became Prey at that point, as anyone with a stake and some garlic (anyone else just get hungry?) could theoretically hunt it down. So, you see, the classification system is more of a guide than a law.

What? Oh, the vegetarian Vampire incarnate? An incident with a tempting mortal virgin ruined the whole thing. But I get it: diets are tough.

I AWOKE to the smell of bacon wafting through my childhood bedroom. Is there anything better? Sorry to all you vegans out there; you can pretend I said "tofu."

After dropping Rachelle at her apartment last night, the Watchman had dropped me off at my mom's, who still lived in the house I grew up in. Well, technically I hadn't, of course, but I had all the right memories. I hadn't plugged my phone in before falling asleep, so the low-battery symbol was flashing. I also had a new voicemail from Rachelle; I'd check it after addressing the breakfast that was calling my name. Priorities are an important part of the Monster Hunter gig. I popped my phone on the charger, then quickly showered and dressed before slipping downstairs to join Mom in the kitchen.

"Morning, sweet pea," she said. Even though I knew it was the first time I was hearing her voice, I felt love and safety in her company. This was my home, this time at least.

She was still cooking, but I snatched up a strip of bacon cooling to the side of the stove before she could swat me aside. "Morning," I said cheerily around the mouthful of sizzling bacony goodness.

Mom was short and soft, hinting toward comfortably plump, reminding me of nothing so much as a gingerbread woman. Grayish white, honey, and brown all vied for dominance in her hair, which was pulled back into a half-pony. Pale brown skin, much like my own, proclaimed her mixed heritage, and she wore a red-and-white checkered apron over blue jeans and a tee. She had a robust energy as she bustled about the kitchen; she rarely held still. And damn, did we have good genes. She was in her early fifties, but she still got carded on occasion. She was also radiantly beautiful, but I didn't know if that was objectively true or if I only thought that because she was my mom.

It was a good thing Mom had so much energy, because she lived here alone and managed the house by herself. She was an independent contractor with a degree in technical communications, and she worked with several of the start-up tech firms that flocked to Seattle. She brought in a healthy income, and we'd always lived comfortably.

I didn't have a dad. I never did.

"I heard about the fire," she mentioned, keeping her tone light. "I'm sorry, sweet pea. What happened?" She placed a heaping plate on the table in front of me. Eggs scrambled with onions and veggies, bacon, toast, hash browns... Mom was the best.

I dug in, talking between mouthfuls. "Gas leak, they think. Not really sure. Most of my things didn't make it, but I'll file an insurance report. I'll be able to replace most of it. Feel bad for the landlord, though."

We chatted while we finished breakfast and a little beyond, and then I gave her a hug and excused myself. I had a lot to do.

Someone else was hunting monsters. I wasn't sure how to feel about that. Concerned? Angry that they were stepping on the toes of my identity? If I pushed my emotions down and tried to approach the situation with logic, I was forced to admit there was a chance my impostor's intentions were noble. They could be trying to keep my enemies off balance or give me time to reincarnate under the radar, so to speak. But I doubted it. More likely, someone wanted to take advantage of my hard-won reputation.

Mom let me borrow her compact sedan, and I hit the streets. First stop: my office. I needed to assess the damage and salvage what I could. Second stop: the bank. Time to find out exactly how much money my backstory squirreled away for me before I reincarnated. I wasn't too optimistic.

Anger gnawed at my gut as I thought more about the impersonator. Someone using my reputation as the Monster Hunter incarnate was an enormous threat to my credibility among incarnates. Moreover, I was very discerning in what I hunted. There's a reason I wasn't called the Incarnate Hunter. What if my doppelganger was using my title as an excuse to kill incarnates? I would need to pay attention to any suspicious incarnate deaths... maybe I could track down my imitator by keeping my ear to the ground.

My phone rang. I realized with a curse that it wasn't paired up with Mom's car, so I answered it and put it on speakerphone. "Hello, Emery here."

"Emery Luple?" a soft-spoken voice on the other end asked. "My name is Caden. I called yesterday and spoke to your assistant." Oh, right. I had his contact information on the business card... in my other pants.

"Yes, hi, Caden," I said, striving to sound apologetic. "I'm sorry I haven't gotten back to you. Yesterday was a very busy day. You were calling to report a lead for my channel, right?" I pulled off the freeway and began making the short trek to my office on the outskirts of Seattle proper.

A pause. "More or less," came the response. "I was hoping you might be interested enough to come to New York." Another pause. "Have you heard about the beheadings?"

I frowned. Three times in two days. "I have." Of course there was something supernatural about them. The Watchman was right: I was rusty. This wasn't eighteenth-century France. Beheadings weren't commonplace these days.

I pulled up to the wreckage of my office. It was still taped off, and I wondered if I needed to get permission from someone before I entered.

"I thought you might be interested in the case," Caden was saying over the phone. "I think there might be something supernatural going on with—"

My phone beeped, and I glanced at it as Caden continued. Rachelle was calling. Crap, I never checked her voicemail.

"What do you say?" Caden asked, infusing this last question with extra cheery brightness. "You up for a visit to the Big Apple?" He sounded like he had come to the end of his sales pitch and was crossing his fingers. It dawned on me that his smooth voice was covering up nerves. A fan of my blog, perhaps? That, or maybe he really was hoping I could help solve the murders happening in his backyard.

My phone beeped again.

"This number is my cell," I told Caden quickly. "Text me your info. No promises, but I'll look into flights and hotels"—and my bank account—"and I'll see what I can do." I glanced at the time on the car's dashboard; it was still morning. "I'll get back to you later tonight with a response."

Caden was clearly relieved, though he did his best to hide it. I disconnected the call and swapped over to Rachelle.

"Morning, Emery!" came Rachelle's clearly-I'm-a-morning-person greeting. "You on your way yet?"

"Huh? I'm sorry; I haven't listened to your voicemail yet. On my way where?"

Rachelle said something to someone on her end. It sounded suspiciously like she was complaining about me. "My place. I figured you'd be going to your office this morning, and you could use the extra hands to help you out."

I looked up at my office. It was a disaster. I thought for a moment. Rachelle's apartment was maybe twenty minutes away. I could handle cleanup by myself. Moreover, I probably *should.* I'd already involved her a lot. "Thanks, Rachelle, but I think I've got it."

There was more talking on her end, followed by soft laughter. "Oh, just come over. I had a surprise for you, but you spoiled it. I bumped into a friend of yours." She lowered her voice. "From a previous life."

That got my attention. "Who is it?"

"Her name is Morrigan."

My blood froze. I saw Huntington's lifeless body again.

"I'll be right there."

I drove recklessly fast, trying to out-speed my demons. I was at the door to Rachelle's apartment building nine minutes later.

"Are you all right?" I asked her in a low voice as soon as she answered the door. She looked unharmed; hell, she looked great. A night's rest and a shower had restored her to the bubbly girl I knew only in my fabricated memories. No longer smudged and disheveled, she had her hair pulled back into a loose loop and wore athleisure clothes that suggested she'd already completed her morning jog. Productive much?

"Other than my entire understanding of life changing in the last twenty-four hours, I'm superb," she said, beaming. "Come on in!"

I grabbed her wrist and gave her a sharp tug, trying to convey the utmost importance and urgency in my motions. "We need to go *now*."

"And leave without saying hello to your oldest friend?" a honeyed voice said from behind Rachelle. "I'm wounded."

Rachelle opened the door wider with a grin, revealing Morrigan coming down the steps to greet us, walking with grace and panache that were somewhere between Cinderella descending the grand staircase and a tiger stalking its prey.

Morrigan. If evil were an incarnate, this was surely the form it would take. They say the devil's in the details, and Morrigan was *all* details. Not tall, she towered over you with her presence. Her voice was pure and dulcet, but her words had more knives hidden in them than Ali Baba and all of his thieves. Her long, dark tresses were lustrous, like the sheen of a serpent, coiled and cascading down one shoulder, framing discerning eyes that missed nothing. She was old enough to be refined, young enough to be coveted; cunning enough to devise any scheme, and patient enough to see it through to completion. Worst of all, she was unpredictable, with no regard for anyone but herself.

If I was the Monster Hunter incarnate, Morrigan was the Monster.

Destiny brought us together time and again, in many lives, many forms. Often, it left one of us dead.

"What are you doing here, Morrigan?" I spat. Rachelle flinched away from the naked hatred in my voice. I didn't care. She didn't understand, *couldn't* understand.

Morrigan smiled, red lips parting. Oh yes. *She* knew. How ironic that my immortal enemy would understand me better than my best friend.

There were small signs of Morrigan's age that hadn't been there when last I'd seen her: a few lines, little else. It was quite the feat—I hadn't seen her in nearly two decades. I remembered our last meeting with vibrant, unwanted clarity. I'd spent two incarnations running from that encounter. Huntington's death. The little girl's terror. Morrigan's mocking laughter.

Needless to say, seeing her pissed me off. And the fact that she was still in the same body only angered me further. It was like a trophy she carried, proof she'd outlived me. "You've been gone so many years, recently," she purred. "*Someone* needs to look after your friends, with you gone." Her eyes flitted to my clenched jaw. "Put your claws away, kitten. I simply wish to speak with you."

"Then why not just call me? Instead, you threaten my friend—"

"Threaten?" Wide-eyed innocence masked something sinister.

"Rachelle has been a most gracious hostess. Your mortal *associates* always provide me with such joy; why ever would I threaten them?" Her hand covered her heart. As though she had one.

I bit back my response, taking a deep breath instead. She was trying to get under my skin. If I let her, then she won this exchange.

Morrigan pouted. "Not in a playful mood? It's so hard to catch you in one, these days."

"What. Do. You. Want?" I growled.

"Eggs Benedict."

I blinked. "What?"

Rachelle had been watching the exchange with visibly rising unease. At the mention of eggs Benedict, however, she brightened. "We made breakfast, Emery. Come in and have some?" She pitched it as a question—her way of telling me she'd follow my lead, I hoped.

Morrigan arched one eyebrow.

I weighed my options. If I left now, with Rachelle in tow, we'd likely be safe. Morrigan wanted something, or she wouldn't be here. The chance that she would kill Rachelle (and possibly me) in broad daylight, in front of an urban apartment complex, was slim. Not nearly as slim as it would be for anybody else, but slim nonetheless. But Morrigan also knew where Rachelle lived. If I disappeared to New York for the next couple of days without hearing Morrigan out, did that make it more likely I'd return to find Rachelle's death on the local news?

"I already ate. But I'll stay for one cup of coffee." I turned to Rachelle. "Would you mind grabbing us some coffees? You can take my mom's car." I held out the keys.

She didn't take me up on my offer to escape. "No need!" she chirped. "I've got a Keurig." Her cavalier attitude shouldn't have surprised me; her enthusiasm and fearlessness had led to plenty of thrilling high school escapades... but I could already see those same traits were likely to land her in trouble now that they could put her in real danger.

I swallowed my retort and nodded. Once.

Rachelle bounced up the stairwell. I tensed as she neared Morrigan, but my nemesis only watched me with mounting amusement in her eyes.

I hissed, "You expect me to dance to your tune when you show up at my friend's house like this?"

Morrigan's smile widened. "You wouldn't respond to my friend request on that mortal blog of yours. Two incarnations, Emery, and no hello?" She shook her head in mock sorrow, then ascended the stairs to join Rachelle in the kitchen.

I took a moment to compose myself. Recollections of previous encounters with Morrigan tumbled in my mind, tangled and confused, too twisted with raw emotion to fully separate into distinct memories. The most recent stood out: The smell of salt and brine. The cries of a small girl. A gunshot. And over it all, I saw those eyes, the light extinguished, staring blankly, blankly...

I shuddered. I was not ready for this encounter, but Morrigan likely arranged it that way. I needed to get out of this, put her off balance.

I needed a loophole. That thought comforted me. *I can do this.*

Morrigan had settled at the metal table in Rachelle's small kitchen. I pulled out a chair, scraping the floor a little too loudly, and joined her. I put my back to the door, not letting Morrigan between me and our escape route. If she noticed, she didn't comment on it. She was still too close for my comfort—by a few continents—but, wonder of wonders, it seemed she was telling the truth: she'd come for conversation and eggs Benedict, not murder.

"Do you know who's impersonating me?" I asked as I sat, more to take control of the conversation than with any real expectation that she'd answer. Still, if anyone would know, it would be Morrigan. The serpent had found my new best friend a day after my reincarnation, after all.

"*Impersonating,*" she repeated slowly, then shrugged. "No."

I grunted. That was about as helpful as I'd expected.

"But if you're asking about the Monster Hunter incarnate," she added, "I believe you'll find her in New York."

I looked up, but she was accepting a mug of hot coffee from

Rachelle, uninterested in my reaction. Rachelle placed another mug in front of me. "What do you know about her?" I grated, despising myself for asking. She was walking me down a path of treats, and I was gobbling them up. I could see the pit of snakes ahead, but I couldn't veer off the path. Had Emery Luple *ever* been a match for Morrigan?

"She's staying in Manhattan. I'll give you the address."

Rachelle remained standing by the Keurig, apparently trying to be unobtrusive. I felt her eyes go back and forth between us as we spoke.

"And why would you do that?" I asked, blowing on my coffee to cool it and watching Morrigan through the curling steam.

Her eyes sparkled over the rim of her mug. "An amends." She sipped her coffee without wincing at the hot liquid, her gaze not leaving my own. As if an address were an even trade for a murder.

"That's a terrible deal," I said, testing my coffee and then taking a swallow. "Even more so because the Monster Hunter incarnate is sitting in this very kitchen."

"Indeed." Morrigan met Rachelle's gaze. "He isn't always this inso-lent, you know. Several of his incarnations were polite, even gener-ous." She sighed, feigned disappointment etched deep into her features. Yet she was unable to mask those glittering eyes. "I blame his upbringing," she said conspiratorially. "His mother did her best, naturally, but Emery keenly misses his father's influence."

I narrowed my eyes. "I don't have a father," I said slowly, seeing the direction of the conversation she was dangling in front of me but unable to find the barb. "I never do."

Morrigan shared a look with Rachelle, as though I'd proven her point. "What a coincidence."

I shrugged. "Part of my incarnation."

She took another sip. "Oh? Are you the Bastard incarnate, then?"

I lifted my coffee mug, showing it to her. "I said one drink. When this is gone, so am I."

The spot just above her left eyebrow twitched. I'd struck a nerve. I kept the smirk off my face. Morrigan would undoubtedly win this bout, but at least it wasn't a shutout. Emery Luple was on the scoreboard.

"I do hope your feminine wiles will rub off on him," Morrigan told Rachelle. "I find that Emery is most accommodating when he's in love with a mortal." Rachelle and I had different, yet parallel, responses to Morrigan's taunt: Rachelle *colored* red, and I *saw* red. She avoided my eyes, and all I could see were eyes. Dead eyes. His eyes.

Snap out of it, Emery. I was breathing hard. I glanced at Rachelle... and realized with a jolt that her reaction meant she was concealing feelings for me. *Oh no.* I groaned inwardly, thinking over the memories of my relationship with Rachelle. It was pure innocence, congenial, not even a hint more than platonic. But I could see it now. In her body language, in her blush, in her averted gaze. *Crap.* She was going to be severely disappointed. I would need to find a way to let her down gently.

All those thoughts and feelings rushed through me like I was a straw. Only a moment or two had elapsed, Morrigan watching me with undisguised, exquisite pleasure.

My fury and emotions made me a fly in her web, each thrash sending a tremble down the threads, letting the spider in the center know exactly where I was, vulnerable and caught. I would not play into her hands that easily. I banished my emotions to a corner of my mind. They'd resurface, I knew, but not right now.

"I accept your amends," I told her calmly, soaring above her trap.

She blinked, the only evidence of her surprise, and then dipped her head in graceful acknowledgment. "Oh I'm *so* glad," she purred.

My victory soured in my mouth even as she slid an envelope across the table toward me. "What is this?"

"Two tickets to JFK. One-way, just in case you don't return for, oh, I don't know, say... exactly one thousand and one days." Her attention slid to Rachelle. "Or ever."

I went cold, despite the warm coffee in my belly. "What makes you think I would take Rachelle with me to the dangers in New York?"

Her eyebrows shot up, mock surprise written on her face. "You mean you'd leave your mortal behind?" She doctored up a false note of concern, one finger tapping her chin. "I suppose I *could* be convinced to check in on her while you're gone..."

My heart sank. In the end, I'd walked right into her snare anyway. And I still couldn't see the shape of it. What was it that Morrigan *wanted*?

"No, I couldn't expect you to do that," I said evenly, as if reconsidering.

"*Excuse me.*" Rachelle crossed her arms. "I know I'm just a measly *mortal* and all, but don't I get a say in this?"

Morrigan dabbed her lips with a napkin. "Of course you do," she said magnanimously, proffering a sympathetic smile. "I'm sorry, my dear, I overstepped. In my eagerness to offer you this gift, I forgot my manners." She put on a pleading look. "Oh, but you will go, won't you? Say that you will. I'll feel so much better knowing that someone is looking after Emery for me."

Rachelle was intelligent enough to see through Morrigan's charade, I was sure, but Morrigan had baited her hook with care. Rachelle, for all that she wasn't buying the act, also really wanted to go. Hesitation and indignation warred in her expression. It was a battle I recognized. I was in the same damn boat. And if I was going to New York in part for *There's Always a Loophole,* I would need Rachelle's services anyway. A fact reflected in her dilemma.

Every fiber of my being wanted to avoid New York. I wanted to go somewhere—anywhere—else, just not New York. It was the center of Morrigan's web, the bottom of her pit, the end of her candied road. Frustration roared like a caged animal inside me as I considered. I knew far too little of her schemes. Was this visit to get me out of Seattle, or into New York? Why did she know the very address of my impersonator? It now seemed impossible she was not involved in my impostor's appearance. But in what way and to what end? One thing was certain: if Morrigan wanted me in New York, the only reasonable response was to avoid it like the Plague incarnate. And yes, that's a thing.

"I'll go," I said and snatched the envelope from the table. I looked at Rachelle. Her lips thinned into a fine line, but she nodded.

Morrigan's expression was unreadable, giving no inkling of her thoughts, which were hidden behind a silken smile. As my eyes met hers, I knew I'd fallen headfirst into the pit she'd dug for me. Probably with less resistance than she expected.

And yet New York called to me. The decapitations. Caden's request for aid. My impostor. Morrigan's well-lit path of inevitable treachery was my destiny.

If I ever met Destiny incarnate, I owed her a punch in the face.

*A*stute readers may be wondering what happened to chapter eight. *If you noticed, congratulations! You don't win anything, but you're a perceptive person, and that's its own reward. If you didn't notice, I can hardly blame you. Counting is hard.*

Chapter eight was a boring affair—Rachelle and I did some packing, I forgot my toothbrush, and we had an uneventful flight the next morning. Morrigan proved her dastardly villainy by giving us both middle seats in coach. And then we landed. You're welcome for sparing you the riveting read.

WE WALKED out of the drugstore, I with a new toothbrush triumphantly in hand, towing our luggage behind us. New York City had a different feel from Seattle, and it was... a lot. It felt like everyone was in a hurry and we were an impediment to their busy schedule. Our luggage branded us as tourists, and by the impatient glances we received on the subway, that was a bad thing. Not everyone was cast from the same mold, though. One woman pleasantly informed us how to get to the hotel district in Manhattan and helpfully recommended we not stop on the sidewalk. I'm fairly sure she wasn't being sarcastic about it, either. Since this incarnation was from Seattle, I felt optimistic about my abilities to spot passive-aggressiveness. A skill that would likely not come in handy in New York, as there wasn't a whole lot of *passive* to the aggressiveness around here.

All that said, New York City was not unpleasant. As long as Rachelle and I didn't block the subway doors, we were widely ignored, which was almost the same as being accepted. There were so many people, each of them with a life and backstory all their own. It was overwhelming. It put things in perspective, too. Every life is important—almost as important as mine—and here I was in a city *teeming* with life. This wasn't my first visit to NYC; I had lived here in previous incarnations, but many years had elapsed since then. Moreover, I'd long ago learned to appreciate my "firsts" with each new incarnation. That mentality kept me from becoming too frustrated by my lack of memories and enabled me to be excited by "new" things. It kept immortality fresh, you know? Well, you undoubtedly *don't* know, but you get the idea. To all of you incarnates reading this, I recommend you try it. The reincarnation experience is typically considered the worst part of our deal, but each new life presents a new opportunity. Damn, that's wise. Maybe I'll write a self-help book for all my incarnate fans out there.

The address Morrigan had supplied for my impostor was located in the southwest corner of Manhattan, along the Hudson River. Our rough plan was to head to Midtown and seek lodging there. With our HQ thus established, we could begin investigating said impostor and connect with Caden—and hopefully take down two birds with a single stone.

Our journey was punctuated by frequent stops as Rachelle took out her camera, sometimes snapping photos and sometimes sweeping it slowly around, recording our adventure. On the top of the camera, she mounted a microphone that looked a little like a fuzzy, black shuttle rocket. Occasionally, she would have me turn around and smile or wave. I humored her with as much patience as I could muster. It was difficult to put into words, but something had changed between Rachelle and me, a tiny, unspoken snag in our friendship. Whether it was because of the hatred I'd displayed for Morrigan, or Rachelle's discomfort due to my realization of the feelings she harbored for me, or something else entirely, I couldn't say. On the surface, nothing had changed, but beneath... something had shifted. It wasn't expressly bad. Maybe it was simply an awkwardness that would dissolve back into our friendship and make us stronger in the end. For the moment, however, I felt an intuitive warning to be cautious with her feelings; they were, perhaps, more fragile than they had been a day before. So I tempered my sense of urgency and waved at the camera Rachelle handled expertly. It took an embarrassingly long time for me to realize what she was doing: documenting our travel for *my* blog.

It had taken a bit of stumbling around to find our way to the E train that took us into the city. It wasn't the fastest option, but Rachelle and I agreed it was better to opt for the cheaper route. I had a surprisingly hefty balance in my savings account, but we both wanted to see more of the city anyway. I wasn't too worried about lodging. We didn't have a hotel booking, but we were spoiled for choice in Manhattan. And maybe Caden could help us find something more affordable after we'd met with him.

The fast-and-loose nature of my so-called plans did not sit comfortably with me, but it was only one of many problems taxing my mind. I kept replaying the conversation with Morrigan in my head, trying without success to suss out the scheme lurking behind her words. I thought and overthought our exchange. Had I handled myself well? Could I have asked a question I hadn't asked that would've provided a peek into her agenda? Done something to get under her skin, the way she'd crept beneath mine? Should I have put on a performance, like she'd done, to convey the pretext of civility? What would such an act accomplish? Even if I'd been able to crack her perfect veneer of composure, it would have been worth it.

Seeing Morrigan had exacerbated a worry that had been nettling me since my reincarnation. My previous two incarnations had been damaged, plagued by the tragedy of three-incarnations-ago Emery. Huntington's murder. My failure to save the mortals who counted on me. Yesterday I had reincarnated into a younger body with a healthy mind, largely unburdened by the trauma of my pasts, but those memories still clung to me, unwilling to be wholly forgotten or overcome. Additionally, another concern crowded in among the others: who had killed me? Previous me, I mean. The memory of my skirmish with the Yeti wasn't clear; there was something I was missing, oddities I couldn't place and couldn't quite remember. But the gunshot and my subsequent demise were not so muddied. My initial inclination was to blame Morrigan, but I dismissed the thought immediately. The voice behind me, even muffled, had *not* belonged to Morrigan. Not enough gloating, for starters. Morrigan wanted me to know when I died at her hands. No thief-in-the-night—or, in this case, shadow-in-the-sandstorm—shenanigans from her. The victory of killing me would be cheapened, hollow if the last thing I saw was anything except her smug expression.

Which meant, I deduced sourly, that there was *another* person who wanted me dead. Yay. It also suggested the Genie served not Morrigan but this other unknown enemy. Which wasn't entirely unexpected: being the Monster Hunter incarnate, I had more than one enemy. All of this could simply be a revenge plot, with me as the lucky target.

Which brought me to my next worry: why was someone in New York hunting monsters? Were they claiming to be the Monster Hunter incarnate, or were they just trying to fill my shoes during my absence? Being the Monster Hunter was an enormous burden; I was responsible for keeping people and other incarnates safe. Why anyone would take on the weight of that mantle was beyond me. I mean, sure, dropping my name could open a few doors, but—according to Gregory—this impostor hadn't even claimed to be Emery Luple. Which made the whole thing even more bizarre. And then the bombshell: Morrigan knew exactly where the impostor was. Down to the very address. Sure, she could have done her own investigative work to unearth their identity and then drop it in my lap as a lure. But it seemed unlikely. More likely, and scarier by far, was that Morrigan was involved in the deception. I just couldn't find the angle.

And to top everything off, this fraudulent Monster Hunter was living in a city that was the epicenter of a string of grisly murders. If I were a betting man... but no. Better not to jump to conclusions. The coincidences were piled high, certainly, but that sometimes happened around me. I attracted drama like a flame draws moths. Best to keep an open mind.

"Whatcha thinking about?" Rachelle asked. I jumped, then looked sheepishly at the camera she was holding.

I put on my best showman's smile. "New York City," I answered, gesturing around to indicate the grand city around me. The buildings here were tall and fit together seamlessly, no alleys or driveways between where one business ended and the next began. Every block or so we crossed a major street with major traffic. Foot traffic was heavy, too, but we'd turned down a smaller street and the sidewalk was wide enough for passersby to skirt around us. "We're only a couple blocks away from Times Square." I pitched my voice to sound serious and mysterious—mystserious?—at the same time. "And what sinister plot is bubbling beneath the everyday bustle of the Big Apple? My friend and I have traveled across the States to unearth the mystery of the decapitations. Police and press are baffled, but gumshoe Emery 'Loophole' is on the case."

Rachelle laughed. "Gumshoe? What are you, a 1920s mobster?"

I pretended to be offended. "Oh, and what impressive nickname do you kids call a detective these days? 'Private eye'?"

"What?" She snickered. "Are you sure you aren't the Grandpa incarnate?"

My mouth dropped open in genuine shock. "Nice burn," I said, appreciating her vernacular. "You sound like one of us."

She scoffed. "As though it's hard." She mimicked a posh tone and said, "You simply talk down to *those mortals* and throw in a joke about reincarnation every once in a while for good measure."

I'd opened my mouth to retort when a strange sound caught my attention. It was on the extreme edge of my hearing, a whistling *whoosh* that...

"Don't tell me I bested the invincible Em—" She cut off as I raised my hand sharply. Cocked my head. It had come from that parking garage, there. I could faintly hear *something* echoing from the mouth of the garage.

My skin crawled. The sound was the pale imitation of the source, nothing but an echo of an echo. A crunch, like metal splitting bone, followed by a wet rasping sound.

"Stay here," I hissed, motioning for Rachelle to remain on the sidewalk. I crouch-walked up to the entrance of the garage and peered around its corner. A person shied away from us on the street, giving us a wide berth.

The garage wasn't terribly large, its entrance only wide enough for two vehicles to squeeze by each other. The resemblance to a mouth was further emphasized by the downward slope just inside its interior, as though the garage swallowed the vehicles that entered. I took a deep breath—it smelled dry and musty at the same time—to calm my nerves, then walked cautiously into the garage. Rachelle, naturally, followed me. I shot her a glare, but she ignored it, keeping close behind me, her camera recording our descent. No time to argue. I moved forward more cautiously than I would have alone, unwilling to put her in harm's way without knowing the exact nature of what lay ahead. My senses were electrified, dialed up to catch a whiff of danger before it was upon us.

"Help!" a voice cried out, making me flinch. The word echoed up from the tunnel, loud. It was close.

We rounded the corner to the first floor of the parking garage. The looping drive continued to descend, but the scene before me was what I'd come to find. A short, bearded man stood over a lump that, I realized with sickening shock, was a fallen body. The man looked up as we approached, his eyes wild. "Help!" he called again, frantic. His voice was higher pitched than his barrel chest and thick brown beard suggested. I rushed over, barely getting out a "What happened?"

before the man began to stammer and point. He held a phone in his hand.

"Call the police," I told him, trying to sound both calm and authoritative. He nodded and dialed, his hands shaking.

Swallowing hard, I looked at the body. The body belonged to someone who wore a long-sleeved gray undershirt beneath an olive-colored quilted vest, with old jeans, accented by white rips and scuffs, tucked into brown boots. And that was it.

What did their face look like, Emery? you may be wondering. *What gender were they?* From their build, I would guess male. Without turning the body over, I couldn't be certain. Oh, and one other little detail made it a tad challenging to determine.

The body was utterly devoid of a head.

here wasn't enough blood. The wound was still grisly.
Gaping and raw, red and seeping, little drips of blood
pattering on the pavement. A sort of puffy ring encircled the wound,
looking *way* too much like raw chicken. Moldy raw chicken.

I just threw up in my mouth a little.

Despite all that, the amount of blood reminded me of an opera-
tion, as though the head had been severed carefully from the shoulders as opposed to torn or hacked. I had seen my fair share of death. I
often reincarnated into backstories that put me on the frontlines:
investigator, law enforcement, soldier, etc. Anything to get me close to
incarnates. I had also doled out my fair share of slayings. There was
almost nothing to which the mind could not become accustomed.
But some things, you didn't *want* to. I looked down at the body with a
profound sadness. It was at times like these that I pondered the existence of mortals. Did they reincarnate like we do, but without the
memories? Did they go on to an afterlife? Or did they return to the
world that gave them life, becoming one with it? In spite of my many
incarnations, that mystery yet eluded me.

If ever a death *screamed* that an incarnate was involved, it was a
headless corpse that didn't bleed. There was something gut-wrench-
ingly *wrong* about this, something surreal. The other man had moved

a little ways away, speaking with the 9-1-1 dispatcher, and Rachelle...
Rachelle! I spun to her, cursing myself for not thinking of her sooner,
not protecting her from the scene.

Her hair framed a pale face set in a grim, determined mask. Her
mouth trembled slightly, but her hand guiding the video camera was
steady and careful, sweeping the scene. I was struck by her poise and
her fierce resolve; this was a modern-day warrior. She noticed me
watching her and gave me a weak smile, then pointed with her other
hand. Not at the body, it turned out, but at the concrete pillar above it.
I frowned, not seeing what she was... hold on. It was dark in the
parking garage, the low-powered lights nothing compared to the
daylight outside, and I'd been distracted by the dead body.

Hacked into the pillar was a word, scrawled as if in haste, but
literally *gouged* into the concrete as though someone had carved it
with a knife in a tree trunk. I squinted to make out the letters.

AHEDRIAN

"What does it say?" Rachelle asked, and to her credit, her voice
sounded almost conversational.

I sounded it out. "Ahedrian," I told her in a low voice.

Rachelle looked at me blankly. "Does that mean anything to
you?"

I shook my head slowly.

A car, presumably exiting the parking lot, approached. It started
to pass us but stopped when the driver saw the body. A large woman
climbed out, asking us what was going on. Rachelle began speaking
with her in quiet tones. Giving me time to investigate, I realized with
a start. Damn, she was a *good* sidekick.

I was at a loss, though. The body was prone and headless, and I
didn't want to disturb the scene before the police arrived. There was
the strange word carved into the pillar, along with some speckled red
graffiti. No, that wasn't graffiti, was it? It was blood. An arc of blood
sprayed across the pillar, as though the swing that decapitated the
victim had splattered the surface behind them. Then what? Had the
wound immediately closed? That made no sense. But the blood told
me something important. I had begun to question whether the

murder had happened here, or if the murderer had simply dumped the body after killing it somewhere else. The spray of blood, if it wasn't planted, meant that the killing happened right here. Which was further proof this was an incarnate's work. Only a supernatural or paranormal force could decapitate someone with so little blood spilled, then disappear without a trace.

The bearded man who'd found the body rejoined us. I nodded at him, hoping to capture his attention. He was shaking and avoided looking at the body. "Did you find them like this?" I asked, gesturing to the victim.

"Yeah, man. I was just getting into my car when I heard a weird sound. Came over here to see what it was. And found... this."

"Did you see anyone else?"

He shook his head. "Thought I heard footsteps, though. Like, running. But this place has a lot of echoes. It could have been on a different floor."

I pointed at the word carved into the cement. "Any idea what that means?"

He looked at it in surprise, then swallowed and visibly paled. "Whoa." He licked his lips. "D-d-didn't even see it there."

I watched him carefully. "You know what it means." I didn't pitch it as a question.

His eyes were glued to it, but he pulled them away, glancing at me with apprehension. "Yeah, man. Haven't you seen the news?"

I shook my head. "I just arrived in New York," I told him. I looked around to point out our luggage—and groaned. Rachelle had brought hers with her, but I'd left mine outside, on the street, in my hurry to come down here. I should go get it before it disappeared, but I didn't want to leave the scene yet. "What does it mean?" I asked.

"Not entirely sure, but it's been found at all of the decapitation sites. People talk, think it might be a name or a curse." His eyes were drawn back to the carving. "The murderer's calling card."

Another car pulled up and honked at us to get out of its way. When we didn't comply, a man in a business suit rolled the window down and started cursing, only to fall quiet as he noticed the body. In the distance, I could hear approaching sirens. The area would soon be swarming with police officers and news crews.

I thanked the bearded man for the information and walked over to Rachelle. "Sounds like the murderer leaves that word as their calling card," I informed her. "Been at the other murder sites, too."

"Some sort of incarnate word?" she asked in a low voice.

I hesitated. "Could be, but not one I've heard before." I gave a helpless shrug. "Most of 'our' words are real words, though, just with different meanings. This is new to me."

A white van had driven up, and I glimpsed a logo on the side; a local news channel. Police cars with flashing blue lights crammed in and around the van, men and women in uniform shouting instructions to the gathering crowd even before shutting off their vehicles.

"Maybe we should go," I said, watching the news team haul their equipment out and scramble to get a piece of the action before the police shooed them away.

"Excuse me!" one of the news crew shouted. As I turned, I hid my dismay. A tall, leggy woman in a tailored black skirt suit was striding toward Rachelle and me, rummaging in her clutch. Her mane of cascading red curls bounced about her shoulders and back. From her small purse she produced a wad of folded bills. "Two hundred dollars for your footage," she offered, giving us a disarming smile.

Rachelle blinked, taken aback. I stepped forward hastily. "Thanks for the offer," I said, "but we really didn't see anything."

The woman's smile didn't falter. She dug a USB cable out of her clutch. "I'm Sabrina Miles, NYBC News. Look, I'm not asking for your camera, guys, just the footage." She leaned in, her green eyes sparkling above freckle-dusted cheeks. "Don't worry; it doesn't have to be professional quality. These first-on-the-scene phone videos are all the rage with the public right now. The more amateur it looks, the more authentic it is." She shrugged, as if to say, "Who knew?"

I felt myself fighting a smile. Sabrina Miles was persistent. Three-incarnations-ago Emery would have *liked* her. They could have been friends. "It's not that," Rachelle said, finding her voice. "It's just...

Emery here runs a blog. We couldn't sell it, knowing that we have the exclusive first look."

Sabrina's smile wavered for a moment, but she didn't let it slip. "A blog, huh? No problem." She took out a small spiral notebook and a pen and flipped a few pages. "What's the name of the blog? I'll give you the two hundred bucks, and I'll credit your blog. You'll get national recognition." She glanced at me. "Emery, you said? What's your full name?"

I was openly grinning now. She was *good*. She didn't phrase the offer as a question, just expected we'd cave. And made us feel good while doing it. Never mind three Emerys ago. I liked her *now*. "Emery Luple," I told her. "My blog is called *There's Always a Loophole*."

Sabrina scribbled, nodding along. "Nice. Kindred spirits, you and I. Sabrina Miles: 'going the extra *mile* for you.'" She snapped her notepad closed and stowed it away. Held up the money again.

Rachelle pushed forward, almost in front of me. "Three hundred, and it's yours," she said. I was glad she'd taken over. It was her footage, after all.

"Only got fifty more, guys," Sabrina responded, digging out another bill from her clutch.

"Deal." Rachelle accepted the wad of cash, then helped Sabrina hook up her phone to Rachelle's camera.

"Know anything about 'Ahedrian?'" I asked Sabrina while they worked.

She looked up sharply. "Yes. Why?"

I pointed over at the crowd surrounding the body. "Because it's carved into the wall over there."

She gave a low whistle. "You two got it on the cam?" Rachelle confirmed she had. "I got a good deal on this, then. Ahedrian is a headline, these days."

"Almost sounds like you respect this killer," I commented.

Sabrina snorted. "I respect anything that gets me on the front page." She shook her head. "Tragic, what's happening. No doubt about it." She looked up at us and veiled her expression with another smile. "But tragedy sells. Especially in my line of work."

I nodded, understanding.

"Sabrina, we're up," one of the cameramen called.

The file transfer finished, and Sabrina thanked us again. She paused, considering us. "You guys want to be on TV? Give a statement?"

I shook my head. To my relief, Rachelle followed suit. I wanted to keep a low profile until I knew more about this murderer. And my impostor.

Sabrina shrugged and handed Rachelle her business card. "Call me if you change your mind."

Rachelle sidled up to me, speaking low. "You sure that was a good idea?"

"I don't see the harm." I blew out a breath. "Honestly, the content was probably too graphic for my blog. This way we get the recognition *and* get paid."

Rachelle looked dubious, but she dropped it. "What's the plan?"

"Time to get out of here. We'll be trapped down here all day otherwise." I grinned. "And thanks to your local news channel, we can upgrade to a swanky hotel for the night!"

"Umm, Emery? I think you underestimate the cost of a New York City hotel."

11

Formal Incarnate Lesson Two: Benign Incarnates
By Emery Luple

*W*elcome back, class. Today we are going to discuss my favorite classification of incarnates: the Benign. And even though you should always shoot to be a ten, I'm going to tell you why it's even cooler to Benign. Get it?

Benign incarnates are gentle and kind, unthreatening to human life or health. We often try to improve the existence of mortals and human society. Think of us as the Social Workers incarnate, working tirelessly to bring joy, charity, and world peace to all. We truly are role models of selflessness: virtuous, wholesome, giving, and—above all—humble.

Remember how Prey incarnates dwell in Safe Havens? Well, each classification of incarnates has its own version of a domain. For us Benign types, it's called a Sanctum. It's a sort of retreat, our happy place where we can go to recover or reflect. Sanctums are sometimes public venues, too, places where mortals may tread to seek sanctuary from the woes of the world. Like Camelot. We're just generous that way.

Some other examples of Benigns include the following esteemed roster:

the Santa Claus incarnate, the Watchman incarnate, and the Fairy Godmother incarnate.

My Sanctum? Oh. Well, I suppose I did bring on that question, didn't I? To be honest, I haven't had one since Huntington's death, three incarnations ago. I guess I lost my happy place when Morrigan killed him. I suspect that until the specter of that tragedy stops haunting me, I will not find my Sanctum. Um, I'm sorry; please excuse me. Class dismissed.

~

MY LUGGAGE WAS GONE. Of course.

And so was the sun. In the relatively short time we'd been inside the garage, day had succumbed to evening. Rachelle and I checked into the Starboard Hotel, less than a mile from the parking garage. The hotel had a nautical theme, as you may have guessed, with rich blue carpets accenting shiny hardwood floors, wooden paneling, and naval murals in the lobby. We were undeserving of the warm welcome we received from the staff, given that we hadn't made a reservation ahead of time and we both looked like we'd hiked from JFK Airport. Plush seating and plenty of low lighting gave the place an intimate feel. Our room continued the theme, with thick rugs over hardwood and—most thematically of all—round windows that made it seem as if we were looking out the portholes of a sea vessel. We were on the seventh floor, and our room commanded an impressive view... of the next building over.

Rachelle began unpacking her things, and I called Caden. As I waited for him to pick up, my stomach rumbled. I hadn't eaten since the biscotti and chips on the flight.

"Hello?" Caden's voice came over the line.

"It's Emery. I know I said I'd call you yesterday—sorry about that —but I have a surprise for you."

"No, not at all," came the response. "I'm glad to hear from you. A surprise, huh? Does that mean you've decided you'll come to New York?"

I grinned. "As a matter of fact, I have. Where can I meet you?"

There was a pause. "When do you arrive?"

I glanced at the clock on the nightstand. "About three hours ago."

"Really?" Caden's voice became eager. "Where are you now?"

"Do you know the Starboard in Manhattan?"

"I'm not far from there, actually," he said. "Want to meet up tonight?"

"As long as there's food," I said, "you can convince me to meet you just about anywhere."

Caden laughed. "I know just the place."

ONE MUCH-NEEDED SHOWER LATER, I came out into the room wearing my jeans and a sheepish smile, shirt in one hand. Rachelle was seated on her bed, reviewing the cam's footage. As I walked toward her, she looked at my exposed torso and blushed slightly, covering it by looking back down at the footage as though she'd missed something important.

"Um, do you have any deodorant I could use?" I asked. "Mine was in my suitcase."

She stared at me for a moment too long, her eyes straying from my face, before ducking her head and saying, "Yeah, of course."

I sighed as she leaned over the bed and unzipped a pocket in her bag. I needed to address this, and soon. But... it was so uncomfortable. In all my lifetimes, nothing was quite so awkward as an unrequited crush. Flattering, certainly—but awkward.

"Sorry," I said as she handed the deodorant to me with averted eyes. "I'll pick up some of my own tomorrow."

She shrugged and made a noncommittal sound in her throat.

I hesitated before taking a seat on the bed. "Rachelle," I tried again, "you know that, uh..." Good grief, now she was getting up and avoiding my eyes. "Where are you going?" I asked, barely managing to keep the exasperation from my voice. In hindsight, I probably should have put my shirt on first.

"Bathroom!" she said with forced cheer, and then she proceeded to close the door firmly, leaving me half-dressed and nonplussed.

I shook my head and rubbed my face, at a loss for words. I threw on my shirt quickly and considered heading out to meet Caden alone, but immediately dismissed the idea. The awkwardness with Rachelle would pass, once she was ready to hear it, and I didn't want to damage our friendship. Plus, she'd come all the way to New York with me. I wasn't going to start leaving her out of things now.

An irrational part of my brain wondered if this was part of Morrigan's scheme. Had she provided not one, but two tickets to New York in order to jeopardize—or straight-out ruin—my friendship with Rachelle? I trashed the idea as unworthy as soon as I thought it. I couldn't blame Morrigan for all my problems, much as I would like her to be my scapegoat. But she *had* pressed for Rachelle to be here. Why? How did Rachelle fit into Morrigan's plans?

Regardless of the answer, I needed to rebuff Rachelle's feelings and salvage our friendship before the whole thing imploded. Rachelle was not fragile. She'd demonstrated her warrior spirit on several occasions already since I'd reincarnated two days ago. I knew she was resilient, strong, and capable. She'd survive hurt feelings. It wasn't as if it was *love* or anything. Just a crush. We'd both manage.

She came out of the bathroom, her hair fixed and her face washed. Makeup reapplied. "Ready to go?" she asked without preamble.

I nodded, sensing (I can take a hint!) that she did not want to talk about it. I grabbed my wallet and the hotel keycard, and we descended to the lobby.

The restaurant, Los Mares, was a festive spot specializing in Mexican seafood. It was busy but not slammed, with a short line of people and most of the tables filled. The floor was concrete, the walls white tile, and the whole place had a nautical theme... again.

I was from Seattle. The city is a major seaport. Our sports teams are the Mariners, Seahawks, and Kraken. And yet I don't think I'd ever experienced this much in the way of seafaring motifs. To be completely fair, I had only technically been from Seattle for three days. But I had the memories and experiences of living there my entire life—so it counts.

Rachelle and I stood in line, waiting to order, when my phone buzzed. I looked at it. A text from Caden. He was here.

I looked up to see a young man enter Los Mares only a dozen feet away or so. His eyes swept over the crowd, seeking us out. This had to be Caden.

He was cute, and his look perfectly matched the soft voice I'd heard over the phone. He was younger than I expected, perhaps our age, maybe a year younger. I suppose that made sense, given his familiarity with my blog. The entrance to the restaurant was cheerfully lit to ward off the late-winter darkness, creating the illusion that his white outfit glowed. The light caught in his feathery golden hair, which shimmered in the sharp illumination. Eyes the color of seafoam alighted on us, and his boyish features brightened. He gave a tentative half wave, which Rachelle and I returned automatically.

In a tiny, oft-forgotten corner of my mind, in the place where the *immortal* Emery dwells, a thought began to build, trying to push through to my conscious brain, but guttered out before I could catch hold of it.

Caden threaded his way through the other diners, his lean frame easily navigating the line. He stepped up to us—he was a little shorter than I'd first thought—and gave us a shy smile. "Emery?" he said. His voice was light.

"Guilty." Something seemed familiar about him, but it was probably just his voice; his appearance matched it perfectly. "Sorry for the short notice."

"Not at all, I'm really excited you came." He turned to Rachelle. "I'm Caden."

She was regarding me curiously, her expression one I couldn't quite identify. After a moment, she pulled her eyes away from me and smiled at Caden. "Rachelle," she said, by way of greeting. "I'm a friend of Emery's. We came from Seattle together."

"Your voice sounds familiar," Caden observed. He thought for a moment, then snapped his fingers. "You're Emery's assistant. We spoke the other day."

"I play that role sometimes." Rachelle shot me a mischievous look. "He's pretty helpless without me, if we're being honest."

"Hey, now." I raised my hands defensively, laughing despite myself. "Nothing wrong with knowing when you need help."

"I agree," Caden said earnestly. He looked down at his feet for a moment. "Thanks again for coming. Let's order food, and then we can talk more about why I called you."

Rachelle and I agreed, and while we waited our turn we talked about the flight and our first impressions of New York. We all ordered fish tacos, and Caden insisted on treating us, since we'd "come all this way."

By the time we got our orders, all of the tables in the small restaurant were occupied, so we took the food out to the street. Maybe in the warm summer months there was outdoor seating, but on a chilly evening in March, we'd have to make do on our own. We put our backs against the exterior wall of the building, the sidewalk large enough for pedestrians to pass us unhindered, and ate in companionable silence for a few minutes. I ate eagerly, licking juice off my fingers.

After a few minutes, Caden asked, "So, what do you two know about the decapitations?"

"More than we'd like to," Rachelle mumbled between bites.

I nodded my agreement. "I heard about the first few from the news. Three, I think. The one today makes four." Caden stared at me, and I chafed under his direct attention. "Did I say something wrong?" I asked.

He shook his head, tousling his golden hair. "I'm just impressed. You work fast. The fourth body was just found a few hours ago."

"Actually, we came across the body before the police did," I told him. Rachelle seemed content to have me speak while she finished her fish taco at a much more graceful pace.

Caden blew out a breath, and I watched it curl into the night air. "Whoa. That's... intense. I'm sorry." He hesitated, winced, then asked, "What was it like?"

I described the scene to him. How I'd heard a strange noise—I tried and epically failed to articulate the *crunch-scrape* sound—and we'd descended into the parking garage, finding the body. I told him some of the details, too, not holding much back. There was something inherently trustworthy about Caden, and he proved an attentive listener. I made no mention of incarnates, of course. I didn't want to scare him off. He was a fan of my blog, and *There's Always a Loophole* was the antithesis of the incarnate world; it was all about *disproving* the existence of the supernatural.

His nose scrunched up in distaste at hearing the word Ahedrian. "Ever come across it before?" he asked.

I shook my head. "New to me. Do you know what it means?"

"Some sort of warning, I think." He brightened and flashed me a smile. I felt a stab of something from that corner of my mind again. I tried to grab hold of it, but it was like trying to remember someone's name when it was on the tip of your tongue. The more I forced it, the more it evaded my grasp. "Actually," Caden said, "it's the reason I called you. The word Ahedrian has been found at each beheading. There have been rumors about ghosts and monsters, that Ahedrian is a word to ward off evil"—he looked up at me, tone fierce—"or to *summon* it."

I felt a thrill down my spine. "Ridiculous," I scoffed.

Luckily, he didn't take offense at my skepticism. "You're the expert," he said, shrugging. "Which is why I called you." Suddenly, he looked shy. "I've been a fan of your show from the beginning, and it just struck me the other day that the police are missing the supernatural connection. Or, you know, the 'loophole.' They may be the best at solving normal crimes, but no one solves supernatural mysteries better than you."

I opened my mouth to reply, but then screams split the night.

*C*aden and I responded in lockstep, both springing forward at the same time.

Rachelle had been paying more attention than we had. One hand covered her mouth to stifle her startled yelp, the other pointing out into the night, off to my left. I looked in that direction, squinting into the darkness. Another scream pierced the silence, and my eyes were drawn to a writhing shadow, my mind at first refusing to understand what I was seeing.

A beastly silhouette slithered out of a manhole thirty paces away, in the dead center of the street. I shaded my eyes from the bright illumination of Los Mares, trying to force them to adjust. It was like waiting for a Polaroid picture to develop as you watched impatiently, shadows slowly shifting and parting into individual shapes, then people, then... an alligator?

The reptilian behemoth was easily sixteen feet in length, from the snout to the tip of its tail. Bulky and low to the ground, with deep ridges along its back and a long, wet jaw. It opened its mouth, strings of saliva stretching between curved teeth the size of my fingers. A throaty roar rumbled down the street, followed by exclamations and screams from nearby pedestrians. A vehicle driving toward us on the other side of the gator caught the reptilian beast in its headlights, throwing its mammoth shadow against the buildings all around me, jaw spread like the silhouette of a tyrannosaurus.

The alligator sprang forward, its low belly almost scraping the pavement. Shock threatened to glue nineteen-year-old Emery to the sidewalk, but immortal Emery shrugged it off as though it were a cobweb and raced forward to meet the oncoming creature. It was enormous and, up close, I realized it was albino, with pale, milky-white scales and red eyes that glowed like embers in the night. I threw the bag of empty dinner wrappers and fish juice at its head in hopes of distracting it, then dove aside. The gator snapped the plastic bag out of the air without even slowing, its raptor jaw slamming shut with the speed of a sprung mousetrap. I landed in a crouch and watched in horror as the creature continued toward Rachelle and Caden. I launched myself after it, but I could already tell I wouldn't make it in time.

Caden watched the oncoming alligator with wide eyes but surprised me with his quick thinking. As the gator neared, he shoved Rachelle to the right and pushed off of her, launching himself in the opposite direction. Over a thousand pounds of lean, coiled muscle went thundering through the space Caden was still exiting, and he cried out as one of his legs caught in the alligator's right haunch. He was pinned, his ankle disappearing under the folds of leathery underbelly. The gator swung its immense head around to bite at him, but Caden had bought me the time I needed to catch up. Without stopping to consider, I kicked at the monster's head as hard as I could.

It didn't do much, really, but the gator recoiled and then snapped at my foot instead of Caden's head, so it served its purpose. I was already reaching down, wrapping my arms under Caden's armpits and heaving him out from under the alligator's bulk. The monstrous creature went for us again, but the white tennis shoe on Caden's free foot caught it sharply under the chin. He was suddenly free, scrambling to his feet, using me as leverage to pull himself up and out of the reptile's toothy reach.

On the other side of the gator, Rachelle was just getting to her feet from where Caden's push had thrown her. Even though the reptile's red eyes were focused on Caden and me in front of it, its tail—a heavy appendage roughened by scaly skin and thick knots—curled up into the air and slammed down with sickening force. Rachelle let out a grunt of surprise and pain, and I heard a *crunch* that made my heart sink.

The alligator didn't give me time to worry about her, though, as it bunched and lunged again, crossing the distance between us in a blink. Time seemed to dilate, stretching as my life filled with nothing but a widening maw encircled with daggerlike teeth.

Then Caden was there. He blurred in from the left like an all-white battering ram, hitting the reptile shoulder-first with all the weight his slender form could rally. Aided by momentum, he managed to drive the creature off course. I sidestepped instinctively, gravity carrying the gator through its lunge and beyond me. Caden, stumbling from the tackle, caught himself on the edge of the building.

Seeing Caden's quick reactions, I felt indignation spike through me. I was the Monster Hunter incarnate, wasn't I? I should be saving him, not the other way around. The feeling built, filling me with the need to prove myself, to *act*. I might not be a hero, but I was equipped to deal with this incarnate. And it was slowly dawning on me that this alligator was most definitely an incarnate.

The Alligator in the Sewers incarnate. A New York City urban legend. The story goes that kids flushed baby alligators down their toilets and the gators grew into monstrous albino creatures that roamed the sewer system. I grinned. A ludicrous enemy required an equally ludicrous solution. With a cry that was half anger and half exhilaration—a shout that screamed "I'm about to do something foolish"—I leapt onto the reptile's back, straddling it like a rodeo bull. I wrapped my arms around the beast's snout and locked them together with as much desperation-fueled strength as I could muster. I felt its sharp exterior teeth ripping into my sleeve and piercing my skin, but I dared not falter. I continued to squeeze, hugging the jaws closed, my legs burning as they fought to keep purchase on the Alligator's knotted hide.

Caden screamed at me. "Emery! What are you doing?"

"Cowabunga!" I whooped in reply. This overgrown lizard was not teenage, mutant, or ninja enough to be the incarnates I *hoped* to run into within New York City's sewer system. That ridiculous idea kept running through my mind as I focused on fighting the pain and keeping my knees and arms locked in place.

I needed a plan, quick. No, not quick. *Now.* The reptile thrashed beneath me, not bucking as much as I thought it would but rather *squirming* in a way that made it difficult to keep from slipping off. If I lost my grip, even for a moment, I'd be gator chow.

Think, Emery! Hard to do while riding a gator, its teeth tearing at my arms. It was a beast incarnate, which meant its fatal flaw might be capture, like the Yeti's. There weren't any tranquilizer darts on hand, though. Maybe I could improvise—a net or makeshift cage could work. No problem. Simple.

Abruptly, a *crack* rang out, and I felt rather than heard a *pop* beneath me. My whole body was squeezing the reptile when it shuddered and then went limp. I realized my eyes were squeezed shut, too, following the lead of my arms and legs. The body kept twitching, but the fight had gone out of it. Slowly, with extreme caution, I unclenched my body.

Adrenaline ebbed, and pain hit me like an unexpected gut punch from a friend. I rolled off the creature, hugging my arms to me, trying to cradle both at once. The gator's teeth had carved deep into my right biceps and both forearms. My legs were trembling from being clamped so tightly. Blood smeared my sleeves.

I lay on my back, staring up at the towering skyscrapers and dark sky beyond. I panted hard, a fierce grin splitting my face. I was alive. I'd taken on an alligator *with my bare hands*. I'd like to see my impostor do that!

A face suddenly filled my vision, blocking part of the night sky. It belonged to a woman with Japanese features. Very angry Japanese features. "Are you okay?" she asked. Her gentle voice contrasted with her obvious fury.

"Fine," I managed through gritted teeth.

"Let me see." She pried my arms from my torso and—with surprising tenderness—prodded each one, scrutinizing my wounds. "That was very brave," she said, but her mouth turned down in distaste. "And very irresponsible. Next time you come across something like that, you run." She pinned me with a look. "Understand?"

Huh. I didn't think I'd ever been lectured by a mortal about how to wrestle a gator before. This was a really real "first." "I'll try to remember that." I grimaced, turning my head to the side as her fingers found an especially tender wound, and saw a metal baseball bat lying on the pavement. Was that *slime* on it?

"Who are you?" I asked.

"The woman who just clubbed a gator to save you. You're welcome, by the way," she replied darkly. She was tying a strip of cloth tight around my biceps. I winced, and she noticed. "Trish," she offered, softening ever so slightly.

"Nice to meet you, Trish."

"Uh-huh."

Caden's head popped into view. "You okay, Emery?" he asked, concern written on his face.

I smiled. "Never better." A chill suddenly went through me. "Is Rachelle..."

He glanced off to the side, in the direction I couldn't see with Trish blocking my view. "She's okay, Emery. She'll be all right. But we should get you both to the hospital."

I nodded my agreement, my head brushing against the concrete, and settled in to wait for the ambulance.

Formal Incarnate Lesson Three: Predator Incarnates
By Emery Luple

ello again, class! Today's lesson is all about the Predators. I am intimately familiar with this classification, because they are my day job: hunting down Predator incarnates is what I was born to do. Well, that and tell you about my exploits. I can't stuff and mount the monsters I hunt the way mortal hunters do, so my version of displaying my trophy is to regale all of you with my hunting tales. You're welcome.

First and foremost, unlike the Benign and Prey incarnates we've already discussed, Predators are inherently dangerous. They're sort of like... grizzly bears. They won't break into your home and murder you (that dubious honor belongs to the fourth classification, but I won't get ahead of myself). However, you also don't want to cross paths with one. Keep your distance, and you're fine. Provoke them, or just stumble across them, and you're dinner.

And yes, for you A+ students out there, Predator incarnates also have a domain of influence. They reside in Territories, and they're absurdly protective of them. Territories can range from... well, the expansive New York sewer system to a cave in the Himalayas.

Predator incarnates include the Yeti, the Troll, and the Dragon. I've personally slain two out of three of those. I'll let you figure out which two.

~

THE NEXT COUPLE of hours passed in a blur. Rachelle and I were taken to the hospital by ambulance. The paramedics allowed me to sit under my own power, but Rachelle was strapped to a stretcher and moved with care. She was conscious and embarrassed about the fuss, but Caden and I assured her she was holding up admirably. And she was. Not just any mortal could stand up to a sixteen-foot urban legend with teeth the size of crayons. Wait, does that sound menacing enough? I'll try again. Not just any mortal could stand up to a thousand-pound urban legend with teeth the size of paring knives. Those are the small vegetable knives that are extra sharp, right?

Which forced me to consider Caden. In a fair and just world, his pristine clothes would have been stained with grime and greenish slime like mine, but he sat next to me in the ambulance with no evidence of the encounter except for his wide green eyes. Not a single golden strand of hair was out of place. A suspicion crept into my thoughts, but he turned to me, noticing me studying him, and smiled wanly. The idea worming through me shriveled away like the Vampire in sunlight. He was so trustworthy, with his honest and open face; how could I harbor any distrust for him?

Trish, my baseball-bat-wielding savior, had bandaged me up and then moved on, helping Rachelle as best she could until the ambulance arrived. She saw us safely aboard, gave me a mocking salute, then disappeared from my sight as the ambulance doors swung shut.

The gator, meanwhile, had bubbled away into green slime shortly after being dispatched. That was the way of inhuman incarnates that hid from the public. Like the Yeti, these incarnates had to elude capture in order to stay alive. That also refueled the myth, breathing new life into it and ensuring the reincarnation process continued unabated. The system was pretty ingenious, really. Whoever designed it—whether it was nature or Mother Nature incarnate. God? God incarnate?—should be proud of themselves; it was self-sustaining and self-perpetuating at the same time.

One thousand and one days. The magic number. That's how long it takes to reincarnate. It, too, fits perfectly into the cycle. For the next several months, experts and myth seekers alike would be meticulously combing the sewers, searching for clues about the alligator or hunting for others like it. Months would crawl by with no such evidence, and the hype would gutter out, fading to mere embers of interest. A few zealots, refusing to let go, would persist in their search. After a year passes, even the zealots start to falter, venturing into the sewers only occasionally, obsession fighting against logic and a disappointing lack of proof. More months tick by, and obsession recedes to hobby. Another year, and even the hobby has surrendered to fancy. Everyday life and the next big deal rolls in, and by the time the reincarnation happens, all eyes are elsewhere.

For the alligator, it would lurk beneath the sewers of New York for years, maybe decades, before it was sighted again. For me, I would wake up in a new body in a random corner of the world, new backstory threatening to drown out my past lives altogether. It wasn't someone else's body. I didn't take over a life already in progress, snuffing out the existing person and assuming direct control. It was subtler than that. I was reborn, new body constructed at that very moment, and reality just... slipped me into it, rearranging the memories and experiences of the people "in my life." Three days ago, Mom hadn't had a son, but she'd probably always wanted one. Then Emery Luple came back from the grave and, with a nudge here and a poke there, every person in my backstory remembered me as if I'd been there all along. The illusion was so powerful, it would slip me into photographs and affect the people Mom worked with, so that no one ever remembered that her last name hadn't been "Luple" the day before. And as simple—and mind-bendingly complex—as that, Emery Luple was back.

That's why I called myself "Loophole." I was a loophole in reality itself.

The hospital was busy, but arriving by ambulance fast-tracked us.

Two hours later, I was bandaged in fresh linens in a shared room with Rachelle, reclining on a stiff hospital bed and drinking from a sippy cup. Ah, the life.

The lacerations down my arms looked—and felt—worse than they were; the cuts were mostly superficial. That's the medical term for "hurts like hell but sounds like it doesn't." The mostly shallow gashes crisscrossed my biceps and forearms, burning from wrist to shoulder. The rest of my body, while unmarked, was exhausted. I kept getting little muscle quivers in strange spots, reminding me they were overworked. It didn't hurt, really, but I was sore. I winced as another spasm fluted through my upper thigh. If this was how I felt now, tomorrow was likely to be a nightmare.

Rachelle and I had both endured X-rays. My wounds were limited to my torn flesh and blood loss, but my bones were fine. I'd also taken a knock on the head at some point, and the docs wanted to keep me for a few hours to monitor my condition and be certain I was as fine as I felt. Rachelle was not so lucky. It turned out her leg was broken. The doctor reported that it was an oblique displaced tibia fracture. I didn't know what that meant, so the doctor explained it to me. Her shinbone (tibia) had broken at an angle (oblique) when the alligator's tail slammed down on it. Her bone had shifted slightly out of alignment (displaced), so the bone did not completely connect in a straight line. Unfortunately, the displacement was significant enough to warrant surgery; she'd need to wear a cast and would not be monster hunting with me for months. I don't know which upset Rachelle more: the broken leg or the end of monster hunting. But I could guess.

I felt riddled with guilt. The immortal corner of my mind was berating me, reminding me that this is why I didn't get mortals involved in my world. Rachelle, even knowing the dangers, had fallen victim to them. I couldn't protect her. Was I foolish for trying, for trusting again? Would I never learn?

Before I could fall deeper into despair, Caden entered the room and tossed me a bag of chips he'd obtained from a vending machine. "Thought you could use some real food," he said.

I looked down at the bag of chips and back at Caden, arching one eyebrow. He blushed. "It's better than the cafeteria food," he deflected.

I laughed, banishing the guilt. I knew it would wait for me. "Thank you. For the chips, but also for the assist with that gator. Even though I had everything under control."

"Oh, absolutely," he agreed with a completely straight face.

Rachelle snorted from the other bed. "You owe me a night in a fancy hotel," she said. I was glad she still had a sense of humor. If her merciless teasing of me stopped, I'd know something was *seriously* wrong. "How long until they take her into surgery?" I asked quietly.

Caden glanced at the hospital clock. "Anytime now." We'd been lucky in this, at least. The hospital had surgeons on call 24/7, and the orthopedic team had just finished up with another after-hours surgery.

"Guys," Rachelle interrupted, "look." She was pointing at the TV in the corner of the sterile room. The sound was low, barely audible, but there were subtitles. It was the news, I realized, and the footage... it was ours. "Turn it up."

Caden fetched the remote and increased the volume. "—be warned, the following footage may be disturbing for some viewers." The scene jostled as the camerawoman—Rachelle—moved closer to the body. The camera swept up, taking in my profile in the gloom, then down toward the headless lump on the ground. It wasn't perfectly in focus, but that was probably a good thing. After a moment, the perspective glided upward again, to the cement pillar where the word "Ahedrian" was carved into the stone.

"This footage was provided to NYBC News by two young responders who were first on the scene," the anchorwoman's voice continued over the images. "Video bloggers, they happened upon the murder while shooting content for their own show. We've posted a link to their blog at the bottom of the screen. Now we'll go to field reporter Sabrina Miles, who arrived on the scene only minutes after the body was found."

Sabrina's familiar face appeared on the screen, police lights flashing behind her and splaying their colors over her wild shock of red hair. She had adopted a sober expression. "The scene here is chaos as police and detectives swarm the area. It is only thanks to the two young entrepreneurs I met earlier that I was able to get a glimpse of the scene to bring to all of you at home." Rachelle's footage began playing again as Sabrina spoke. "Of special note, you can clearly see the word carved in the stone here. 'Ahedrian.' The word found on the tip of every New Yorker's tongue these days. What does it mean? Present at each of these crime scenes, it has left police and experts baffled. I turn now to the man who found the body."

The camera angle shifted as she began to interview the bearded man, and Caden lowered the volume and turned to us. "What do you think?"

"She's hyping up the mystery of 'Ahedrian' quite a bit," I observed, "but that's sensationalism at work. Decapitations and an unknown word left at every crime scene. It's like a real-life murder mystery."

Caden nodded in agreement. "She's also not wrong. Everyone is talking about Ahedrian. Each time another murder is discovered, it fans the flames."

"That's probably what the murderer wants," Rachelle said, her voice laced with pain.

Caden nodded again, walking over to Rachelle's bed. He surprised me by putting his hand gently on her forehead and brushing her bangs back. "You feeling okay?" he asked.

Rachelle closed her eyes and took a steadying breath. "Just hurts," she murmured. "I'll live."

Watching the two of them, I felt a surge of affection. Caden had known Rachelle for a matter of hours, but the compassionate note in his voice was sincere. The room was dim, the low light lending the three of us a companionable intimacy. The large window afforded little view aside from the towering structure of an adjacent building, so Caden had drawn the thin curtains, a couple of light sources outside filtering through it hazily. He looked over at me and met my eyes, the green light from Rachelle's heart monitor playing across his smooth face. There was an abiding sense of serenity about Caden, something ineffably peaceful about him. Which prickled at me. I'd seen him fight off a monstrous alligator with surprising fearlessness. I remembered the way his body had rocketed into the creature, driving it off balance and sparing me an embarrassing, toothy demise. There had been nothing *peaceful* in that action.

A few minutes of bustle disrupted the quiet as nurses arrived to wheel Rachelle off for her surgery. It would be a few hours, they informed us, and encouraged us to get some sleep while we waited.

Caden stepped around my bed to approach from my right, settling into the reclining chair there. He shared a tired smile with me.

"Thank you for looking after Rachelle," I said, feeling awkward but unsure why.

He shrugged. "The least I could do."

"Not really what you expected when you called my number, huh?"

"Wrestling an alligator?" he asked with a hint of incredulousness. "That was definitely not on my radar."

I frowned at him. "I'm pretty sure *I* was the one wrestling the alligator."

"Yes," he said, raising an eyebrow, "but that's not how the story will go when I'm telling my friends about it."

I broke into a grin at the laughter dancing in his eyes. We stayed that way for a moment, and then I asked in a lowered voice, "How *are* you doing? Really?"

"I'm not the one in the hospital bed," he pointed out. Or deflected. He reached up and brushed his fingers over my bandages, feather light. "These wounds looked painful."

"They're not so bad," I assured him. And they really weren't. Whatever meds the doctor prescribed must have been kicking in. "I can stay with Rachelle if you need to get back home for the night," I offered, my jaw creaking into a yawn.

"Then who'd be here to watch out for you?" he asked mildly. I smiled, assuming he was teasing. But his face remained serious, his eyes large in the dim light as he watched me.

"I'm rather good at watching over myself," I replied, the bravado only slightly undermined by my bandaged arms and sippy cup. "Been doing it a long time."

Caden kicked back, reclining as far as the chair would allow. He spoke to the ceiling. "Well, you can start doing it again in the morning, if you'd like. For tonight, I'm staying here."

I regarded him thoughtfully. Although I wouldn't admit it out loud, I was pleased he had decided to stay. I settled into a slightly more comfortable position on the hospital bed, thinking. I felt surprisingly... safe. Like someone had my back, was looking out for me—and not simply because my backstory set them up to. Was it genuine affection, though, or was Caden just a naturally caring person? Moreover, did it matter, if it felt good to have someone watching over me? My knee-jerk reaction was to laugh this feeling off, to banish it with some self-disparaging thought. But I'd been doing that for a long while. It was time for a change. A new incarnation, a new start. So I reflected on it instead. This was the reason I wanted to trust again, I realized. It was a weight I'd borne without even knowing it, buried beneath the guilt I'd carried for so long. My attention on it now, it stirred awake, demanding to be named, to be known.

Loneliness.

The realization levered its way beneath my defenses. Had I always felt so alone? No. I hadn't, I knew. Then the next inevitable question: how long had I felt this way? The answer came instantly, reflexively, unwanted and unstoppable. Since Huntington's death. Snippets of that scene played out before me. Me, holding his body, blood soaking into my knees and pooling on the cement floor. Morrigan's laughter. I squeezed my eyes tight and clenched my jaw, trying to shut out the little girl's sobs, the terror of her wails mingling with the horror of my own grief... but they would not recede.

Breathe, Emery. I remembered, with unwelcome clarity, how Huntington's death hounded me wherever I went, chasing me through two—albeit short—lifetimes. Both times, a thousand and one days had not been enough of a respite.

I concentrated on my breathing to calm myself. In and out.

In.

Blank, dead eyes. I couldn't hide from them. I wanted to curl into a ball, to physically wall myself off. But I knew it wouldn't help; this pain wasn't physical. It was deeper, a scar on my psyche.

Out.

Huntington. Tragedy. Murder. Kidnapping. Death. So much death in a single night.

In.

Never again, I'd sworn to myself. I had thrown myself into hunting monsters, removed myself from the world of mortals. Fled from my memories. But for all the monsters I stalked, I avoided the worst one of all.

Out.

Tears pricked the corners of my eyes. I wasn't strong enough to confront that memory yet, not fast enough to outrun it, not brave enough to accept it. Where did that leave me?

In.

No way out. Focus on something else.

Out.

Anything else.

In.

The hum of hospital machines. The soft ticking of the clock on the wall.

Out.

Caden rested in the chair next to me, eyes closed, breathing even. I didn't think he was asleep yet, but he was peacefully unaware of the internal struggle occurring right next to him.

In.

Seeing him dragged me back to the present. That night was my past. Three incarnations ago. What was the point of a new life, if not a fresh start? I needed to move on, to put it forever behind me. But I wasn't quite ready yet.

Out.

So I reflected instead on the here and now. It was just after midnight. It was a funny time, midnight, if you were awake to experience it.

In.

"Today" and "tomorrow" blurred together, blended, became nearly indistinguishable from one another. You couldn't say, "Tomorrow I will hunt down my impostor," because it already *was* tomorrow.

Out.

It's a loophole, I thought, *like me.* It wasn't. But somehow, that thought made my lips quirk in the barest semblance of a grin. I made no sense.

In.

Whether it was today or tomorrow, it marked day four of Emery Luple.

Huh. "Emery Luple." Not "this incarnation."

Out.

I felt more like... *me.* Tears flowed hot over my cheeks, and I tasted salt. For the first time in several incarnations, since Huntington's death, my thoughts were about this day, rather than "this time." With a hint of desolation, I realized I hadn't felt like me in quite some time. Being around Rachelle—and now Caden—made me recognize that fact. Made me feel more like myself.

It filled me with a profound sense of hope. Maybe a bit of desperation, but hope was definitely in there, too. Tomorrow—or today, or *whenever*—I would start fresh. I would begin my hunt in earnest. I would discover the mystery of Ahedrian, learn the identity of my impostor, uncover the murderer. I didn't expect to succeed in a day, but I *would* succeed in the end.

Watch out, New York: Emery Luple is here. Perhaps not the Emery I once was, but perhaps that was a good thing. I couldn't decide if that last thought was empowering or pathetic.

Empowering, I decided. I would not be defined by tragedy.

Overwhelmed by exhaustion, I let sleep claim me.

I wheeled Rachelle down the hallway of the hospital, heading for the exit, cheerfully narrating our bland adventure through the hospital hallways as though I were her tour guide. One successful surgery later, she now sported a bubble-gum-colored cast from her ankle to just above the knee. Unfortunately, the hospital would not loan us the wheelchair beyond the lobby, so she would need to use the aluminum crutches they provided. Despite all that *plus* an uncomfortable and short sleep, her spirits were impressively high this morning.

The three of us grabbed a yellow taxicab from the hospital's front roundabout and headed back to the Starboard. It was a tight fit with Rachelle's leg, which was propped up on my lap, and the crutches at our feet.

"What's on the agenda today, boys?" Rachelle asked brightly. When I didn't respond immediately, she added, "I know I won't be tagging along, but at least let me live vicariously through you. I know you have a plan brewing, Emery. You've been uncharacteristically quiet this morning."

Caden, sitting on the other side of Rachelle, gave a short laugh. "This is him being *quiet*?"

"Oh yeah. You're in for—"

"All right," I interrupted good-naturedly, holding my hands up in surrender. "We're going shopping."

"Shopping?" She was taken aback, but then nodded. "I guess that makes sense, with you losing your luggage and all."

I shook my head. "Not just for clothes. Last night showed me how woefully underprepared I am for this investigation." I glanced at Caden, unable to say anything too specific in front of him.

Luckily, I'm pretty sure Rachelle caught my meaning. "Pick out something cute for me while you're out." She gestured to her leg cast. "Something matching my newest accessory."

The cab pulled up to the hotel, and I paid our fare. We settled Rachelle as comfortably as possible in the hotel room, then Caden and I proceeded downstairs and I paid for another night.

"What's our first stop?" Caden asked.

I had awoken first this morning, maybe an hour before the other two, and I'd spent the quiet time thinking. I needed a few essentials: clothes first and foremost, and yet another toothbrush. But I also needed gear. Weapons. I was tired of fighting incarnates on their terms. It was well past time for me to start fighting on *mine*.

"I need some new clothes and a toothbrush," I told him. "Since you're the local, you want to lead the way?"

We walked down the streets of Manhattan. It was Friday, colder and clearer than the previous day. Caden, clad in his white tee, must have felt it more keenly than I, but he gave no sign that it bothered him. He commented on a few things as we passed: a building, a landmark, or just an anecdote. I listened with half an ear, the other part of my mind engrossed in planning. Caden was going to ask about the alligator, eventually, and about the decapitations. Since *There's Always a Loophole* was about debunking myths, I began to piece together an idea for how to cover up the gator story. It... wasn't great. If I truly wanted to debunk the myth, I'd decided, Caden would most likely expect me to investigate it. Which was a great cover-up for buying some important weapons, like a tranquilizer gun.

"... an incarnate?"

I froze, giving Caden what I'm sure was a shocked look. "What did you just say?" I asked, heart pounding.

Caden had stopped walking when I did and turned to face me, bewilderment in his soft green eyes. "I'm sorry," he said, "I didn't mean to overhear. I just figured it was a word you two used, like when ghostbusters say it's a 'manifestation,' you know?"

I relaxed, understanding dawning. "You heard Rachelle and me say it?"

He bobbed his head, golden hair flashing. "In the ambulance, right when I was getting in. Rachelle asked you if it was an incarnate. I figured she meant the gator."

Worry etched into Caden's face, my response clearly leading him to believe he'd made a misstep. I forced a smile, hoping it came across as light and disarming. "You guessed it in one," I said, striving for a casual tone. "It's the word we use—in the 'biz'—to describe an urban legend come to life." That... actually wasn't a lie.

He looked as though he wanted to say something more, then indicated the entrance of the building we'd stopped in front of. "This is our destination," he said instead.

"Caden..."

"Come on," he said with forced excitement, waving me forward. "Let's get you some new clothes." He walked quickly toward the store.

I followed, feeling somewhat disappointed. That was odd. I'd recovered perfectly, hadn't I? Obviously not *perfectly*, I supposed, or Caden wouldn't be acting strange. I sighed. Should I tell him the truth? About incarnates, me, all of it? I hadn't hesitated to tell Rachelle, after all. But that was different. Even though I hadn't *actually* known her for years, I felt as though I had. She was my best friend, had earned my trust... through memories that hadn't happened, sure, but they *would* have, if I'd known her. They still showed me her character.

I'd only just met Caden. And while he seemed so quintessentially trustworthy, I hesitated. I wanted to tell him, but it could endanger him. I watched him disappear through the store entrance, a couple dozen paces ahead of me. I followed him slowly, trying to wrap my head around our conversation—around his reaction, and mine. He had called me from across the country, put faith in me that arguably was not deserved. Did I owe him the truth in return?

Thoughts of last night flickered across my mind. I didn't want mortals near me, did I? I certainly didn't want them hurt or killed because of me. So why was I drawn to them?

I needed to follow Caden inside, needed to be my 'normal' self. I squeezed my eyes shut, trying to expel all this indecision.

"Emery?" Caden's golden head poked out the front door, looking back at me.

"Coming!" I trotted over to him, flashing him my signature smile, my signature mask. "Time to make me look good."

At first he was subdued as I picked out a few outfits to try. I was nowhere near as adept at fashion as Rachelle, but lifetimes spent in body types of varying ages, structures, and genders equipped me with a sense for it. My first shopping trip was secretly one of my favorite parts of reincarnation; it was all about crafting my new look. I was a few days behind, but I could still reimagine myself through my choices, find a style to reflect my new individuality. Like donning a persona, it cemented my self-image, made me feel more connected to my new incarnation. It wasn't about looking good, it was about looking like *me*.

As I became engrossed in perfecting my appearance and conveying my personality through it, my earlier fears and concerns began to melt away. Caden, picking up on my energy, opened back up to me. I held up a long-sleeved shirt replete with a pocket chain, and he made a face. I laughed and put the shirt back on the rack, selected another, and held it up for his approval. As he pointed out an ensemble he especially liked, combining a few different looks, I realized that he wasn't the only one opening up. This activity, so innocuously human, yet so personal to my immortal self, drew me like a magnet. I'd spent many an incarnation designing my look, a lone artist with paint and brush; as Caden chose another shirt I wouldn't have considered on my own and held it up to me with eyes squinted in thought, it was as though another artist approached and offered me a new palette of colors, filled with hues and shades and tones I'd never seen. Emery Luple, the sum of two artists; the result bolder and more vibrant than before.

They're just clothes, Emery.

But it wasn't about the clothes, or fashion, or shopping. It was about the experience, the shared reinvention. It didn't matter that it meant nothing to him.

It meant everything to me.

I couldn't express these things to Caden, but I could reciprocate. As we completed my shopping, I spied a sporty white tee with colored sleeves and panels down the sides. I snatched it off the shelf and spun around, keeping hold of my own selections under my other arm, and evaluated it against Caden's slim form. The colored areas were almost exactly the same shade as his eyes. He held up his hands in protest as he caught what I was doing, but the warm surprise in his eyes betrayed him.

Before leaving, I picked out a pink scarf and a bubble-gum-flavored lip balm for Rachelle, both to go with her new cast. I even found a bubble-gum-scented candle as a joke, surprised to discover they were quite popular.

Naturally, I changed out of my slimy, stained clothes and into my new ones the second the tags were off. To my delight, Caden put on the shirt I chose for him too. As we walked out of the store, *damn*, we looked good. But there was still one thing missing from the Emery Luple signature look. I grinned, barely refraining from rubbing my hands together in anticipation. This was my other favorite part: *weapons*. Trust me; Emery Luple *always* looks cooler with weapons.

An hour and a half later I walked out of the sporting goods emporium with a backpack slung over my shoulder, the comforting weight of several (safely capped) tranquilizer darts, a blowgun, a fishing net, pepper spray—both aerosol cans and grenade-style—a Taser Pulse+ with two live cartridges, a pair of hunting knives (they had a buy-one-get-one-half-off sale), a camera with an extra-bright LED flash attachment, an empty can of Pringles in case my Genie friend reappeared, and an air horn assuring me I was ready to take on many, if not most, of the incarnates we'd be likely to encounter. You may doubt that all those items can be found at a single store, and to you I say: stop interrupting my story. It's far more exciting the way I tell it.

Caden had followed along like a puppy as I'd hunted down specific items, eyes widening further with each selection. "Aren't you going to get a baseball bat?" he asked, amusement—and maybe concern—evident on his face.

"What for?"

"Well, isn't that what got the alligator in the end?"

I looked at him. "You don't think I got enough to handle another gator?"

"A gator army, I'd say."

"Good." I took a deep breath. "Let's talk about the alligator in the room."

"You don't need to," he said quickly, looking apprehensive.

"I do." I held his eyes. "You're involved in this, so you need to know enough to protect yourself." I held out one of the two hunting knives. Sheathed, of course.

He backed away. "Um, no, thanks." The look of horror on his face was almost comical.

"It's just for protection," I told him. He shook his head firmly, and I shrugged, putting the knife back into my bag. "Guess you'll have to rely on me, then," I said lightly.

"I seem to remember holding my own against that gator," he protested.

"True enough," I agreed easily. "*There's Always a Loophole* sometimes leads me to dangerous encounters, like that alligator. I like to be prepared."

He grinned. "Nailed it."

I returned his smile. Then I began telling him the story I'd been preparing all morning. "You've heard of the urban myth, right? About kids that flush baby alligators, and they grow into monsters that lurk in the New York City sewer system?"

He nodded, waiting expectantly.

Someone probably planted that gator as a hoax, and There's Always a

Loophole *is going to find out who did it, and why.* A simple explanation. Not without its flaws, but I could convince him while we "investigated." I knew I could; Caden's trusting face was intent on me, receptive to whatever story I fed him. I opened my mouth to say it. "It's all true." *What?* What was I doing?

He smiled uncertainly at me. "I'm pretty sure they would have found alligators in the sewers before now if it were all true."

"Not alligators plural," I said reflexively. "*The* Alligator in the Sewers." This was it. If I didn't stop talking, I was going to tell him everything.

Caden licked his lips, then said, "You mean it's all true, don't you?" He looked down, the next part coming out as a mumble. "Urban legends are real?" I could hear the uncertainty in his voice. He was probably afraid I was going to mock him.

Seeing him like that, I caved. I was a good judge of character, wasn't I? "Yes, urban legends are real," I confirmed. "They're called incarnates."

Caden's face snapped up, and he searched my eyes for any trace I was teasing. Then a radiant smile broke over his features. "I *knew* it!"

I blinked. "What?"

He brushed my question aside and leaned forward, eager. "Tell me everything."

I hesitated, searching my memories; this wasn't the usual response. I was pushed off balance—first by my traitorous conscience, then further by his response. I shook my head but found my voice before his excitement faltered. "Better to show you."

Formal Incarnate Lesson Four: Malevolent Incarnates
By Emery Luple

*H*ey class. Who out there can tell me the four classifications of incarnates? Anyone? You need to speak up; it's really hard to hear you from in here. All right, well, if you said "Benign, Prey, Predator, and Malevolent," then—ding ding ding!—we have a winner. Bonus points if you yelled it out loud. I still couldn't hear you, but I appreciate you following orders. Good little mortal.

Malevolent incarnates. I've saved the worst for last. Where to begin? You know how some people seem bad, but they're just misunderstood? Malevolent incarnates are nothing like that. They are active threats to humans and/or society, with the ands being even more dangerous than the ors. Malevolent incarnates exist as manifestations of legends dredged up by humanity's fears. Creatures that feed on terror, human flesh, souls, and anarchy the way children gobble down breakfast cereal. Some, like Morrigan, are masterminds and schemers, the embodiment of villainy. Others, like the Succubus incarnate, are Malevolents because their sustenance is dependent upon harming, or killing, people.

Malevolents dwell in their Lairs, where their powers are strongest.

Since Malevolents are deadliest there, it is always best to lure them away before attacking them. That is, if one were foolish enough to attack them in the first place. After all, the tactic with the highest chance of survival when dealing with Malevolents is to stay away from them entirely. Sadly, this does not guarantee your safety.

I told you: they're just the worst.

~

GRAND CENTRAL STATION. A legend. So much so that if anything ever happened to it, it would likely reincarnate.

An immense structure, it stood as a testament to the capabilities of mortals. A starry sky adorned the vaulted ceiling high above Caden and me, playful constellations wheeling about on their two-dimensional plane. The distinctive, ornate architecture soared above me, fanciful stone-wrought edifices and sculptural art atop squared pillars. The building made me feel small. Not just in comparison, but also because being here felt like I was stepping through history. This was a crossroads, literally and figuratively. I was just another person among billions to visit the famed terminal. More than that, it was a personal crossroads: I'd been here in other incarnations. If I closed my eyes, I could almost cross paths with my previous selves; I remembered meeting the Watchman over by that vending machine; getting off the train and walking through the main terminal for the first time, the building new and exciting, almost terrifying; the Princess incarnate giving me a peck on the cheek on that upper level before heading down the stone staircase to catch her train. Remembered crisscrossing the station dozens of times. Different lives, different years, different people; the same building.

Caden turned around to see what was holding me up. Something about my face made him pause, and he swung slowly around to take in the building, as if trying to see what I was seeing.

We had swung by the hotel, brought Rachelle a late lunch, and dropped off our shopping bags. She had been delighted at receiving the scarf and made me model one of my other new outfits—I was lucky to limit her to one—before Caden and I left for Grand Central to catch a train. With the fresh reminder of Rachelle's busted leg weighing on my conscience, I decided to take no chances with Caden. I would introduce him to the incarnate world as safely as possible. To that end, I'd brought as many of my new supplies as I could comfortably carry. No sense taking unnecessary chances. Now, surrounded by a horde of people, Caden and I proceeded through the terminal. My new outfit included a beige overcoat that stopped just above my knees, the creamy color bringing out the best in my skin. We were headed for the train to Harlem. Caden seemed confident in the crowd, and I let him lead us to the platform.

Eight minutes later, we boarded the sleek metal train. It was wider on the interior than I remembered, although that was mostly countered by the sheer number of people. We picked out two plastic seats, and I slid in first so I could look out the large window. Caden slipped in beside me. The empty seats around us filled quickly, only a few remaining unoccupied. I could hear an older Korean couple talking quietly in a language I recognized but couldn't understand. Bummer. It was always extra helpful when my backstory included multilingualism. Sometimes, as I aged—or if I reincarnated into an older body—I'd remember chunks or whole languages I'd learned in a previous life, but not always.

Caden lowered his voice and moved in close to avoid being overheard. "So, where are you taking me?" I could feel his breath on my cheek as I leaned in to hear his quiet words. His excitement was infectious, bubbling up inside me, demanding I show him everything. Something in my mind stirred as he spoke, but I couldn't quite place the nagging feeling that I was missing something. It probably wasn't important.

What am I doing? It was bad enough I'd involved Rachelle; why was I getting *another* mortal involved in this? Less than three days of adventure with Emery Luple, and Rachelle was stuck at the hotel, wounded. I was lucky that was all; she could easily have been killed. So why didn't I tell Caden to go home, then proceed on my own? Was there something wrong with me?

I turned to look at him fully. His lips were quirked in a smile, waiting with barely restrained anticipation for my response. For a moment, I saw the gator attack again—how he'd fought side by side with me, kept up with me after a fashion. It hadn't dimmed his enthusiasm in the slightest. That was very, *very* dangerous. Rachelle was fearless in her curiosity, but Caden was... eager. That should have terrified me. But I found it thrilling, too. Compelling.

"You're hesitating," he said, not moving any further away. "Emery, you don't have to tell me anything you don't want to."

But that was the problem. I wanted to show him everything. To share. His earnest nature tempted me to lower my carefully constructed walls. I briefly considered again the trusting nature of this incarnation's personality overlaid with my normal, cautious immortal mind. It colored me like a drop of red dye in white cream; no matter how much I stirred, the whole thing became pink, forever changed by that single drop.

Or maybe, just maybe, my immortal scars were healing.

I pulled away, looking out the window as the train jerked into motion. Moving forward. The timing of that felt anything but coincidental.

I made up my mind. Safe incarnates only. I flashed him a grin. "Oh no, you aren't wriggling out of this that easily."

"So, then, what's in El Barrio?"

I tried to look mysterious. I'm sure it worked. I'm a pretty mysterious person. "The start of our journey, my friend." I sobered. "I really did travel to New York to solve—and stop—these murders. But I need more information. You and I are going to get that information."

The solid station wall slid past, opening to an urban scene as the train picked up speed. I had wanted to visit the address Morrigan gave me and investigate my impostor, but, one, if there was some sort of ambush waiting for me, the longer I put off visiting, the likelier I was to foil Morrigan's plans, and two, it was too dangerous to bring Caden to that possible trap. I'd pay my impostor a visit tomorrow.

I wondered, as the train sailed past buildings and the populated streets of New York, if the murders and my impostor might be related.

The ride to East Harlem was short, just over ten minutes. The sun hung further west in the sky, afternoon fully settled upon us, as we disembarked the train and I pulled up the directions to the shop I was seeking. It wasn't far.

"Who all knows about these incarnates?" Caden asked, trying out the word.

I looked up from my map app (mapp?) and said wryly, "Well, there are thousands—probably more—of urban legends and myths, so quite a few people."

The directions said we were a couple of blocks away. Harlem's streets were blocks of long, interconnected buildings, rows of similar limestone constructions divided into dozens of individual residences and storefronts. Little staircases that looked like tongues dotted the structures at even intervals, and the bottom levels of the townhomes were sometimes apartments and sometimes shops. It was difficult to tell them apart, and if not for the striations in color, it would be nearly impossible to tell where one building ended and the next began.

Caden regarded me with a flat expression. "I meant how many people have you told. Like me. And Rachelle."

"That's pretty much the whole list," I told him, searching the fronts of the buildings as we passed. I knew it was around here... somewhere.

"Really? What about Trish?"

I looked at him blankly. "Who?"

"The young woman who took down the alligator."

Oh. The one with the bad temper. "You know, when you say it that way, it really undermines the role *I* played in bringing that gator down."

He laughed.

"I don't actually know her," I admitted. "She just showed up."

"What are the chances of that happening?"

"Around me? Quite high, actually."

Curiosity stole over his expression. "And you don't think that's weird?"

He was right; the timing was suspicious. But I'd become accustomed to coincidences in my line of work. When it came to incarnates, they were simply par for the course. "Trust me, Caden, that doesn't even scratch the surface of 'weird.'"

At last I spotted the shop I was seeking, squatting at the base of a towering townhome. An old, weathered porch fronted the building, surprisingly solid, with fading gray paint that undoubtedly once was the color of the building itself. Vivid flowers poked out of an old vase, more welcoming than the dirty old mat lying at the front door with the word "Welcome" on it. Overall, the place felt like a relic, quaint but imperfect, tucked like an old, gnarled tooth among updated buildings.

Caden kept pace with me, his eagerness resurfacing now that we'd arrived at our destination. "Madam Zerona's Spirits and Seances," Caden read aloud from the yellowed sign in the window, which sported black letters in a spidery font. He shot me an excited grin. "No tricks," he said warningly, the threat spoiled by his enthusiasm.

I rolled my eyes good-naturedly. "No tricks," I agreed. I knocked.

"Come in," came a muffled voice from inside.

I opened the door and entered, Caden hot on my heels. The smell of cigarette smoke hit me as I walked in. An older woman sat knitting in a rocking chair, her knobby fingers deftly weaving lines of thread with two overlarge needles. Slate gray hair with fingers of black in it was tied back in a loose bundle, her eyes magnified by large spectacles. Despite the quintessential fortune-teller image, she wore modern clothes, including a knitted maroon infinity scarf.

"One moment," she said without looking up, her needles clicking together as she finished the segment she was working on. "Please sit." The room was set up much like a living room, comfortable and homey. A floral-print couch and a matching plush chair sat opposite the woman, a small, oaken coffee table in the center. There was a modest tea cart with delicate china, as well as a mini fridge.

Caden and I exchanged a glance, and I shrugged, walking into the living room and plopping down on the couch. I sank deeper than I expected. A moment later, Caden settled beside me. He inspected the room with interest, craning his neck to take in some of the oddities. His undisguised excitement again reminded me of a puppy, and I grinned at the image in my head. He caught my bemused expression and stilled.

The old woman completed something indistinguishable to me and set aside her things, giving us her full attention. I felt her pause as she took us in. "Welcome to Madam Zerona's, gentlemen," she said. Her voice sounded raspy. The smoky haze and ashtray on her side table weren't just from her customers. "I don't believe you have an appointment, but I'm happy to help you, if there's something you need."

I leaned forward. "Hi, Zelda," I said. "It's Emery Luple."

I watched her blink, twice, three times. With the spectacles, the surprise in her eyes was magnified. "Emery?" She studied my new form with pursed lips. "Iris told me to expect you, but you know how she is. Good to see you again. How long has it been?"

I grinned. "A while," I admitted. It was surreal, seeing her like this. The last time I had visited her, I had been several decades older than she, and she had probably been closer to twenty than thirty. The trek had taken quite a bit longer, but she had lit up at seeing me. Looking at her now, I saw that same spark in her tired eyes. I wasn't sure which had aged more gracefully: her, or her shop. The years had not been overly kind to either of them.

She pulled out an unlit cigarette and waved it as though clearing smoke. "How may I be of service to you?"

"I have some questions, and I'm hoping you can help me get answers." She was the Medium incarnate, able to pierce the veil between the living and the dead. Capable of speaking with the spirits of the deceased and giving them a voice in kind.

She lit her cigarette. "Ask away."

"Actually," I said, turning to look at Caden happily, "My questions are for the Ghost."

*C*aden and I watched as Madam Zelda Zerona lit the final thick, white candle in her summoning circle. The heavy curtains, drawn shut, created an artificially dark atmosphere, the candles providing the only source of illumination. There were thirteen candles in total, almost like the numbers on a clock, completing the ring of fire. I glanced at Caden, seeing the candlelight flicker over his youthful, excited face. Even though he had already witnessed one incarnate, it was still an alligator, which wasn't fantastical. Like Rachelle and the Genie, you really needed to experience something right out of mythology to begin believing in earnest. I mean, you've read my entire journey so far and you still probably harbor doubts. But trust me—if the Unicorn traipsed through your front lawn, *then* you'd believe.

Looking at Caden, I felt a tremor of worry in my stomach. His eagerness, while contagious, unnerved me. I thought again of last night, of how he'd brushed back Rachelle's hair soothingly at the hospital. There was a tenderness to him that made me protective, even though he was quick on his feet. Maybe I just felt protective of all mortals.

Caden stepped up to me and whispered, "So, how long have you known her?" He asked it casually, and I understood immediately what he was doing: letting me decide how much to tell him, asking questions without pressure.

"What makes you think she's not just a fan of my blog?" I teased.

Caden grinned at me in the darkness, seeming to understand I wasn't going to give him an answer. "What, exactly, is she doing?" he asked instead. "You said you need to speak with a ghost?"

"The first thing you need to know about incarnates: there is only one. A single incarnate to represent the various myths out there. Madam Zerona is the only real medium in existence: the Medium incarnate."

He nodded, following along. "So she isn't summoning *a* ghost, she's summoning *the* single ghost in all existence?"

"Exactly," I replied approvingly. "The Ghost incarnate."

Caden considered that as Zelda leaned down and lit another cigarette using one of the candles. She took a long drag and blew out a big plume of smoke. I admit, I'd thought this was part of her summoning ritual. Nope. Just a smoke break.

"So, then, what about Bloody Mary?" Caden asked suddenly.

"What about her?"

"Does she exist?"

"Yes," I replied. "Pretty much every legend or myth you've heard of—and many more you probably haven't—exists in the form of a single incarnate."

"Okay," Caden said, drawing out the word. "But isn't she also a ghost?"

I opened my mouth, then closed it. Damn. He'd gone straight for an advanced incarnate question, and he'd gotten there surprisingly fast. Yes, I realize many of you may have had this same question, or one similar. Rest assured; I'm equally impressed by your intelligence. You were also smart enough to read or listen to my tale thus far, so I never really doubted your intelligence in the first place.

"That," I said with a raised finger, "is a very good question." He didn't puff up at my compliment, just waited for me to continue with interest written all over his face. "There are two types of incarnates: personas and archetypes. The Ghost incarnate is an archetype. She embodies all myths and legends of ghosts, and the result is a bit of a hybrid. She can do all of the things you'd expect of a ghost: walk through walls, go invisible, float through the air, that sort of stuff.

"Bloody Mary, on the other hand, is a persona. She exists as a single myth perpetuated across different cultures. She shares many similarities with the Ghost, but she also has very specific specialties: she appears when summoned by her name, always out of a mirror, and usually with murderous intent." Something about that last line pricked my subconscious.

Caden thought for a moment. "What about synonyms?" he asked.

"What about them?" I asked absently, trying to catch the elusive thought. *Something with murderous intent.*

"Is there both a Ghost incarnate and a Spirit incarnate?"

I shook my head. "No. But it wouldn't surprise me if, in some cultures, The Ghost incarnate is called the Spirit incarnate. Ultimately, for both personas and archetypes, there is only ever one."

He accepted my words and said, his voice light, "She's not summoning the murderous ghost, is she?"

There it was. Murderous ghost. Beheadings. New York as the setting. It dawned on me. There was one obvious suspect.

"Caden," I said excitedly. "What if 'ghost' is what we've been missing from the Ahedrian murders?"

He looked at me, puzzled. "What do you mean?"

I raised my hand in front of him, fingers in a loose fist. I held up one finger. "Decapitations." Another finger. "New York." Finger. "Ghost persona." Last finger. "Incarnate, a.k.a. urban legend."

Caden's face was pinched in thought. "I can't think of any famous ghosts in New York City history known for decapitating people," he said at last, sounding crestfallen.

I grinned triumphantly. "What about just outside the city?" I insisted, warming to the idea. "Say, to the north?"

It took a moment, but then his face lit up. "Sleepy Hollow," he breathed.

"The Headless Horseman," I crowed. "It makes so much sense."

Caden nodded slowly, but his brow furrowed. "Not everything fits. The word 'Ahedrian,' for starters."

"We'd be foolish not to investigate, though." We both subsided into our own thoughts. It wasn't perfect. The man who had found the body in the parking garage had told me he thought he'd heard footsteps, not hoofbeats. Surely he would have noticed *that* detail.

Zelda puffed one last time on her cigarette and then ground it out in the ashtray. "All right, kiddos," she said in her raspy voice, "feel free to ask your questions."

I looked at the summoning circle and frowned. I needed to think. Should I pivot, ask questions about the Headless Horseman, my new suspect? *No, don't get tunnel vision.* I needed to ask questions that would give me clues to find the murderer, not fit the clues *to* the murderer. My attention wavered as I noticed Caden looking over my shoulder with widening eyes.

I spun around, already knowing what I'd find. The translucent body of a young girl, vaguely effervescent, suspended in the air, hanging upside down. With chubby cheeks, dark pigtails tied off with yellow bows, and a sunflower dress over thick stockings, she was surprisingly adorable. Even with her pink tongue poking out at me. "Boo!" she squealed.

I threw up my hands and feigned a theatrical scream, backing away and pointing. "It's a g-g-g-g-ghost!"

The Ghost incarnate giggled and twirled in the air, reorienting herself right side up. She looked no more than six years old. She'd been six a long time. "It *is* you, Emery!" She laughed in delight.

"It's great to see you again, Iris. I'm sorry it's been so long."

I'd met the Ghost several times throughout my many incarnations. Rarely had I seen her so vibrant, though. The yellows of her dress were normally subdued by both her translucence and her illumination. Her voice, too, often sounded like it came from the other end of a tinny connection. This time, however, it sounded like the little girl was in the room with me. All of this was due to the power and presence of the Medium.

Only the Medium could summon Iris. I don't know if the ritual with the candles was necessary or not, but I do know that it wouldn't work for me. If I wanted to track down the Ghost, I would need to do it the old-fashioned way, by searching her usual haunts. The Medium could summon Iris from anywhere, sparing me the trouble of tracking her down. And yes, for those few of you who are as quick as Caden: as far as I know, the Medium *could* summon other persona incarnates possessing ghostly traits. But doing so could prove fatal, if she attracted the wrong kind of ghostly attention—like Bloody Mary, for example. And that, my friends, is three times. I hope you aren't reading this out loud in front of a mirror! Just sayin'.

Iris was swimming around in the air, encircling Caden and me. "This is a good look for you, Emery," she said with childlike sincerity. Then she anchored herself in midair in front of Caden, eye level, even though her yellow sandals only reached down to his thighs. "Hi, Caden!" she said cheerfully.

His eyebrows shot up in surprise. "You know my name?"

"Of course!" She wrinkled her nose at him. "I hear lots of things, even if you can't see me." Her little face became suddenly, uncharacteristically serious. "I'm the only Ghost, but those who are close to death cross into my Sanctum." She reached a little hand out and placed it on his shoulder. Since she was incorporeal, Caden wouldn't be able to feel it, but Iris held her hand there perfectly, unwavering, giving the illusion it rested on his shoulder. "Thank you for the work you do. You can tell your... family that, too."

Understanding bloomed on Caden's features and turned his smile radiant. His eyes shone. "Thank you for saying that, Iris. I will tell them."

Well, now I was lost. I filed it away for later. "Iris," I said, feeling uncomfortably like I was intruding, "I have a few questions for you."

She cartwheeled away from Caden, and her legs passed right

through my head. Given her unusual solidity, I flinched, but they phased through me as I knew they would. "You want to know about the Wookiee!" she said in a self-assured, knowing voice. Before I could respond, she said, "Wait, wait, no. I know! I know you said it's important! But so many things have happened since then. I can tell you all about the mirrors!" She said it in a singsong voice, full of excitement. I always forgot how much of a little girl she could be. Sometimes getting her to pay attention was like trying to saddle a squirrel. "I don't have a reflection, so it doesn't really work on me. But I bet *you* could make it work!" I opened my mouth to try to corral her, but she waggled a finger in my face as if I was being naughty. "You're trying to interrupt me. I gave you your message. Now I get to talk about what I want. You promised."

I tried to keep up with her. Wookiee? Like, from *Star Wars*? Let me assure you, there is no Chewbacca incarnate. He's a legend, to be sure, but he's also fictional. And copyrighted.

So, no Wookiee incarnate. Why, then, had I told Iris to tell me about it? And mirrors? That made me think of the compact I still had from Kolby's treasure collection. But it was at the hotel with Rachelle.

Focus, Emery, don't get distracted.

"Wait, Iris. You had a message for me specifically?" I asked, trying to pick the thing that stuck out from her stream of words. It was like trying to catch a mosquito with chopsticks. "From whom?"

She looked at me incredulously. "You mean you don't even remember?" She threw up her hands in childlike pantomime of utter exasperation. "You told me to tell you it was a Wookiee. I remember because it rhymes with 'cookie.'" She puffed up, proud of herself. "That's the whole message."

I pondered for a moment. It must have been from a previous life. I'd work it out later. Iris's attention span was... let's call it *finite*. I needed her help while she was here and cooperative.

"Iris," Caden said gently, "Emery and I have some questions about the beheadings around New York."

"Huh? Those?" She hung her head, her arms dangling down as if exceedingly disappointed in us. "What do you want to know about them?" she asked in a voice that sounded like we were *so* boring.

"Were you present at any of the deaths?" I asked.

"Yeah, two of them!" She said it proudly, like she'd won two gold stars.

"That's great," I encouraged her. I felt a surge of relief. She was drawn to death like ants to sugar, especially uncommon deaths, but I still hadn't known for certain if she'd be able to help me. "Did you see who murdered them?" I asked her quickly.

She folded her arms across her chest. "No. I got there too late. They were already gone." I couldn't tell for sure if "they" meant the murderer or the victim. From what I could tell, Iris could sometimes speak with dead people for a very brief time after their demise.

A deep chill went through me as I processed that thought. *Iris could speak to the recently deceased.* My mind replayed the message she said she'd delivered. *It was a Wookiee.* The message, she'd said, had come from me. I sucked in a breath. "Wait. Iris, this is very important. Did you speak to me in *Saudi Arabia?*"

She stamped her foot and squealed. "That's what I've been trying to tell you!" She was clearly growing bored with my inability to keep up with her.

I remembered the fight with the Yeti incarnate now. The oddities. Its white fur dyed brown, the dye dripping off. The ridiculous bandolier strapped to its barrel chest. Its presence in the *freaking desert.* And a human had been there. I'd never seen them, their voice coming from behind me and muffled, presumably by a headscarf. They'd pulled the trigger. Killed me.

Someone was trying to imitate a Wookiee, using an incarnate. But why? Far more importantly, why would they kill for it? Was it related to the current murders, or had I stumbled onto yet another puzzle? Did Iris's comment about mirrors play into this, or was that just her six-year-old mind jumping topics like a jump rope?

I had more questions now than before we'd summoned her, but Iris was drifting toward the rear of the building, a profoundly bored expression on her little face. I worried she might leave. *One mystery at a time.* I needed to ask my questions. Even if the Medium could force the little girl to stay, I didn't want to ruin my goodwill with Iris. And there was something just plain mean about holding a six-year-old against her will, even an immortal one.

"These beheadings," I asked quickly, "is there anything the victims had in common?"

She kept drifting slowly, up and away from us, toward the back of the building. She pulled her attention away from whatever drew her there, though, to look back at me. "They didn't have their heads," she reported. "And they weren't very nice."

I nodded, mind racing. "Were they not nice people, or were they bad people?"

She thought about it for a moment, continuing to drift. I took a step forward to keep abreast with her. "I think they were bad people," she finally said.

Caden stepped forward and asked, "Do you know anything about Ahedrian?"

She went stock-still. Tilted her head like she was listening to something only she could hear. Then she crooked a finger at us, serious again. "Follow me." And she disappeared through the rear wall.

We stood there, frozen. The Medium rocked in her chair, teacup in hand. When had she filled it? "What are you waiting for, a tip?" She laughed, which devolved into a hacking cough. "Get out of here," she wheezed between breaths.

We did, thanking her profusely as we rushed to the back of the building. There was a door leading out to the back of the townhome. Evening was approaching, the sun lower in the sky, casting the clouds in beatific hues of golden pink. This entire block of buildings pressed up against a wall. Iris hovered in the air about six feet above us, nearly transparent now that she'd left the Medium's Sanctum.

"Come on," she called, and slipped over the lip of the wall and out of view.

Caden eyed the wall dubiously. "After you."

I assessed the height. It was only about eight feet tall. "No time." I cupped my hands to form a step for him. He hesitated only a moment, then stepped into my hand and put his hands on my shoulders. I lifted, and he caught the edge of the wall easily, pulling himself up without any apparent effort. I tossed him my backpack and then ran up the wall, using my height and momentum to lever myself up with surprising ease. Have I mentioned that I *like* this body? Looking back at the ground behind and below me, I was impressed with myself.

"Nice," Caden said approvingly.

Beyond the wall was a neighborhood park. We jogged together, following a runner's path that angled in the same direction Iris had disappeared.

"This way," she called from my left and disappeared toward a playground and a basketball court. We took off after her. There were a few people about. It was that odd time of day in March when the sky darkens and families turn to the indoors for entertainment. In a few months at this same time, the park would be thronging with people.

Caden and I approached the court, Iris phasing through the chain-link fence while we used the built-in gap in it. There were two youths, a boy and a girl, playing basketball with each other. We gave them a wide berth, and they watched us cross the court, not noticing the ghost girl who led us. She was probably invisible to them. Or they were very nearsighted.

We crossed the court and exited on the other side, where a small dirt path cut from the court back to the looping joggers' trail. Iris had stopped in the middle of the path, which was occluded with bushes that mostly hid this area. We could be seen from the court and the trail, but only barely. Caden and I spotted it at the same time, the thing that drew Iris. Scrawled in the dirt to the side of the path in deep, persisting grooves, a single word.

AHEDRIAN

I looked around frantically, peering under the bushes and sweeping up and down the footpath. There was no body. No victim. "Iris," I called out, low and urgent. "Did someone die near here?"

The Ghost shook her head, pigtails flying. "Not yet."

I felt like I'd swallowed ice. I didn't like the way she said that. It instilled a sense of urgency in me. "Iris, could the murderer be the Headless Horseman?"

She shivered, though she certainly couldn't feel the chill in the air. "I suppose," she replied, "but he couldn't do *that*." She pointed at the dirt.

Of course. The Headless Horseman would be incorporeal, ghostly, incapable of affecting the real world except in very limited ways. Specific ways. Like decapitation.

"An accomplice?" Caden asked, looking to me.

I wondered. "Malevolent incarnates don't usually work with others." Neither did I, though, until recently. "Maybe." My mind was racing, spinning.

"What if the accomplice scribbles the word and leads the victim here," Caden said slowly, thinking it out, "and then the Headless Horseman..." He looked at me and drew a finger across his throat.

"That would mean we have time to stop it," I realized. "The question is, how long until the murder."

"A couple of hours, at most," Iris said, catching me off guard. She crossed her arms at my expression. "I can tell. Not exactly, but..."

"Caden, how long to Sleepy Hollow from here, by car?"

He calculated. "Half hour, maybe a little longer."

I considered. Decided. "I need you to go back—"

"Emery," Caden said. "I'm going with you." He said the words softly. Not a plea. Not an argument. A statement.

I rubbed my temples. "I don't have time to debate this, Caden. You can't come with me. It's dangerous."

"Exactly," he said. Surprisingly, he looked to the Ghost. "Iris, do you see me dying anytime soon?"

I stood up. "That's not how it wo—"

"Of course not," she piped, her voice sounding tinny and far away.

I felt a stab of irritation and a light sense of betrayal, but it was nothing beside the rushing sense of urgency. I balked, my hands squeezing into fists, relaxing, squeezing. Caden surprised me by reaching out and taking my hand in his. "We can stop this murder, Emery. Both of us. Together."

I stared into his eyes and caved. Again. "Promise me you'll follow my lead," I said, hating myself.

"I promise."

I pulled my hand free, angry, but not really with him. "Let's go."

L ess than five minutes later, Caden and I piled into the back seat of a yellow taxi. As the cab pulled up, I'd thanked Iris wholeheartedly for her help and promised I would visit with her again soon. She waved goodbye as we drove away, fading from visibility before we hit the first intersection.

Sleepy Hollow. The Headless Horseman incarnate. *Shit.* This was all happening so quickly. I checked my supplies, glad I'd thought to bring them along. The Taser made me feel a little safer. With Caden along, I'd do everything I could to keep this from becoming a full-blown hunt. Just a simple *chat* with the Headless Horseman, and, if I was wrong, we'd be back before the murder in Harlem. If I was right, there'd be no murder in the first place. Easy. No problem. Right?

Right.

I drummed my fingers on the armrest. My mind was rocketing ahead, planning, *worrying,* and I felt a time bomb of urgency and impatience ticking away in the pit of my stomach. I was staring at the numbers, willing them to stop counting down—but also wishing they'd just reach zero and be done with it. I needed to chill.

Caden sat on the other side of the cab, the gap between us feeling wider than it had all day. He looked out the window, expression and posture unreadable. He didn't appear angry with me, nor hurt at my irritation. He was contemplative. And, dammit, he gave off peace and calm like he radiated particles of the damn stuff. In this moment, we were opposites. I was all white rapids, surging water, a river hurling itself toward a waterfall with careless speed. He was a mountain lake, deep and crystal clear, every ripple absorbed into its depths, mirroring serenity and the splendor of the landscape around it. I breathed. Borrowed some of his composure, let it calm my racing mind.

"What was that about Iris and your family?" I asked him, striving to bridge the distance between us. My voice sounded tense, though.

He didn't answer. Studying the passing city, he silently witnessed day's final breath before night claimed it. I found myself feeling frustrated. If it were Rachelle there, I'd know what to do, what to say. Rachelle was all fire and a little ice. If she gave me the cold shoulder, I'd crack a joke and the ice at the same time, maybe something at her expense to stoke the fire with which I knew she'd retort. Her temper was swiftly lit and swiftly spent. If Rachelle was fire and ice, then Caden was just... warmth. A candle to her firework.

Finally he turned to me, face serious. "We should call the cops. Have them stake out the murder scene. Just in case we're not able to take care of the problem in Sleepy Hollow."

I saw the taxi driver give us a strange look in his rearview mirror at the mention of cops and murder. I flashed him a smile. "We're on a scavenger hunt," I lied. "A murder mystery scavenger hunt." Ooh. That sounded kind of awesome.

He shrugged, uninterested, and threw over his shoulder, "Sounds fun."

I considered Caden, then said quietly, "All due respect to New York's finest, I don't know that they'll dedicate an officer to sit there for hours on evidence that boils down to less than graffiti." I rubbed my jaw. "The Headless Horseman is a solid suspect," I reasoned out loud. "And if we're wrong, we'll be able to get back in time."

He nodded, but he didn't look wholly convinced. "You're the expert," he said, giving me a tiny smile.

For some reason, that worried me more. "You might be right," I told him. "I have an idea."

I pulled out my cell and phoned Rachelle.

"I'm so glad you called," she said. "This *Top Chef* marathon has been going on all day. I can't seem to stop watching, but there's only so much ceviche a girl can take. Are you going to be back soon? This show makes me hungry; I was thinking of ordering room service."

I grinned. "Not for a while yet, sorry. Caden and I are en route to Sleepy Hollow."

"Oh? *Ohh.* That makes sense! Headless Horseman incarnate, decapitated bodies... You, Emery Luple, are a genius. You should do this for a living."

"I'll consider that," I said wryly. "Do you still have that reporter's business card? Sabrina Miles?"

"Yeah, but it's all the way across the room." She heaved a sigh. "The things I do for you."

"Can you call her and tell her we found another sighting of..." I paused, glancing at the driver. He'd probably recognize the word Ahedrian. "Of that word we found in the parking garage? There wasn't anything else at the scene, but she'd probably want to report on it, and she'll get extra kudos for being the first one there." I thought for a moment. "And make sure she brings a crew with her. The last thing I'd want is for anything to happen to her."

"Safety first. Got it."

With Caden's help, I gave her the address of the park, then disconnected the call.

"We're almost there," he said quietly.

I looked out the window. Night had claimed most of the sky in the twenty minutes we'd been in the cab. The city had all but disappeared, replaced with buildings and streets that looked like something out of a history book. Colonial-style houses, large swaths of maple trees, and low stone walls gave the area an antiquated appeal. As the taxi drove by a cemetery with gravestones standing like sentinels in the night, I couldn't help but recall Sleepy Hollow's reputation for being one of the most haunted places... ever.

We left the taxi and tipped the driver for taking us outside of New York City limits—it was ridiculously expensive—and he wished us luck at our game. We found ourselves in front of a picturesque chapel with cobblestone sidings and arched windows that reminded me of eyes. The structure was topped with a pristine white roof and a matching bell tower.

"This is the south end of Sleepy Hollow Cemetery," Caden reported, getting his bearings. There's a river just south of here, and the famous Headless Horseman Bridge crosses it."

"How well do you know the myth?" I asked.

He shrugged. "Two guys fight over a girl, one is a local hero and the other is Ichabod Crane, a superstitious miser after her family's wealth. Ichabod's unwelcome advances are rejected, and he makes his way back to the farmstead where he's staying but runs afoul of the Headless Horseman and is never heard from again." His tone assumed a spooky cant. "Was the Headless Horseman the other suitor, playing on Ichabod Crane's superstitious nature to run him out of town? Or was the Headless Horseman real, a specter that ferried Ichabod Crane's spirit to the underworld? No one knows." He considered his words for a moment. "Well, I guess maybe *you* know."

"Nice rendition." I applauded. "I would have mentioned the race, but otherwise spot-on." I paused. "And I don't, actually. Know if he was real or not."

Caden frowned. "What do you mean? I thought they're all real."

"Incarnates are given power by their myth. Without it, they don't exist." I started walking in the direction Caden had indicated was toward the bridge. "So, at the time, it could have simply been Brom Bones—that's the other suitor in your story—in a costume, and the incarnate came later." I shrugged. "Or it could have been the first sighting of the Headless Horseman incarnate, perhaps based on the ghost stories already told in the area, and the retellings have made him grow in popularity and power."

The road was surprisingly wide, and an occasional car coasted by as we walked. To my right was a small wooden fence, with looming maple trees on the far side. To my left, the cemetery was bordered by an unexpectedly low, Gothic fence. As we walked, I read a sign in front of the chapel that read, "Old Dutch Church of Sleepy Hollow, 1685." Caden pointed ahead to where the road spanned a tiny river— more of a stream, really—before widening to accommodate a side road and a gas station.

"That's the bridge," he said. "In the legend, it's said he disappears when he tries to cross the river there."

I eyed the gas station, then the rather unimpressive bridge. I had been expecting something old and preserved, a wooden construction perhaps, remodeled throughout time but reflecting the original. This was... well, it was more or less a continuation of the road. A four-laned, crosswalk-sporting, modern-sewer-grated road.

We walked to the stone railing of the bridge and looked down. A stream babbled maybe ten feet beneath us, the noise of running water muted each time a car cruised by. I swung my gaze up and down the street. Sleepy Hollow was charming, despite it not meeting my expectations. The buildings were quaint compared to the towering New York skyscrapers I'd been among all day, and trees and flowers shook slightly in the breeze. Cast iron lanterns lit the walks, forlorn in the darkness. I pulled my coat closer around me.

I pondered where we might find the Headless Horseman. "We need to either stalk the graveyard or walk along this river." Caden's hands were on the stone railing, his body craned to look down at the water. I put my hand on his shoulder to emphasize my next words. He looked at me, surprised. "Caden, you must do exactly as I say. Incarnates are not all as adorable as Iris or as harmless as the Medium. This could be very dangerous."

He nodded firmly, earnest. "I promise." Then his face split into a grin. "But relax! Iris said nothing can happen to me."

I frowned. "Did we hear different things? She said you don't die, Caden. You could still be hurt, maimed, put into a coma—"

His hands shot up in a show of surrender. "Okay, okay. You've made your point. No death, injuries, or comas for me today."

I held his gaze for a moment longer to hammer home that I was serious. Then I dug into my bag and rummaged around, bringing out the flash camera and the air horn. As much as I wished to give him my spare stun gun, I knew he wouldn't accept it, so I handed him the camera instead.

"Not entirely sure getting pictures of this will help your blog, since *There's Always a Loophole* is about debunking myths," Caden said lightly, "but I'm more than happy to be your photographer in a pinch. I'll even waive my usual fee."

"How generous," I replied drolly. "It's actually for self-defense."

He held it up and snapped a shot of me. The flash was blinding, my eyes having adjusted to the night. I let out a yelp and covered my eyes with my hand, blinking the burning afterimage away. When my vision cleared, Caden was looking at the camera appreciatively. "Works better than I thought it would," he admitted. "But you have eyes. It's the *Headless* Horseman, remember?"

"That's it," I declared, "you're staying here."

He stowed the grin, but it sparkled in his eyes. Or was that the afterimage, still? "Emery, I *swear* I'll follow your lead."

I eyed him suspiciously, but I wasn't going to leave him here by himself. As much as I hated to admit it, he would be safer with me nearby to protect him. What had I been thinking, bringing him along in the first place?

"Incarnates often rely on secrecy to survive," I explained, "so they have a weakness to anything that threatens to expose them."

I could see understanding dawn. "Like a camera."

"Like a camera. Ghost personas are especially susceptible. When you take a photo of one, they tend to go invisible and intangible."

"What happens if I actually manage to get a picture of him?" Caden asked.

"It won't turn out. It'll be blurry, out of focus, just good enough to spread the *possibility* that the image is authentic."

"Huh. That explains a lot. Alien sightings, reports of ghosts, even the Loch Ness Monster... never a clean photo." Caden shook his head wonderingly. "To think that all this time, that would be evidence *for* the myths instead of working against them."

"Only once you know the secret." I handed him the air horn.

He hung the camera around his neck and took the air horn from me. He turned it over and over in his hands, then suddenly held it up in triumph. "Does this call attention to the incarnate, which they want to avoid, so they run away from the sound?"

I gave him a sheepish smile. "I was just hoping it might spook his horse."

"Oh."

"One more thing." I hesitated. "According to the myth, the Headless Horseman wants a new head. Is desperate for one."

Caden nodded. "Which is why none of the victims' heads were found."

"Exactly." I grimaced. "I know what Iris said, but do everything you can to protect yours, okay?"

"Got it."

"Let's go," I said, taking point. "We need to find his Lair. I'm guessing it's likely to be along the river, wherever the horseman showed up in the myth to chase down Ichabod Crane. If only I knew the legend better." I walked to the end of the bridge and started to forge a path down the steep drop off the main road toward the river.

"If you want to follow the river," Caden pointed out from above, "we can just take this road. It follows it north and east for a ways." He waggled his phone at me. I couldn't see the screen, but he must have had a map pulled up. Because of course he did.

I closed my eyes and took a deep breath. "Good idea," I said when I'd hiked back up the incline and reached him. "You passed the test. A-plus."

He grinned as I stalked past him.

I kept an eye on my phone as we walked, worried about the time. 7:49 p.m. It had already been an hour since we'd left Iris. We needed to hurry.

The road was empty, but there were a few houses along the left, and a low rock wall to the right separated us from a forest. Tall pines towered overhead, seeming to grow taller and more sinister as night fully settled around us. Sprinkled throughout this greenery were skeletal trees, their branches reaching upward like twisted, gnarled bones. The homes ran the gamut from short, squat houses to contemporary buildings with garages big enough to park a small plane. A few of the houses had lit windows, but far fewer than I expected. With most of the lights out, the houses had an abandoned quality to them, as though they watched passersby with empty, hungry eyes. Once or twice I thought I caught the pale face of someone looking out a window, watching Caden and me trek down the road. But when I looked again, the windows were empty. I wouldn't admit it out loud, but I was grateful for Caden's company.

We crept closer to our inevitable encounter with the Headless Horseman. As we pushed onward, my instincts guided us more than anything. We were going the right way. I could feel it. The distance between the houses increased as we walked another mile down the street, time *tick tick tick*ing away in the pit of my stomach. Had Rachelle convinced Sabrina? Or were we already too late?

As we approached our destination, it was as if we were walking backward in time. Here, nature fought to regain control of the land. The houses became run-down things, overgrown, surrendering to the persistent, whispering trees. The trees themselves thinned, becoming emaciated, devoid of leaves to soften their haggard appearance. The Lair pulled me toward it. We were close.

We came to a spot where a trail led off from the main road, angling into the forest and quickly swallowed by it. I felt my hackles rise as I looked down that dirt-and-pebble path, and I knew in my heart—which had sunk to my stomach—that we'd find our culprit in that direction.

"It's spooky, huh?" Caden said, following my gaze.

I looked at him and felt steel creep back into my spine. I was the expert here. I was the Monster Hunter. He was counting on me to protect him, to lead him, to keep us both safe.

"All incarnates have a domain, a place where their powers are the strongest," I told him. "Take the Alligator in the Sewers, for example. No way a girl with a baseball bat could drop that thing on its home turf. But it had exited the sewers, its Territory, and that weakened it."

"Are you telling me that"—he pointed at the path—"is the front door to the Headless Horseman's Territory?"

"Yes. Well, almost. There are four types of incarnates, and I don't think we're lucky enough for this one to be a Predator." I listed off the four incarnate classifications and quickly outlined the difference between them. "Each one has a different type of domain," I said. "Sanctum for Benign, Safe Haven for Prey, Territory for Predator, and Lair for Malevolent."

Caden picked it up immediately. "So this is the front door to his *Lair*."

I took a deep breath and nodded. "Unfortunately, I think so."

He hooked a thumb over his shoulder. "Last house was back that way, maybe three minutes. Want to meet there if something goes wrong?"

"That's a good idea," I murmured. "But if I don't show by morning, you need to leave."

He looked at me incredulously. Then, seeing my grave expression, he nodded once. "But let's call that Plan Z."

"Deal." I hesitated. "Caden, let me do the talking. I've never encountered the Headless Horseman before, so I don't know what to expect. But I've been dealing with incarnates for a long time."

He regarded me somberly. "I understand, Emery."

I took out my Taser. Ghostly incarnates shared a fatal flaw: electricity. In ancient times, only legendary relics like Mjolnir incarnate —that's Thor's hammer, by the way—could threaten ghosts. But in our modern world, I had more options. Hence the Taser. It was brand-new, but I checked the battery level out of habit. It was full, of course. I secured the holster around my waist but kept the Taser in my sweaty hand. Prepared as I could be, I took my first step down the path, Caden a step behind me.

18

 econd step. The nape of my neck tingled. The wind soughed through the surrounding trees, susurrations passing from leaf to leaf. They whispered wordless warning of our trespass, sighing at our folly, consigning us to our fates. Chilly night air brushed against my clothes like the ghostly fingers of a phantom taking my measure.

Third step. Goose bumps washed down my arms. Our footsteps were loud on the crunchy gravel. The breeze carried the scent of wet, rotting wood and kicked up fallen leaves like we were in the flush of autumn instead of the final days of winter.

Fourth step. The darkness ahead seemed deeper, a tunnel of trees instead of a path. The dark, overcast sky somehow seemed to grow murkier, heavier. A low rumble of thunder sounded, like a dog's menacing growl as you reach your hand out to steal its bone.

Our fifth step took us beneath the stretched branches of a skeletal tree, its fingers extended overhead like an archway.

A crack of thunder and a jagged flash of lightning struck simultaneously, assailing all my senses at once, the blazing afterimage of hot white light making Caden's camera flash from earlier seem like a weak flicker. I ducked, hands protecting my head, as the tree detonated above us, throwing a shower of sparks and molten bark spiraling down. The resulting crash was deafening. The tree was torn like a sheet of paper, wood curling like the legs of a dead spider, small fires glowing along the charred pulp.

I stumbled, feeling embers pattering like rain on my head and the back of my new coat. The flash and fire had seared my vision. The world hummed from the tree's explosion. I spun, trying to get my bearings, to locate Caden, make sure he was safe. My eyes watered, vision swimming. There! He was kneeling on the ground, right? Yes, his back to me, facing the incinerated remains of the tree. The scene came into focus, sound slowly pushing through my daze. There was something moving in the smoke rising from the tree stump. No, not moving. Rearing.

The squeal of a horse pierced the buzzing in my ears.

Shit. So much for talking.

The shapes and colors in my vision finally resolved into a nightmare. An enormous black horse stood on its hind legs, its front hooves flashing eight or nine feet in the air, its eyes burning like demon fire. With Caden kneeling in front of it, the stallion looked like some sort of dark horse god, wisps of smoke from the tree wreathing it, still-dying embers matching its glowing face. Where Iris was all effervescent translucence, this horse was condensed shadow, its silhouette blending and merging with the night's shades of black.

The horse's rider was mostly obscured by the bulk of the nearly upright horse, but he was large, with a long cape flowing down and out as though caught by an updraft.

Move, Caden. Move! I was trying to scream the words, but everything was happening so fast.

A flash lit the scene and I tensed, expecting another bolt of lightning. Of course, I reacted far too late; had it been lightning, I'd have been blinded again. This flash was feeble in comparison, a gunshot to a cannon. But it caught the rearing horse full in the face.

The camera.

The horse let out a scream (if you've never heard a horse scream, consider yourself fortunate; it's *terrifying*) and spun around, its hooves cleaving the tree—and passing through the knobby bark as though it weren't there—and then it galloped in a straight line away from Caden, passing through trees, the rider's cape billowing behind like silky night. I lost it almost immediately in the shadows.

Caden had hunkered low to the ground, probably recoiling from the tree's explosion. Somehow, even though he'd been closer to the detonation than I, he'd managed to orient himself to face the Headless Horseman *and* had wits enough to use the camera.

I was stunned.

I also had no time to appreciate his impressive stunt. The camera would drive them away for only a moment. Even as I thought it, the horse swept out of the underbrush to my left—not stirring so much as a leaf—trying to run me down. I threw myself to the ground, barely avoiding getting trampled. How did something so terrifying and immense move so quietly? As I fell, my arm snapped up to aim at the Horseman's retreating back, but I refrained from pulling the trigger.

The Taser Pulse+ works by using a compressed gas cartridge to eject two probes. The probes are attached to conductive wires, which in turn are connected to an electrical circuit. The barbed probes fire off at slightly different angles and stick themselves into skin. Since electricity follows the path of least resistance, it courses through flesh, locking up the muscles between the two probes. The charge persists for half a minute, essentially warping the victim's body into the worst charley horse you've ever imagined. Incapacitating spasms and a dose of pain encourage... *compliance* in the person on the business end of the weapon.

It doesn't work quite that way with ghostly incarnates. Don't get me wrong; the science is the same. But these incarnates—I think of them as "incorporeal incarnates"—are made up of plasma. Well, plasma and myth. But let's focus on the plasma, because I don't really understand the scientific interaction between electricity and fables. Incorporeal incarnates don't have any physical muscles. Or physical anything, for those of you keeping score. But they have plenty of plasma, and plasma is highly conductive.

This all led to one very satisfying conclusion: 50,000 volts of electricity coursing through the Headless Horseman would keep him from any further murders until he reincarnated. That's 1,001 headless-free days.

Unfortunately, he had to be corporeal enough for the probes to take hold, otherwise they'd pass right through him harmlessly. Which meant I had to hit him while he was trying to hit me. Joy. Moreover, if I missed with those probes, I was going to need to get a lot closer than I liked, or a lot more creative than I wished, to send him packing. The Taser could be used like a stun stick in a pinch, but I really didn't want to get that close to this Malevolent.

I heard the barest rustle of leaves, and then the Headless Horseman made another pass at me, materializing out of the woods on near-silent hooves. I rolled, barely getting out of the way, gravel and dirt kicked up and spraying into my face. Then the specter was gone, vanished into the trees without a sound. Looking at the spot in the road I'd been at a moment before, I saw deep grooves where the ghost horse had tried to trample me.

A blast from Caden's air horn brought me slamming back to *now*. I spun and shouted, "We need to get out of these trees!" Farther down the dirt road, through the tunnel of scrawny trees, the path opened onto what looked like a clearing. If I had more space to time my shot, to see the incarnate coming, I'd have far better luck. "Back to the road!" I yelled, hoping Caden would leave the Lair and allow me to fight the Headless Horseman on my own.

Caden didn't even hesitate. He bolted *toward* me and gasped, "I think there's a clearing this way. We can fight him easier if we have some room." He swept past me, throwing over his shoulder, "Come on! That horse is fast, but it can't turn on a dime."

I tore off after him, cursing under my breath.

Behind us, over my harsh breathing and our crunchy footfalls, I heard the sound of hoofbeats. I looked back. The Headless Horseman was galloping down the path from the direction of the road, his horse's hooves making solid clopping noises but not actually connecting with the earth; no gravel flew, no dust kicked up. Somehow, despite the darkness, I saw the Horseman fully for the first time. A giant of a man, wearing dark riding leathers studded with black-lacquered metal, leaned forward in a saddle that would have easily accommodated both Caden and me. His massive shoulders sported raven feathers that fluttered as he bore down upon us. They were the top part of his cloak, I realized: a mantle of feathers and then a long, flowing cape that looked woven from the night itself. And that was all the shoulders sported; where his neck and head should have been, he bore instead a smooth, shadowed indentation. He looked like a doll with its head removed. The scariest freaking doll in existence.

I had planned to use the clearing to get a good shot, but as the Headless Horseman bore down on me, I reconsidered. I raised the Taser with a steady hand, doubtful I'd get a better opportunity than this. Especially if I was wounded... or dead. I could see the red dot of the little aiming laser on the center of the nightmare riding down on me. Fifteen feet was the limit of my Taser's range. With the speed of the Headless Horseman's approach, I'd need to fire and roll to the side almost at the same time.

The next few moments happened so quickly, it was as if someone took still frames and displayed them in quick succession. I snapped down the safety and squeezed the trigger. The barbs snapped forward like the twin fangs of a snake. I dove to the side. Felt the barbs bite into something solid. Heard the clicking sound of discharged electricity. Looked up.

The Headless Horseman bore down on Caden. There was another camera flash, followed by the frustrated neighing of the horse as it phased *through* Caden, who was dashing toward the clearing. The camera must have forced the Headless Horseman to go incorporeal and rendered him unable to strike his prey in the physical world.

I followed the Taser wires and found them embedded in... a *pumpkin*? It sat in the center of the path with both barbs sunk into it. In the legend, Ichabod Crane nearly escaped the Headless Horseman's clutches, but at the very last moment, the rider threw a pumpkin that caught the fleeing Ichabod across the back of the shoulders, smiting him. In the morning, the remains of the pumpkin were the only evidence the Headless Horseman was real. It was the entity's ace up the sleeve. His last-ditch—and successful—attempt to reach his original quarry. And evidently, it could be used as a last-ditch defensive measure, too. That was one damn versatile gourd.

I swore and leapt to my feet, detaching the now-useless cartridge from the front of the Taser and letting the wires fall to the ground. I had another cartridge in my bag, but I couldn't reload while Caden and I were in immediate danger. I sprinted down the path and into the clearing. It was larger than I'd thought, lined on all sides by trees, giving the illusion that we'd entered some sort of natural arena.

The creak of leather sounded from right over my shoulder, and hot horse's breath gusted against my neck. I hit the ground by instinct, but I felt something heavy and painful slam into my upper back as I fell. I somehow avoided the horse's flashing hooves as the Malevolent raced past me, heading for Caden.

Caden scrambled up one of the nearest trees with surprising alacrity. *Good,* I thought—he was trying to get to safety and leave the monster hunting to me. But the Headless Horseman's gallop suddenly slanted upward, as if there were a ramp between him and Caden's perch instead of nothing but air. The horse's hooves continued to clop like they were on solid ground but lifted the Horseman to Caden's height. Fortunately, Caden saw the Horseman coming. Just as the incarnate reached him, Caden dropped through the twisting branches and caught a lower one, then swung gently to the ground. I'd give him a ten out of ten. Hot damn. The Headless Horseman continued his trajectory through the spot Caden had been a moment before, wood splintering and then spraying across the clearing beyond.

Caden's distraction—intentional or otherwise—gave me the time I needed to clamber back to my feet, rolling my shoulders. Nothing broken. I had, however, dropped the Taser in the grass. I looked around for it, but the Headless Horseman was back in an instant, riding me down. I hesitated, not wanting to leave my precious weapon—

The incarnate slammed into me with the impact of a car, driving the breath from my lungs and lifting me from the ground. Pain exploded in my chest. My hand whipped out by reflex and caught something—the horse's reins. I was yanked forward, my arm nearly pulled out of its socket, and dragged along with the Horseman. My heels connected with the ground and bounced, skipping, sending my legs akimbo.

Then the damn incarnate went all *ghost* again. My fingers lost their purchase and slipped through the entity like it was nothing but fog, and I hit the ground, kicking up a plume of dirt and fallen leaves with my momentum.

Caden's hand gripped my shoulder. "Are you all right?" he asked, worry and urgency pitching his voice high.

"Doing great," I assured him through clenched teeth. I got to my feet yet again, trying to assess my body. Everything seemed to work, though my arm felt stiff and I knew the pain was waiting, adrenaline holding it back like a handler struggling to control a pack of frantic, barking dogs.

"We need to cross the river," I told Caden. "The myth. He can't follow us there."

Caden bobbed his head in quick agreement, then scanned the area. "That way, I think" he said, pointing.

We ran. Well, Caden ran. I sort of hobble-limp-skipped, but I kept up. The clearing was a good size, but the river was just beyond the line of trees on the other end.

Twice the Headless Horseman looped around and struck at us. The first time, he cleaved his way between us, scoring a shallow groove in the grassy dirt and forcing us to spread apart. On the second pass he came at Caden, and I saw a sickle in the Horseman's hand, held low and to the side. There was very little light, but it glinted nonetheless as it came arcing down. Caden cried out, and I saw something go flying from his torso, spiraling off into the night.

My horrified mind and hummingbird heart screeched to a halt, thinking the object was Caden's head.

"I'm fine!" Caden gasped between breaths, not slowing.

It had been the camera, I realized. The incarnate had sliced so close to Caden's neck that the sickle had caught the strap and severed it.

We made the tree line. The downward slope beyond it was not steep, and we plunged down without hesitation. The river was thirty feet away.

The Headless Horseman sped toward us again. Even so, we were going to make it! The "river" here was little more than a brook, five feet across at most, and so shallow that rocks were exposed in its center. Caden and I ran side by side, movements in sync. The Headless Horseman was a split second away, sickle poised like a scorpion's tail. Caden and I sprang across the river, legs outstretched, as the blade sliced the air just behind us.

We landed, stumbled a few more steps, and turned almost as one. The Headless Horseman, on the other side of the river, was rearing up, stallion and rider stretched to full, monstrous height.

I put my hands on my knees and gasped in huge gulps of air. Caden followed my lead, panting hard.

The Headless Horseman guided his horse back several steps, the beast tossing its head and mane in frustration.

"There's a building back there," Caden pointed out between heavy breaths. "Looks like an old farm, maybe?"

I glanced behind us, away from the Horseman. There was a low, dark structure amid the trees. It didn't look like a house; maybe a low barn. Even in the dead of night, I could tell it was derelict, devoid of inhabitants.

The Headless Horseman's haunting laugh crossed the river, drawing my attention. He was walking the horse toward the river with slow, deliberate steps, like an expert equestrian showing off his prized stallion at a horse fair. I frowned. What was he doing? The horse reached the water's edge, less than a dozen feet from us. It nickered and tossed its mane, then stepped *forward,* its hooves stopping just above the river, crossing the water as if it weren't there.

"This isn't the right spot," I breathed, a sinking feeling washing over me. "Get to the building, Caden. Now!"

Thankfully, he didn't argue. He loped back into motion, flying back toward the dark structure.

"I name you," I screamed at the incarnate. "Brom Bones, desist!" It was my last-ditch effort, my Hail Mary. Sometimes, incarnates whose identities were not well known or shrouded in myth could be influenced by naming them.

It was no good. Either the name was wrong—the Headless Horseman may not have been the other suitor after all—or it wasn't enough to penetrate the incarnate's metaphorical armor here in its Lair. Or maybe the accursed incarnate couldn't hear me. He had no ears, after all.

I needed to buy time for Caden to get to safety. As much as I despised dying—and hated the idea of losing the chance to get to know Caden better—at least I would reincarnate. I watched the Headless Horseman walk toward me like an executioner, comfortable and infinitely patient in his certainty that I was his. I could see the sickle rising high above my head, could feel the horse's breath as it snorted, its huge head within arm's reach of me. *Screw that.* If I could feel its breath, then hopefully that meant it was solid enough to feel *this.*

I swung my backpack off my shoulder and into the side of the horse's face with all the strength I could muster. The heavy bag connected and the horse screamed, rearing back in surprise. The bag was torn from my fingers, but I was already dashing back toward the structure. My action had bought me precious seconds, but only a few. Desperate to reach the structure ahead, I bolted through the unkempt grass with such speed that my feet barely touched the ground.

It was a broken-down building, little more than an elongated shed, with a fenced-in, overgrown yard. The fence was falling apart, more missing than otherwise. I felt the specter at my back, bearing down on me.

But as I flew across the threshold of the enclosure, I felt a cleanness, a sense of refuge that could never emanate from the dilapidated structure in front of me alone. Like a drowning man, I heaved breaths of precious air. I knew instinctively I had departed the Headless Horseman's Lair.

Caden was there, catching me as I plowed into him, his braced body keeping me from knocking us both over.

I collapsed to the ground anyway, and he plopped down beside me, our breaths ragged and uneven. The Headless Horseman trotted along just beyond the fence, clearly unable to cross the threshold. He circled the building twice but apparently found no weaknesses to the barrier, despite the fact that his horse could have passed through the fence at a dozen places even without phasing through it. We were safe, for the moment.

Caden caught his breath and looked from the agitated incarnate to me. "Well," he said, injecting a breathless sort of cheer into his tone, "*now* what?"

I watched the Headless Horseman pace the boundary of our little shelter again and felt more secure by the minute. The withered farmstead was far stronger than it appeared. I pulled out my phone and was unsurprised to find I had no service. I was growing certain that this was a place out of time, perhaps Ichabod Crane's abode, his refuge against things that went bump in the night. It was now our sanctuary. And given that my bag of tricks and all my weapons were scattered throughout the woods, we'd likely be here for a while, waiting out the Headless Horseman. I figured (hoped) that he'd disappear with the night.

"What is this place?" Caden asked, wiping sweat from his brow. "It looks old."

I told him my theory.

"So how'd we find it?" he asked, accepting my explanation with little trouble. I tried to see it from his perspective: I guess, if the Headless Horseman was real, why couldn't a farmhouse appear in the middle of the night?

"This kind of thing happens with incarnates," I told him. "If the Headless Horseman exists, so too does that which defies him. That sort of thing." I shrugged. "I could be wrong. Maybe he just doesn't like fences."

I held up my new coat. It was destroyed, smeared with dirt, grime, and grass stains. It reminded me of one of those commercials where the kids go outside and play in the mud, then come back inside to show Mom, who rolls her eyes while the jingle plays, then the garments miraculously look brand-new again, like... well, like Caden's clothes.

"How do you do that?" I grumbled at him.

He gave me a quizzical look.

"Keep your clothes so perfect, even after a battle like that."

He chuckled, taking in my ruined coat with sympathy. "I don't get jackhammered into the ground, for starters." Not *loads* of sympathy.

We explored our little oasis of safety within the Horseman's Lair. The structure—if such a word could be applied, given the sad state of repair of this thing—sat low to the ground, roof only about six feet high, so we had to duck our heads. Half of the building stored supplies: cut firewood stacked up in one corner, bales of hay in the other. The other half of the shed was vacant, containing only a few empty feed bags and a straw-strewn floor interrupted here and there by weeds. The whole thing was open to the air, more like a lean-to than a true shelter.

Caden slid in first and put his back to the rear wall. I ducked inside and paused, listening to the soft neighing of the incarnate's horse. It sounded like it was maybe a dozen feet beyond the shed's rear wall. Which was not far enough away to make me feel at ease, but I was at least confident a sickle wouldn't come crashing through the structure's flimsy wall. I stretched my stiff muscles as best I could in the cramped space, then settled down beside Caden, my ruined coat discarded at my feet.

"Good thing you thought ahead about putting someone at that crime scene," I told him, still reeling from our defeat.

He cocked his head. "You're the one who came up with the idea to have Rachelle convince that news reporter to do it."

I groaned. "She's going to kill me."

"Sabrina?"

I shook my head. "Rachelle."

"Oh, I don't think so," Caden said with a grin. "If you'd gotten yourself killed, *then* she'd kill you." We laughed softly, sharing the simple joy of escaping that situation with our lives.

The mundane sounds of night, entirely absent during our battle with the Headless Horseman, returned as we rested. Wind rustled through shivering leaves, crickets chirped to one another, and an owl hooted, all interspersed with the horse's soft tread and occasional whinny.

Caden smiled at me in the darkness. "It's not so bad out here, I guess." He knocked his knee into mine playfully. "Being stuck here with you, I mean."

"Could be a lot worse," I agreed. I'd put him in so much danger, though. Worse: I'd known it would be dangerous, and I'd done it anyway. It was so selfish. I'd simply wanted to show him everything, to *show off*. Look at me, I'm Emery, the Monster Hunter. Look what I can do! Was my ego so insatiable that I deemed it more valuable than Caden's life? If not, why had I brought him along? Was it the fear of being alone? I didn't think so. I'd done it before. Two lonely incarnations, zero mortal deaths. Well, none on my conscience.

"Emery?" Caden asked softly. I turned my attention from my internal turmoil to him. How did his golden hair catch the moonlight inside the shed, of all places? "Can incarnates be killed?"

"Yeah."

He picked up a piece of straw from the ground and began twisting it around his finger. "What happens to them? Does the myth just... die out, too?"

I shook my head, my gaze captured by his fingers playing with the twine. "No. As long as the legend survives, the incarnate does, too." I sighed, surprised that I could see my breath in front of my face. With the adrenaline finally ebbing, I began to feel the chill in the air. Except my right side, warmed by Caden's body. "A thousand and one days. Dead incarnates disappear for that exact duration, then reincarnate like new."

His hands paused. "A thousand and one days? That's... specific. What is that, just shy of three years?"

"Yeah. Two years and nine months, just about. Which means after taking out a Malevolent, you get to enjoy a nice reprieve before they pop back up. Sometimes with a hankering for vengeance."

He nodded and went back to playing with the piece of straw.

I should stop this, I knew. I should quit telling him things about this life, this world. It hadn't scared him away, and that was so dangerous. I couldn't protect him. I needed to admit that.

Where is Huntington? I thought suddenly. Always before, when I'd put mortals in harm's way, his eyes appeared to remind me of my impotence.

But not this time. Caden had held his own against the Horseman, true, but it didn't stop me from feeling remorse; my stomach clenched at the thought of his coming to harm. And I had knowingly walked him into the Lair of a powerful, hateful Malevolent. Did the memory not appear because Caden had survived unscathed? Was it biding its time, waiting for Caden to fall victim to my mistakes?

I knew I couldn't control him, couldn't dictate where he went. But I certainly didn't have to welcome him into my world, walk him down the path, lead him directly into the waiting jaws of the Headless Horseman. So why didn't I feel more guilty, more ashamed? If anything, I felt... relieved. And safe, in this place. It tried to undermine my guilt.

"Emery." Caden's voice came again, soft and close in the dark. His dilated pupils swallowed the luminescent seafoam green of his eyes. "You... you're an incarnate, aren't you?" His fingers froze again as he waited for me to answer.

I hadn't told him, I realized. Despite everything we'd shared about ourselves, I had held back. Old habits die hard. The moment stretched between us. My mind swam, part of me wanting to tell him, to accept this brash, new part of myself that welcomed Caden's interest. A part of me wanted to swallow that foolish, optimistic side of me and remain brittle. Remain unyielding. Save lives.

"Yeah," I breathed.

Caden tossed the bent, broken straw aside and blew out his

cheeks. "It makes so much sense. How you know all this. Why you think you're invincible, but you're afraid for everyone else."

Had I said that out loud?

"Making me promise to leave in the morning if you didn't return," he continued. "Your hesitation when I ask questions about the world of incarnates. It's *your world*." He shuffled closer, his shoulder and leg resting against mine. I felt his warmth and didn't shy away. Was my heart, so recently rested, beginning to beat faster again? "Thank you," he whispered fiercely, infusing the words with sincerity.

I blinked, confused. "What are you thanking me for?"

"For taking a chance on me. For sharing your weird, wonderful world with me. For putting your faith in me. I can't imagine what my life must look like to you. So short. Are human lives like... like a candle, to you?"

I sucked in a sharp breath. *Human lives,* he'd said. As if I weren't human.

But was I?

"Hey now," I said, "I may not be precisely mortal..."

Caden was my equal, wasn't he? He had stood toe to toe with me. Arguably, he'd fared better than I had against the Headless Horseman. *But how can he be my equal, when he's so vulnerable?* The thought was the second punch in a one-two combo. I felt gutted. When had I become so arrogant? When had I stopped thinking of myself as *human?*

"But I'm still human," I finished feebly, tears springing unbidden to my eyes. This was how Caden slipped under my guard. It wasn't about trust or magnetism. It was his humanity. He reminded me that I was human too, not above it at all.

I found myself smiling at him, so close in the dark. "Mortals' lives are more like... shooting stars than candles. They flash through my life quickly, true, and sometimes they seem so far away. But they're brilliant." A tear slid down my left cheek, hidden from Caden. I pulled my knees up to my chest, unable to hide the warmth in my voice as I looked at him. "And special."

He leaned forward and snatched up my discarded coat. He shook it once, twice, then draped it over my legs and his like a blanket. "I wish I could be a regular star instead," he said after a moment. "Their light is a constant, something you can rely on."

"The beauty of something isn't really found in how long it lasts," I said. "Sometimes it's beautiful precisely because it's impermanent. Everyone treasures rarity."

He considered my words, closing his eyes. Out front, the horse neighed again. The inside of the shed was slightly shadowed, the moon's illumination pushing through the overcast sky outside and through the wooden slats in the wall we sat against. I studied Caden's upturned face, the moonlight sculpting his soft jaw. I felt my heart flutter in response to the light playing on his skin. It caught me off guard.

"So, did you reincarnate like twenty years ago," Caden asked suddenly, not opening his eyes, "or do you reincarnate as a teen?"

"It depends," I answered. "It's different every time. I reincarnated four days ago, actually."

His eyes popped open, and he blinked at me in surprise. "Really?"

"Really. Well," I hedged, "probably five days ago now. I think it's after midnight."

His brow furrowed. "But your blog has been around longer than that."

"Yeah. Reincarnation is tricky." I tapped my finger on my knee in thought. "I'll do my best to explain it. Pretend reality is a lake. When I reincarnate, I'm plopped right into the middle. Actually, no, not the very center, but at a random spot. When I splash in, I make a few ripples. People closest to the spot I entered are affected by the ripples most, but the rest of the lake isn't even touched. Reality patiently smooths out the ripples... by, um, scrambling everyone's memories so everyone thinks I've been there all along. Sometimes it's easy, and sometimes it's... elaborate. Creating a blog over the course of years is a little on the elaborate side." I puffed out a breath. "I'm not making this any clearer, am I? I guess what I'm saying is that, until a couple days ago, those blogs didn't exist. You have memories of watching them, but those are fabricated by reality itself.

Or whoever manages all this." I laughed. "That doesn't make sense at all."

"No, it does, I think," Caden said. "So *you* haven't ever made a blog, but they exist now and everyone remembers you making them, even though they never actually watched them in the first place." He grinned. "Which means you don't have fifty thousand views at all."

I snorted. "To make it even more complicated, I remember making the blogs. Reality plays havoc with my memories, too. But I still remember my past lives, or chunks of them." My voice lowered to a whisper. "Sometimes I wonder, if reality creates all this, and everyone remembers it happening, then is it even an illusion?"

He considered that, shrugged, then scanned my face and the visible parts of my body. "Do you always look like this?"

"Nope. I come back in all shapes, sizes, ages, colors, and genders."

His eyebrows shot up, but the only emotion on his face was wonder. "That's incredible," he breathed. I felt pleased by his response, though I wasn't entirely sure why.

We sat for a few minutes in comfortable silence, and I realized that my stiff muscles and the uncomfortable wooden wall weren't really bothering me. The pacing Headless Horseman, the cold air, my aching body, the prickly straw I sat upon... it all paled next to the soothing sounds of the night and the warmth of Caden's body leaning against mine beneath my ruined coat.

Caden tilted his head back to rest on the wall behind us. "You asked me about my family earlier," he said, his gaze on the low-hanging ceiling.

"You don't have to tell me if you don't want to," I told him, echoing his words from the train. I wanted to know, but given his response in the taxicab, I wasn't sure he wanted to tell me.

His lips quirked. "I'm an orphan. Tale as old as time: baby left on the front porch of a convent, reared by the nurturing nuns who ran it. But as I grew up and no one came to claim me, the nuns couldn't continue to harbor me without breaking their vows about living with a man. It was fiercely debated, of course. I was one of them, their communal son, and they couldn't bear to relinquish me to the foster system after caring for me for so long." His eyes were windows, and I saw anguish there... but also love. "The decision divided them. Six of the thirteen nuns abjured their vows, abandoned their former lives, and moved to the big city with a young boy as their ward."

The night was quiet, as if listening to Caden's story as raptly as I was. "What happened next?" I asked, adjusting myself so I was leaning just a little into his warmth.

He didn't pull away. "They didn't have much money, or many worldly possessions. But the new abbess—the former being one of the six who left—supplied them with what they could afford to lose, for my sake, and my six moms opened a small care center. It eventually became a hospice. My moms and I take care of people who are dying, people in need of a comfortable place to rest before the end." He looked at me, his eyes shining. I saw his throat bob as he swallowed. "We've even had a few miraculous recoveries, but that only resulted in our wait list growing longer and longer."

"What a beautiful story. Your family are healers."

His face glowed at the compliment. "They are saints," he agreed, "and I do my best to assist. They won't allow me to live my entire life at the center, though. They say I grew up sheltered enough. They want to send me off to college." He gave me a mischievous grin. "I managed to buy myself a year by swinging a few scholarships for next term. They couldn't get rid of me that easily." He sighed. "But they really want me to leave New York, to experience living elsewhere. I think that's why Iris really touched me, back there. Knowing she'd visited with some of the folks we cared for, knowing they were grateful for tending to them." He swallowed hard. "My moms would say, 'It's payment enough.'"

I, for once, was unable to come up with words. But Caden seemed lighter, and we shared an intimate, comfortable quiet. A light breeze blew cool air between the slats of the wood and grazed the back of Caden's hair. I heard again the soft whinny of the ghostly horse from out beyond our refuge. I felt remarkably safe, given our shelter was being circled by a Malevolent. The sensation of security tickled something in the back of my mind, reminded me of a feeling I'd known, a long time ago, a feeling I'd forgotten. Sitting close to him, my heart hammering so loudly I feared he might hear it, I slipped my hand over his. It was warm and soft, and I left mine there as if by accident.

Caden glanced at me in surprise, then quickly looked away. "I... I was thinking of moving to Seattle, actually," he said. He didn't move his hand. "There's a good nursing school there. And your blog made me fall in love with the Pacific Northwest." I felt his fingers slide between mine, entwining them. It made me feel elated and very, very mortal. No—very *human.*

"I've lived just about everywhere," I told him. "I don't even remember all the homes I've had." I licked my lips, then said, "But I've learned that it's more about who you spend your life with, rather than where." I yawned, sabotaging the beauty of my statement.

"Looks like we're going to be here for the long haul," Caden said. "You were roughed up more than me. Why don't you get some rest? I'll watch over you."

I wanted to argue, to insist I be the one to watch over *him,* but I smothered the impulse. *I'm not better than him just because I'm an incarnate.* The thought rang profoundly true, and I nestled against Caden, my head falling onto his shoulder.

I dreamed.

The smell of the sea, of salt in the air. A wharf. It hadn't happened like this, but I could hear the girl's whimpers from out here, hear them over the crashing of waves against the dock, the creaking of wood.

The entrance to the warehouse was a cross between a hungry mouth and a roaring furnace, somehow glowing red while still remaining recessed in darkness. Morrigan, cloaked in shadows, beckoned me forward with a pistol in her hand. It was smoking as if it had recently been fired. Her form slipped into the open maw of the warehouse and vanished, leaving me alone on the dock.

No, not alone: my hand was interlaced with Huntington's. He was already a corpse, his eyes blank, empty, dead.

Morrigan's voice echoed in my head. *"They're just bugs, Emery, so easily squashed."*

Caden was there now. He was asking me to take him inside, to show him everything. I wouldn't do it. For once, please, don't cave—don't give in. Only death lurked therein, ready to pounce with gloating words. I had to protect him, keep him safe.

Caden did not relent. He looked at me, soft steel in his expression. "*But who's going to watch over you?*" He stepped confidently through the door and I lurched after him, my heart in my throat.

I awoke then. I'd shifted position, no longer leaning against Caden's shoulder; instead my head was cushioned in his lap. He smiled down at me, reassuring me I was still watched over.

Safe.

PART II

Ahedrian

"Where the *hell* have you been?" Rachelle demanded from her perch on the bed as we entered the hotel room.

I shot a look at Caden. "I told you." He just grinned.

"I've been worried sick about you guys." She eyed me critically, taking in my dirt-stained clothes, disheveled hair, and shabby backpack. Her eyes traveled from me to Caden's immaculate clothes and hair. "I see I only needed to worry about one of you."

"I'm taking a shower," I grumbled, stalking across the room and closing the bathroom door firmly behind me. I undressed in front of the mirror and inspected my body for bruising. I hurt less than I expected, muscles—especially my arm—sore, but nothing like I'd anticipated. And after sleeping on the hard ground all night, too. I marveled at my skin, unblemished by scrapes, cuts, or bruises. Absurdly, I felt cheated. I'd survived being utterly thrashed by the Headless Horseman, but I had nothing to show for my efforts.

"That's a good thing, Emery," I said aloud to my reflection, exasperation creeping into my tone. "Stop standing around in uffish thought. Get moving."

I turned the knobs of the unfamiliar shower until the bathroom steamed, then stripped and stepped under the spray. Hot water coursed down my body, washing away the dirt and detritus from my battle with the incarnate. I'd awoken this morning with my head on Caden's outstretched legs, his back still upright against the wall of the wooden structure. He hadn't relaxed his vigil, watching over me throughout the night like my own personal sentinel. I grinned, feeling the individual jets hit my teeth. I gargled and spat, savoring the water streaming over every inch of me, making me whole and fresh and new. Which, I realized, is how I felt.

From the jaws of a sound defeat, I had snatched a small but profound victory. It wasn't the win I'd been expecting. It hadn't been the triumph for which I'd hoped. But it had been a victory I needed. I had confronted a darkness within me, forged in my past—and I felt confident it was the first step in overcoming it.

As I scrubbed my body with soap and watched the water rinse the foamy residue from my flesh, it wasn't just dirt and grime dribbling away down that drain. It was hesitance. It was fear. It was two incarnations with whom I'd now started to make peace. That left me naked, clean, and a bit vulnerable. I didn't mind. There's a hidden strength in being vulnerable, one I'd neglected for too long. It was a shared strength, owned not by a single person but by those who opened to one another and became more than the sum of their parts.

Maybe, just maybe, I could learn to forgive myself. I had owned my failures, borne them dutifully across countless hunts, accepted the fault, shouldered the blame. I should learn from it, grow from my experiences, prevent it from happening again—but it would not define me forever.

The Headless Horseman had disappeared with the dawn, so Caden and I had gathered our things—*my* things, strewn across the clearing—before finding a cab to take us back to the city. I had texted Rachelle while we were on our way back, but she hadn't responded. Whether she'd been sleeping, furious, or both, I wasn't sure. Caden and I hadn't spoken much during the drive, but it was a comfortable silence, punctuated with occasional shared, private looks.

I thought about Caden, and my smile returned. He confused me.

No, that wasn't true. My budding feelings for him were what confused me. I couldn't deny I had them: just placing my hand in his had elicited electricity, sent my heart racing. The immortal corner of my mind analyzed that and found it... startling. Perhaps even unsettling. After lifetimes, I exceled at figuring people out. But he was different. I couldn't quite describe him, couldn't put him in a box. With how many romantic trysts I'd been entangled in over the course of countless incarnations, the emotions had become... rote. Unchanging and expected. Excitement without the thrill. But this beginning, the stirring in my stomach, it reminded me of Huntington... No, best not to tread there. Yet after countless romances, the same courtship time and again, this felt like something *new*.

I'd become familiar with the rules of the game, but Caden changed them, and thus, the game. He was... my loophole.

I found myself hoping he felt the same way. I hadn't even known if he would be attracted to guys. To *me*. But I'd picked up on the subtle signs: the way he leaned into me, or how he didn't pull away when our faces came too close. The small smiles he shared with me, making me feel as though he only looked at me that way. Those were possibly imagined, but then he'd entwined his fingers in mine. There was a connection there, right?

A tiny, guarded corner of my mind worried I'd misinterpreted simple kindness as something romantic. Huh. What a *human* thing to wonder. I dislodged the worry and inspected it coolly. A wholly human sentiment, almost *adolescent*. I wondered when I'd last indulged in such a thing. I washed it down the drain to follow my fear.

My excitement emboldened me. If this was indeed something new and unexpected, I would follow it to its inevitable conclusion, grateful for the journey.

I completed my shower and emerged from the bathroom with my towel around my waist. I admit, this time I did it on purpose. I was curious what Caden's reaction to seeing me half-naked would be. He was sitting on Rachelle's bed with her, their heads together over her tablet. As I crossed the room, I felt both of them following my movements. I dressed in my corner of the room, hiding my grin. I was entirely too pleased with myself. Maybe accepting my humanity made me a little *too* mortal.

Nah.

"What are you two talking about?" I asked as I joined them, dressed in one of the new outfits Caden had helped me pick out yesterday. The bed creaked as I sat down; it really wasn't designed to accommodate all three of us.

"I told her about our run-in with the Headless Horseman," Caden told me. "But don't worry, I made sure to tell her how heroic you were in battle."

I groaned.

"It's true," Rachelle said, eyes wide, looking serious. "My favorite part was where you Tasered a pumpkin. Really showed it who's boss."

Of course Caden had seen that. "Well, you know how I feel about vegetables." I made a face.

Rachelle shook her head, looking amused. "Nice try, Emery, but pumpkins are fruit," she said.

Caden came to my rescue. "We were also watching this." He gestured to Rachelle's tablet. "It's this morning's news." Rachelle tapped the screen to resume a video.

"—'Ahedrian' cropping up in three different places throughout the city." The familiar red-haired reporter delivered the news with a sort of professional excitement. "My team and I camped out all night at one such site in El Barrio but, as with the other two locations, we found no evidence of a body. Could this be a shifting tide in the beheading cases? We turn now to several residents of Harlem for their take on 'Ahedrian.'"

The news cut to a middle-aged man providing his opinion, but Rachelle muted the report. "Just goes on to say that maybe appeasing Ahedrian by scribbling his name all over the city may reduce the murders." Rachelle shook her head in disgust. "Are you sure Ahedrian isn't an incarnate?"

"Fairly certain," I replied. "I've never heard of it before, which kind of defeats the point of an urban legend."

They nodded in unison.

I indicated the tablet. "She stayed there all night?"

"She really came through for us," Rachelle confirmed. She looked at me pointedly. "So, what's our next step?"

"We need a game plan."

Rachelle pulled out a stylus and opened a notepad app on her tablet, situating it so we could all see the screen. "I'm ready."

"First of all, decapitations: what do we know?"

Caden spoke up. "Iris said all the victims were possibly 'bad people.'" Rachelle wrote "Decapitations" and underlined it, then scribbled "Bad guys?" underneath. Then she raised her hand as though she were asking a question in class. "Who's Iris?"

"Before going to Sleepy Hollow yesterday, we visited the Medium," I explained. "Iris is the Ghost incarnate." I recounted our visit with her as best I could remember. Rachelle wrote "Wookiee?" "Yeti," and "Saudi Arabia" on her tablet in a section removed from the rest.

"What else do we know?"

"The word 'Ahedrian' has been found at each beheading," Caden volunteered.

"And," I recalled, "there wasn't enough blood at the scene."

Rachelle dutifully recorded "Crime Scene: no head, Ahedrian, not enough blood." She tapped her stylus against her lips in thought. "Can we rule out the Headless Horseman?"

I hesitated, then shook my head. "Not unless there was another beheading last night. The fact that we stopped a murder from occurring is actually evidence *for* the Horseman."

Rachelle created another column, labeled it "Suspects," and wrote "The Headless Horseman" under it. She paused, then added "Ahedrian?" beneath that.

"I don't know how it fits in yet," I said, "but I think we'd probably better add my impersonator to that list."

"Huh?" Caden gave me a puzzled look.

"Someone has been going around slaying monsters in New York," I told him. "For all I know, they're even claiming to be the Monster Hunter."

156 | JUSTIN SCHUELKE

He looked baffled. "And that's a problem?"

"Yes!" I gave him an incredulous look. "That's *my* role!"

He blinked, then looked away, a blush climbing his cheeks. I clicked my mouth shut, but Rachelle pounced, a smile on her face. "What incarnate did *you* think he was, Caden?" she asked sweetly.

He put his face in his hands, clearly embarrassed, and mumbled something between his fingers.

"What was that?" Rachelle pressed, barely holding back laughter. "Couldn't quite hear you."

He threw up his hands and blurted, "I thought you were the Hero incarnate."

Rachelle, on the verge of laughter, suddenly dropped her teasing. Her mouth popped open in surprise. "Awww," she cooed. "You know, Emery, that actually fits. I vote to change your incarnation." I sputtered, but she bowled right over me. "All in favor?" She raised her hand in the air.

Caden looked back and forth between us, face still red, and then raised his hand with an apologetic smile.

"It's settled," Rachelle announced. "And I get to be your sidekick." She gasped. "No, wait! I get to be *the* sidekick. The Sidekick incarnate!"

"That's not how incarnates work," I objected, shaking my head.

"Sure it is," she argued. "What comes first, the myth or the incarnate? Emery, we could start the urban legend, and *bam*! You'd have a beautiful new immortal sidekick."

"Why do you get to be the Sidekick incarnate?" Caden demanded.

"No one gets to be the Sidekick incarnate," I interjected with a grin. I was entertained by their banter, and it *was* flattering to see them argue over who got to spend eternity with me.

"Why not?" Rachelle huffed. "If someone can make a Wookiee incarnate, then I can most certainly become a Sidekick incarnate."

I started to laugh, then froze. "Wait." I repeated her words in my head, realization dawning. "You're right," I breathed.

She smirked. "Of course I am."

"No. No, Rachelle, don't you get what you just said? You're right.

Someone was trying to create a Wookiee incarnate by using another incarnate, the Yeti. Someone was trying to *create an incarnate.*" My mind struggled to wrap around the concept. I started pacing again, thinking it through. "It's not possible. But what if someone thought it was? Would they kill to keep it quiet?"

"And why go to such measures?" Rachelle asked. "Why use an existing incarnate instead of"—she shrugged—"I don't know, just dressing up in a Wookiee costume?"

"Authenticity," I replied. "In today's world, hoaxes are spotted quickly. But by using a real incarnate, they'd get all the perks."

"Like not being able to be caught on camera," Caden chimed in.

I ran my hand through my hair. "It doesn't work," I said slowly.

They both looked at me. "What doesn't?" Rachelle asked. I peered down to see she'd added an equal sign and a plus between her words so that it now read like an equation: Wookiee? = Yeti + Saudi Arabia.

I sighed. "The Yeti can't be captured. That's its fatal flaw, its Achilles' heel. Upon successful capture, it just... disappears. Comes back a thousand and one days later." I let out a frustrated noise. "None of this makes sense."

"Then we're missing something," Caden said around a yawn. "Can you tell us what happened in Saudi Arabia?"

I hesitated, and Rachelle took the opportunity to finish writing "Someone tried to create the Wookiee. Emery definitely not the Hero. I'm not the Sidekick... yet!"

"It's where I died, last time," I told them. Rachelle's stylus went still, and Caden sat up straighter. "I was tracking down the Yeti, confused why it had left the Himalayas—its Territory. I tracked it, found it, killed it."

Rachelle frowned. "You didn't realize it was dressed up like a Wookiee?"

I scowled. "I had a few other things on my mind while I was fighting for my life!" I shook my head. "Besides, it was still dying when someone snuck up behind me, put a gun to the back of my head, and pulled the trigger."

Watching their jaws drop open together, as if they were two marionettes operated by one puppeteer, put a bit of humor back into me. "Before you ask: yes, they snuck up on me in a desert, but in my defense, we were in the middle of a sandstorm. And no, I didn't see their face."

Rachelle adjusted her position, giving her leg cast a stretch. "Is that your kryptonite?" she asked.

"A bullet to my head?" I asked. "That's fatal to just about everyone."

Caden yawned but smothered it with the back of his fist and leaned forward. "You were distracted by the Yeti and killed by someone else. Which means there's a history of incarnates and mortals working together."

"If the shooter is a mortal," Rachelle countered.

But I saw where Caden's mind was going. "You mentioned yesterday that the incarnate behind the murders might have an accomplice," I mused. "I guess you could be on to something."

"There's a lot of question marks on this list," Rachelle said, writing "Accomplice?" under "Suspects."

"We need more information," I agreed. "Rachelle, I'm putting you on research. Find out whatever you can about the beheaded victims. See if you can find a link between them." She flashed me a thumbs-up and wrote "Rachelle, Sidekick Extraordinaire: research victims."

"Caden," I continued, after only a moment's hesitation, "you and I will follow up on the address we got from Morrigan, see what we can find out about this impersonator of mine." Only a day ago, I had convinced myself not to take Caden into that potential trap. But much had changed in a day—in a night, really—and if I had decided I was going to trust them, treat them as my equals, then there could be no half measures. I wouldn't run headlong into this without planning, though. And Caden *would* understand the danger, which meant I needed to fill him in on Morrigan.

Caden saluted with a grin, but it was sabotaged by another yawn.

I came to a decision. "But first, we need to refuel." They both looked at me quizzically. "Rachelle," I said, "you want to stretch your leg and come with me to grab some lunch?"

"Like you wouldn't believe," she replied, already levering herself off the bed and reaching for her crutches.

I walked over and sat down next to Caden in the spot Rachelle had just vacated. "You stayed up all last night," I told him. "I won't leave you behind, but you need to rest."

He tried to protest but was betrayed by yet another yawn.

"Take a nap while Rachelle and I have lunch." I waited until he nodded in agreement. "I promise I will come wake you up before leaving." I placed my hand on his leg. "We're in this together, now."

"Together," he agreed, smiling.

Decapitations
Bad guys?

Crime Scene:
No head
Ahedrian
Not enough blood

Suspects
The Headless Horseman
Ahedrian?
Emery's Impostor?
Accomplice?

Wookiee? = Yeti + Saudi Arabia
Someone tried to create the _Wookiee_

Emery definitely not the Hero.
I'm not the Sidekick... yet!
Rachelle, Sidekick Extraordinaire: research victims
Caden to investigate impostor with Emery

id you catch the things we missed? If so, send me your business card; I could use you on my next investigative case. Maybe I'll even feature you as a guest on There's Always a Loophole.

I must apologize. For Rachelle's chicken scratch on the previous page, yes. But also because when I lied to you earlier, I expected to have owned up to it by now. Hang in there—I promise it's all part of the story. Maybe, with the way I've been telling it, you'll understand how I felt when I learned the truth.

"LOOKS LIKE THIS IS THE PLACE," I announced, holding up the slip of paper and comparing the address written there to the one on the front of the building. It was a swanky apartment building tucked away in the southwestern corner of Manhattan, overlooking the Hudson River and a small park. The side of the high-rise building was more window than stone, accented with balconies. If the spacing between the windows was any indication, the builders had packed as many apartments in as they could to capitalize on the premium location.

Caden and I stood across the street from the main entrance. Caden, having napped while Rachelle and I lunched, finished off a caffeine-laced smoothie we'd picked up on our trek here. Between the nap and the drink, he looked alert and ready to go.

I drew in a long breath and blew it out. No more stalling. I was literally on the doorstep of my impostor's abode; it was high time I told Caden about Morrigan. "Before we go in, I need to tell you about the danger."

He looked like he might object, but I must have looked as serious as I felt. "I'm listening," he said earnestly.

"Associations between incarnates are like any other relationships, except ours can span multiple lifetimes. Throughout my incarnations, I've forged friendships with other incarnates—like Iris. These friendships usually endure through reincarnations, but because of the cyclical nature of our lives, sometimes we go centuries without seeing one another. Unfortunately, incarnates also make enemies, and those associations are just as enduring."

Caden gestured up at the apartment building. "Like the Monster Hunter incarnate?"

"No. I've actually never met them—and they're *not* the Monster Hunter. My guess is they're either a mortal working for my true enemy or they're some sort of shape-shifting incarnate, like the Doppelganger."

"And who's your 'true enemy'?"

"Morrigan."

Caden grinned. "Is it wrong that I think it's cool you have an immortal archnemesis?" He contemplated a moment. "Are you sure you're not the Hero? I mean, you have your own Villain incarnate."

I rolled my eyes, though I couldn't help but feel a thrill of pride. "Morrigan is no joking matter, Caden," I said, trying to get us back on track. I needed him to understand. I licked my lips. "She's killed me more times than anything else. Worse, she sees mortals as expendable. No, not just expendable: she sees their deaths as nothing more than tools to cause me pain." I swallowed. "She has killed people I care about before. It nearly undid me. I can't have that happen... again." I changed the last word, unable to say "to you."

Caden seemed to understand. "Your fatal flaw."

I blinked. "What?"

He gave me a smile and moved closer to me. "I understand. I won't be used against you, Emery. I'll be careful." His eyebrows furrowed. "But what does this have to do with your impostor? You said they might be working for Morrigan?"

I waved the sheet of paper I held. "She provided this address. Said I'd find my impostor here."

Caden's eyebrows shot up. "If they're working together, why would she volunteer that information?"

"That, my friend, is the million-dollar question." I shrugged. "It might be nothing. Morrigan loves to gloat—"

"As villains do," Caden interjected, nodding sagely.

"And she especially revels in staying two steps ahead of me. Which is easier to do when I've recently reincarnated."

He considered. "So which is more likely? That she orchestrated all this, or that she wants you to know how superior she is?"

"Probably both," I admitted. "But until I find out why, I don't think I have any chance of understanding her motives."

"Which means all roads lead to you worrying we're walking into a trap?"

I smiled grimly. "Nailed it in one."

"Then it's a good thing you brought me along," he said. "We can watch each other's backs."

I shook my head in wonder. A too-large part of me was filled with panic. I was going against everything I'd promised myself: I was involving a mortal in something I knew was dangerous. I did my best to muffle that panic. I had deliberately chosen this path. I would ensure he knew the dangers. I would do everything in my power to protect him, to minimize the danger he faced. And I would respect his choice to accompany me. It was his to make.

I couldn't quite make myself believe that yet. But all things take practice. Fake it till you make it, and all that.

I swallowed my fear. "Let's go, but tread carefully."

We walked across the street, Caden tossing his empty smoothie cup in a recycling bin, and entered the building together. The lobby was smaller than I expected, with three branching hallways making a lowercase t. The right branch contained rows of metal mailboxes. The left branch ended before it truly began, the space used for a small office, the window dark and the door firmly shut. A Closed sign hung from the handle, red letters on black. The final branch, directly ahead, was a short hallway with two elevators on the right and a door leading to the stairwell on the left. I looked at the address on the piece of paper: my impostor's apartment was 1005.

We tried to call the elevator, but to our dismay, it required a keycard of some sort. So instead, I opened the door to the stairwell and started up. But on the first landing, I saw that a keycard was also needed to unlock the doors leading to the individual floors. We retraced our steps and stood in front of the elevator, considering.

It dinged, the doors swung open, and a young woman wearing headphones emerged.

"Hi," I said, adopting an embarrassed expression. She looked at me in surprise. "I'm so sorry; I forgot my card upstairs. Can you just swipe yours so I can go grab it?"

She shrugged and swiped her card over the reader, then walked off without a word. I punched the "10" button, and Caden and I rode the elevator up to that floor.

"Nice," Caden said as soon as the doors were closed.

I shrugged. "Amazing what you can get into if you just act like you belong."

The doors opened, and we stepped out of the elevator. It took a few minutes of hunting, but we eventually found room 302. We stood outside the blue-painted door with gold lettering. My heart was beating faster now. Behind this door, I would finally confront my impostor.

"Should we... knock?" Caden asked.

"Be ready for anything," I warned in a low tone. Then I rapped my knuckles against the door.

I waited, my heart in my throat.

I tried to watch everywhere at once, to be able to react quickly if needed. My entire body felt tense, ready to spring, like a coiled snake.

Nothing happened.

I knocked again, this time putting my ear against the door to listen for sounds from inside. Nothing.

"I don't think anyone's home," I said, feeling disappointed.

"Did Morrigan happen to give you keys along with the address?" Caden asked in a whisper, testing the door handle. I shook my head. "This is kind of the worst trap ever, then," he pointed out.

I couldn't disagree. "Maybe we should stake it out, wait for whoever lives here to come home?" I muttered.

Caden shrugged. "I'm here to support you. If you think we should wait, then I'm with you."

Just for kicks, I tried the door handle too. And flinched when it turned. "It's unlocked," I said, disbelieving.

"What?" He frowned. "I *swear* I tried it."

He had. I'd seen him. "Must not have turned it far enough," I offered, turning an apologetic smile his way.

It was a thin excuse, and we both knew it. Worry thrummed through me. Could it have been rigged to only open for me? Some trap only I could trigger? I brushed the thought aside, but my senses stayed on high alert.

Turning my attention back to the door, I nudged it open. Nothing moved inside.

And *damn*, it was a nice apartment. Hardwood floors, cherry cabinetry, and a matching entryway table greeted me. I pushed the door the rest of the way open, taking in the sparse furnishings, the low glass coffee table, and the enormous sliding glass door leading onto a private balcony. The view was stunning. Not only did it look out over the Hudson, I could see the Jersey skyline on the far side of the river even from where I crouched in the doorway.

"Hello?" I said into the apartment, making sure it was empty.

"Emery," Caden said nervously, "are you sure we should go in there?"

I looked at him, bemused. "Says the guy who tried the handle first?" I teased. "We aren't going to take or break anything. I just need to find a picture, to see who it is that's been going around the incarnate world claiming to be me."

I took a step inside, my heart racing again. I felt goose bumps run down my arms, the little hairs standing on end. I took a steadying breath, then moved further inside. Caden followed me, closing the door behind him.

The unit, for all its chic design palette, was devoid of many personal items. It felt staged, like my impersonator had taken up residence in a fully furnished apartment. Which was possible, of course. The kitchen contained a set of china, a personal espresso machine, and an empty drying rack. A dark gray towel dangled from the handle of the oven, and several sharp cooking knives hung from a magnetic strip above it. The kitchen exuded a pleasant cinnamon smell.

Caden moved to the living room, inspecting the wall art. It was as tastefully generic as the rest of the apartment: no personal baubles or trinkets, and certainly no photos.

It was so frustrating. I felt on the verge of discovery, but even here, it eluded me. Since the Watchman had told me about my impostor, the desire to discover their identity had been hovering at the edge of my mind, a constant nagging worry. Morrigan providing the very address we were now at compounded the anxiety, made me feel almost desperate to uncover the truth. But this apartment was about as revealing as a shoebox. No pictures of friends or family. No discarded clothes, and the two coats on the coat rack were as neutral as they came. Not even a damn cat to indicate anything about this impostor.

I moved past Caden and ventured into the bedroom, certain that if there were anything personal to find in this place, it would be there. At the very least I could inspect the impersonator's closet and see whether their fashion choices provided any clues to their identity. I wasn't very optimistic.

I stopped in the doorway and took in the room. The bedroom was larger than I expected and the only carpeted area in the apartment. A queen-sized bed nestled in one corner, neatly covered with a dark blue duvet. A small dresser mounted with a flat-screen TV, a closed closet along the right-hand wall, and a nightstand completed the room's décor. There was a single window overlooking the park and the Hudson, but its curtains were drawn, casting the room into unnatural darkness.

Nothing immediately grabbed my attention, but my eyes drifted to the closed drawers of the dresser. With luck, there would be something personal stashed there or in the nightstand. As I walked in to inspect the room more closely, I felt more than heard the movement behind me.

Suddenly, something hard and metallic pressed against the back of my head. My eyes went wide, and my breath caught. In my mind, I was thrown backward in time to Saudi Arabia, someone standing behind me with a gun pushed into the base of my skull. Memories of a trigger pulled, a shot fired.

"What the hell," a female voice growled in my ear, bringing me back to the moment at hand, "do you think you're doing?"

$\mathcal{J}$ raised my hands, fingers splayed, to show I was unarmed. I thought I recognized that voice, but not from my previous death in Saudi Arabia; from something more recent.

"I'm sorry," I said at normal volume, hoping to catch Caden's attention from the other room. "I just needed some answers."

The woman behind me laughed quietly. "Yeah, you're not the only one." She tapped my skull with the barrel of her gun. "Turn around slowly."

Barely daring to breathe, I eased around.

A familiar, angry face glared at me from the other end of a pistol.

I gaped. "Trish?"

Recognition flickered in her eyes, and she put some distance between us, stepping backward into the bedroom door's shadow, where she must have been hiding when I entered. She didn't lower the gun. "You again?" she asked in annoyance. "Shouldn't you be recovering in a hospital or something?"

I shrugged. "It was just a short visit." I eyed the gun. "And I'd prefer not to go back. Any chance we could talk without the weapon?"

Caden had approached the bedroom on near-silent feet. From my angle, I could see him on the other side of the door from Trish. It required every ounce of my willpower not to glance at him and give away his position. He was poised, waiting. He could slam the door into Trish from his current position, if it proved necessary.

"Let's try talking *with* it, first. Tell Blondie to get in here."

"No," I replied calmly. "I won't let him risk himself like that. Let's just talk, incarnate to incarnate."

She stiffened at that. "I should have known you were an incarnate as well as a fool. Mortals aren't so quick to throw their lives away." She hesitated, then lowered the gun. Didn't holster it, though, I noticed.

"Thank you," I said. Then added, "For putting the gun down, not for insulting me."

She looked at me with disdain. She was really quite good at it—I bet she practiced that look in the mirror. "How did you even get in here? I know I locked the door behind me."

I grunted, doing my best to ignore the gun still in her hand. "Guess you're wrong. It opened for me."

She stared at me. "What are you supposed to be, the Rogue incarnate?" When I didn't answer, I saw her jaw flex. "Who *are* you?"

I swelled up with indignation. "That's *my* line." I glared. "I am the Monster Hunter incarnate. Who the hell are *you*?"

Her expression didn't change. To be fair, I don't think it changed very often. "You're kidding."

Caden, apparently having decided that the danger was over, poked his head out from the other side of the door. "Hey, Trish. Sorry to burst in on you like this."

Her eyes shifted back and forth between Caden and me. "How did you even know I was here?"

I dug in my pocket. Seeing her gun arm tense, I slowly withdrew the piece of paper Morrigan had given us. "Got the address from Morrigan." I said the name intentionally, watching her face for any sign of recognition.

I was rewarded with a look of disgust. "You shouldn't get entangled with that snake," Trish said. "She's nothing but trouble."

I was taken aback, but I felt a grin tugging at the corner of my mouth. "You aren't working for her?"

"Of course not. I'm in New York *hunting monsters*." She said the words like she was explaining something to a toddler. She looked again at the paper in my hand and then at Caden's face. She scowled and finally holstered the gun. "And so are you," she realized, connecting the pieces. "Because, for some reason, you think you are me." She stepped out from behind the door, grabbed it, and opened it further, like she was holding it open for us. "You need to go."

I gawked. "You aren't the least bit curious about how two incarnates both think they're the Monster Hunter?"

She glowered. "Not really. You're wrong. Besides, I'm close to finding a monster, and you losers could get hurt."

I rubbed my temple. "Trish, please, listen to me. I'm just as concerned for your safety as you apparently are for mine."

"Touching," she said, "but I was only being polite. I just don't want you in my way." She gestured again to the open bedroom door.

Caden, however, was looking perplexed. "Wait," he said slowly, trying to capture our attention. "Trish, how can you be close to finding a monster in your own apartment?"

Trish shot him a withering look. "This isn't my apartment," she snapped.

I traded a look with Caden, a sinking feeling in my stomach. He paled, too.

I realized what I'd been missing a moment too late. The smell of cinnamon in the apartment intensified.

We'd sprung the trap.

The wall to my left, the one with the draped window, *burst* inward. A storm of noise, stone, plaster, and glass shards pelted me as I threw myself onto the bed. I raised the thick duvet to minimize the impact of the debris.

As the dust settled, I saw there was now a gaping hole where the apartment wall had been moments before, and a male silhouette filled the space. The Genie incarnate hung in the air, ten stories above the ground. He looked much as I recalled: Middle Eastern features. Black hair tied back into a tail; dark goatee. The dangling earring and the studs. The only difference was that he was now bare-chested, and gold rings pierced his exposed nipples. Two gunshots cracked in quick succession, loud in the small room despite the hole in the wall. The Genie flinched but did not seem overly bothered by the bullets.

He drifted lazily into the apartment, soft-soled shoes gently alighting on the thick carpet... and the layers of wreckage from the implosion. "Emery," he said, the word thickly accented, "so good of y—"

He was cut off as Trish flashed across the room and brought the butt of the gun down sharply on the back of his head. The strike dissolved the Genie into red smoke. The cloud streamed like it was expelled from a fog machine, flinging itself to the corner of the room before re-forming. The Genie cocked his head toward Trish.

"And you brought guests." His devilish smile cut his goatee in half. "Even though th—" He was forced to stop talking again as Trish leapt across the small room and aimed a heavy kick at his groin.

I'll give her this: she was fast and no-nonsense. I felt a surge of annoyance—and maybe some excitement. No way was I going to let her outfight *me*.

The Genie had *poof*ed again—a handy defensive measure for avoiding kicks to the tenders, I must admit—and the scarlet cloud was re-forming by the closet. I threw the duvet cover at it and was rewarded with a muffled exclamation. I tackled the thrashing bed covers at about waist height, driving us both to the ground. I expected the duvet cover to go limp at any moment, the Genie doing his favorite disappearing trick, but I was wrong. Instead, the Genie made the *duvet* disappear... into flames. Suddenly it felt like I was wrestling with a campfire.

I yelped at the intense heat and leapt free of the burning fabric, rolling across the rubble-strewn carpet in an attempt to extinguish my now-smoldering clothes. Yeah, that's right: the new clothes that I was wearing for the first time.

The Genie towered over me, flaming bit of cloth flittering through the air on the wind coming through the wall-hole. He grinned down at me, and I swear I could see the fire reflected in his eyes.

Then Caden was there. He rammed the Genie from the side, using his shoulder like he'd done with the gator. The Genie, apparently caught unawares, was knocked back and through the hole in the wall. But Caden's momentum carried him with the Genie, and he teetered at the edge of a hundred-foot drop. Started to go over the edge.

Trish caught him and yanked him back, keeping him from stumbling out into a ten-story fall.

The Genie, unfortunately, could fly. He snarled at Trish and lobbed a fireball at her, launching it softball-style, like he had in my office. Trish somehow managed to avoid the projectile, which rocketed into the room and detonated against the closet, the entire wall going up in roaring flame. A wave of heat assaulted us.

Why hadn't the building's fire alarm gone off yet? As soon as I thought it, a shrill siren pierced the apartment. I regained my feet, wincing at the harsh sound. I wasn't sure how to combat an enemy who floated a hundred feet in the air *outside* the apartment building, but I began looking around for anything I could improvise with.

Trish fought her way to a standing position and waved us off. "Move, both of you," she yelled. "Get out of here!"

Caden dashed toward the living room, and I followed. I had no intention of retreating, but the rest of the apartment was a much larger space. That would make surviving the exploding softballs easier.

"Find a container," I said to Caden. "Any container will do."

We heard a crash, followed by a *whoosh*. Trish and a roiling cloud of black smoke ejected from the bedroom at the same time.

The Genie must have circled the outside of the apartment, and he came into view from the balcony. He lobbed two more bolts of flame, and the sliding glass door shattered, spraying knives of glass into the apartment. Trish threw her smaller body in front of me, shielding me from the worst of the glass. Unfortunately, the second ball of fire exploded at our feet, and I felt myself lifted into the air and thrown backward by the force of the detonation. We slammed into the apartment wall, cracking the plaster, and became entangled as we tried to regain our feet together.

I could see Caden searching the kitchen, throwing open each cabinet and heaving the contents out before moving to the next. So far, no luck. Which made sense, given this was the incarnate's apartment.

In the confusion, I'd lost the Genie. That may sound silly to you, but trust me, the fight was not nearly so *neat* as I've laid it out for you. Sweat, heat, pain, fire, competition, and the scent of cinnamon swirled around me like a tornado; making heads or tails of it simply demonstrates my impressive ability to tell a story.

Trish shoved me to the side as fire sheared through the air where I'd been standing and the wall between us went up in flame. Damn. This incarnate liked fire a bit too much. He had also ventured indoors and now stood in his living room, staring at us.

"As I was saying," he sneered. "You are late, Emery. And you bring rude guests to invade my home. Roasting you has become personal." He rested his hand on the posh sofa, and it caught flame as though it were doused in kerosene. With a flick of his wrist, the burning piece of furniture slid across the room like it was a flaming race car and I stood at the finish line. It drove forward, directly at me, and I barely managed to get out of the way. It slammed into the wall and punched through it, out into the hallway beyond.

The Genie, keeping a keen eye on Trish, now flung another ball of fire at her to keep her from advancing. She grabbed the coat rack by the door and swung it like a baseball bat, connecting with the fireball and sending it ricocheting into the living room, where it detonated off to the Genie's right, setting another corner of the room ablaze. She followed the swing without hesitation, leaping across the apartment in a blink. She looked like the Valkyrie incarnate—a warrior queen, soot-stained and steely-eyed, lance (ahem, coat rack) held before her, banners (coats) streaming as she drove the "lance" forward to spear her foe. The Genie was forced once again to vanish into a plume of vermilion smoke.

"Any time now with that container," I called out to Caden, shouting to be heard above the blaring alarms. He looked desperately at the discarded items. The kitchen was the only room untouched by the fire, but smoke was billowing against the ceiling.

It was difficult to track the Genie's red cloud amid the glaring flames. Embers and sparks swirled through the air from the entrance and two other walls. The Genie manifested suddenly, coalescing into his shining bronze skin at the kitchen's entrance. "Burn for me, little man," he cackled. The hardwood floor in the kitchen ignited at the Genie's words, flame spreading like the floor was made of kindling.

"Caden!" I cried.

A counter separated the kitchen from the living room, and Caden launched himself through the gap between the countertop and the base of the cherrywood cabinets, landing in a crouch in the living room.

I desperately needed to think, to find a way to beat the Genie. He wouldn't have his fatal flaw here, in an apartment designed to be a trap. So it would need to be something we'd brought in. But the only thing I could think of was the gun.

The gun!

"Get the gun!" I screamed.

Caden looked up, ducked under a bolt of fire, then dashed into the bedroom where we'd first encountered Trish and the Genie. I felt a flash of guilt as he slipped into the open doorway that flickered with the light of the fires within, smoke coughing out of the room like it was a chimney.

Then I had my own problems as the Genie, hands outstretched, sent a spiral of flame at me. I hit the ground, the tongue of flame streaming over my head, burning the little hairs on the back of my neck. I looked up to see the incarnate, eyes alight, take aim at my prone form.

And stagger as something heavy smashed into him and shattered into thousands of pieces of glass. I ducked and covered my head as shards rained down on me. The Genie vanished into his red mist with a howl of pain and anger.

Trish had dropped the coat rack and grabbed the glass coffee table. Her strength astounded me. She'd spun to build up momentum, like she was throwing a discus, and then launched the table across the room with deadly aim. The thing probably weighed upwards of fifty pounds and was as long as she was, but she'd thrown it like it was nothing.

Caden came dashing past her from the bedroom, holding the pistol distastefully, pinched between two fingers and held out in front of him like it would bite him.

The Genie reappeared near Trish, staring at the cuts that dribbled blood down his bare chest. Shards of glass would probably be lodged in his skin if he hadn't dematerialized. Furious, he began hurling spheres of fire at her in a savage rage. *Shit.* It was as if an angry tennis ball machine and a two-year-old's tantrum had a fiery demon baby.

I snatched the gun from Caden's hand. Popping out the magazine, I discharged the bullet still in the chamber and tossed the gun aside. *Please let this work.* I advanced on the Genie from the side and behind, hoping he wouldn't notice me in his fury. I wasn't going to give him the chance to flee this time.

But I paused for a moment to watch Trish. The Genie advanced on her a step at a time, hurling softballs of fiery death. From less than *ten feet away,* she dodged. Again and again and again. She was a blur, moving like some sort of superhero, sidestepping, ducking, and leaping over the bolts of flame like the two had choreographed the entire fight.

I shook myself and sprang forward, but the Genie saw me coming and sent a fireball my way. I instinctively tried to shield my face with my hand. The ball of fire exploded around my closed fist... and dispersed, the heat that washed over me strangely muted. *Of course,* I realized, uncurling my fingers to reveal the magazine in my hand. *He can't damage it. It's his fatal flaw.*

I had done it. I'd found a container. It was an unconventional one, granted. But it would work.

I stalked forward, emboldened, and the Genie hesitated, eyes flicking from annoyance to confusion to fear as he realized what had happened. Trish closed the space between them in a blink, taking advantage of his distraction, and her elbow snapped up toward his cheek. He flinched, dissolving into red smoke. I tried to swipe the magazine through that smoke to capture him, but it rocketed away like the trail of a bright firework, re-forming outside the balcony, out of reach.

"This isn't over, Emery," the Genie snarled, shaking with rage. I considered chucking the magazine at him, but if I missed, we would be weaponless once again. "Three is *my* number, and our third encounter shall be mine!"

He disintegrated into crimson mist that blew away on the wind, leaving us exhausted and sweating in the inferno that had been his apartment.

"*Ha!*" I crowed. "See?" I said to Trish, pointing at myself in triumph. "Monster Hunter incarnate." A flaming hunk of plaster fell from the wall behind me, crashing to the scorched hardwood and sending up a shower of embers.

She turned to me, livid, her finger in my face. "The only thing you are," she said, "is lucky. I'd have had him five minutes ago if I hadn't been saving your sorry ass."

"Um, guys?" Caden interjected, looking around at the flaming apartment. Smoke and shimmering waves of heat distorted visibility. My eyes watered, heat and smoke drying them out.

"What are you talking about?" I demanded. "I vanquished him while you were playing dodgeball!"

"*Vanquished?*" A single sharp laugh escaped her. "He got away because of you. Maybe you're the Monster *Chaser*, because you certainly didn't *hunt* anything today."

"Funny, I don't remember him saying anything to *you*. He called me out by name."

She stared at me with a look that was part incredulity, part derision. "Why the hell would you ever want a monster to know your name?" Her hands curled into fists. Something in the kitchen popped loudly, sending up a shower of sparks. "I've spent *lifetimes* hiding my identity from them. I'm their hunter, not their friend!"

"*Emery,*" Caden cut in, putting his hand on my shoulder. "We need to go. All of us."

I looked around at the apartment and grimaced. "He's right," I told Trish through gritted teeth. I eyed the shattered remains of the coffee table. "Truce until we get outside?"

She glared at me. "Whatever." That was like getting a "Hell yeah!" from anyone else.

Trish retrieved her gun from where I'd dropped it, and the three of us quickly left the apartment. We had to duck through the flaming doorway, emerging in the hallway where residents were scrambling to evacuate.

"Is anyone still in there?" an older woman with horn-rimmed glasses asked me. I wasn't sure if she saw me push through the flaming barrier or if she just took in my soot-stained face and clothes and made an educated guess. "I haven't seen the nice young lady who lives there, but she's so rarely home."

Lady? "Everyone's out," I told her, looking around at the surrounding apartment doors. "How about the neighbors?"

"I think everyone's accounted for," she replied, patting a red carrier next to her. I realized it was a kennel with two silent, terrified cats inside. "Fire department is on its way."

"Then let's go," I said, hefting the cat carrier for her. As we made our way to the elevator, I noticed several people stationing themselves in the hallways to direct others down the stairs. It was always fascinating to see mortals in an emergency. If panic didn't set in, they could be quite cooperative and caring. We helped the cat lady down ten flights, and even in a crowded staircase, I noticed how much cooler it was away from the burning apartment.

I also registered the pain for the first time. You know when you go to the beach and get sand everywhere? And three showers later you still find it in your clothes? This was like that, but with freaking *shards of glass.* Every time I turned my head, I felt little slivers poke my neck.

My skin felt raw, like I'd been badly sunburned. I kept wiping away tears, too, as my eyes compensated for the smoke.

When we reached the street, the woman thanked me for carrying her cats, and Caden, Trish, and I slipped away from the crowd, angling toward the small park by the Hudson River. I stared up at the building we'd just vacated and winced. The Genie's apartment looked like a nasty wound. A thick column of black smoke poured from its garishly lit, flickering interior as the firefighters worked to contain the blaze. I turned away.

My companions were inspecting the damage, too. Caden, as usual, looked untouched by his time in the bowels of a hellish conflagration. I couldn't spot a single smudge of soot or ash on him, but he *was* shining with perspiration, so that made me feel a tiny bit better. Trish, on the other hand, looked like she'd been through a war zone. Her black leather jacket was intact but, warped and burned by the heat, looked more like shrink wrap than leather. Her tank and jeans were shredded, and even with their dark coloring, I could see flecks of blood on them. But... I frowned. Her skin, visible beneath the tattered garments, was unblemished. "You're not injured," I said in surprise.

Trish glanced back at me, impatient. "What?"

"You stood in front of the balcony door when it shattered—saved me from a face full of glass." I paused. "Which I appreciate. I rather like this face."

"Your point?"

"You aren't bleeding," I said, leaning in to examine her wounds more closely.

She yanked the jacket closed and shrugged. "I told you. I'm the Monster Hunter. After a hunt, my wounds just... close. Or heal, or whatever."

Caden took a seat on the park bench. I wanted to follow suit, but I wasn't about to sit down while Trish stood. But hot damn—emphasis on *hot*—I hurt. Everywhere. I felt like I'd been microwaved, then rolled on a bed of crushed glass and served to order.

"Is that how you threw the coffee table, too?" I asked, keeping the exhausted strain from my voice. "You... what, get stronger around monsters?" When she didn't answer, I continued, "Maybe you're some kind of Hercules incarnate."

"Nope. Monster Hunter. Strength comes with the package, at least when I'm around monsters." She sighed. "Look, you did a good job, even if it was foolish not to run. I"—her mouth curled into an expression of distaste, like she'd bitten into an apple and found it sour —"appreciate your help. But please don't do it ever again," she concluded hastily.

I opened my mouth to argue, but Caden cut in smoothly. "We make a good team. We could use your help investigating Ahedrian."

Trish looked back and forth between us, and I swear I caught a flicker of amusement on her unforgiving face. "What are you guys, good cop/bad cop?" She shook her head. "I work alone. If Ahedrian brought you to the city, you should leave. I'm handling it."

"You think Ahedrian is a monster, then?" Caden pressed, speaking quickly so I couldn't butt in. I realized what he was doing, of course, but he was probably right. For some reason, Trish didn't respond well when I spoke.

"What else do you call someone or something that goes around beheading people?"

"A problem," I said firmly.

She looked annoyed but nodded in agreement. "Yeah." She hesitated, seemed to chew on our words, then asked tersely, "You have info?"

Caden bobbed his head. "Some. We could use more, though."

She pursed her lips, then came to a conclusion. "Okay, fine. We'll trade. What have you learned?"

Caden volunteered the baseline. "The bodies are beheaded, and the word Ahedrian is scrawled nearby."

She looked unimpressed. I added, "There's not enough blood at the scene, though."

Trish frowned. "They just cleaned it up before you got there."

I shook my head. "No. The most recent body—we got there before the cops."

Her eyebrows went up. "What else?"

"No, it's your turn," I said. I decided that sitting down while she stood would make me appear nonchalant and unthreatened, so I settled down next to Caden on the park bench. It had nothing to do with exhaustion or pain.

She considered. "I went to the morgue," she said matter-of-factly, like she was announcing the color of the sky. "Three of the bodies have superficial wounds. Two were stabbed, the other slashed. The wounds aren't defensive, though, and they don't make sense: one stabbed in the leg, the other through the hand. Unrelated to the cause of death. Which is, of course, decapitation."

"Any idea *how* they were decapitated?" I asked.

"An incarnate." Trish shrugged. "The separation of head from neck isn't natural. The wound is almost surgical."

"I noticed the same thing, but it's useful to get corroboration," I acknowledged. "Our turn." I felt like we were in a competition. "We spoke with the Ghost. She thinks the victims were all 'bad guys.'" I made quotation marks with my fingers. "We're looking into the possibility that they're linked—possibly all criminals."

"Not completely incompetent, I see," she said approvingly. She didn't even frown as she said it. "Iris isn't always reliable," she said, "but I should have thought to speak with her myself."

I grinned. "Not just a pretty face."

"You've been doing your homework, Trish," Caden said. "Any chance you got any official information on the crime scene?"

"Naturally." Bah, she didn't even sound like she was bragging. "Only interesting fact is that there was nothing interesting about it. The DNA found at the crime scene matches the people you'd expect: police, news crews, the people who discovered the bodies." She shook her head. "And not much of it, either. Nothing on the bodies of the victims."

I nodded slowly, then told Caden, "That's not overly surprising where incarnates are involved. Just like the gator turning into ooze after we killed it—"

"*I* killed it," Trish corrected.

"—incarnates stay hidden by not leaving much physical evidence behind."

"You know your shit," she said, "I'll give you that."

"Thanks?" I replied.

Caden, though, was nodding. "So forensics aren't very useful. Bummer, but it makes sense. Ever since you explained the camera trick, I've come to realize how much we rely on science and tech to verify what's 'real.'" He smiled at me. "But incarnates are loopholes."

I returned his smile. "And 'there's always a loophole.'"

"All right, Boy Scouts," Trish said, looking back and forth between us with a look of irritation, "that's my cue to leave." Well, it was an upgrade over "fools."

"Wait," I told her, leaning forward. "Something isn't right here. There are never two of the same kind of incarnate."

She hesitated, then nodded sharply. "Agreed."

"So what about you and me?" I intentionally worded it in a noncombative way, hoping it would advance the topic.

Trish looked at me, pity in her eyes. "There is no 'you and me.' Maybe you *were* a monster hunter, one time, one life. Maybe it was your job, like being a lawyer or a doctor. Hell, maybe you walked this Earth for lifetimes before I did, and it was your deeds from which I came." Her eyes held mine, her own hard and certain. "But you have never been the Monster Hunter incarnate." She pulled away. "Anyone can slay a monster, Emery, but only one person was *born* to."

The finality in her tone smothered the angry response sitting on my tongue. Her certainty cast a shadow of doubt over me. It was like someone telling you that your eyes aren't the color you've always known them to be. It was inconceivable. It was absurd.

I mean, sure, *mine* aren't always the same color, but that's not the point.

How did you argue with someone who was wrong yet emphatic in their certainty that they were not? My thoughts raced back to Huntington, to the tragedy that befell us. I'd thrown myself at monsters to run from my pain. Did that memory somehow imprint itself on my identity? Did it cast a shadow over my incarnation, make me identify as the Monster Hunter so I could forget I'd failed at that which I embodied? *No,* I thought. *Trish is wrong.* I hunted monsters because it offered solace from the memories, but also because it was who I was. If I concentrated, I could remember hunting monsters in antiquity, in eras long since forgotten. Dracula incarnate in his castle. The Medusa on her island. The Frost Giant in his cave.

Trish reached down and reclaimed the pistol's magazine from me. "Thank you for the information about Ahedrian." Even her gratitude sounded annoyed. "I have a monster to hunt. Stay out of my way."

I let her walk away while I sat there, stunned.

Caden fidgeted, looking like he wanted to say something but wasn't sure what.

I thought about our encounter with the Genie. Trish had been incredible—superhuman, even—but *I* had been the one to chase him away. Her comment about chasing monsters instead of hunting them stung me again.

Her certainty had rattled me, but conviction didn't make a thing true. To prove to her—and maybe myself, if I was being totally honest—that I was the Monster Hunter, I needed to figure out what incarnate she was. Preternatural strength and speed could fit into quite a few incarnates' repertoires. Some sort of Ninja incarnate, perhaps? But the supernatural healing after a fight didn't really make sense.

Caden put his hand over mine. "Are you okay?"

I shook off my line of thinking, giving him a smile. "Of course," I said, but the words sounded meager. I hoped my grin was more convincing. "She's wrong, and I'll find a way to prove it." I tried to put Trish's words behind me. I would reexamine them later, whether I wanted to or not.

"Even if she's not wrong," he said softly, looking down at his lap, "you can still be my Hero incarnate." His words felt like a hug after a hard day. I melted. Even some of the pain ebbed, the discomfort of hundreds of slivers of glass waning. The breeze off the Hudson caught his golden hair and tousled it, making it shimmer. I breathed deep, inhaling the scent of him. He smelled clean, like mountain air in the spring. It centered me, brought me into the *now.*

I exhaled and said the first thing that came to my mind. "Thank you for not dying."

He shrugged and smiled at me. "Not all of us have extra lives," he teased. "There were a few moments up there when I would have killed for immortality, though."

I laughed. "A lot of people would," I said, making to stand up from the park bench.

I froze halfway, though. Then sat back down, heavily. The words replayed in my mind, the implications shoving aside my worries about Trish, pushing away thoughts of Caden's scent. Realization hit me like a hammer.

"Caden." I turned to face him, our eyes meeting. "What if somebody *is*?"

"Killing to become immortal?" he asked. "How would that work?"

My mind raced. "Well, what if someone were killing to create an urban legend?"

His eyes widened in realization. "Ahedrian," he said. "They're trying to create an incarnate."

I nodded, horrified. "Or to *become* one." I jumped off the bench. "Come on. We should include Rachelle on this."

Formal Incarnate Lesson Five: Incarnate Titles
By Emery Luple

*H*ello, class. Today's lesson is a quick one, so I'm giving you a two-for-one deal.

First lesson: incarnates usually drop the "incarnate" title with each other. You've probably noticed me doing this more and more. Like with the Genie, the Headless Horseman, the Ghost, the Medium, etc.

So when do we use the full title? There are times when we need to be clear we're speaking about the incarnate versus a real-life concept. Most of the time, "incarnate" can be dropped, but some incarnates' names may be prone to confusion, such as the Princess incarnate. Similarly, the Diablo could refer to the incarnate, the Spanish devil, the video game, or the Lamborghini model. "The Diablo incarnate" is more specific.

We also add the word "incarnate" as either an honorific or—let's be honest—for simple dramatic flair.

Second lesson: we incarnates love our drama.

CADEN and I grabbed a bite at a food truck while we waited for the ride service he'd called to take us back to the hotel. I wasn't very hungry, but he'd napped through lunch. After what I'd just put him through, I owed him a much finer meal, but I looked like a dumpster diver. A dumpster-fire diver, actually. I promised him I would make it up to him, and he deflected, saying I didn't owe him anything and some of New York's food trucks were secretly the best dining experience in the city anyway.

Even with Caden's presence to ground me, my mind wandered. So many mysteries, entangled with one another, all spiraling around me. It was like an enormous puzzle—one of those with thousands of pieces and all the colors nearly identical—was blown into a tornado and I stood in the eye of the storm, catching glimpses of the pieces that flashed by me, occasionally able to grab and hold one but unable to complete the puzzle itself. I needed to think, yes, but I also needed to talk it out. I perform best with an audience, after all. Plus, Caden and Rachelle were bright and insightful. I hated the idea of retreating to the hotel once again, but let's face it: I needed a shower. And their input.

Caden finished his lamb gyro and sucked the juices from his thumb. He saw me watching him and blushed. "You should see your face, Emery," he said, his nose wrinkling.

I could only imagine. It was why I'd let Caden call our ride; even by NYC standards, I looked scary. I had missed a text from Rachelle while we were in the heat of battle—emphasis on... sorry, you get it: fire puns!—so I replied and let her know we were heading back to the hotel. When the black SUV drove up, I saw my reflection in the dark glass of the passenger rear window. I looked worse than I had feared. Black soot smudged my entire face, and tear tracks streaked through it from when my eyes wouldn't stop running. I'd smeared those further by wiping at my eyes and cheeks. I looked like a cross between a raccoon, a homeless person, and Wile E. Coyote after being blown up. Very intimidating, Emery. If you're the Monster Hunter, monsters are surely quivering in their boots.

If? Damn. I needed to rest. I was exhausted.

In contrast, Caden's face was bright and shining, free of dirt or grime—or any other evidence of our fiery battle. He examined my reflection, and if his quirked smile was any indication, he found my ashen state amusing.

He turned to look at me in person. "You look like you lost a fight with a chimney," he noted, trying to contain his grin.

"This," I countered, pointing at my face, "is what it looks like when you *win* that fight."

"Sure, sure," he said, looking at me in the car window's reflection again. "Come on. It's nearly brillig, and you know how frumious Rachelle gets when we don't check in."

I turned to him in confusion, about to ask him to repeat himself; what the hell was a *brillig*? But while I opened my mouth, I didn't speak. As Caden reached to pull open the vehicle's door, the late afternoon sunlight caught him in just the right way, and he seemed to *glow*. It wasn't my bias making him out to be brighter than he was, either—this was actual luminescence. Light pooled around his shoulders and fanned out, crowning his golden hair. For an instant, he was radiant.

I blinked and the light shifted, the door opened, and Caden hopped into the SUV. He slid to the far end of the bench seat and looked up at me, expression curious. He patted the seat next to him, as if inviting me to join him.

Caught off guard, I blushed, but the soot and ash were finally good for something: they hid my embarrassment. I slid in beside Caden, and he exchanged pleasantries with the driver.

I shook myself. I was so exhausted, I was hallucinating. Or my poor, overtaxed mind was seeing and hearing things.

No. That could happen, certainly. But the immortal corner of my mind drowsily awoke, grousing at me that something was amiss. It reminded me that I had been through far more stressful situations than today and kept my wits about me. *Trust your instincts.*

"What did you say back there?" I asked Caden. "About it being nearly... 'brillig'?"

He frowned. "I..." He looked away, but not before I saw two pink spots appear on his cheeks. "I meant to say it's nearly four in the afternoon."

"But you didn't," I prompted, leaning forward, trying to capture his evasive eyes.

He looked at his phone as if it were suddenly fascinating. "I think it just came out wrong, Emery," he mumbled. He risked a glance at me, and I was surprised to see an embarrassed smile. "You just looked so adorable in the reflection, with your chimney-face," he blurted, reddening further. "My words got all tongue-twisty."

"Oh," I said articulately, feeling a strange sort of glow in my stomach. "Well, that's okay, then." I masked the awkwardness of my response by laying my hand on his leg, just above the knee. "Um, thanks." *Nailed it, Emery, great save.*

Caden glanced up at that, his cheeks glowing. Our faces were surprisingly close. His embarrassment melted into a nervous smile.

He reached up and brushed some of the soot from my cheek, his warm fingers sending tingles that somehow spread down my spine and into my stomach. Then he blinked and snatched his fingers back, dusting the black residue off his thumb with a chagrined expression. I felt a stab of disappointment, but he slipped the same hand into mine, still resting on his leg. He gave me a small smile and looked pointedly toward the driver, then sat back with a sigh.

We spent the remainder of the short ride in companionable silence, our fingers occasionally entwining or squeezing, enjoying each other's touches like it was some kind of game. It made me feel silly, and mortal, and reassured and confident—all at the same time.

Back in our room, Rachelle sat on her bed poring over her tablet, sheets of paper strewn about her. She had a stylus tucked behind one ear and a pencil on the other side. Her bright pink cast stuck out awkwardly, while her good leg was tucked under her. She looked up as we walked in, smiling at Caden, and then her eyes widened as she took in my post-apartment-fire appearance.

I could see three or four reactions flit behind her eyes before she settled on, "Did you two go to different places?"

"Har, har," I responded wearily.

"I hope this hotel doesn't charge by the... *shower.*"

Caden laughed and said, "Go on, I'll fill Rachelle in while you clean off."

"So soon?" I gave him a crooked grin. "I thought you liked this look."

Rachelle snorted. "Emery, you know how cute it is when a puppy rolls around in the mud and comes up to you, tail wagging, face caked in dirt?"

Caden grinned and pointed at her.

Rachelle rolled her eyes. "At the end of the day, you still gotta wash the damn dog. Go clean up."

I glowered at Caden. "Traitor." Then I yelped and ran for the shower as Rachelle threw a pillow at me. The two of them were laughing as I closed the bathroom door.

I had a thousand things to think about as I stood in the shower and scrubbed a battle off me for the second time that day. The water ran black with the soot and ash, my thoughts weaving together the discordant clues at my disposal.

Morrigan had wanted me to go to New York, had sent me into a trap sprung on Trish and me simultaneously. The timing of that seemed suspicious—I had put off visiting my impostor, so how could Morrigan have accounted for my random delay? The apartment almost certainly was hers, as Horn-Rimmed Cat Lady had mentioned that the apartment belonged to a woman. That connected Morrigan to the Genie, but it didn't explain how Morrigan knew the moment I would reincarnate. Only my murderer in the desert would know that. Had I been duped, and it was Morrigan all along? Or was she conspiring with yet another incarnate? What was this, the Malevolent League of Evil? Perhaps my murderer was the so-called Ahedrian, the one responsible for the decapitations around NYC. But how did all of this fit with Ahedrian killing for immortality? Could Morrigan and the Genie possibly be working with... a mortal?

My mind spun around these facts, trying to fit them together, but I ultimately needed more information.

When I was thoroughly washed, I dried off and inspected my

handiwork in the mirror. I looked clean and fresh, and, surprisingly, my skin had lost much of its redness and hadn't roughened from burns or heat exposure. I ran my hand through my hair and inspected it, satisfied I hadn't missed any soot. Looking in the mirror, however, I was reminded again of the strange words Caden had said. *Brillig* and... *frumious*? Something bothered me. Iris had mentioned something to do with mirrors, I recalled, and it had nudged me to remember the compact mirror, Kolby's "treasure." Rachelle still had it, right?

There was something to it. Something I had missed before.

I left the bathroom. Caden had pulled the only chair in the room to the foot of both beds and was sitting back in it, answering questions Rachelle tossed his way about the fight with the Genie. I dressed quickly, pulling on my third new outfit. I'd bought a few more shirts, but this was the last complete outfit I'd purchased. I was fairly certain I wouldn't be engaging with any monsters tonight, so I felt comfortable wearing the outfit I'd been saving: the one Caden had picked out for me that I never would have gravitated toward on my own. The long-sleeved brown Henley featured contrast stitching on the shoulders in a color that matched my skin. It hugged my torso and fit snugly through the arms, showing off my musculature. Thinking back to my first day, it was the kind of shirt that went with the cocky grin I'd sported. I loved it.

As their conversation drew to a close, I sprang onto my bed and swung my legs around so I was facing both Rachelle and Caden. "All caught up?" I asked Rachelle.

"I think so. But you aren't." She plucked several sheets of paper off of her bed and held them out to me. "While you were off playing with your friends, I was busy holding down the fort." I took the papers from her. They were personnel files—no, criminal records, I realized. "I was able to get Gregory Gregorius's help," she announced smugly. "I called him up, and he pulled some strings and sent me these."

"The Watchman incarnate," I said in answer to Caden's questioning look. "He's in Seattle. Rachelle, what am I looking at, exactly?"

"These," she said proudly, "are the criminal histories of the *unreleased identities* of our victims."

I skimmed over them. "Auto theft, manslaughter, grand larceny, aggravated assault, possession..." I shook my head. "So this confirms our theory that all the beheaded victims are criminals."

Rachelle was holding up a sheet of paper that read "Applause!" in her handwriting. "I figured you'd need a reminder to admire my brilliance."

"Excellent work, Rachelle," I said. She had a suspicious stack of papers next to her, and I reached for them but she snatched them away. Not before I saw "Laugh!" written on another one, though.

"Which means," Caden concluded, ignoring our antics, "the murderer has done their homework. Maybe Ahedrian is an attempt at some sort of Vigilante Justice incarnate?"

Rachelle shot him a sour look. "That would suck. That sounds way too cool to be our murderer."

"Hollywood at work," he shrugged.

"I think we need to start at the beginning," I said. "Comb over everything we know to find out what we're missing."

The two of them nodded.

"So it starts with the first murder?" Rachelle asked.

"No. It starts with Morrigan." I looked at them grimly. "It always starts with Morrigan."

"Your archnemesis?" Caden said into the silence that greeted my proclamation.

I considered the best way to impress upon both of them how dangerous Morrigan truly was, but the most accurate word, "Super-callous-hag-malicious-hateful-and-atrocious," was too upbeat, and it didn't *show* them.

Rachelle sniffed and said, "'Archnemesis' is a little theatrical. Essentially, she's a very friendly and engaging woman... who, okay, kind of transforms into the most terrifyingly cunning thing you've ever seen when Emery walks into the room."

Caden grinned at her. "Then she's a lot like you?"

Rachelle blinked in surprise, then begrudgingly held up the "Applause!" sign.

I needed to get them back on track. Morrigan was no laughing matter. By bringing mortals back into my life, I needed them to understand her lethality. To fear her. They needed to respect her deviousness *for* me, since I often didn't mistrust her enough. To my detriment. I would not allow Morrigan to use them against me. Not if I could help it.

"I don't remember my first life," I told them, "but I remember my first *death*." That wasn't entirely true, but it was the first time I'd been murdered—I was certain of that. As the centuries slipped by, the past became hazy, distant and forgotten, even by me. Those rare times when I survived to old age, my venerable mind could pierce some of that haze, recall things I'd forgotten for lifetimes. And sometimes, when I reincarnated into an older body, I'd remember events with startling clarity.

"Morrigan killed you?" Rachelle asked quietly.

"Morgan, actually," I replied. "We were friends, I think, in life. Betrayal, one of the oldest stories ever written." Images of that first death, like photos in my mind, haunted my dreams to this day, persisting through countless reincarnations. Looking up at the pale sky. Morgan's curled smile beneath a grief-stricken mask. My chest, stained in bright blood. "Time and again, Morrigan and Emery, Emery and Morgan. Different faces, the same dance, the same conclusion. A story eternally retold." I sighed. "Every time Morrigan surfaces in my life, it feels like inevitability nudges us toward a cliff and we tumble down together, picking up momentum, fighting and clawing until we inevitably reach the bottom. One of us broken, bloody, dying, survived by the other." I shook my head. "There is no escape. Each time I reincarnate, I limp forward, hoping against hope I won't see her again. Sometimes the respite will be lifetimes, sometimes it will be a thousand and one days. But never forever."

"That's horrible," Caden said, pain and sympathy in his big eyes.

"Emery," Rachelle asked, "how old *are* you?"

I flashed them my signature smile, burying the pain that had crept into my voice. "Nineteen." I shrugged. "You know the expression 'age is just a number'? Well, I'm pretty sure it was coined by an incarnate. I'm not like a classic immortal from the fairy tales: I live, I age, I die. To me, it makes sense to track each life's progress instead of my overall total. It makes each life feel more meaningful."

She looked thoughtful. "Huh. But could you and Morgan be, like, the first incarnates?"

I grunted. "I'm not *that* old," I protested. "From the beginning, I assumed there must be others like me. But it took me a few lifetimes to hear whispers of their existence, and even longer to finally find them." I smiled, the memory unfolding like a blossom as I spoke. "In due course, I found a community of incarnates. Some of them sought, as I did, others with whom to share their lifetimes. Others were already ancient, passing down their knowledge and experience to those of us who were new." I sighed. Accustomed to the vigilant and cynical nature of the corner of my mind I associated with my immortal self, I was surprised to feel nostalgia, poignant and fond, flowing from it instead. "Many of them are gone now, their legends forgotten, their stories no longer told. But I remember," I finished in a whisper.

Caden put his hand on my knee. "Like stars," he reminded me. "Their light reaches us even after they've vanished."

"Right," I said, sharing a smile with him. I cleared my throat, storing those precious memories with my other seldom-visited treasures. "Morrigan. Everything always starts with her. The last time I saw her, before this week, was three incarnations ago. She murdered a..." I swallowed. "A friend. A mortal." I felt a surge of guilt, both from my memories of his death and from hiding the nature of our relationship. It felt cowardly, and it didn't do his memory justice. I didn't want to dredge up past relationships in front of Caden. But with his hand still resting on my knee, his eyes wide and reassuring, I knew I needed to do the right thing. "His name was Huntington." My throat felt dry. "Throughout countless lifetimes, I've been exposed to everything from deep and abiding love, to dalliances and passionate affairs, to unrequited love. I've experienced love in a thousand variations, but this one seemed special. Looking back at it now, maybe it wasn't. Maybe it was simply love lost. Tragic love." I almost flinched as Caden removed his hand from my knee, but his open expression didn't change as he sat back. Our eyes met and he gave me an encouraging nod, so I continued. "Morrigan thrilled at finding such a weakness in me, of course. Huntington and I were investigative journalists, so she schemed until she'd created the perfect story, the perfect trap: she became a serial killer, leaving crumbs behind at each murder to taunt us. We followed like good little sheep, never suspecting our story was a den of wolves." An angry tear slid down my cheek. "She lured us to our deaths. It was... cinematic. Perfectly constructed in every way. A kidnapped child, an empty wharf. Hints casually dropped, leading us to the girl's whereabouts. Timed impeccably: we could save her, just the two of us, if we acted immediately. But it would have been impossible if we'd involved anyone else." Rachelle and Caden were rapt, watching me with expectant sadness on their faces. "I remember our arrogance, our overconfident—almost cavalier—attitude on the dockside as we envisioned ourselves heroes." I barked a short, bitter laugh. "I feared no mortal killer. Even if it was an incarnate, then surely only a monster awaited us. Only a monster would kidnap a child, right? And who better to slay a monster than I?" My voice was ice. "The girl was bound and gagged, her whimpering screams sounding the moment we entered the building. We weren't completely reckless, but our caution wasn't enough. As I worked to untie the child's bonds, to soothe her terror, I heard a gunshot." My voice broke, and I took a few deep breaths before continuing. "I didn't even see him die. Just spun around to see Morrigan, smoking gun in hand, Huntington's body still falling to the ground. His body collapsed; his head bounced off the cement floor with a crack like the sound of my heart breaking." A tear slid down my cheek. "She *laughed*. A bubble of amusement. I cradled his body, but his eyes were already empty. He died, and I had missed it. Like it didn't matter. As if"—in my memory, I saw Morrigan's red lips mouth the words, gloating as I held his corpse—"'mortals' lives are nothing.' She blew me a kiss. Then ended me, too." A few more tears leaked from my eyes.

The end of my story was met with silence, pregnant with grief and sympathy. Rachelle's hand covered her mouth in horror. Caden's wide eyes watched me, brimming with compassion.

"You and your precious mortals, Emery. Really, I'll never understand your weakness for them. How do you fall in love with an insect? They are insignificant, their accomplishments no more meaningful than an ant toiling its entire life to... to what? Build a hill no higher than my knee? How

have you not yet learned? Mortals' lives are nothing to us. So easily squashed. Like bugs."

Rachelle maneuvered herself across the gap in our beds and sat down beside me, giving me a hug. After a moment, Caden joined us on my other side, and I felt his arms around my shoulders as well. I'd carried the shame, the anger, and the desolation of that memory for years, anchoring my soul to a haunted landscape of darkness. In the course of a single retelling, simply by listening and caring, these two 'insignificant' mortals lifted me into the light.

Morrigan—the thought fought its way through layers of scars and guilt—*I'll take these 'insects' over you every last time.*

I shuddered, composing myself. Wiped my eyes and sniffled. "Sorry," I breathed. "I spent two lives avoiding her. She found me in this one."

"Okay," Rachelle said unsteadily, "it always starts with Morrigan." She gave me a forced thumbs-up. "Got it."

I met their gazes and held them, demanding their attention. "Promise me," I said, emphasizing each word, "that you will not underestimate her. Swear to me that you understand and that you will do everything you can to respect our enemy."

"I promise," Caden said solemnly, seafoam eyes holding mine.

I turned to Rachelle. In a rare moment of somberness, she said, "I promise."

I smiled wearily. "Now that you better understand the stakes," I said, "let's piece this puzzle together. Just remember, always keep Morrigan in mind. If things don't make sense, or some motive seems veiled, you should always consider her."

They nodded together, patting me on the back and reclaiming their spots.

"Then I think our second puzzle piece, after her, is Saudi Arabia," I declared, feeling the weight of our conversation disappear into the depths like a leviathan's silhouette beneath a boat in the ocean. "One thousand and six days ago, I stumbled upon a person who achieved an impossible feat: they'd captured the Yeti incarnate."

"Isn't that a bit dramatic?" Rachelle cut in. "Impossible? Really?"

"The Yeti's kryptonite is capture," I explained. "Knocking it out, tranquilizing it, caging it, collaring it." I ticked off each item on my fingers. "No matter which way you slice it, imprisonment proves fatal to the big guy."

"So someone found a loophole?" Caden guessed.

"Exactly. Somehow, they figured out how to capture it and relocate it to the desert." And as staggering as it was that someone had managed to catch it, the next part was even more bizarre.

Rachelle, keeping pace with my thoughts, concluded, "Then they tried to recreate Chewie from *Star Wars*. They were hoping to create enough rumors to create a new type of incarnate: the Wookiee."

"Flash forward to now," Caden said, "and someone is trying to do the same thing. They've learned from their mistakes: this time they aren't using an existing legend or character, they're creating one from scratch." He met both of our gazes. "Ahedrian."

I held up my hand. "I think that's right, but let's not get ahead of ourselves. The next mystery is the Genie. He tried to kill me within *minutes* of my being reincarnated."

Rachelle gave me a flat look. "Not just you. He didn't care much about collateral damage."

"The important point," I continued, "is that only my Saudi Arabian killer would know the exact time I'd reincarnate."

"I think my point is pretty important, too," Rachelle muttered darkly.

Caden had caught on. "So your Saudi Arabian killer is likely to be the Genie's master."

"Which points us back to Morrigan," Rachelle said with a frown. "Right? I mean, she gave you the address that led you to a trap. And that trap was in the form of the Genie."

I'd been shot from behind. The shooter's voice had been muffled by the sandstorm and, presumably, their protective headgear, but it hadn't been Morrigan. I was sure of it. Wasn't I? In any case, what would she have achieved by killing me from behind, by disguising her role in my death?

Morrigan was not predictable. It would be utter foolishness to rule her out entirely, but my gut told me it wasn't her.

"It seems pretty likely," I agreed. "But I just don't think she's the one who killed me in Saudi Arabia. I can't shake the feeling that it was someone else."

"Well," Caden said, "you've convinced me that Morrigan is a schemer. Maybe she is involved, but she's not actually the murderer. We've already entertained the idea of an accomplice. What if the accomplice is Morrigan?"

"Not a bad theory," I said, "but there's at least one other incarnate involved: the one doing the actual beheading. From what we know about the lack of blood coupled with Trish's info, we can be reasonably certain the decapitator is an incarnate."

"But that doesn't make sense," Caden countered, his face drawn in thought. "If someone is trying to become immortal by turning themself into an incarnate named Ahedrian, then wouldn't *they* have to be the thing everybody fears and talks about?" At our uncertain nods, he continued. "Well, then they can't be an incarnate already, right? They can't become immortal twice."

I grimaced. "Yeah, good point. But as I said, a mortal wouldn't be capable of killing in this exact way."

"Can an incarnate ever be two incarnations at once?" Rachelle asked suddenly.

"What do you mean?"

She sat forward, adjusting her leg. "If the human is working with a well-known incarnate, like the Headless Horseman, then if Ahedrian was created through the beheadings, maybe it couldn't affect the existing incarnate. He couldn't become the Ahedrian *and* the Headless Horseman. Then the incarnation would default to the human, right? Or at least, someone might figure it would work that way."

I shook my head in exasperation. "This is all conjecture," I said, "because it isn't possible to intentionally *create* incarnates. For all I know, if the legend of Ahedrian grew, an entirely new incarnate would appear."

"But the human doesn't know that," Caden said. "Maybe they think they've found a loophole."

"And given the Yeti loophole they *did* find," Rachelle added, "maybe they're right."

We all chewed on that thought for a few moments, then I cleared my throat. "Three more mysteries." I held up three fingers. "In order: mirrors, my impostor, and why Morrigan wants me in New York."

Caden perked up. "That's right," he said. "Iris mentioned something about mirrors, didn't she?"

"Yeah." I looked to Rachelle. "Do you still have Kolby's treasure?" She pointed at her bag, across the room. I jumped up and fetched it for her. I'd spent enough lifetimes as a woman to know better than to go through her purse without asking. She dug around, then proffered the compact to me. It was just as I remembered: peach-colored and smooth, devoid of ornamentation or anything particularly exciting. I kept it closed.

"Ever since I reincarnated, I've said some strange things when I've looked into mirrors. I didn't notice, really, until this afternoon." I gave Caden a meaningful smile. "Rachelle, will you please say 'four o'clock' while looking into this mirror?"

I tossed her the mirror. She frowned and inspected it for a moment. "All right," she said slowly. She shrugged and popped it open. "Brillig," she said deliberately. Then she blinked, eyes narrowing. "*Brillig*," she said again. Her eyes widened, then cut away from the mirror, looking up at us. "Four o'clock. The hell? Is this thing enchanted?"

I shook my head, smiling. "I thought that at first, too. Well, sort of. I thought maybe it was the Magic Mirror incarnate, or something like that." I waved away their questioning looks. "This mirror isn't anything special. It's *all* mirrors. It first happened in the bathroom at my office when I was inspecting my—new—self; then again in Kolby's room with this compact. It happened in our hotel room and again a little while ago when Caden was looking at our reflections in a car window. I think the mirrors are trying to tell us something. Something we've been missing."

Rachelle chewed her lip. "Where have I heard that word before? And remember at Kolby's, you called yourself a 'beamish boy'?" Her eyes lit up. "Yes! I think it's from *Alice in Wonderland.*" She grabbed her tablet and started typing it in. "I was close. It's from the poem "Jabberwocky," which is in the sequel to *Alice in Wonderland.*"

I indicated her tablet. "Does it have the word 'frumious' in it?"

"Sure does." She grinned at me, excited. "And do you know who the villain of *Alice in Wonderland* is?"

I frowned. "The Queen of Hearts?"

"And do you know what her catchphrase is?" she pressed.

Caden's wide eyes met mine. He quoted quietly, "'Off with their heads.'"

he Queen of Hearts incarnate.

  Class, it is imperative to remember: incarnates are not the originals. They are manifestations of legends retold by humanity over the course of time. Time is an important variable when factoring in the resemblance between the current incarnation and the original. Why? Thank you —yes, you—for asking that very insightful question.

  As you've witnessed through my own recollections, memories fade even among my kind. If you are an incarnate hearing these words and still have memories of your first incarnation... treasure them. In time, you will forget. There is no shame in it. The passage of time spares neither mortal nor incarnate.

  With every reincarnation, new personality is infused in the immortal's soul. Whether the personality comes from variants in the telling of the myth or simply from the new life inherent in each reincarnation, I cannot say. I have my opinion, of course, but I will let you form your own.

  The Queen of Hearts incarnate is not Lewis Carroll's Queen of Hearts, though his character certainly inspired the incarnate. The Queen of Hearts incarnate is also not Walt Disney's interpretation of the Queen of Hearts, though that rendition and retelling of Alice in Wonderland *certainly fanned the flames of the legend. And yes, that means she is also not Tim*

Burton nor American McGee's adaptations; and she certainly isn't Kathy
Bates or Helena Bonham Carter. But every retelling strengthens her legacy,
ensuring that every time she is defeated, she will manifest again 1,001 days
later.
  Long live the queen.

CADEN GLANCED out the window of the Starboard at the sunset. "I
think it's time for me to get going," he said regretfully. "If I head out
now, I should be able to make it home before dark."

I tried not to feel a pang of disappointment. For some reason, I
had assumed he would stay with us in the hotel overnight, but at his
words I realized that made no sense. I jumped up from the bed,
where I'd lain on my stomach considering the possibility of Morrigan
befriending the Queen of Hearts. The two would probably hit it off.
"I'll go with you," I told him. "Keep you company."

Rachelle quirked an eyebrow at that but stayed silent. Caden
grinned and agreed. I felt pleased; I had entertained a momentary
worry that he might not desire my companionship.

We bid farewell to Rachelle, and Caden promised he'd return in
the morning. We made our way through the hotel and slipped out
into the crisp evening air. The sun descended rather swiftly, the sky
darkening while the buildings of New York flickered awake. The brilliance of Midtown Manhattan as twilight settled over the skyline took
my breath away. Illuminated billboards, floodlit signs, steady street-
lamps, glowing food trucks, skyscrapers with hundreds of windows
giving off soft yellow light... even the headlights of cars twinkled like
stars—which, ironically, were drowned out by all the other lights.

Caden and I ambled side by side, and I was happy to see he wasn't
in a hurry. Despite the evening hour and the March bite in the air, the
streets were packed with people bustling with brisk purpose, pulling
coats tight around them as they pushed past our meandering pace. I
kept trying to think of things to say—which is usually *not* a problem
for me—but the streets were noisy and people crowded on all sides,

so I kept pace with him in silence and settled for the occasional bump of our hands.

We came to a stop on a busy corner, and Caden suddenly turned to me, the thousands of lights all around us framing his silhouette and dancing in his eyes. "Hey," he said, "I want to show you something. Seems thematically appropriate." He flagged down a taxicab as he spoke, a true New Yorker. "You ever seen Central Park?"

I stopped myself from automatically saying yes. Memories flashed by of various visits to Central Park—I think I actually lived there once, as a young boy, homeless, observing the lives of strangers. But there were other memories, too, of sipping coffee and strolling past the carousel, morning joggers zipping by. Of sitting at the lagoon, counting the ducks. Of a family of tourists stopping me and asking I take their photograph. I shook the memories away, looked into Caden's excited eyes, and said, "Not in this lifetime."

He opened the taxi door and beckoned for me to hop in. He slid in after me and told the driver to take us to Columbus Circle. The drive was short, no more than ten minutes, and we emerged from the cab at a round plaza surrounded by fountains and crowned with a central spire. The crowds here were thicker than they had been in Chelsea, this entrance to Central Park by no means deserted.

Caden led the way north along the path, cutting through the park proper before the crowds lessened to a point where we could stroll side by side. He pointed to a stone monument. Hellenistic statues adorned its base, while golden figures crowned the column. "That's the USS *Maine* National Monument," he told me, seemingly excited to play tour guide, "and it marks the Merchants' Gate entrance to Central Park." We passed the monument and entered Central Park. The history here was palpable, eliciting shivers of anticipation not unlike the feeling upon entering an incarnate's domain.

For those of you who have never been to Central Park, it may not quite be what you imagine. At times, the paths are exactly that, twisting through the trees and lawns—but at other times, they meet with roads and cross busy intersections, with cars, bikes, buses, and skyscrapers directly next to your walk through the park. It's an odd sort of urban escape, but most of it certainly isn't a forest or jungle. It's populated at all hours of the day, as inherently New York as the Statue of Liberty or Times Square.

We walked down the path, spacing ourselves so we weren't too close to any other pedestrians, granting cyclists and joggers plenty of opportunity and allowance to pass us by. There weren't too many as evening sped toward night, but they weren't altogether rare, either. Ahead, the route ducked beneath a stone bridge, forming a shallow tunnel.

"Does it hurt?" Caden asked suddenly.

I was caught off guard. "Does what hurt?"

"Dying." He watched my reaction, his face curious.

"Oh." *Well, it isn't fun.* I thought about how best to reply. "Yeah, sometimes." A biker whizzed by, disappearing into the tunnel ahead. "But it isn't really about the pain, most of the time."

On impulse, I reached out and captured his hand in mine. He turned to me in surprise, then softened into my touch. After a few steps, we found our stride, ambling forward hand in hand.

"What's it like, then?" he asked.

"It depends." I realized no one had really asked me this before. Or, perhaps more accurately, I'd never answered honestly before. "Most of the time, it's a lot like going to the dentist." He looked at me suspiciously, and I held up my hand. "No, really, I'm going somewhere with this. Think about it. You usually don't *want* to go to the dentist, but you know you must. While you're there, it's not enjoyable, but it's also not as bad as you feared it was going to be. Then, when it's over, you walk out feeling better, fresher... and grateful you won't have to do it again for a while."

Caden laughed, shaking his head, his arm bumping into mine.

"Sometimes I look forward to it, anticipate it," I continued. "Usually after living a long life. The thought of a new adventure, then, is exciting."

We stepped into the tunnel. The sudden darkness and Caden's hand in mine made him seem very near.

"It can be painful," I admitted, "but usually it's more of an emotional toll. Regret at not being able to continue living as my current incarnation, of possibly not remembering my friends. Sorrow at losing my family and at the anguish I know it will cause those I leave behind. Remorse at being unable to stay longer, of leaving things unfinished." My voice echoed off the stone walls.

"It sounds... lonely," Caden said. I could see the lighter patch of night as we approached the other side of the tunnel.

His words struck me as true. Dying *was* lonely.

I stopped walking, and he did, too. I could barely see him, but his eyes seemed to glow. "I don't feel alone right now," I told him. I reached up and put my fingertips on the side of his face, cupping his cheek. His skin was soft and warm. My heart began pounding so hard I swear I could feel its beat in my finger pads. Even in the dark, I saw his eyelids go heavy, felt him lean into my touch.

"Good," he mumbled, his breath tickling my wrist. "I don't like the thought of you going through that all alone."

I leaned in and rested my forehead against his. My stomach did a flip. I felt a tremor in his breathing, warm against my face. I inhaled the scent of him, feeling almost lightheaded. He was clean and fresh, just like earlier, just like always. "Thank y—"

Caden cut me off with his mouth over mine.

Warm. I melted into him, felt him respond in kind. The kiss was soft. There was a breathless sort of hunger to his lips, but at the same time he wasn't too needy or overeager. I returned his silken kiss, my lips moving against his. In that moment, we belonged together.

The moment stretched, but it was still too short. I didn't want it to end, and the way he leaned into me instead of pulling back made me realize with a giddy delight that he didn't want it to end, either.

At last we separated, and I felt his lips graze mine in a slow, leisurely retreat. He didn't pull back very far. Our foreheads resting together once again, we shared a moment or two of quickened breaths. "I've never met anyone like you," he whispered, the openness of his admission stirring something inside me.

I chuckled against him, wrapping my arms around his smaller frame and pulling him close. "I think," I said in a low voice, "that I can say the same." I let a bit of lightness creep into my tone. "And given my many, many lifetimes, I think that means I win."

I felt his quiet laugh. "Let's call it a tie?"

"Deal. But not very many people can talk me into a draw, I hope you know."

We left the tunnel feeling like two silly teens who stole kisses in the dark, high on the thrill of sharing something private, intimately ours. I idly wondered how long it had been since I'd truly been a teenager.

We walked together for a time along the path, the hush of the night special and close. People still occasionally passed us, but the frequency dipped, the distance between them growing longer.

Finally, we came upon a still pool, reflecting not the light of the moon but of a few skyscrapers towering above the treetops. "We're almost there," Caden said. He pointed to a path that diverged from the one we'd been following. "Over here." We walked down a hedge-lined path and emerged at a pavilion with several bronze statues. I inspected them in the dim light and saw a young girl sitting on a giant mushroom, surrounded by figures in Victorian attire. A bronze statue of a diminutive man sporting a top hat, and... a rabbit wearing a waistcoat.

"It's Alice in Wonderland," I realized belatedly.

"I figured it was appropriate."

I smiled. "Agreed." I shook my head ruefully. "So many clues, in Seattle and especially around New York, if only I'd been open to them."

"Don't beat yourself up," Caden said, leaning against me. "You've been in New York, what, three whole days?" He grinned. "At this rate, you'll have solved the murders and hunted all the monsters in New York by next week."

I nodded, a strange reluctance coming over me. "Caden," I asked quietly, worried at the fragility in my voice, "what if I'm *not* the Monster Hunter incarnate?"

He didn't answer immediately. "You've never encountered Trish in a previous life, I take it?"

I kept my eyes on the Alice sculpture. "No. And, dammit, she makes a stellar case for it, doesn't she?"

"I suppose," he responded tactfully. "Let's examine the facts. Her strength and speed increased dramatically during the fight, then her wounds healed afterward. It's compelling, sure, but I'm sure there are other things she could be."

"But then why don't *I* get those advantages?"

"Honestly?" Caden searched my face. "I think you do. Have advantages, I mean. They just aren't the same ones."

I narrowed my eyes. "Okay, I'll bite. What are you thinking?"

He kept his attention on me, but I noticed his fingers began fidgeting. "I *know* that door was locked, Emery."

"So... I can get into places I'm not supposed to?"

He shrugged. "Or places you *are* supposed to. Think about it. How long were you in New York before you *randomly* stumbled upon a crime scene?" He held up a finger to forestall my response. "The very crime you crossed the country to investigate."

I sighed. He didn't understand. That kind of thing happened to me quite often. "I think that's just part of being an incarnate," I told him.

"I don't know as much about all of this as you," he admitted, "but I thought about calling you a hundred times, from the first time I watched *There's Always a Loophole.* Even before the murders. They were really just an excuse." He blushed, visible even in the low light. "I've always been drawn to you. But more than that, I've been drawn to what you do. Or, I suppose, what I thought you did. My dreams have always been filled with the supernatural. Being so close to death at the hospice center, I've always felt a connection with the..." he struggled for the right word, "the... *beyond*, I guess. When we met Iris yesterday, I felt like I'd known her all my life. I think it would have surprised me more to find out she *didn't* exist." He blew out his cheeks. "What I'm trying to say is, I called you the day you reincarnated. Not the day before, not the day after. I was compelled to finally act right when you needed to come to New York."

I felt a strange sort of glow at his words, but I knew the truth.

"Caden," I told him gently, "the reason you acted when you did is because that is when reality shifted, putting the memories in your mind that you watched my blog. I know you feel like you've been following my channel for years, but that isn't the case. That's just reality slipping me into this existence, this incarnation."

"Exactly," he insisted. "Coincidences and conveniences. Everywhere. Reality bends around you, Emery. What do you think that means?"

I opened my mouth, but nothing came out. I didn't know what to say. Reality had always bent around me—but I wasn't unique. All incarnates were slipped into reality when they reincarnated. I just... made a bigger splash than most.

But to Caden's point—why?

"I think," he said, slipping his fingers into mine, "it means you're special. Maybe you're not the Monster Hunter. But I think you're something even better, Emery."

I looked at him and swallowed. "Caden, I'm *not* the Hero incarnate." I felt something break inside me as I said, "Heroes save people. But I couldn't save him." I felt shame flood through me again. But it swirled with a new guilt: my mounting feelings for Caden. I felt I was somehow betraying both of them.

Caden, however, echoed my earlier gesture and cupped my cheek, forcing me to attend to the present. "Anybody can be a hero, Emery— and being a hero doesn't mean winning every battle. Heroism isn't an incarnation, it's risking your life to protect your friends from an alligator. It's six women abandoning their oaths to raise an abandoned boy. It isn't about battling a Headless Horseman in the night. It's not about being a monster killer. It's about finding the strength to stand up to the mistakes that haunt you and make a conscious decision to persevere, to move forward. To save again. To love again." His smile was colored by a touch of sympathy. "No one can be a hero all the time. That's too much responsibility for anyone."

I felt the sincerity behind his words, the compassion and understanding in them as profound as it was inexplicable. Those words, spoken with as much certainty as anything Trish had claimed, found purchase in my heart. It didn't mean I believed I wasn't the Monster Hunter, just like that. But for the first time, the doubt didn't hurt. "Then what am I?"

"A good person."

I snorted to cover the moisture that pricked my eyes. "You haven't known me very long."

"I'm an exceptional judge of character."

I raised my eyebrows in mock surprise. "A boast? From you?"

He puffed up his chest. "It's not a boast if it's true," he countered. The way he said it, I think he was trying to impersonate me. "If it's all the same to you," he said, modest once again, "maybe we can figure it out. You know, together. You and I."

"I think I'd like that."

We exited Central Park at the Alice in Wonderland sculpture, heading into the Upper East Side. We began walking along Madison, the night deepening around us, the pools of light becoming farther apart. The buildings here were quieter, dimmer, felt older. Though they were four or five stories tall, they felt small compared to the looming structures of Midtown.

"Here's my stop." Caden gestured to a bleached brick building. A few steps with a railing, as well as a ramp for less mobile pedestrians, led up to an archway with heavy wooden doors. The arch was topped by stone angels, and the stained-glass windows of the upper floors had delicate black bars in front of images depicting acts of peace and floral scenes evoking calm.

A stone tablet named the building: "Malek Care Center."

"Caden Malek," I tested aloud. "I like it." I realized I hadn't heard his full name spoken aloud since we'd met.

Here, at the doorstep to his home, I realized I didn't want our night to end. I felt the same reluctance from him. We spoke quietly for a few moments, but we both felt the night drawing to a close. Eventually, he stepped into me and I slipped my arms around his shoulders, embracing him. "Thank you for... everything," I whispered in his ear, floundering for words. I brushed my lips against his cheek.

"Stole the words right out of my mouth," he murmured. He

stepped back, then hit me with his beautiful smile. "Good night, Emery."

Caden slipped up the stairs, opened the heavy wooden doors, and disappeared through them.

I heaved a sigh, feeling the New York night wallop me with sounds and sensations that had been hushed or forgotten in Caden's company. Cars drove by on the street; horns honked in the distance. The March breeze sent chills through me, carrying the faint smell of food and wet concrete.

I shot a quick text to Rachelle: OMW BACK TO YOU, SEE YOU SOON.

I felt... happy. Content. I had much to think about, to analyze. But not tonight. Tonight belonged to Caden and me.

A sleek black limousine cruised up in front of the care center just as I began to consider ordering a ride service back to the hotel instead of chancing a New York cab. To my surprise, the limo pulled over, sliding to a smooth stop in front of me.

The window began rolling down, black reflection slowly giving way to reveal the dimly lit, scarlet interior. "Why, hello there. You look as though you could use a ride."

My joy froze. I recognized the voice coming from the shadowed recesses of the luxurious vehicle.

Morrigan.

I felt a stab of panic. Morrigan was here, in New York? How long had the black limousine been lurking, following me? Following *us*. Had she seen me walk up with Caden? Had she taken particular interest in this building, somehow anticipated my arrival?

Think, Emery. No. The limousine had turned the street corner a moment ago, hadn't it? I couldn't be certain, but I thought I remembered seeing its smooth, glossy finish come into view from the intersection, which would mean she hadn't been waiting for me here.

But how could she have known exactly where to find me?

"The air has a bite to it this evening, doesn't it? Please, do join me."

I'd been caught off guard, unaware. *Fight back!* A large—and I mean *large*—man was coming around the rear of the car. His chest was twice the size of mine, and I didn't have a small frame. His roped-muscle arms were long and menacing, the knuckles seeming to drag on the ground as he walked, like those of a human-ape hybrid. Not really, of course; that was my panic-induced exaggeration kicking in. He opened the door of the limo and gestured inside, surprisingly polite. I had the sense he would equally politely knock my teeth out if I refused.

I needed to consider my options. If I spurned her offer, what would she do? *Had* she seen Caden? Would he be in danger if I refused her?

"Emery, darling." Her voice slid from the interior of the limo like a hand slipping out of a velvet glove. "The Starboard is not so terribly far from here, and we have much to discuss. Do come to the decision we both know you're going to make, so that we may begin."

The Starboard. I should have guessed she would know where I was staying. It was a not-so-subtle threat. She could see I was not with Rachelle. I could see the pieces tumbling in my mind like a chain of dominoes, leading me to the conclusion she wished me to reach: if I didn't get in, Rachelle was in danger.

If I did get in, *I* was in danger. For a selfish moment, I compared the two options.

No. There was no option. I wouldn't risk Rachelle's life.

I finally found my voice. "Well, as long as it's no trouble." I slid into the limo. The door shut behind me like the sound of a cell door being slammed, lock clicking.

Morrigan sat primly in the plush interior, a slender glass of champagne held in one gloved hand. Her silken, raven-black hair was pinned up, held in place by delicate netting and a red silk lily. She wore a flattering white dress, the cut prominently displaying her smooth, crossed legs. The scarlet lighting of the interior played across her, shading her dress, gloves, and heels a sharp red hue, giving the illusion she was draped in crimson. It also cast her face in ruby-tinged shadow as she regarded me.

Her eyes penetrated me, peeling back the layers of my guard, analyzing everything from my new attire to the perspiration on my forehead.

I settled into the comfort of the limo as it smoothly accelerated back into traffic. Grabbing an open bottle of champagne and a matching flute, I poured myself a glass. My nonchalance was a weapon to throw her off guard—and a shield to buy me time to think, to plan. Most importantly, enabled me to assume the carefree visage I needed. I was proud that my hands didn't shake as I poured the pale liquid.

She watched me without comment, her red lips quirking slightly, as though she saw right through my performance. I held my glass up to hers, and she tipped her head, clinking my glass. "To old friends," she purred.

I refrained from rolling my eyes and sipped my champagne. It fizzed against my tongue. I know, I know; I shouldn't have accepted any food or drink from her. Not only was I underage according to US drinking laws, she could have poisoned it. Relax. I've lived far longer than twenty-one years. The poison thing, though, that's a good point. It was a foolish risk to take.

But when playing games with Morrigan, only risky plays were possible. Nothing else had a chance at success. We were at the top of our mountain, the edge so very near, the slope steep. Let the scratching and clawing commence.

"I'm surprised to find you here without your little mortal," she said. I fought to keep my expression neutral. She was not as well-informed as I had feared. She didn't know Rachelle had broken her leg, been sidelined. She also likely didn't know about Caden.

I covered my relief with another sip. "Needed to clear my head."

Morrigan did not respond to my nonanswer. "I do hope you aren't tiring of this one too quickly. From what I can tell, she's got more fire in her than your average mortal."

I narrowed my eyes. "Why are you so invested?" I asked, calling her out, dragging her damned machinations into the light.

If it bothered her, she gave no sign. "You've spurned your precious mortals for years, Emery." Her eyes widened in mock sympathy. "I *loathe* to see you denying yourself the pleasure of their company."

Uh-huh. They were just ammunition for her to use against me.

"Oh, don't give me that look," she said, waving a gloved hand as if shooing away an insect. "Have I been anything but helpful to you?" I thought it was a rhetorical question, but she paused, awaiting my reply.

I sat up straighter. "Helped me? Helped me into a pit of vipers, maybe."

A single eyebrow snaked upward. "Oh? Did you not find what you expected at the address I provided?"

I snorted. "An ambush? Yes, I found *exactly* what I expected."

"Spare me the puppy-dog act, Emery." She inspected a spot on her glass and wiped at it with a gloved finger. "I led you by the hand to that which you sought, and I tossed in some entertainment for you as a favor. Frankly, I expected more gratitude."

"You admit to being the Genie's master?"

Morrigan paused, expression unreadable. "So disappointing," she said at last, clicking her tongue. "Spoon-fed, and still unable to piece the puzzle together." She sighed. "I had such high hopes for this incarnation, you know. You were handed everything: the athletic physique of a warrior, the agile mind of a youth, the fiery temperament of a fighter." Her eyes glittered. "The perfect playmate."

She set aside her champagne flute in a side pocket housed in the limousine's doorframe. In the same motion, she drew a small black pistol with a suppressor attached. "Oh well," she announced, sounding bored, "there's always the next one."

I stilled, the .22-caliber pistol's narrow barrel aimed at me before I truly registered it in her hand. Far too late to act.

My mind raced, but I kept my features smooth, the panic buried deep within my chest. What would get me out of this? The driver had locked the doors, and I could not escape—the limo or the bullet. Funny, the vehicle had seemed so roomy a moment ago. I couldn't risk anything physical, then.

Could I stall her? Yes, of course I could. If she truly wanted me dead, I'd already have a hole in my forehead. I avoided eyeing the gun. It was like having a live serpent in my lap but ignoring it as it slithered its way around my throat, its forked tongue tickling my cheek.

It was a threat. One she might well follow through on, but I wasn't dead yet. She still wanted something.

I deliberately tipped the rest of the champagne into my mouth, savoring the bubbly taste. When I lowered the glass, I thought I saw the trace of a smile on her lips.

Don't look at the gun. Don't look at the gun.

I mirrored her sigh from earlier, adopting a disappointed expression. "Really?" *Don't look at the gun!* "What, haven't met your murder quota for the month of March?"

She let out a tinkling laugh. "That's better. Perhaps the misstep was mine." She waved the gun slightly. I *just* managed not to watch the movement. "I'd forgotten that subtlety is wasted on the young." She indicated her gun, but I kept my gaze rooted on hers. "I should have resorted to something more direct from the beginning."

Without taking my eyes from hers, I grasped the champagne bottle by its neck and poured myself another small serving. "You want me to ask you how you found me on the side of the street in New York City," I told her, careful not to make it into a question. With every word I spoke, I half expected to hear the crack of the gun. I couldn't risk a glance to see if the safety was off or if her finger hovered over the trigger. My instincts told me I already knew the answer to both of those questions.

Morrigan pursed her lips. "No." I tensed, barely able to breathe, but forced myself to relax. "I want you to already know the answer to that question."

What did she want? Why had she sent me to New York? Why had she given me the address to find my impostor, only to have laid a trap? *Wait.* The question I'd been asking myself in the shower earlier resurfaced. How had she known I would run into Trish there, if it wasn't Trish's apartment? I had chosen a random time, delayed my visit, but still crossed paths with Trish. How had Morrigan accounted for that? And if she didn't know Caden, how had she found me on the street outside his family's clinic?

My thoughts traced back to Caden's words in front of the sculpture. Coincidences and conveniences. Reality itself bending around me. Could Caden, of all people, have nudged me onto the path I needed now, with Morrigan?

That would be one hell of a convenience, wouldn't it?

I shrugged from my forcibly relaxed position. "You expect me to identify the pattern in the coincidences I've experienced in the last few days."

Because I was watching her eyes instead of that damnable gun, I caught the flicker of surprised approval before she masked it. "Finally, a glimmer of intelligence," she said, her tone like a caress. It made my skin crawl. Her fox-like smile widened in delight. "And you haven't so much as *glanced* at the gun. Bravo." She met my eyes, and her expression shifted into something predatory, like a hawk about to swoop on a juicy mouse. "This one's for all the marbles: *Why do I care?*"

We fell together down the mountain in my mind, our civil conversation a masquerade for our sparring. The ground loomed closer, now, but I'd begun to get my footing. If I stuck the landing, we could both walk away to find another mountain. If I didn't... well, I had no illusions as to who would be left broken and bloody on the ground.

I sat forward, ignoring the gun and the threats. Tried instead to surprise her with an earnest response. "I think, if I had that answer, *then* you'd shoot me," I said. "But you can rest easy, comfortable in your superiority." I raised my glass as if toasting her. I let a smile slide onto my face. The cocky one. "I'm only on day five. I'll have you figured out by the end of the week."

Morrigan considered me, gun poised in her gloved hand. She looked like she was mulling over my words, tasting them, savoring them like a fine vintage. "We are bound, you and I. Destiny has pulled us together more times than either of us can remember, Emery. Why do you suppose that is?"

I sat back. "Because there's no such thing as Justice incarnate?"

I recoiled as the gun went off and the side of my face was sprayed with liquid and glass shards. My heart lurched. She'd shot me.

No, not me. The champagne flute I'd been holding was now a glass stem ending in a ragged stump.

"Don't be trite," she said, her face unperturbed, no more bothered than if she'd swatted a puppy on the nose with a rolled-up newspaper.

Her words were muffled, nearly inaudible. "Silencers" are not like they are portrayed on TV. They suppress the sound from the level of, well, a gunshot to the level of a rock concert. Instead of a *crack,* the shot makes a sort of *click-phtt* sound. You know, if that sound were made directly into a microphone whose speaker was located inside your ear.

Remembering to breathe, I plucked a linen cloth from limousine's bar and wiped my face dry. I was relieved to see the cloth did not come away bloody—I had feared some glass might have caused damage I didn't immediately feel.

Morrigan continued, "Whether or not you yet realize it, our stories are entwined, our fates meaningless without each other's existence." I kept the skepticism from my face. It wasn't hard. After relating my lengthy connection with Morrigan to Caden and Rachelle, I felt her words too keenly. That made me angry, but I kept that, too, from my face. "All that I have achieved in your absence—and I assure you, I have a staggering tower of accomplishments"—she gestured with the gun as if the limousine were evidence of her claims—"is hollow compared to our last meeting. Much to my chagrin, I find myself eagerly anticipating our next meeting, our next dance. I've searched for years, Emery, to find out why that is."

My curse? I swallowed my response. I felt the limousine pulling over, but I dared not glance away to see where we'd arrived—at the Starboard or somewhere else, a destination of her choosing.

Morrigan set the gun down in her lap and, for a brief moment, I considered lunging for it. I could snatch it up and continue this discussion in a thousand and one days, but I hesitated. Do not misunderstand—I *would* kill her; I would pull that trigger in a heartbeat. I am not a saint, not the hero Caden saw in me. I wasn't afraid or unwilling to end her life; I'd done so before. Survival of the fittest. But killing her now would only defer my troubles for a thousand and one days. Then she'd be back, unknown to me and scheming, and I would have no idea what she would look like, who she might be. Better the enemy I knew. Besides, putting her away in prison would buy me years or even a lifetime of peace. I'd done that before, too.

She withdrew a folded sheet of paper and a needle from some hidden pocket in her dress. "I have decided to bestow upon you a parting gift," she announced. She held up the sheet of paper in one hand—a map of New York, I realized—and the needle in the other. She closed her eyes. I had to give her credit for arrogance. The gun sitting in her lap, me a few feet away, and she closed her eyes. She waved the map in the air theatrically, then flourished the needle. What was she doing? With eyes still closed, she pricked a random spot on the map. Then another. Then *another*. Her gloved hand blurred as she punched hole after hole in the map, all around the city of New York.

At last, she put the needle away and opened her eyes. Holding the map as one might a treasured artifact, she presented it to me.

I frowned. "What is this?"

"Proof. When you're ready for it." She waved the map in front of me, impatient, and I plucked it from her, my eyebrows drawing downward. I hated leaving Morrigan when I couldn't see the shape of her plans. Which, I imagined, was the reason for her arcane theatrics.

"Choose one, Emery. It matters not which." Her scarlet lips quirked. "You'll agree I could hardly set a snare at every location, chosen at random?" I did, but somehow I knew I'd still end up in her trap. "When next we meet, I expect you to better answer my question." She leaned forward as my door opened, Polite Ape dutifully holding it for me. "We need one another, Emery. I would have you learn *why*."

I left the limo, half tensing for a bullet in the back. The crisp air felt unreal, like I'd emerged from the dungeons of hell alive, if not triumphant. The limo peeled away, leaving me holding a punctured map. Riddles and unasked questions swirled around me but never quite landed, my concentration too scattered to form coherent thoughts.

The entrance to the Starboard awaited me like the arms of a mom and, in that moment, seemed to me like the gates of heaven.

I sat on the stairs leading up to the entrance of the Starboard Hotel, taking some time to recover from my encounter with Morrigan. The puzzle pieces were beginning to tumble into place, even while other mysteries eluded my grasp. My death in the Saudi Arabian desert, the Yeti-slash-Wookiee, my murderer, the Watchman finding me and leading me to Kolby's treasure, Ahedrian, Zelda, Iris, the Headless Horseman, the timing of the beheading in the parking garage, the timing of running into Trish in the apartment, the timing of Caden's suggestions about me, the timing of Morrigan's limousine pulling up. The timing, the timing, the *timing*. Was Caden right? Was it evidence that my incarnation had nothing to do with hunting monsters? That I was something different? *Something better,* he had said.

A van stopped in front of the hotel.

There were fragments of the bigger picture at my very feet, begging me to pick them up and start to string them together. Mysteries wrapped within mysteries—but the answers crept tantalizingly nearer, if only I expanded my mind to locate the one missing piece. The spider at the center of the web, the person whose strands connected everything. I needed to find the Queen of Hearts.

I needed help. To see an angle I hadn't considered, an angle that eluded Rachelle, Caden, and me. But who could provide that help?

Raised voices sounded from the back of the van.

"—don't care, Gustav. It's taken me months to get this interview." I frowned. Did that voice sound familiar?

The reply—presumably from Gustav—was lower in volume, but it sounded mollifying. I peered over the balustrade to get a better look at the van. Its side read "NYBC News."

"Oh, for heaven's sake, it's a four-star hotel. What's going to happen to me here?" I grinned as I placed the woman's voice.

"But Sabrina," Gustav countered, their voices coming nearer as they made their way around the van and toward the hotel entrance. "Between your place and the report from this afternoon, it just isn't safe."

I jumped up from my perch and headed down the stairs as the two came into view. Sabrina was lugging a heavy suitcase and fighting with two other bulky bags. The man with her, Gustav, had his hands full with video equipment *and* another couple of bags that matched Sabrina's set. Damn. Gustav tossed the van's keys to a valet and hurried after Sabrina, who hadn't stopped to wait for him.

"Safe?" Sabrina was saying. "There's more security on that island than all of Manhattan." Two bellhops were trailing after her, trying to offer their assistance, but they obviously did not want to interrupt.

She looked up at me and started. Recognition flashed in her eyes and, despite her ongoing argument, she managed a smile. "Hey! It's..." She hesitated, then seemed to remember. "Emery, right? Loophole?" She looked down at her burden. "Give a girl a hand?"

I laughed, stepping forward and nodding to the bellhops to indicate that I'd help her. They slipped away as she hefted a weighty bag into my arms. "Umph," I said, "when you 'go the extra mile,' you don't pack light."

She shook her curls, abruptly looking exhausted. "What can I say? It's been a long day."

Gustav, a flat-nosed man who looked too young for his receding hairline, pushed past us and called back over his shoulder, "It'll be a long night, too, if we don't get you checked in."

I relieved her of the second bag, too. "The news never sleeps, right?"

She threw me an appreciative smile. "Amen to that, kid." She took in my stained shirt. "Rough day for you, too?"

I shrugged, an impressive feat given the weight of her bags. "You could say that."

We walked into the Starboard, and I hung back while they checked in. Gustav, not content to let his objections wait, argued with her quietly as they stood in line. I caught snippets of their conversation, but not much. Something about an island, Gustav needing a raise, and Sabrina being unwilling to budge from whatever stance she'd taken. My ears perked up when I heard them say "Ahedrian."

It reminded me I needed to talk to her and try to buy some time to deal with the Queen of Hearts. After all, an incarnate could only be born if the urban legend continued to spread. If I could convince Sabrina to stop, or at least slow, her reports on Ahedrian, my murderer might panic, do something rash or sloppy. Maybe even reveal themselves.

Or, equally beneficial, it might panic Morrigan, unraveling her carefully laid plans.

Sabrina was a reporter, and a damn good one. Given my history as a journalist, I could tell. More than that, Sabrina and her crew had come through for me: when Rachelle called her to watch over the site in Harlem, she'd stayed there all night. She'd saved a life. Maybe I could convince her to help me one more time.

Besides, her van had pulled up right when I'd been thinking I needed help, right? Coincidence *and* convenience. Caden would be proud.

Sabrina received her room assignment and keycard, and I helped her haul her things up to the fifth floor. Two floors below mine. Sabrina and Gustav acted like lovers at the end of a long fight. He stood with his jaw clenched, all huffy silence, while she covered her annoyance by trying too hard to seem cheery with me. It made for an uncomfortable elevator ride.

I thought about cutting the tension by asking what she was doing at the hotel but decided against it. With the strange energy in the air between her and Gustav, I didn't want to press my luck.

Fortunately, Sabrina broke the silence. "I meant to thank you for the lead the other evening," she said to me. "You and your friend Rachelle make quite the team. Ever consider going into journalism?"

"A time or two," I replied with a grin. "My blog reaches quite an audience, but nowhere near as many people as you do."

She regarded me critically. "You've got the right attitude for it, that's for sure. Don't get into the business for the paycheck, though." She laughed and poked Gustav with her elbow.

Despite his obvious irritation, Gustav let out a chuckle. "You get paid more than the cameraman."

I laughed, too. "I'll need to get that in writing, otherwise Rachelle will never believe me."

The elevator stopped and we exited, carrying our heavy load the short distance to her room. "Come in and set that down anywhere," she said when we got there.

Her room was, unsurprisingly, nearly identical to mine, but with a single king-sized bed instead of two smaller ones. The nautical theme and the porthole windows were beginning to feel more like home to me than Seattle.

I set down the bags at the base of her bed. "I'll let you unpack and turn in," I said, "but I did have a favor to ask of you before I go."

"Oh?"

I looked back and forth between her and Gustav. "I know it's a big ask, but I was hoping you could stop reporting on Ahedrian."

Her eyebrows shot up, and she put her hands on her hips. "Why would you want that? And why would I agree to stop reporting on the thing that's given my career a much-needed face-lift?"

While they'd been arguing in line downstairs, I had carefully crafted the lie I thought had the greatest chance of convincing her. I opened my mouth, but Gustav cut me off, throwing up his hands.

"Because it's *dangerous,* Sabrina! If we keep this up, we'll end up in the headlines... but for all the wrong reasons!" He jabbed his hand sharply in my direction. "Take this as a sign, huh?"

She shook her head and rubbed her temple, then directed her reply at me. "You won't get anywhere in life if you don't take risks, kid. This Ahedrian business is terrible. But for field reporters like me? Investigative journalists? This is striking it rich." She turned to Gustav. "We can't call it quits now. We're one report away from the biggest story of our lives."

I considered. "One report away? Would you stop after that?" I asked. I quickly added, "Just for a few days."

She frowned. "What's happening in a few days?"

Time for the lie. "Rachelle and I received an anonymous letter," I told her. "Claiming to know where the next murders will take place."

Her cynical look said she wasn't buying it, but I saw something else flicker behind her eyes. Was that interest I spied? "I shouldn't be telling you this," I said, "but we want to work with the police. Set up a few traps. And," I let her see eagerness creep into my expression, "catch it on film for my blog."

She snorted. "The cops will never let you that close." I saw a gleam in her eye, though. She wasn't hooked, but she was nibbling on my bait.

"Oh." I wilted, then brightened, as though a thought had just occurred to me. "Well, maybe *you* could help me, then?"

Sabrina began unpacking her clothes and sliding them into drawers next to the bed. "I hate to break it to you, but it's just someone messing with you, Emery."

"But what if it's not?" I pressed, pulling Morrigan's folded map out of my back pocket and gesturing with it. "You give me, say, three days, to investigate it on my own. You stop airing anything about Ahedrian. If I haven't found anything in three days, I'll give you the map. You can have the whole story. I'll go back to Seattle."

She laughed, but not unkindly. And I could tell she was stalling, putting another pair of folded jeans in a drawer. Then she straightened and turned to me. "Two conditions," she said. "First, we already

Incarnate

Incarnate | 225

have a big story slated for tomorrow. The three days start after that. And second, you let me see the map first, to make sure it's not a waste of my time."

I hesitated. I dismissed her first condition without concern. At this point, a single story wasn't going to be the tipping point for creating an incarnate. Urban legends needed to grow over hundreds of retellings. And the three days would buy me time I didn't currently have. Time to find the Queen of Hearts. Time to unveil Morrigan's plans. Time to make the murderer panic that their story wasn't being told. What was that I had been thinking on the stairs outside? Timing, timing, *timing*.

The second condition worried me, though. I guessed that several of the locations marked with punctures would be duds. Morrigan had poked a lot of holes, seemingly at random. On its own, without the background I had... it was a map of New York with holes in it. Something a toddler could do by accident.

"Deal," I decided, giving her my cocky grin. "You drive a hard bargain, Sabrina Miles."

"Funny," she said as she walked toward me, eyeing the map, "I was just about to say the same thing to you, Emery Luple."

My pulse raced as she moved in to inspect the map. *Please let this work, please let this work.* "No pictures," I said lightly.

She took the map in her hands and held it up, letting the light shine through the pinholes. Gustav walked closer and poked his head over her shoulder. He seemed to hold his breath while Sabrina came to a decision. I wasn't sure what she was looking for, but after a moment she gave a grunt and handed the map back to me. "This better not be some trick," she said with a disbelieving laugh, like she could not believe she had brokered this deal.

"It's not," I told her. I didn't even feel guilty. My lie could save lives and afford me the chance I needed to catch up with my killer.

I left her room a few moments later, exulting at the fact that, finally, I had won an exchange today.

Formal Incarnate Lesson Six: Intersection of Gender and Reincarnation
By Emery Luple

*C*lass, today we are going to learn about incarnates and gender. A controversial topic, at times. Before we begin, I'd like to make a disclaimer: I may have different views than you, and that's okay. You're only human... probably.

There are two types of incarnates when it comes to gender. No, not male and female. The division is between those incarnates who are locked to a certain gender and those who are not. Those locked to a certain gender are rarer than those who are not and include some pretty famous examples. The Santa Claus incarnate, the Mermaid, Dracula, and the Queen of Hearts always reincarnate as the same sex, the concept of gender more or less built into their identity. One reason for this is that their identity—such as that of Kris Kringle or Saint Nicholas—is an important distinction in recognizing the incarnate. Another reason is that their very title—like Mermaid or Queen of Hearts—is not a gender-neutral word.

The vast majority of incarnates, however, reincarnate across the spectrum of genders. Like me. Each time I reincarnate, everything about my identity may change. Some aspects of my personality persist, it's true; I'm

almost always witty, perceptive, brilliant, attractive, and humble. And I like
cheese. Heaven and Hell have mercy on your soul if I reincarnate lactose
intolerant.

Some incarnates may surprise you with their gender variability. The
Knight in Shining Armor, the Fairy, the Valkyrie, and the Leprechaun are
just a few incarnates that may reincarnate as any gender, even though
most people have a predetermined notion of how they should appear.

Important note! The so-called gender-locked incarnates may simply
have a strong bias toward one gender type. We all thought the Tooth Fairy
always reincarnated as a woman until an incarnation ago, when he rein-
carnated as a man. So I wouldn't rule anything out; we're learning more
about gender every day. Oh, and as a side note, I'm pretty sure that's what
inspired Dwayne Johnson to star as the Tooth Fairy. I can't say for certain,
but the timing is suspicious.

RACHELLE LOOKED up from her phone as I entered our room, a flash of
annoyance flitting across her face. "About time. I was beginning to
think Caden lived in another state."

"Sorry," I said. "I ran into some... friends."

I removed my champagne-stained shirt—it was stiff where the
liquid had splashed and then dried—and replaced it with a plain
white tee. Rachelle watched me furtively, but when I caught her looking, she quickly turned to her phone.

I refreshed myself in the bathroom, washing my face to get rid of
the champagne smell. I refused to take a *third* shower. The conversation with Morrigan replayed in my head. It had been so long since I'd
seen her—until this incarnation, that is—that I had forgotten: this
was a ritual of mine after an encounter with her. I would revisit our
conversation a thousand times, finding nuances I'd missed before,
generating witty comebacks and snappy one-liners I should have said
in the moment. I would consider every angle of her words, searching
for unspoken meanings and testing the outline of her plans. If I didn't
know what her schemes were, I couldn't hope to counter them.

That wasn't entirely true, I realized. I could leave New York, fly back to Seattle, and wash my hands of this whole mystery. That would undoubtedly sever the noose Morrigan was trying to slip over my neck.

But I couldn't do it. Leave people to die? How could I abandon the mortals of New York City to fend for themselves against an incarnate they knew nothing about? Especially when I knew, deep down, that I had the power to stop it?

I scrubbed at my face.

I could stop it. I realized the truth of that statement. But did having the power to stop something evil obligate me to step up? To fight it? Why did *I* need to be the one to right the wrong?

Damn it all, was Caden right? *Was* I the Hero incarnate?

Or did I just *want* to be? Maybe it wasn't my incarnation but instead my fatal flaw. Morrigan had exploited my hero complex before. Hell, she was exploiting it now, wasn't she? She'd sent me to New York, knowing that even my desire to oppose her plans would not be enough to dissuade me from coming here to save the day.

I splashed water on my face, rinsing away the soap.

No, Caden was right: anyone could be a hero. I was not destined to be *the* Hero. Likely no one was. Heroism was too colossal of a concept to incarnate, too common to be an urban legend. Heroes weren't fictitious, some myth or legend. They were all around us.

Which led to another, equally profound, conclusion. I could walk away from this, choose the selfish path—the safe path—and someone else would step up. Maybe Trish. Maybe someone I had never met. But the fact that I would not walk away meant that, while I was not the Hero, I was still capable of being one. Of doing the right thing for its own sake. A hero, not born or destined, but *made*, choice by choice.

That was enough for me. The responsibility exacted a toll, as Caden had noted. It made me predictable, easily exploited by the likes of Morrigan. I wouldn't always be able to do the right thing. Which was another reason why it was important I do so when I could. Like now.

I looked up into the mirror, water droplets dribbling from my chin, and said, "Looking good, you beamish boy." I chuckled and dried my face on the towel. "Thanks, looking glass," I told it, my voice muffled by the cloth, "but I already figured you out."

I walked out into the room and sat down next to Rachelle, careful not to bump her leg. "Thanks for coming to New York with me. I feel kind of mean for not saying that before now."

She looked at me in surprise, and color rose in her cheeks. "Don't be silly. You'd be lost without me." She looked at her phone again. It looked like she was perusing a social media site. "But thanks," she mumbled. "I just wish I could do more to help. This busted leg sucks."

"Is it painful?"

She hesitated, then shook her head. "No. Not really. The docs gave me meds, but I haven't taken them." She lifted the cast and let it drop back to the bed. "I thought it would. The night it happened, it hurt just lying there. It's only been two days, but it doesn't even hurt when I move around." She grimaced. "Big inconvenience, though. And going to the bathroom is the *worst*."

I grinned at her. "Well, don't heal too fast, or we won't be able to get sympathy seats on our flight back."

She rolled her eyes. "Oh, gee, I hope my quick recovery doesn't mess things up."

"I think," I said slowly, "maybe you are recovering quickly because I'm going to need you soon."

"Oh yeah?"

"Maybe." I squirmed. "I'm beginning to believe that reality bending around me might be part of my incarnation."

She frowned. "That's... conceited." She flushed but didn't apologize. "What I mean is, what makes you think reality is bending around you?"

"It's not my theory," I said defensively. "Caden mentioned it first. Then Morrigan."

Her eyes widened. "Morrigan? She's here?"

"Unfortunately. I ran into her on my way back to the hotel." I

230 | JUSTIN SCHUELKE

quickly told her what happened, doing my best to relate the conversation exactly as it had occurred. Rachelle listened attentively, only asking a clarifying question once or twice.

She rested her hand on my arm when I finished. "I'm sorry, Emery. That sounds intense." She met my eyes, then pulled her hand away, her cheeks rewarming. I sighed. I needed to deal with her feelings, now, before I hurt her more.

I hesitated, though. The conversation would require a delicate approach. It wasn't that Rachelle was some dainty snowflake who would crumble at the slightest touch. It was quite the opposite, really. She was a warrior, strong and brave, but her feelings for me were a chink in her armor. If I stabbed her there, the wound could bring down my courageous friend. Sitting there on the bed with her, thinking of her fighting spirit, I realized I loved her; it just wasn't the kind of love she hoped for.

"Rachelle," I began.

"Show me," she said, cutting me off.

I blinked. "Show you what?"

"The reality thing. Show me."

I stared at her, dismayed. I was trying to come up with words for what I needed to tell her, and she was asking for magic tricks? It was like trying to pin down a hummingbird with a dart. Eww, that's a terrible metaphor. Please don't try that. "How?" I shook my head. "I don't think it works that way. It isn't deliberate, it... it happens *to* me."

She gave me a flat look. "That's convenient."

I returned her expression. "That's the point."

"It can't be that hard. Just"—she shrugged—"guess the number I'm thinking or something."

"Twelve?"

Rachelle's eyes went comically round. "That was the *exact* number I was thinking!" Her eyes gleamed. "It must be *fate*, Emery."

It was my turn to roll my eyes. "Oh, ha ha." I considered for a few moments. "Okay, I have an idea."

I pulled out the map Morrigan had given me and flattened it on the bed. She watched me with thinly veiled amusement. I closed my eyes and jabbed my finger down at the map. I'm sure I looked like a fool.

"You look like a fool," Rachelle said. "But let's see it."

I opened my eyes and looked down. Lifted my finger. It was on a hole, which half surprised me. The hole marked Rikers Island, the famous New York prison. I waited. I'm not entirely sure what I was expecting: a thunderclap? An epiphany? Maybe my phone would start ringing and the warden would be calling me.

After a moment, I sighed, and Rachelle whistled. "Impressive." Her eyes met my frustrated ones, and her expression softened. "It's okay, Emery. I believe you." She gestured to the map. "Want to try again?"

"I think I've made a big enough fool of myself, thanks."

She laughed and placed her hand on my shoulder. "Well, while you're already at it, you've been wanting to tell me something I don't want to hear." She gestured to her leg. "I'm not going anywhere. Might as well tell me now."

I looked at her in surprise. Damn. She knew me so well. Caden, Morrigan, now Rachelle. Even Trish thought she knew me better than I knew myself. Oddly, the idea didn't make me angry. It made me... think. I'd only been alive—this time round, anyway—for a handful of days. My new personality always settled over my immortal one when I reincarnated, but it took time for me to adjust, to become accustomed to it. Even with the lifetime of memories that reality planted in my head, figuring out who I was—and who I wanted to be—was one of those things that kept me feeling human. I was reasonably certain Morrigan didn't go through this crisis of self each time she reincarnated. She didn't need to; she felt immortal, the body and life she received no more or less consequential than a bag of bones wrapped in flesh. A means to an end, like everything with her.

My mind teetering between Rachelle in front of me, my evening with Caden, and my conversation with Morrigan, Morrigan's words came back to me. She had said that I'd been handed everything, this incarnation: youth, brains, physique. She was right, but for the wrong reasons. I *had* been given everything I needed, but it wasn't the physical or mental traits... it was the *people.*

"You already know what I'm going to say, don't you?" I asked.

She bit her lip, then dipped her head. "But I need to hear you say it, I think."

I took her hand in mine. "Rachelle, you mean more to me than you probably know. Yours was the first voice I heard after reincarnating. You were the first person I saw in this lifetime." I smiled at the memory of her calling out my name while I inspected my reflection for the first time; of her walking in, hefting a box too large for her small frame.

She smiled at me, too, but her eyes were guarded. "But?"

I braced myself. "I love you, Rachelle, but I don't have feelings for you." I took a deep breath, saying the words as gently and earnestly as I could. "And I'm sorry, but I don't think I ever will. Not the feelings you want me to have."

Her eyes misted, and her smile diminished but didn't disappear entirely. "I know."

"You are very important to me, though." I thought back to Kolby's house, how she'd boldly strode in behind me, unafraid of the dark. "I value your intelligence, your wit, your courage, and your friendship." She nodded, and a tear ran down her cheek despite her brave smile. She was trying to make this easier on *me*, I realized. I reached up and brushed the tear away. "I'm undeserving of your friendship," I told her.

She rolled her eyes, another tear following the first. "Damn right you are." She let out a half laugh, half sob. "I know I've only known you a couple of days. I *know* that. But it feels like I've been admiring you for years, Emery. How is it possible to have had a crush on you *before you even existed*?" She sounded exasperated, but her shoulders didn't sag and no further tears fell. She was so strong, it hardly seemed fair. I appreciated, even relied on, her strength. She needed someone who could return it.

I leaned forward and gave her a hug, pulling her against my

shoulder. "I don't know," I said, honest and unhelpful. "But if it brought you into my life, it can't be all bad."

She bobbed her head, a little too quickly. "Well, not all bad for *you*," she said into my armpit, but I could hear the smile underpinning her words.

"Not for me," I agreed quietly, holding her tight, comforting her. A full minute passed in near silence, then she wiped her cheeks on my sleeve and sniffled. "You better not blow your nose on my T-shirt," I told her. "I've gone through more clothes in the last two days than in entire *incarnations*."

"You paid money for those rags?" she asked, smiling as she recomposed herself. She pulled back to look at me, and I was surprised to see the undamaged face of the Rachelle I'd come to respect. I wouldn't have judged her if she'd emerged with red patches blotching her cheeks, her nose all puffy and pink. But there was none of that. A few tears, a few jokes, and we were right as rain. I suddenly hated that I'd waited so long to speak with her. I really was undeserving of her.

"I think I'm ready to hear the next part," she said, for some reason sounding stoic.

I started. "The next part?"

She nodded, a small grin pushing through her melancholy. "It's Caden, right? You have feelings for him."

"I..." I paused. I was suddenly aware I hadn't said anything about that out loud. "I... yeah," I stammered. "Yeah, I do." I felt suddenly shy. "How did you know?"

She made a disgusted sound, humor in her eyes. "Because you two are so effing cute, for starters." Her voice turned whimsical. "I saw the way you looked at him, that first time, when he walked into the restaurant. Like he was the only person there." She let out a brief laugh, and there was only a hint of resentment hiding in it. "I studied him from head to toe. I was so confused, wondering if we were looking at the same person."

"I'm sorry," I said, not sure how to respond.

She rolled her eyes. "Don't be." She put her hand over her heart.

234 | JUSTIN SCHUELKE

"We can't choose who we fall head over heels for." She shrugged. "Besides, it makes sense you'd fall for an incarnate."

I was glowing when that last line hit me. "What?" I croaked.

"I'm not offended," she assured me. "I figured it's no different than you falling for a boy instead of a girl."

"You think Caden is an incarnate?" I asked, my words coming from far away.

My world shrank around me. Rachelle blurred as my mind began flickering over memories, thoughts, moments. As my immortal senses sprang awake and alert, I leapt from the bed. I felt something building on the horizon. Something weighty, threatening to bowl me over. I needed to move, and keep moving, or it would knock me on my ass.

"Emery, what's wrong?" Rachelle asked, alarmed, as I paced the floor. "You knew, right?" She suddenly looked less sure. "You had to have known."

My fingers pulled through my hair. Ever since the moment Caden had walked into Los Mares, my immortal senses had been trying to tell me something was amiss. Every time he asked me a question, I spilled everything. I'd thought I was just responding to his openness. But I'd been *compelled* to tell him.

"He's an incarnate," I breathed, stunned.

"God," Rachelle said. "Emery, I'm sorry, I... I thought you knew."

It was so obvious. The signs were everywhere. He'd been in three battles with me, without even a scratch. Without so much as a speck of dirt! Within a day, I had told him about incarnates. Taken him to my contacts. I'd been drawn to him, as if by... by magic.

Glamour. The thought threatened to drop me to my knees. Like the Kobold tricking the owners of his house into thinking he was Kolby, their little boy, Caden had duped me with glamour. That corner of my mind had flared, tried to warn me. But he'd fooled me into telling him everything I knew. And every time I'd grown suspicious, his glamour had smoothed it away. Why? Surely he had memories of his previous lives; why had he deceived me into showing him a world he must have already known about?

I looked at Rachelle's stricken face. "How long have you known?"

She gaped, words coming out, but I wasn't listening.

He had tricked me into developing feelings. And despite all my lifetimes of experience, his glamour had obliterated my caution, and I'd fallen for him.

I slumped down onto my bed, everything collapsing on my shoulders, weighing me down. I couldn't breathe. My chest tightened; my lungs felt made from lead.

Caden was an incarnate.

Caden was an incarnate.

Gears whirled and clicked into place, jarring clockwork that began to answer my questions but left me with so many more. I stared at my hands in helpless horror, suddenly terrified that Morrigan and Caden were working together. It would explain how her limo found me waiting outside of his residence. Explain why Caden hadn't been harmed in the fight with the Genie—he had never been a target. Caden had even been the one to call me, luring me to New York before Morrigan dangled her honeyed trap. *No, no, no.*

I pictured Caden in my mind. I tried, but I couldn't come to see him as anything but beautiful. Our shared smiles, his fresh scent. My head spun, my heart too heavy, tears in my mind unable to find their way to my eyes.

Caden was an incarnate. Was he somehow involved in the murders? During the time he'd been with me, no more murders had taken place. Even when one was scheduled to occur, Caden had been with me all through the night and *no one had died.*

I pictured his face, and I couldn't reconcile it with that of a murderer. I couldn't even begin to shade him evil. He was too pure, earnest, innocent.

But, of course, glamour would make him appear that way, wouldn't it? I grabbed my head. I couldn't bring myself to believe it. Better the murderer was *me* than Caden. Anyone but him.

"Emery!" Rachelle sat on the floor, leg splayed awkwardly as she knelt, her hands gripping my knees. "Talk to me. I don't understand."

"He's an incarnate," I said again, hating that my voice sounded like a whimper.

Her concern threatened to send me back into lightheaded space, but something in my eyes seemed to warn her and her expression hardened. "Yeah, so?"

The challenge in her stare gave me something to focus on. "He duped me," I said, my words still sounding far away.

She threw her hands into the air. "Oh, for the love of..." She trailed off, searching my face. "That's ridiculous."

I blinked, trying to focus. "No, you don't understand." I took a deep, steadying breath. "It's glamour."

Her eyebrows shot up. "Like... Kolby? The thing that makes you go all starry-eyed in front of some incarnates?"

Exactly. "I've been such a fool." I heard the defeat in my voice and tried to amend it. "Glamour is a spell. Incarnates use it in different ways—Kolby used it to hide, to appear meek and needful of help. But the Siren incarnate, for example, uses glamour to appear beautiful and lure unwitting men into her snare."

Rachelle gave me a flat look. "And you think Caden is the Siren?"

"No, of course not. But he duped me completely."

"Really?" she said, deadpan. "*Caden?*"

I blinked at her. What was she getting at?

She hit me upside the head, and I flinched, surprised into speechlessness. "You really are a fool if you think Caden duped you. If you think he's even capable of it." I stared at her uncomprehendingly. "I don't know much about incarnates, Emery, but if I had to pick one out for Caden?" She tucked a strand of hair behind her ear. "He might as well be *Goodness* incarnate."

"I..." I measured her words with as much rationality as I could muster, which admittedly wasn't much. I wanted so badly to believe her, but what if I was deceiving myself? "That's what his glamour is for," I objected weakly. "It makes you think things like that."

She levered herself back onto her bed, facing me, her lips compressed into a thin line. "And is his glamour affecting me now?"

I hesitated. "Well, no, probably not." I knew I had to be careful. I couldn't just let her convince me of what I wanted to believe.

But Caden *had* saved me from the Alligator, and then later, the Genie. My terrified conviction gave way to introspection. Caden had been with me when we'd found "Ahedrian" written in the park. He clearly could not have snuck away to inscribe it. He had called me to come to New York to join him in *catching* the murderer. While an arrogant murderer might do such a thing, Caden didn't strike me as arrogant—he was modest, humble even, his face eager and bright. I loved the way the light always caught in his golden hair...

I shook my head to clear it. Lousy glamour.

"It's still affecting *me*," I muttered.

Rachelle's brow furrowed in confusion, then cleared with a knowing look. I could practically see the spark of her humor conflict with her desire to be compassionate. "Oh, Emery." She put her hand over her mouth, and I didn't know whether it was to smother a smile or a frown. "You have lived lifetimes, and yet you're just as clueless as any human." I opened my mouth to protest, but she cut me off. "No, it's okay. It's... cute." She leaned forward. "Picture Caden, right now, and tell me what you see."

I almost sulked instead, but I didn't like the mental image of myself sulking. I did as instructed. "I see his glamour," I replied sourly. "From the moment I met him at the restaurant, I was drawn to him."

"I wasn't."

I paused. That's right. She'd said she had examined Caden, trying to figure out if we were looking at the same person. But... "That doesn't make any sense."

Rachelle's smile had turned smug. "What if *I* said it?" She affected a moonstruck expression, her voice mockingly wistful. "'From the moment I met him at the restaurant, I was drawn to him.'" She rolled her eyes. "Take away the glamour, Emery. With what affliction would you diagnose a silly mortal like me?"

Infatuation. Attraction. A crush.

It *wasn't* glamour. It was a spell far older. More powerful, more mysterious. It wasn't supernatural... it was the most natural thing in the world. Caden hadn't deceived me into falling for him. I'd fallen for him and then deceived myself. The corner of my mind where immortal Emery slept had tried to wake up and warn me that he was an incarnate, but I'd refused. I hadn't been confused by Caden's glamour, though, but by the magnetism between us and my own growing feelings.

There *was* glamour there. I saw that clearly now. It kept Caden's incarnation hidden, maintained the illusion that he was a regular guy. Changed the way the light played over him so it looked closer to natural, so others rationalized it away. Made him appear worthy of trust, playing on those around him, encouraging the truth from their lips. But, I realized, I had already wanted to share the truth with him. Maybe I could have resisted the glamour alone. But it wasn't just the glamour that attracted me. It was Caden himself.

I felt like my world had come crashing down around me, and now I'd grabbed all the pieces and flung them back up, held together by grit, hope, and still-drying glue. It was fragile. If I thought too hard, I feared it would all fall apart again. I groaned and slumped backward on the bed.

A moment later, the bed jumped as Rachelle plopped down next to me. "It's okay," she said, like she was talking to a toddler. She patted my head. "Anyone can get lovesick."

I swatted her hand away. "You really think so?" I asked. My voice sounded vulnerable, but I could feel my confidence growing, the glue drying. My world was going to be okay.

"Of course. Caden's cute, but he's *so* not my type. I think, if it was glamour, then he'd *become* my type, right?"

"That's... surprisingly wise."

"I'm going to ignore the 'surprisingly' part." She threw a piece of cloth at my face. The shirt I'd been wearing, I realized. "Now go wash this so you can wear it again tomorrow for Caden, and I'll *consider* not telling him about this meltdown of yours."

I groaned again. "You wouldn't dare."

"Hell hath no fury like a woman scorned, Emery." I cringed, and she laughed. "Nah, I wouldn't do that." She nudged me. "Now go! Before I change my mind."

I gathered our dirty things and fled to the hotel's laundry room, my head crammed to bursting with thoughts. Caden was an incarnate. But then, if he wasn't deceiving me, why hadn't he told me about himself? The answer was obvious: he didn't know.

Which was impossible. He'd have memories of his previous incarnations. He'd confided in me that he'd always felt connected to the supernatural, that his dreams overflowed with it. Was he dreaming of past lives?

The answer dawned on me as I sat there, listening to the washing machine churning. I remembered his story about the baby dropped on the doorstep of the convent. It explained everything, even though Caden didn't know it.

Incarnates recalled more and more of their past lives as they aged. Being reincarnated into an older body helped, too. But Caden had reincarnated as a baby, all memories of his previous lives obliterated by a whim of fate—or whatever entity dictated our reincarnations. He would recover those experiences, slowly, as he aged. No wonder his dreams were haunted by the supernatural. His subconscious must be working double time trying to funnel memories into his mind. But every morning when he awoke, the all-too-mortal world around him convinced him his dreams were nothing but figments of his imagination. Then I'd come along and shown him an entirely new world, filled with possibilities he'd literally dreamed of but never believed real.

I was suddenly ashamed of having imagined Caden was deceiving me. He was a lost incarnate, unable to remember the truth about who he was, always questing for answers. His search had drawn him to me from across the country.

The next logical question was, which incarnate was he?

He personified goodness, Rachelle had said. I was inclined to agree. He was innocent, clean and pure. His reflexes were sharp; he'd turned and faced the Headless Horseman faster than I had. He had rescued me multiple times in our skirmishes with the Alligator in the Sewers and the Genie. His compassion had helped me confront two lifetimes of pain. Swept me off my feet and extinguished the guilt that burned hot within me.

Damn. Was *he* the Hero incarnate?

I rubbed my eyes wearily, throwing the wet garments into the industrial-sized dryer. I needed sleep. I needed to figure everything out. I would see Caden in the morning, but suddenly that seemed so far away. I wanted to tell him everything, to see his face light up when I told him he was an incarnate, like me.

I suddenly realized the implications of that. I'd never fallen for an incarnate before. We could... I swallowed. Theoretically, we could spend not just one but multiple lifetimes together. Like the Prince and the Princess, we could find each other time and time again. The thought brought a smile to my face, even though I cautioned myself about jumping ahead. This was just a crush, right? Life was not a fairy tale. The Prince and the Princess got to live happily ever after with each incarnation, but that wasn't written into *my* story. Telling myself that did not keep me from feeling a little giddy.

My thoughts turned to the Monster Hunter. Trish had claimed, in no uncertain terms, that everything I believed about my incarnation was based on one false premise: that I was the Monster Hunter incarnate. Caden seemed to agree with her; he saw me more as... the Destined One, fated to be where I was supposed to be, precisely when I was supposed to be there. Morrigan's words led me to believe Caden was on the right track, that somehow fate was a tangible force guiding my hand. It was important to Morrigan, for some reason, that I discover my personification. If I was not the Monster Hunter, did that make her not the Monster? Could that be why it was so important to her? I doubted it. I thought she would be honored to be the Monster incarnate.

Hell, how could I ever expect to figure out Caden's incarnation if I couldn't even identify my own?

I stewed in my thoughts for some time before taking the clean clothes and returning to the room. It was nearing midnight, and I was exhausted. I hadn't even slept in a bed last night. I folded the laundry while waiting for Rachelle to finish in the bathroom so I could brush my teeth. With her leg, she couldn't move very quickly, so I stretched out on the bed to wait.

I must have fallen asleep, because I dreamed.

I was on a precipice. Far below me, hungry, blue-black waves crashed against the face of the cliff. My two most recent incarnations stood inland from me, their backs toward me, only recognizable because it was a dream. They stood with arms clasped, separating me from whatever lay beyond them. They faced...

Scores of dead, accusing eyes, intermixed with smoking guns, mocking laughter, and the wails of a little girl—somehow all my fears and feelings from that tragedy pressed against my two most recent incarnations. They tried to push back, to keep those haunting images from overwhelming me and driving me over the cliff.

Those two incarnations turned and screamed at me over their shoulders. *Be smart! Be terrified.* I looked back out over the ocean behind me and so far below, swirling with eldritch shadows in its depths. It *was* terrifying. A long plummet into unknown waters eager to swallow me.

The incarnations warred with the dreadful memories, the full weight of the tragedy held at bay by the two Emerys with interlocked arms. Over their shouts of defiance, though, I heard a voice coming from the sea behind me.

"—putting... faith in me...

"—find... strength... save again... love again...

"—a good person..."

I wasn't alone. A feeling of confidence cut through the uncertainty and began building my resolve. I turned and looked down. The water wasn't deep, terrifying, or blue-black.

It was seafoam green.

The last two versions of Emery Luple had died alone, unhappy and unloved. I'd lived two—admittedly short—lives terrified, haunted by the eyes of a dead man. Two lives spurning the company of mortals, living in isolating cold for fear of the flame. I took a step forward and placed a hand on each of those incarnations' shoulders, thanking them for their sacrifice. Then I pulled them backward and over the cliff's edge with me.

We didn't fall. The air rushing around us, welcoming waves rising to meet us, excited to share in our freedom, we *flew*. The two incarnations with me broke into smiles, twin expressions of fear evaporating in the sky.

Even in the depths of a dream, I felt a peace I hadn't experienced in some time—coupled with a sense of triumph.

When I awoke, light was streaming through the drawn curtains of our room. It was wan and pale, the first rays of dawn. I dozed for a while longer, nonsensical dreams drifting through my consciousness like balloons at a parade. An hour—maybe two—later, I finally yawned, stretched, and decided I needed to get up before Caden came knocking. I grinned at the thought. I couldn't wait to see him again.

I slipped into the shower, mentally preparing for the day ahead. I would start it off by revealing to Caden that he was an incarnate. Maybe treat him to the hotel buffet before breaking it to him gently. Hmm. I owed him something better, though, didn't I? Maybe I'd need to look at cafes nearby. Afterward, Rachelle, Caden, and I needed to strategize. We had more information and Morrigan's map. We could split up, check out as many destinations as possible. I frowned. Rachelle wouldn't be able to contribute much in that regard. I briefly wondered if I might be able to find and recruit Trish. She wanted this murderer caught almost as badly as we did. I just needed a way to get in touch with her.

As I put on my clean clothes, the morning light brightened my spirits. Rachelle awoke and turned on the news while I opened the curtains to let in the sun. There wasn't much of it, to be honest. The day was gray and overcast with the threat of rain hanging in the air. I didn't mind—for a Seattleite, this kind of weather was like a familiar, comfortable blanket.

"Yesterday," the news anchor reported in a rich baritone, "an NYBC News field reporter, Sabrina Miles, was the target of a malicious attack."

Rachelle and I exchanged startled glances. The headline for the story read **"LOCAL NEWS REPORTER VICTIM OF ARSON."**

I froze as I took in the accompanying image: the same apartment Caden and I had been to yesterday. Where the Genie had been waiting to ambush us.

"Turn it up," I said quickly.

A bushy-mustached anchor with salt-and-pepper hair was speaking into the camera. "Good morning, New York, and welcome back to the morning news. Yesterday, calamity hit even closer to home than usual, as a member of this very news team became the victim of arson. The fire department's initial findings determined the blaze was set deliberately, though the full details remain undisclosed at this time. The Chelsea apartment belongs to NYBC News's own Sabrina Miles."

My heart was pounding. I met Rachelle's gaze. "What are the chances of that?" she asked me quietly.

Coincidence. Again.

"Sabrina was fortunately not at home when the arsonist struck," the newscaster continued, photos of Sabrina playing across the screen, "and vows the attack only strengthens her conviction to uncover the mystery of the so-called Ahedrian murders. As many of you know, Sabrina has been the first reporter present at many of the decapitation crime scenes, relentless in her pursuit of justice for the victims' families."

Something was wrong, like black clouds darkening the sky, portending a storm. The anchor went on, somber, his deep voice filling our hotel room. "We are a family here at NYBC News, and an attack on one of us is an attack on all of us. We've launched our own investigation into the apartment fire. And our editors have put together this tribute collage of Sabrina's career to show our support. Sabrina, this time we are going the extra mile for *you*."

A montage began playing, a timeline of Sabrina's career, old news reports and cases showcasing her achievements before and during her tenure at NYBC News.

"What does this mean?" Rachelle whispered.

"It explains why she's at the hotel," I said, while my mind raced through the implications. "But there's more to it than that."

Morrigan had sent us to that apartment. The Genie had been lying in ambush, waiting for us to arrive.

The tribute was ending with Sabrina Miles signing off from various locations.

"From Albany, New York..." The image changed. "Wichita, Kansas..." An ugly suspicion slithered into my thoughts, casting dark shadows over my earlier good mood.

Puzzle pieces I'd been collecting started tumbling into place, clicking as they settled, perfectly balanced, perfectly positioned. Answers. Horrible answers.

Sabrina had beat the cops to the crime scene we found. Had she already been nearby?

"—the heart of Maine..." Another clip. "—sunny Puerto Vallarta."

Trish had said the only DNA found at the beheading scenes belonged to the police, the civilians who had found the victims, *and the news crews*.

"All the way from Riyadh..."

Riyadh? My blood froze.

"*Funny*," she had said, "*I was just about to say the same thing to you, Emery Luple.*"

"From Central Park—"

Those exact words.

"—this is Sabrina Miles."

She'd said them to me last night.

"Going the extra *mile...*"

Those had been the last words I'd heard before a bullet hit the back of my head.

"For you."

$\mathcal{T}$he air between Rachelle and me thrummed with tension. My phone buzzed, and we jumped. I swallowed and picked it up.

It was a text from Caden. *You guys up? I'm here.*

Yeah, come on up, I replied.

Rachelle and I waited anxiously for him to arrive. I slipped over to the door, peering through the peephole. All my emotions about Caden from the night before had been washed away on the tide of our big discovery. Seeing him step up to the hotel room door brought some of those feelings rushing back. He was an incarnate and, incredibly, did not know it. Recollections of lifetimes spent searching the world for others like me zipped through my mind, more impressions than true memories. The world had been a lot different back then, though. Without internet and international flights, the Earth had seemed a much larger place.

I opened the door, but my warm smile was sabotaged somewhat by the concerns lurking beneath the surface. I tried to study him objectively, hoping to unveil some detail I'd overlooked before. To reveal a clue—any clue—as to which incarnate he was. Last night's revelations, however, did not change him. Slender, blond, unassuming, open, honest, and eager. He was the same, and that fact frustrated and delighted me in equal measure. His bright eyes regarded me with a dose of bemused curiosity. He was carrying a tray of smoothies.

"Morning," he said, a bit hesitant, probably due to the way I was sizing him up. I held the door open for him, and he brushed past me and entered the room. "What's going on?"

Rachelle spun her tablet around to reveal the articles she'd been viewing. "We think we found our murderer," she said triumphantly.

"We *know*," I said. "Sabrina Miles. And she's staying in a room two floors down."

His eyebrows went up. "Wow. Coincidence?" He looked down at the smoothies. "I should have brought something with more caffeine." He set them on the small table. "Fill me in. What did I miss?"

"I want the red one," Rachelle called out. She caught my exasperated look and said defensively, "What? Everyone knows the red one is always the best."

"We don't have time for this," I told them. "We can stop the murderer right here, right now."

"Emery," Rachelle said, "we need proof before we just... *attack* her."

"You'd never forgive yourself if you hurt Sabrina and we were wrong," Caden agreed, handing a smoothie—the red one—to Rachelle. He looked up at me with a concerned expression. "Besides, if it *is* her, she has the Queen of Hearts and the Genie on her side, right? The Genie alone nearly killed us."

I ground my teeth but nodded my agreement. First things first: the smoking gun. "Rachelle, can you pull the articles or news reports by Sabrina from her time in Riyadh?"

Caden walked over to me and put a smoothie in my hands, then colored as he leaned in and kissed me on the cheek. "Let's think this through," he said quietly. "We'll do it together. If you rush in alone, you could get hurt. I don't want Sabrina's next report to be your headless body."

"Confirmed!" Rachelle said brightly. "See for yourself."

We leaned over the tablet. Sabrina had written three articles during her time in Riyadh; the dates overlapped my desert death perfectly.

"We got her," I said.

Sabrina Miles of NYBC News was our murderer.

My puzzle was beginning to look complete. I'd filled in the edges, arranged whole sections of the pieces. Sabrina's plan was brilliant, I had to admit. She committed murders and then reported on them, spreading the word of Ahedrian like wildfire. As the hype blossomed, the flames fanned by her own journalism, she cultivated the creation of a new urban legend on her terms. There was only one question yet burning in my mind: was she trying to obtain immortality for herself, or was she already the Queen of Hearts incarnate and scheming to bestow immortality upon another?

Rachelle scowled. "Now we just need a way for you to confront her without her magicking your head off." She paused. "Is 'magicking' a word?"

"Yes," I replied, gesturing with my smoothie, "it's just not a particularly good one."

She responded like a mature adult and stuck her tongue out at me.

"And" Caden added, "we need to face her without starting a war in a crowded, public place. We can't have people getting hurt."

I ran a hand through my hair in frustration. They were right, of course, but I chafed at the idea of not acting when I knew who was behind the murders and where she was. I was there, at the finish line, but the two of them were cautioning me against finishing the race. "Any ideas?" I asked.

"I think," he responded carefully, "if Sabrina doesn't know we're on to her, we can use that to our advantage."

Interesting. I wouldn't have expected him to suggest that kind of strategy. Was that his glamour at work, making me perceive him as more virtuous than he truly was? Or was I overthinking it? "Do you have something in mind?"

He hesitated. "I think our first order of business is to separate her from the Genie," he said finally.

I sipped the smoothie, more because I needed to *do* something than because I wanted a drink. "I like that idea." Mango and peach. Surprisingly refreshing. "And we know the Genie is already champing at the bit for round three."

"Maybe we can provoke her into sending the Genie after us again," Caden said, thinking it through. "But this time *we* set the trap. Turn the tables on them."

"I like it," Rachelle said, grinning wickedly. She gave Caden an approving look. "Setting traps. I'm so proud of you."

"We'll need to manipulate her into doing it on our terms," I said.

"And we'll need to approach her carefully," Caden pointed out. "If we come on too strong, she might be provoked to attack us outright."

"She's capable of it," I told them. "She already killed me once. I won't underestimate her a second time."

Rachelle, though, disagreed. "If she killed you in the desert, Emery, then she knew who you were when we met her in the parking garage. Probably earlier, since she sent the Genie after you at the office in Seattle." Her eyes lit up. "Actually, she tried to kill you twice with the Genie. So we know she wants you dead. There must be a reason she's using the Genie instead of doing it herself."

Caden pondered. "Maybe it would be too easy to link her with the Ahedrian murders," he mused. "We can use that. She can't have headless corpses found in her hotel room."

"She could just shoot him."

"Again," I added sourly. But I weighed their points. "You might both be on to something, though. I don't think she can risk killing me herself. If she's trying to create an urban legend, it's imperative she not get caught. No, not just caught. She can't be *involved*. If a mortal murderer were named or discovered, all the work she put into creating a legend would be undone."

Which means," Rachelle concluded, "if you provide a tempting reason to delay attacking you, she's likely to take that option."

We began hashing out a plan. The three of us made a remarkable team; Rachelle's bold cunning paired with Caden's voice of reason resulted in me breaking the tie or finding the middle road more often than not. I kept us on track, hyperconscious of the passing time and the need to catch Sabrina before she checked out of her room.

As we plotted, my thoughts strayed back to Caden. Our current predicament demanded my attention, but I still needed to inform him soon. To tell him what he was. Except... I didn't *know* what he was, did I? What personification did he embody? I observed the obvious traits: his golden, feathery hair and clean appearance; the goodness inherent in his personality. Hell, he just seemed like the Golden Boy. Which, for the record, is a high school stereotype, *not* an incarnate.

But his uncanny way of coaxing the truth from those around him, his glamour highlighting his sincerity while simultaneously putting people around him at ease, made me think of the Human Lie Detector. Which, I was reasonably sure, was also not an incarnate. But, dammit, urban legends changed and evolved all the time. There were incarnates out there I'd never heard of, despite trying to keep up.

"—sound like a plan?" Rachelle was saying.

"I'm in," Caden said.

I beamed my signature grin. "Let's do this."

I tucked my Taser into my jeans at the small of my back and spent a moment arranging the hem of my shirt around it. Satisfied that the weapon wasn't visible or suspiciously bulging, I looked at Morrigan's map one last time before folding it up neatly. "I just wish I knew where she was going to attack next." I sighed. "It would make our deception much more convincing."

Rachelle, her tablet propped against her leg, looked up. "We do. Rikers Island."

I snorted, remembering I had pointed to Rikers Island on the map last night when I was attempting to prove my point to Rachelle. "That's a big assumption, based off of a random finger poke."

"It would be," she agreed, "but it isn't your mystical finger that convinced me." She swiveled the tablet around to face me. "Read it and weep, boys."

It was a "Breaking News" report about the prison. Overnight, a single word had appeared in graffiti on the walls and scrawled across the grounds, every floor, ceiling, and cell, in various fonts, scripts, and mediums. In tribute to some unspeakable horror, the same word, repeated thousands of times.

I took a deep breath, steadying my nerves, and knocked on Sabrina's door. I waited anxiously, half expecting no answer. If we had missed the opportunity to stage our ambush, confronting Sabrina without the advantage of prudent planning would become unavoidable. I'd been forced to *react* too often since I reincarnated, from my first encounter with Morrigan to my two fights with the Genie. The only time I truly took control, I nearly got myself and Caden killed: death by Headless Horseman. Now that I knew the murderer's identity, it was time to put *her* on the defensive for a change.

Caden lingered down the hallway, out of sight, but I could feel his anxiety from here. He had argued—fiercely, especially for him—to join me in this discussion, to help keep me safe and watch my back. I refused. Sabrina would already be wary of me. Showing up at her hotel room door with someone she'd never met would only heighten her suspicion. He refused to be completely dissuaded, however, and insisted on waiting nearby.

I almost knocked again, but then I heard footsteps inside the room. I waited, breath held. The door opened.

Sabrina stood there, expression caught somewhere between

puzzlement, curiosity, and annoyance. She was wearing one of the hotel robes, and her hair was wrapped up in a towel. "Hey, kid," she said, "you caught me putting my face on. What can I do for you?" *You can stop murdering people, for starters.* My heart beat a little faster.

"Hey," I replied, forcing an embarrassed expression onto my face. It was critically important to keep her from discovering, or even suspecting, that I knew the truth about her. "Sorry to bother you again. I know you said you have a big story today," *and I'm sure you do,* "but I need to talk to you about our deal from yesterday."

She frowned. I wasn't sure if it was an *I wasn't expecting that* frown or an *I should murder him and be done with it* frown. I hoped it was the former. "Come in." She held the door open wider for me.

It felt like an invitation from a spider to enter her web... and I was a juicy fly. So, naturally, I stepped in. My instincts told me I had entered a place that could easily become my tomb, but the room looked innocuous enough. Sabrina had repacked, and her travel bags were piled on her bed, an outfit for the day folded neatly beside them. Her small purse hung on the back of the desk chair. From where I stood, I could see her open makeup kit on the bathroom counter, with a few items strewn about. I don't know what I'd been expecting—shrunken heads, maybe? An enormous cleaver for decapitating victims? A neon "I am Ahedrian" poster?—but the normalcy of the hotel room gnawed at my confidence. For the first time since hearing the news report, my mind entertained the tiniest shred of doubt.

Then I felt Sabrina behind me. My mind flashed back to the blistering Saudi Arabian desert, the voice, the gun to the back of my skull. I felt my shoulders bunch reflexively, but I relaxed them. *Breathe, Emery. She doesn't suspect anything yet.* As if to prove my inner voice correct, she brushed past me and whisked into the bathroom, saying, "I'm running late, so don't mind me. I'll continue getting ready while we talk. I have an engagement early this afternoon before my big story tonight."

Big story. Everything was coming to a head. I could feel it.

But watching her trace her lower eyelid with eyeliner triggered a very different type of flashback. I recalled, with crystalline clarity, staring into the mirror, a bold woman of color looking back at me. Applying foundation, making my skin smooth and warm, my mahogany eyes popping beneath plum eyeshadow. To many, makeup artistry is a daunting concept, the implements nothing but arcane, foreign things. But to gorgeous Emery Luple, field correspondent, they were tools of transformation. With the camera's unflattering lights on me, I needed to look extra stunning. There was something rewarding in sculpting my physical appearance to my standards, highlighting my attractive qualities and subduing those I wished to downplay. Designing my own appearance, transforming it, empowered me to be something simultaneously greater than myself and fundamentally *me*. That incarnation of Emery Luple stayed with me despite her tragic end, the gunshot that concluded that memory bringing me back to the present with a sharp report.

I realized, as Sabrina glanced up at me impatiently, that if I wanted to avoid *this* incarnation dying young, I needed to pull it together. Besides, as I watched Sabrina carefully applying makeup, she reminded me more of an ancient warrior readying for battle. Or maybe a criminal slipping on her mask before robbing a bank. This was the face she presented to the public, but unlike that prior Emery Luple, it did *not* represent who she was. Her true face was masked in blood, not cosmetics.

With her fiery hair caught up in the towel, she seemed less vibrant. Like a colorless shade of her former self.

I needed to say something—anything—to cover my sudden reticence. But I couldn't make it too shallow; she knew who I was, the lifetimes I'd lived. Emphasizing my youth could make her more suspicious, not less.

"Did you hear about Rikers?" I asked, modulating my voice to contain a note of eagerness. I watched her closely to see her response.

Sabrina hesitated, then pulled her eye pencil away long enough to nod. "I was wondering when you were going to ask me about that," she said.

My heart hammered harder in my chest. *Careful.* "I heard you and

Gustav talking last night about a big story at 'the island.' I put two and two together." Was the Genie's "lamp" her makeup kit? Was that why she was standing there seemingly unconcerned? Or could she simply say, "Off with your head!" before I'd reached the door?

"I noticed it was on your map last night. Is that why you've come?"

I kept the surprise from showing on my face. I hadn't expected her to say she saw it on my map. Thinking about it now, showing it to her with a point that coincided perfectly with where she was planning her next strike had been a blunder that could have cost me my life. Likely, the map's many other pinpricks had saved me. Now I needed to convince her I was way off track, or I wasn't sure I'd get out of this hotel room. She probably only mentioned the map to see if I would lie to her. "Yeah," I admitted. "I'm right, aren't I? You're going to Rikers tonight?"

"You're quite the investigator, you know that?" As she contemplated me, I felt like I was balanced on the edge of something sharp.

I shrugged, mustering all the nonchalance I could. "Not really. I figured you got wind of the Ahedrian mess at the jail last night, before the news officially reported on it." I forced a grin. "Makes sense why you stipulated your Ahedrian hiatus start tomorrow when I offered you the deal. You already had this story in the bag."

The silence between us drew my skin into prickles. Had I said too much? I felt like she was holding a knife to my ribs and I couldn't breathe without cutting myself. Then a smile inched onto her face. She reached up—I did *not* flinch—and unfurled the towel, dropping it to the bathroom floor, heavy red tangles falling down her shoulder. "And you want to know if you can get in with me?" she guessed. She began applying product to her hair, running her hands through the curls. I got the distinct impression she was using her morning ritual to keep me off balance.

When I spoke, my voice sounded relieved. I'd been going for smug. "Not exactly. I came down here to make sure I was right."

It was only for a moment, but her hands stilled midstroke. I tensed. She regarded me with narrowed eyes. "Why?"

I needed to get out of here. It was time to set my trap. "As much as

I'd like to go to Rikers with you, I have a bigger scoop on Ahedrian for *There's Always a Loophole*. I was hoping we could split up to cover both places at once."

"A bigger scoop?" The suspicion in her eyes was replaced by a glint of amusement. She finished running her hands through her hair and flipped it back, letting the cascade of red fall into place, framing her face. Now that she was done preening, her attention settled on me like a weight on my chest. Her eyes pinned me in place.

"Rikers seems so *obvious*," I told her. I flashed her a grin and threw in an extra measure of cockiness. "Oldest trick in the book: misdirection. While the eyes of the whole city are on Rikers Island, Ahedrian beheads someone on the other side of Manhattan."

Sabrina weighed me with the tiniest bit of contempt slinking into her eyes. Like a bully flipping a turtle onto its shell, then watching it struggle to right itself. She probably thought I was a fool, denounced me in her mind as a kid who thought he had figured everything out... but was, in fact, utterly wrong.

I, of course, *knew* my claim was wrong. For an urban legend to be born, the event would need to be dramatic and theatrical. With the whole city watching Rikers Island and security increased accordingly, the conundrum was in how Ahedrian would manage to infiltrate the prison and manage multiple—because multiple would be more theatrical—beheadings. A normal human couldn't possibly, right? In achieving the impossible, in spite of the beefed-up safety precautions, the feat would damn well be... legendary. Which, I would imagine, would be the most important ingredient for insta-incarnate. Whereas if Ahedrian struck somewhere else, it would actually undermine their legacy. They might be construed as a dangerous— maybe even clever—serial killer, but ultimately a run-of-the-mill one.

"That makes sense," she said, a little too obvious in her pretense of mulling it over. "In hindsight, it does seem obvious." She sighed. "But I'm a reporter. I have to go to Rikers—there's still a story to be told there." She paused, then asked a little too casually, "Where do *you* think Ahedrian will strike?"

I reminded myself to breathe. "I don't *think*," I answered conspiratorially, "I *know*."

Her pencil-darkened eyebrows arched. "Oh?"

"Remember that anonymous tipster?" I asked, putting as much earnestness into my voice as possible. I pulled the map out of my back pocket and unfolded it.

"Of course." She stood with lips pursed, eyeing me the way a cat watches a bug.

"Well," I said, baiting the trap, "they called me again this morning. They want to meet."

Her eyebrows knitted in genuine puzzlement. "What for?"

"They say they know Ahedrian's identity."

I only saw it because I was looking for it—while trying to seem like I wasn't. A startled apprehension kindled in her eye for a moment before being masked. "Sounds like a dead end to me," she said.

She was a good liar, but she wasn't the best. After fencing with Morrigan last night in the car, discourse with Sabrina was child's play. I amended my thought: discourse with Sabrina was like tricking a child who was holding a gun on me. Terrifying, but infinitely preferable to *Morrigan* holding a gun on me.

I still didn't know if Sabrina was mortal or incarnate. Mortal, I guessed. I would expect an incarnate, with lifetimes of experience, to better hide her emotions. I suppose the Queen of Hearts, however, could be haughtily unaccustomed to concealing her intentions.

I pointed at the spot on the map that Caden, Rachelle, and I had selected. We hadn't had the luxury of time, but given the constraints, I think we chose well. It was a construction site, which would be mostly—with any luck, totally—empty for the weekend. "We're meeting the informant at one," I told her. "We'll find out if they have any real information." I met her gaze. "They were spot-on with Rikers, though."

Sabrina grimaced again, thoughts flitting across her face too quickly to identify. "True," she said at last. Then she did something that froze me in my tracks. She reached for her clutch on the back of the chair.

Panic swelled within me, and I nearly snatched the purse away from her. It took all my restraint not to react. My mind raced. Was she going to pull a gun? The sound of the shot to the back of my head in Saudi Arabia was still fresh in my memory. Or would she summon the Genie to roast me to a cinder? Or pull out an executioner's axe and decapitate me, consequences be damned? She withdrew a tiny spiral notebook. Decapitation by paper cut? No. I felt my tight muscles relax. I tried to keep the relief from my face as she flipped the notepad open, already afraid she'd caught my reaction.

"What's your number?" she asked. When I hesitated, she tapped her pencil against the notepad impatiently. "I can call you from Rikers if we run into anything," she explained.

I nodded, mind racing, fearing some type of trap. I wasn't sure how my phone number could lead to my death, however. And while I could lie, the risk did not seem worth the reward. If she tested it while I was standing there, she'd know I'd lied, and now she held her clutch in her hands. She glanced at me, distrust slowly clouding her features. *No time.* I supplied my phone number, hoping I hadn't created more trouble for myself. She scribbled the information quickly, but... she wasn't writing what I told her. I realized she was using my phone number as a cover to write something else. I smothered my relieved grin. A stolen glance confirmed she was recording the location I'd mentioned on the map.

Got you, I thought with glee. I kept my face smooth.

She snapped the booklet closed, and the smile she wore dipped dangerously close to mocking. "Thanks for the info, kid. Now, if you don't mind? I need to dress and get to my meeting."

"I should get going as well." I was all too happy to leave her room. I'd done it! A thrill ran through me.

As I reached the door, though, Sabrina called out to me. "Oh, and Emery? Be careful out there. I would hate my next report to be on *your* beheaded body." The thinly veiled threat chilled me.

I met her eyes. "You be careful, too." I looked away before my stare could become challenging.

I fled the room.

In the hallway, around the corner, I found Caden practically prancing in place. His relief upon seeing me mirrored my own.

"Well?" he asked, mixing anxiety and hope.

"Let's walk and talk," I said, wanting to put some distance between us and Sabrina's room. We made our way to the elevator, and once we were safely inside, I turned to him with a triumphant grin. "It went well. She took the bait, I'm certain." The elevator descended toward the lobby, where Rachelle was waiting in the restaurant's buffet area.

He nodded. "Now I guess we wait and see what she does with it."

"It'll work." I said it with confidence—it was her likeliest response, the most appropriate tool at her disposal. The Genie could travel great distances with nothing more than a thought, which meant he could almost be in two places at once. Sabrina, unable to do the same thing, would not risk getting caught somewhere far from Rikers Island when she was so close to cementing the legend of Ahedrian.

Our plan was simple. We would provoke Sabrina into attacking us, providing her with the perfect location and time: one o'clock, abandoned construction site. The arena we chose was inconvenient for Sabrina to get to, increasing the likelihood she would send the Genie in her stead. Then came the hard part. I would engage the Genie incarnate in mortal combat for the third and final time. Wait, I guess it would be *immortal* combat. Huh, that actually sounds way cooler. Ahem, anyway. We'd capture the Genie and force him to serve us. Three well-placed wishes later, the Genie would be freed and we'd be in the enviable position of turning the tables on Sabrina.

"I can't help but wish we had backup for the next part, though," I added, thinking through our plan.

It was at that moment that the elevator *ding*ed and the doors slid open.

Trish stood there, arms crossed. Her eyes met mine.

"You've got to be kidding me." I think we said it at the same time.

ongratulations, class! You have completed the introductory courses on incarnates. With the next term will come the more difficult lessons, but we'll save those for another day. I have decided to call this upcoming tutoring "Incarnate University." The best part is that you've passed admissions, tuition costs nothing, and it doesn't require four years to complete. The worst part is that you don't technically receive a diploma, degree, or certificate. But you do get an education, and knowledge is really its own reward, right?

I have never been so proud. You are now members of an elite caste of scholars. Remember, incarnates survive so long as their legends continue to be retold. So do your part. Don't clap for fairies, talk about them. Keep the legends alive.

Share my story.

No, really. Buy it for your friends and family.

My life is at stake here!

I DID SOMETHING VERY DANGEROUS: I grabbed Trish by the arm and pulled.

"Walk with us," I hissed.

She yanked her arm away but followed us with only a moment's hesitation, the urgency in my tone commanding her interest.

"I'm on to something here," she muttered. "This better be good." The punky pixie flipped her hair and transferred her glare to Caden, who was walking on the other side of me.

"Hey, Trish," he said brightly, giving her a wave.

"Hey yourself," she grumbled.

"We know the identity of Ahedrian," I told her, keeping my voice barely above a whisper as I navigated us to the restaurant area.

As expected, that got her attention. She sported a new black leather jacket—and I admit I felt some satisfaction to finally see someone *else* replacing their battle-destroyed clothes. The leather jacket replete with fringe would have made anyone else look like a cross between a motorcyclist and a country music star, but on Trish it, unjustly, looked badass. She followed us through the hotel lobby, tassels swaying with her stride.

Rachelle waited for us amid the nautical finery, crutches propped against a table and a shopping bag at her foot. Her injured leg was supported by another chair. For some reason, she was red in the face and sweating.

"What were you able to find?" I asked her as we approached. I eyed the shopping bags with dismay. I had asked her to go to the gift shop for supplies, not out to a store. Then I noticed the bags had different logos. Two stores? Oh, for the love of—

"Wait," Trish said.

I sighed, glancing back toward the elevators. I'd feel a lot safer if we put some distance between us and Sabrina. But I understood Trish's predicament, too. I'd chafe at being left in the dark, not to mention derailed from my purpose. I braced myself for her questions, ready to fill her in as quickly as possible.

"You sent your friend *with the broken leg* shopping for your supplies?" Trish asked.

"They didn't *send* me anywhere," Rachelle retorted. "I volunteered. I'm just as capable as—no, scratch that, I'm *more* capable than anyone else." She sized Trish up. "You must be Trish. I never got a chance to thank you for helping me bandage up my leg before the ambulance arrived the other night. I'm Rachelle."

Trish inclined her head, her angry expression held at bay by something I hadn't quite seen from her yet. Was that... respect? Sigh. How come when *I* talked back, it just pissed her off?

Rachelle tossed the bag of merchandise at me and waved her phone in my face. "I called you a ride, and it arrived four minutes ago. Get your butt out there." Despite her words, she grabbed my wrist and pulled me closer. "You'll get there about half an hour early. Doesn't give you much time to set up. Be careful." The last part came out as almost a plea.

"I will," I promised, flashing her my crooked grin. I thrust my thumb over my shoulder. "And I'll keep them safe, too."

Rachelle nodded. "I bought a few extra of everything, just in case. There's plenty for Trish."

"You're a lifesaver," I told her, squeezing her shoulder. I leaned down and pitched my voice for her alone. "I know it sucks being side-lined, Rachelle, but I still really need you. I'll keep in touch. Remember to call Madam Zerona as soon as we leave."

"Yeah, yeah." She waved me off, pointing at the rideshare app on her phone. "Five minutes. It costs me more by the minute, you know."

I hefted the bag and gave her a final nod. "See you tonight," I said cheerfully.

We walked out of the hotel and down the stairs toward our waiting car. The overcast sky was heavy with the promise of rain. Trish caught my arm and ground me to a halt. Caden gave us a nod and continued down to the car to continue to stall it.

"I tracked a lead to this hotel," Trish growled. Honestly, she probably just *said* it, but every word she uttered was colored with shades of anger. It probably wasn't even intentional at this point. "I am not about to abandon it for nothing."

I glanced around. We were alone. "I will fill you in," I promised

264 | JUSTIN SCHUELKE

her, trying to infuse my words with sincerity and a sense of urgency, "but we need to get moving. We're going to confront a few incarnates this afternoon, including the so-called Ahedrian. I know we have our differences"—I looked her dead in the eyes and cast aside my pride —"but I'd feel a lot better with the Monster Hunter watching my back."

If I'd expected a smile, I was left disappointed. Trish searched my face, probably for any trace of falsehood, then nodded once, sharply. "I'm in."

The ride to our destination was intolerable. I watched the time like it was a countdown for a bomb taped to my chest. Every red light, every pedestrian, every passing minute filled me with a surge of restless anxiety. Caden, on my left, caught me worrying at my fingernail, and he gently took my hand from my mouth and held it in his lap. But even with his fingers stroking my skin, I couldn't relax.

He was always so grounding, so imperturbable, filled with peace. I tried to borrow from that energy. It helped. A little. For at least a minute.

If Trish noticed the two of us, she gave no sign of it. After throwing a furious look at the driver whose presence meant we couldn't talk freely, she had taken to watching the passing traffic with a faraway expression. Her glower was an apparent fixture on her face even when her mind was occupied. I'm not certain what was going through her thoughts. She may have been considering my words and wondering at them, but she didn't look curious. Maybe she was watching our course and trying to determine our destination. Or maybe she was thinking about kittens chasing butterflies. It was so hard to read her. But I sympathized with the kittens and butterflies; they hadn't done anything to deserve that scowl.

I turned my speculation forward, thinking about the coming hour. The bag of merchandise that sat between my knees included my backpack of anti-incarnate weaponry. It felt like a security blanket. The Genie was formidable, explosive, and infuriatingly difficult to pin down. One of the most challenging aspects of the approaching altercation was going to be defeating him without driving him away. If he fled, like he had at the apartment, it would greatly weaken our position when we went to confront Sabrina later. But if anyone could tame the Genie, it would be three incarnates.

Three incarnates.

I looked sidelong at Caden. With the chaos of our morning, I had not yet had the opportunity to talk with him. I felt a rising desire to tell him. *Caden, you are an incarnate, like me.* I couldn't wait to see his eyes light up at the news. I had already involved him in more of my world than I ever anticipated, but now... now I could share it fully. I just wanted the chance to do it *right*.

He caught me watching him, and he warmed, sharing a private smile. "We've got this," he murmured.

The car finally pulled over. I checked my phone for the time: 12:39. We only had a short window to prepare. We piled out of the car, and Trish looked around, frowning. She surveyed the construction site across the street and looked at us expectantly. "That's our battlefield?"

"Yes." I felt a raindrop on my face. The weather was starting to turn. For some reason, that felt ominous. "Let's get in position."

As we crossed the street, Trish asked, "So is Ahedrian that news chick? Sabrina Miles?"

I stumbled. "Um, yes. How did you figure it out?"

"I did some digging and found out she owns the apartment we trashed. I thought it was just a lead, until I ran into you guys there." She frowned. "But why is she going to such lengths to kill criminals?"

"Our best guess is that she's trying to obtain immortality by creating an urban legend of a monster, Ahedrian, that beheads villains in retribution for their ill deeds. Thus, in turn, creating an incarnate," I explained. "We just don't know if she's trying to obtain immortality for herself or for someone else."

A tall chain-link fence encircled the property, discouraging entry. We followed its perimeter, looking for a spot to scale it that wasn't visible from the road. It wasn't a main thoroughfare—we had tried to

266 | JUSTIN SCHUELKE

choose a building on a relatively quiet street—but it *was* New York City.

Caden added, "There's at least two incarnates involved. The Genie, obviously, but also the one doing the actual beheading. The Queen of Hearts incarnate."

Trish made a face. "That's random."

I shook my head. "Not entirely. Mirrors, or perhaps I should call them looking glasses in this case, provided clues we were missing. I think I figured out why, too: mirrors are the Queen of Hearts' fatal flaw. In the story, a looking glass is the vessel Alice uses to arrive in Wonderland and ultimately overthrow the Queen of Hearts."

Trish looked back and forth between us. "You're wrong," she said after a moment. "You're referring to the Red Queen, the villain from the *sequel* to *Alice in Wonderland.*"

I paused. "What?"

"By your logic, the Queen of Hearts' fatal flaw would be..." She gave me a flat look. "Rabbit holes. That's how Alice got to Wonderland the first time."

"What are you, a Wonderland expert?" I grumbled.

She looked at me pointedly. "Have *you* ever hunted the Bandersnatch incarnate?"

Caden looked puzzled. "In the story, does the Red Queen lop off people's heads?"

"No."

He shot me a worried look. "The mirrors don't need to be precise," I argued, irritated by Trish's know-it-all attitude, "they just need to lead us to the correct conclusion." We'd reached what seemed like a reasonable spot to enter the site. "Let's go."

I boosted Caden over the fence, then offered to help Trish. She ignored me and scaled the chain link like it was a simple ladder. I followed suit after tossing the bag to Caden, managing to get up and back down without ripping any clothes.

The construction yard was dirt, strewn with tools and idle equipment. Ahead was the building proper. The structure towered into the sky above us. The siding of the first several stories was complete, but the doorways and windows had not yet been filled in, so you could peer into the building's interior. It was... a mess. Sheets of plastic hung everywhere, obscuring the walls, and the floor was concrete, the surfacing not yet installed. The load-bearing walls were in place, but the open, empty space between them felt oddly stretched, especially with the low ceilings above.

My phone read 12:46. Fourteen minutes until our "meeting." I retrieved the bag from Caden as fat drops of rain began to fall. We picked our way across the construction yard, cold rain plopping down on our exposed heads at an ever-increasing rate. Dark splotches appeared in the dirt as the skies opened up; the ground would be mud in no time. We hastened into the structure, the rain droning overhead.

I hefted the bag. "I brought some things."

Trish snorted. "Clearly."

I ignored her and withdrew my backpack of supplies, then began parceling out the remaining items. There were four drawstring sports packs with Chelsea Market logos, like skinny backpacks where the straps had been replaced with strings and the pack was nothing more than a polyester sack. They were perfect for our purposes. I handed them out, putting the spare back into the bag. Trish inspected hers, unimpressed.

"Put them on," I said. "They're vessels. The Genie can't cause harm to anything that could be used to contain him, so they should protect you from his fire. But wear them under your clothing so they aren't visible. If he thinks we're too prepared, he might get cold feet again." Caden was already removing his hooded white sweatshirt to comply.

"These"—I held up a fistful of chains with little lockets dangling from them—"serve the same purpose, but to protect your front. Remember, these talismans are like bulletproof vests: they'll provide protection, but they won't fully stop the heat or a well-aimed fireball to the face... or knees, for that matter."

I took out two portable fire extinguishers. They were meant to fight Class A fires, like wood and cloth, not magical fires... but they would have to suffice. They were, I hoped, better than nothing.

Trish threw her pack back to me. "Great idea," she said, the words not sounding very uplifting coming from her, "but I just won't get hit. If you two stay out of my way this time, he'll be dead before he can throw so much as a fireball." She did, however, take the locket and clasp it around her neck, where it looked out of place against her punk brand.

I shook my head while equipping myself with my own set of protective items. "We don't want him dead, Trish."

She stared at me. "You want to *capture* him?" She made a disgusted noise. "How did you ever think you were the Monster Hunter? Have you ever even *hunted* a monster?"

"Plenty of hunters trap their prey," I retorted. "It's actually harder to do!"

Caden finished pulling his hoodie over the drawstring pack and quietly cut off Trish's response. "We need those wishes to save lives," he said. "We think Ahedrian is planning a mass murder at Rikers this evening. We can stop it, but only with help."

Trish jabbed a thumb at herself. "You have help." Caden continued to meet her eyes, and surprisingly, she buckled first. "Killing him will save lives, too, but only if we finish the job. So... no promises. He's not getting away this time, even if I have to end him."

I nodded. "But you'll let us try?"

"*I'll* try," she said. "You will stand right here and not get in my way." She spun away from us and walked deliberately out into the middle of the flooring. Her footsteps were muffled by the increasing roar of the rain drumming against the building's structure and flapping tarps. I was grateful the first couple of floors had solid ceilings.

Caden stepped up to me and put his hand on my shoulder. I wasn't sure if it was a gesture of comfort or just an attempt to keep me from stalking after Trish. I sighed and handed him the fire extinguishers. I wasn't sure how much use they would be, but the marginal protection they afforded would at least make me feel a fraction better.

"I just need a chance at him," I growled.

Heat and light washed over us from behind, baking the back of my neck. Only my Genie-proof sports pack saved me, the back of my new favorite shirt disintegrating into fluttering, flaming motes of fabric. I was thrown to the ground, and Caden let out a cry as he fell away from me.

A familiar, accented voice sneered from behind and above me, "Be careful what you wish for, Emery Luple."

From my belly, I looked up to see Trish spin around and take in what had happened. She cursed and began booking it back toward us, but she was close to a hundred feet away in the expanse of the unfinished floor.

I couldn't see the Genie towering over my shoulder, but I could feel him. The air became warmer, and I imagined him conjuring a sweep of fire, then directing it down and over me. I rolled to the side out of instinct, immortal reflexes reacting faster than the wave of fire that ignited the air where I'd lain a moment before. The dirty concrete heated beneath the flame as I stumbled to my feet, throwing myself forward and striking the Genie with my shoulder... and going straight through a plume of cinnamon smoke as the Genie dissolved.

He reappeared in front of Caden, a fireball springing into his hand even as he formed. The bolt of heat struck Caden across the chest. The locket he wore protected him from the flames, but the force of the fireball was still sufficient to send him flying, both feet in the air as he fell, hard, onto his back. He groaned and raised himself up on his elbows as the Genie's shadow fell over him. Caden watched in horror as the Genie summoned fire between his palms. Caden cringed, his eyes squeezed shut, face contorted against the expected barrage. Trish had covered most of the distance, but she wouldn't make it in time.

"*No!*" I screamed. I launched forward and threw myself across Caden just as he was engulfed by a torrent of roaring flames. The concentrated, direct channel of fire—like that sprayed from a flamethrower—blasted into my back and hammered me down, flattening me against Caden. I felt like I had been shoved into an open oven, but the backpack took the brunt of the blistering heat that swept up and down my body.

I was afraid that, even with protection from the worst of the fire, it would still incinerate me and leave an untouched locket and a sports pack in a pile of ash and charred bones in Caden's lap.

Through the haze of shimmering heat, I saw Trish tear across the distance separating us. She *flew* over us and collided with the Genie. The flames cut off immediately, and I collapsed on top of Caden in relief.

I trembled, unable to move. Caden was looking at me with wide, disbelieving eyes.

"How bad is it?" I asked, pleased at the strength in my voice. I imagined my body might look like a melted lump of wax, despite the backpack's protection.

Caden reached out and touched my back, and I cringed, expecting his hand to touch raw, bloodied skin. Instead, his hand scrunched against my backpack. It had... *worked.* My creative protection had actually worked! My clothes weren't even steaming from the heat exposure.

Trish's grunts as she swung at the Genie pulled me out of my surprise. I scrambled to my feet and offered Caden my hand. Trish lashed out to trip the Genie, bringing him to the ground, but he dispersed into red mist as his bulk hit the concrete. The mist flowed, unnaturally quick, in our direction. Caden blinked the shock from his eyes, then darted away to avoid the oncoming scarlet cloud. As I moved to follow, the Genie materialized behind me, and I felt him reach out and snatch at my protective necklace. I was yanked backward, the chain tight against my throat, cutting off my air. I scrabbled to get my fingers between the locket and my skin.

"You think these mere baubles enough to combat *me*?" the Genie hissed in my ear.

In desperation, I jerked away from him, and I felt the chain snap. The locket plinked to the concrete ground, and I stumbled away from my attacker. The Genie was left holding a broken chain dangling from one fist.

Trish launched herself toward him again, but not before he lobbed a molten sphere my way. Without the locket's protection, I ate a fistful of flame. My head snapped back as the blistering bolt of fire detonated against the left side of my face. Intense, searing pain. The smell of burning hair and flesh. A brief sizzling sound. My face felt like it had been smashed with a furnace, heat and pain clawing their way toward my leaking left eye. Caden caught me before I fell, and I tried to hide my face from him so he couldn't see the damage. I had suffered too many wounds over lifetimes to lie to myself: it was bad. At best, the left side of my face would be inflamed and raw—and the pain would hobble me in the coming confrontations. My face would be forever scarred, possibly beyond recognition.

Caden pulled me back and away from where Trish and the Genie battled. Vanity aside, I was furious. If the pain and damage compromised my condition to fight, how would I confront Sabrina? And *holy hell*. The pain was agonizing, like someone still held a hot poker against my skin.

Caden had reached a plastic-enwrapped wall, and he put his back to it, holding me and stroking my hair. He was muttering soothing words, like someone trying to calm a frightened child. I realized I was gritting my teeth, and groans were escaping my lips. Damn, it hurt. I resisted the urge to reach up and touch the wounds, knowing I would only harm myself further. I controlled my breathing, let Caden's soothing tone at least replenish my composure. I turned my head to watch Trish and the Genie fight, hiding the damaged side of my face from Caden.

Trish was holding her own against her fire-wielding adversary.

The Genie conjured and pitched two fireballs, and Trish spun out of their trajectory, then propelled herself forward in the same motion, her moves elegant and graceful, like those of a dancer. Her foot snapped out and caught the Genie in the abdomen. He doubled over, and she snapped her arm up, catching his face with her stiff-armed uppercut. The Genie dematerialized into red smoke but reappeared almost immediately behind her. Trish was ready. Before the Genie had fully re-formed, her thrust elbow caught him below the sternum, driving him backward.

The Genie's fireball trick was not quite as useful in close quarters, so Trish didn't allow the distance between them to grow. She pressed her advantage even as flames sprang to his fingers. He tried to throw fire, but her hand chopped down and the fireball was thrown harmlessly to the cement flooring. Her follow-up strike took the Genie across the jaw. He evaporated into mist yet again, and Trish tore off toward us. Her speed was superhuman, faster than any living thing I'd ever seen.

Trish reached our side just as the Genie appeared over us. With a contemptuous gesture, the Malevolent incarnate set the sheet of plastic we leaned against aflame. Caden ripped us both away from the curtain of fire. I allowed myself to be pulled along, the agony of my face making me feel dazed and sluggish.

Trish careened into the Genie but was carried *through* him as he puffed into smoke. She skidded past, trailing red fingers of mist, and slid to a stop.

Caden, one hand protectively around me, snatched up one of the fire extinguishers we'd brought. He aimed it at the wall of fire and squeezed the handles. The nozzle sent a surprisingly large cone of white liquid at the sheet of flame, but it barely dampened the raging blaze, and my heart fell. I didn't know if the flames were too hot, too mystical, or simply too large for a portable extinguisher to manage. They shrank away from the chemical solution but did not succumb to it.

My eyes were dragged back to Trish. She wasn't just holding her own, I realized. She... was *incredible*. She'd snapped the chain on her locket and twirled it around her like a cheerleader with a baton. Fireballs streaked toward her with blistering speed and heat, and she slashed them out of the air with the locket. Since it was a container, the fireballs were unable to cause it harm and were deflected away from her. She knocked aside bolt after bolt of fire, untouchable. The deflected fireballs rocketed into the pavement to gouge the cement and send up sprays of stone, leaving behind pitted, black scorch marks. The Genie dematerialized and re-formed again, his stream of fire abruptly coming from a new direction. I held my breath, but Trish didn't even flinch, rotating her defense to meet the new set of fireballs. The Genie, his face contorted in furious concentration and a growl rolling out from somewhere low in his throat, disappeared in a puff of red smoke again. He reappeared, lobbed a gout of flame, then vanished again immediately. Faster and faster, he blinked in and out of cinnamon clouds in a loose circle around her, fire streaming toward Trish from all directions.

I watched with awe, the fierce pain of my injuries easing as I became absorbed in her fight. Caden's litany of soothing words merged into the dull roar of the rain outside, washing over me and taking some of the pain with it. No one—mortal or incarnate—could withstand that kind of heat. Even if I summoned all the incredible luck at my disposal, coupling it with lifetimes of experience, I knew I wouldn't have been able to overcome the Genie's concentrated storm of fire.

But Trish did. Quicker than I could follow, she pirouetted in place, a dancing figure garishly lit by flickering, streaking fire. The tassels on her jacket spun and danced along with her, giving her an almost inhuman appearance. No, *super*human. The chain moved so quickly it blurred the top half of her figure as she slapped away fireballs with graceful contempt. This was it. I had seen this before, albeit rarely. Even in the moment, I knew it in my soul. She perfectly matched each streak of fire, spinning to meet it with her locket before I'd even registered the Genie had catapulted fire from that direction. She was flawless, a deadly vortex of finesse. I was watching an incarnate fully in her element. And it...

It was glorious.

Then she leapt from the mounting fire around her and flung the locket, chain and all, directly at Caden and me. The locket streaked through the air like a dart, trailing a steaming tail from the heat the chain had absorbed. The Genie *poofe*d into existence, right behind us. Somehow, even while fending off wave after wave of fire, with the Genie appearing in a seemingly random pattern around her, Trish had timed her throw precisely. The locket flew past us—

And I realized its trajectory was *just* off. Trish had anticipated the Genie's reappearance and misjudged by a *fraction*. Without hesitation, that corner of my immortal mind opened to me, and with reflexes honed from thousands of lifetimes, I reached out and caught the locket by its chain. I ignored the hot metal in my palm. In a single motion, I swung it around and the locket connected. It bounced off of the Genie's face, slipped from my fingers, and plinked to the cement.

Time seemed to still, the thunderous rain on the unfinished building the only sound.

The Genie froze, staring down at the locket, his eyes bulging in disbelief. Then he let out a howl that drowned out the downpour. He evaporated into a red cloud, but this time the cloud was pulled downward into the locket as though it were a high-powered vacuum.

The flames in the building winked out, smothered as one.

Caden and I collapsed to sit on the concrete. Trish was next to us before I even realized she had moved. To my growing incredulity, she was barely even breathing hard. I felt numb, the pain in my face subdued by the irrefutable realization that I was *not* the Monster Hunter incarnate.

"Are you okay?" she asked, hand gripping my chin, eyes searching my wounded left side with practiced ease. She frowned. "I could have sworn..."

"You were incredible," I breathed. I felt dizzy. She probably thought I was delirious.

Caden's face slid into view. His golden hair shimmered with its own light, and his eyes shone as he looked me over. I felt an urge to pull away from Trish's grip and hide my face from him, but I resisted.

"How bad is it?" I asked, fearful of the response. Caden smiled brightly at me, and he seemed to glow with his own inner light. Maybe I *was* delirious.

Trish glanced at Caden to get his response before offering her own, then did a visible double-take. "What's with the light show?" she asked.

Caden blinked at her, then looked to me, puzzled.

"You're glowing," I told him giddily. And he was. It wasn't just my overactive imagination. It wasn't a trick of the light. It wasn't a metaphor for the way I thought he lit up from the inside.

He was literally glowing. I realized, too, that the pain in my face didn't *seem* to be gone. It had been taken away by Caden's ministrations, his soothing words, his touch. With a burgeoning sense of certainty, I reached up and felt the left side of my face. It was whole and smooth, like the tender new flesh of a freshly healed scrape.

And it all clicked into place. My injuries from the Alligator, the Headless Horseman, the Genie at the apartment. How had I missed it? Rachelle's leg should have been the final clue, but I'd assumed it had to do with me. Even the hospice patients Caden told me about, who had come to die at his family's shelter and then miraculously recovered. My mental scars from three incarnations ago. All of us, we hadn't healed at all. We had *been* healed.

Holy shit. Emphasis on "holy."

The way his glamour compelled me to tell the truth.

His purity, inherent in his personality but also manifest in his immaculate appearance, his clean scent.

The way the light always haloed his golden hair.

"I've been wanting to tell you something all day," I said, meeting his eyes. I cupped his cheek reverently with my hand, feeling like I was touching him for the first time.

"You are an incarnate," I said, putting as much sincerity and joy into the words as I could manage from the concrete floor of an unfinished building. I watched the flicker of emotions on his face as Trish stepped away to give us privacy. Bemusement on the heels of surprise, then chagrin as he realized I was watching him. Dawning realization that I was serious. Consideration, uncertainty, cautious hope.

"Are you sure you didn't hit your head?" he asked me lightly, but with an undercurrent of doubt.

I pulled him close. "There's a reason you have always felt connected to the beyond. A reason you were drawn to the world of incarnates. *Your* world." A laugh escaped me. "*Our* world. The reason you've walked away from each of these fights unscathed. The reason you felt you never truly belonged until the day you came into my life." I peered into his eyes, which shone with an open eagerness I knew so well. "Caden Malek, you are the Angel incarnate."

"I'm an incarnate?" Caden whispered, disbelieving. The rain drummed heavily against the exposed upper levels of the building. I saw him turning the idea over and over in his mind, examining it, deciding for himself.

"You've been healing me," I added. "The Genie incinerated my face, Caden. But look." I gestured to my left cheek. "Undamaged. That was you."

The complicated emotions on his face were difficult to separate, to untangle. I saw wonder there, and confusion. Curiosity, consideration, and then his brow knit in puzzlement. I watched it all, absorbed.

"How come you didn't tell me before this?" he asked, a bit of hurt stealing into his voice.

I chuckled. "You had me fooled, Caden. I had no idea you were an incarnate. Just figured it out last night, actually, and I was waiting for the right time to tell you." I looked around at the unfinished building, the dirty concrete floor. "This wasn't it, admittedly, but I just figured out you're the Angel, and I..." I floundered. "I just couldn't hold it back any longer."

He peered at me suspiciously. "Rachelle figured it out, didn't she?"

My mouth fell open. Then I closed it and nodded in embarrassed confirmation. "In my defense," I said, "I think my feelings for you clouded my normally keen senses." I paused. "That's a terrible defense," I admitted.

Caden, however, was glowing. Both figuratively and literally. His glamour had a much harder time confusing my immortal senses now that I had named him for what he was. He leaned forward and kissed me softly. "I think it's a great defense," he murmured.

From behind him came an annoyed clearing of the throat. He sat back, beaming at me. My eyes were drawn up to Trish, standing a few feet from Caden. She held the chain of the locket she'd thrown. "If you two are *quite* done," she growled, "I was under the impression we were on a time crunch."

I got to my feet, promising in a whisper, "We'll continue this conversation soon." I reached out a hand and helped Caden to his feet.

I was finding it hard to focus. I felt heady, and not just because of the kiss. Caden was the Angel.

Trish indicated the locket. "We should take a moment to memorize the wording of our wishes," she suggested. "The Genie is a bastard; he'll twist our wishes if we don't word them carefully."

That brought me back to the moment like a splash of ice water in the face. "I agree. We planned our wishes out already, but it would be a good idea to make sure they're foolproof."

Caden hesitated. "We're not ready to make them yet, right? Their timing is almost as important as the wishes themselves. Shouldn't we keep him in the locket until we're ready?"

"Even if he's hostile," Trish said, "he won't be dangerous while Emery is his master. We'd be fools not to question him, at least."

I was inclined to agree. The fact that the Genie had ambushed us here at all, though, answered one very big question. He was the smoking gun we needed: evidence Sabrina was our enemy. Only she had known when and where we would be, so only she could have sent him to waylay us.

After several long minutes of sorting out our plans and determining our exact wishes, I said, "Here goes nothing." I rubbed the locket between my thumb and forefinger.

For a moment, nothing happened, and the drone of rain on the building sounded loud again. Then the room seemed to darken by a shade or two, as if someone had drawn the shutters, and the smell of cinnamon reached my nose. Red clouds churned out of the locket, then condensed into the familiar form of the Genie. His arms were crossed, and he looked sullen, spoiling the otherwise magical moment.

"Master," he recited in a bored tone, "your wish is my command." Then he sneered at me. "Let's get this over with."

I ignored his animosity. "We are going to start things over between us. What is your name?" I asked him.

The Genie's lip curled. "I am called Iblis."

I took a steadying breath. "You are not a Malevolent incarnate, not normally. That's your prior master's influence. Help us, and we will set you free."

His stance of haughty distaste did not soften, but I saw a flicker of hunger in his expression. Then he snarled, "I would have been free years ago if not for you!" He shook his head savagely, like a dog trying to escape its muzzle. "Over two years I waited for you, the third wish already made. Freedom so near, yet one person stood in its path. *You.*"

I felt a stab of sympathy. No wonder he had fled when I threatened him with capture. He was starting over now, three more wishes.

"And then you wouldn't *die*," he continued.

The sympathy soured in my mouth. He had tried to kill me and my friends three times too many. "Work with us," I instructed, "and you'll be free before the end of the day."

The Genie mulled over my words, then gave me a brittle smile. "As you wish."

"Can you tell me Sabrina's plans?"

His smile turned patronizing. "You must begin with 'I wish.'"

I exchanged glances with Trish. We both hoped he would talk, but we would not trade a precious wish for the knowledge. We had already uncovered enough of Sabrina's plan; the extra information would not be worth the cost. Trish shrugged.

"If I gave the locket to Trish, would she become your new master?"

"No."

I pursed my lips. "How come you answer some questions, but not others?"

Iblis grimaced, annoyed. "I am only required to answer questions about myself and our contract."

I frowned. "If I want Trish to make a wish on my behalf, is this possible?"

The Genie paused. "Yes, so long as you specify it."

"I do. If Caden or Trish makes a wish, you will respond as though it were made by me."

Iblis spat to the side. "Yes, master."

Interesting. "So you are compelled to tell me anything about yourself? What was *your* role in Sabrina's plans?"

"To spread the physical word of Ahedrian," he replied. Then his smile returned, oily and serpentine. "And to kill you."

Well, that was chilling. Even knowing he had been gunning for me since my reincarnation, witnessing his wicked delight in trying gave me shivers. Spreading the physical word of Ahedrian... the new décor at Rikers was his handiwork. "Anything else?" I asked.

He shrugged, the gesture somehow cruel instead of casual.

Trish narrowed her eyes. "Explain."

His eyes bored holes through her. "I am not required to divulge information about prior master, unless you wish for the information."

Caden had been watching our conversation thoughtfully. Now he spoke up. "Are there any rules or limitations to the wishes you grant?"

"Yes," Iblis hissed.

Trish growled. "List all of the rules to making a wish." I had to hand it to her; even impatient, she phrased her demands with very little room for exploitation.

"I must grant three voiced wishes to the master of my... locket."

282 | JUSTIN SCHUELKE

He spat the word. "Upon completion of the third wish, the contract is complete, the locket will disintegrate, and I shall at long last be granted my freedom." He said the final part with a feverish glint in his eyes. "Three wishes, three rules. Rule one: you cannot wish for anything that would change the structure of the contract itself, such as wishing for more wishes. Rule two: as I am the embodiment of forced servitude, my wishes cannot impose upon the liberty of another."

Huh. That explained a lot. Like how I'd survived her wishes. Sabrina had been unable to simply wish me dead or in chains. Instead, the Genie had to hunt me down.

Iblis seemed to be fighting with himself. After some internal struggle, he bit out, "And finally, rule three: each use of the word 'and' consumes an additional wish, regardless of realization or intent."

I whistled. "Good thing you asked, Caden."

Caden stepped forward, drawing near to the Genie. In a calm and gentle tone, he said, "We want to save lives. Will you help us?"

Iblis spat again. "You imprison me, demand my assistance, *then* ask for help?" He laughed in Caden's face. "Go to hell, little man."

I stepped forward angrily, but Trish beat me to it. "Return to your locket, Iblis. Do not reappear until you are summoned." The Genie evaporated into cinnamon smoke. Trish turned to Caden, who looked troubled. "Spare him your pity. He's an asshole." She glanced in my direction. "And he took an order from me. It appears we're all set."

"We need to move," I agreed, pulling out my phone and texting Rachelle to let her know Plan A was on track.

The Genie's actions had proven that Sabrina was the murderer. With his unwilling aid, our first wish would be to save the people of Rikers Island from her devilish scheme. Our second wish would be to obtain his help in fighting Sabrina and—possibly—the Queen of Hearts. Our last wish would be to erase the memory of Ahedrian from history. I still did not fully believe a new incarnate could be created this way, but I had to admit it was an intriguing possibility. And with the lengths to which Sabrina was going to achieve it, I worried she was right.

Step one was complete. We had separated her from the Genie.

We needed to confront her, but we still didn't know how she beheaded people. Logically, our next step was to either discover that information or circumvent the concern. Fortunately, I knew of a weapon capable of fighting her without fear of decapitation.

*O*ur encounter with the Genie made it undeniably clear that Trish
was the Monster Hunter incarnate.

What then, was I?

*This wasn't the first time I'd encountered this question. I just didn't
know it at the time. I'd come face to face with my fatal flaw three incarnations ago; had died while exposed to it. That experience changed me. Made
me forget who I was. But then, despite engineering it in the first place,
Morrigan grew bored of my ignorance. She needed me for her plans, and for
me to be of any value to her, she needed me to remember the truth.*

*It makes so much sense. The conveniences, such as stumbling across a
murder scene within minutes of arriving in Manhattan. The coincidences,
like being saved from the Alligator in the Sewers when I didn't have a plan
or a prayer. The impeccable timing of Kolby's incident leading to the
Watchman finding me. The way you and I have these little chats right
before the information we cover is relevant to the plot.*

*It all leads to the same place, the answer to the question I posed to you
in the beginning: Who am I? What am I?*

∾

As CADEN, Trish, and I crept toward Harlem in the back of a rather noisy sedan, the pounding rain necessitating fast and squeaky swipes of the windshield wipers, I examined the situation in my mind. From the fragmented picture before me, a whole image was beginning to emerge. As pieces continued to slide into place, the puzzle was now more whole than missing, with only a few glaring empty spaces... and those pieces all seemed to have Morrigan's name written on them. *As usual*, I reflected bitterly.

I reconstructed the facts. Morrigan had prompted me to go to New York in order to meet my impostor—Trish—knowing I would begin to doubt my place as the Monster Hunter. To tempt me into her trap, she'd baited it with two hooks she knew I would be helpless to resist: murder and mystery. To lure Trish into the same trap, she needed a monster: the Genie. Which guided me to a conclusion I'd long since suspected: an alliance between her and Sabrina.

Together, they set up an ambush for Trish and me, which would have been wildly convenient for them if it had succeeded. Luckily— or, I should say, typically—for Morrigan, her success was guaranteed regardless of who limped away from that confrontation. If the Genie defeated us, she would be rid of two pests for a thousand and one days. And if we defeated the Genie, I would realize that Trish, not I, was the Monster Hunter. Why that was important to her, I wasn't yet sure.

As I considered that, several more puzzle pieces clicked into place, the picture resolving itself further. I broke it down: Sabrina was working with Morrigan, because she'd called me by name before killing me in the desert, even though I was reasonably certain we'd never met before that incarnation. And she was likely mortal, because she had used a gun. That last point additionally lent a hell of a lot of credence to the theory that she was not the Queen of Hearts. If she possessed the ability to magically whisk off my head, why resort to using a gun? It seemed likely that her plan was to gain immortality by turning into a new urban legend, Ahedrian. If she was working with Morrigan, that meant my nemesis was also trying to create an incarnate—or was at least amused enough by the idea not to oppose it. It also explained why the great and powerful Morrigan would deign to work with a mortal in the first place: she'd have a murdering incarnate at her beck and call, one who owed her for helping it obtain eternal life.

The master plan—whether Morrigan's or Sabrina's, and you can guess which one I'd put my money on—was a perfect loophole: vigilante killings of criminals in New York attributed to "Ahedrian," and the spreading of the urban legend far and wide through her media outlet.

As I stared at my nearly completed puzzle, I could see only two missing spots, but they marred the bigger picture.

First, the Queen of Hearts. Looking glasses across the country had been handing me clues from "Jabberwocky," nudging me toward the answer: the Queen of Hearts, the tyrant. Much like Bloody Mary, she could probably use looking glasses—which would be just about any reflective glass surface—as a means of transportation. Perhaps the looking glasses felt violated by her passage and turned to me to right this grievous wrong. But why was the Queen of Hearts working with Sabrina—or Morrigan—in the first place? What was her role in this scheme? Trish's assertion that I'd mixed up the queens' identities from the pages of Lewis Carroll nagged at me, too. It wasn't a huge concern, though. The Queen of Hearts and the Red Queen are often confused or conflated by fans, so the Queen of Hearts incarnate—an amalgamation of all the legends told of these figures throughout time —could simply have gained many of the characteristics of the Red Queen. Still, a small part of me worried when things did not align perfectly. It's because I'm a perfectionist, on my mother's side.

The second missing piece weighed much more heavily on my mind. Morrigan's underlying motives. Why send me to New York and set me on the trail to discovering her plans to help create an incarnate? I could hazard a few guesses, but they fell flat. Sure, she would want to rub my nose in her achievements and would delight in watching me fail at foiling her. Similarly, it would provide me with several opportunities to meet an untimely demise, which was her favorite spectator sport. But our discussion in the limousine gnawed at me. She wanted me to discover my personification, to learn my place as an incarnate. To learn, unequivocally, that I was not the Monster Hunter incarnate. I just... did not know *why*. What did it matter to her? I frowned at that thought. There was something to that. She was my opposite. Throughout time, we seemed bound together by a cruel twist of fate. Was that it? Did she hope to discover some mystery about her own incarnation by understanding mine?

The car slowed, and I glanced at Caden. He was lost in his own world of thoughts, undoubtedly about the revelation that he was an incarnate. And not just some random half-forgotten urban legend, either—he was the Angel, a Benign possessing the powers of light and healing. Known throughout the Western world for his beauty, grace, wisdom, and divinity. I found myself smiling as I drank him in, his traits taking on a more mystical cast with the truth of his incarnation revealed to me.

The car rolled to a stop, and Trish opened the door, exiting into the downpour outside. Caden and I came back to ourselves in unison, then slid out after her. The rain was heavy and icy, bouncing off the pavement and forming puddles. Only a few pedestrians cut through the rain, some huddled beneath the dubious shelter of umbrellas, others scurrying down the sidewalk with coats or hats raised above their heads. Despite being let out less than a block from Madam Zerona's Spirits and Seances, we were thoroughly soaked by the time we rushed up the wooden porch and pushed open the door to the tiny shop.

I felt like the Drowned Man incarnate. My hair was plastered to my forehead, cold water dripping down my face and off my nose. My sodden clothes had fared especially poorly today; after first being exposed to the Genie's fiery temperament, my shirt sported many new, black-singed holes. Then the icy March rain had soaked it through to hang heavy and limp on me, revealing my skin through water-logged, charred tears.

In comparison, Trish's all-leather assemblage looked glossy, its sleek appeal unfairly enhanced by the water droplets clinging to its surface. At least her hair was flattened to her... no, wait, she was running a hand through it. Water droplets flicked to the side like a goddamn shampoo commercial, and then her pixie cut slicked back into place, looking as fresh as if she'd just redone it.

And Caden... forget it. He looked pristine, as always. I was contemplating the injustice of the world when he turned his seafoam eyes on me and I couldn't help but smile at him instead. Dammit.

"Took you all long enough," a raspy voice greeted us. Zelda sat in her favorite rocking chair, a long cigarette between her fingers, a curl of smoke disappearing into the air above her. She looked us up and down. "What, did you swim?"

I stared at her shoeless feet and short-sleeved blouse in dismay. "Didn't Rachelle tell you the plan?" I asked. "Why aren't you ready to go?" I glanced out the window. The heavy clouds and dark sky made it seem later than it truly was, an artificial dusk urging me onward.

She took a long drag on her cigarette, held it, then blew it out while I waited impatiently for a response. "Young people," she muttered. "Always in a hurry." She let out a racking cough, and I could feel Trish's pointed stare like a nail gun. "Although," Zelda continued after she'd caught her breath, "I'd expect better from the lot of you."

Caden looked puzzled at her words, and I sighed. "A poor attempt at incarnate humor," I explained. "You'll get used to it." I snatched Madam Zerona's coat off its hook and stepped up to her, holding it out. "We need to get going. Lives are in peril."

She gave me a flat look, ignoring the coat and my outstretched hand. "Good," she muttered. "Business has been slow."

I took a cleansing breath—which did not feel overly cleansing in the smoky haze of the room—and started again. "Zelda, from one incarnate to another, will you please help us?"

"Kiddos, do you know what you're asking?" She indicated her own body with a gesture of her crooked fingers. "I don't know if I have the power to help you."

Trish stepped forward, an expression of deference completely out of place on her features. "Madam Zerona, if I may speak?" And I kid you not, she actually waited for the Medium's smiling nod of approval before continuing. "I do not mean to correct you, ma'am, but you are mistaken. You are the *only* one with the power to help us. You are the Medium, the conduit between this world and the afterlife. And we have need of your voice."

Zelda blew a plume of smoke upward, considering Trish with heavy-lidded eyes. "It's raining buckets out there," she complained, "and I don't have the constitution I once did, young lady." Trish didn't respond, steadily holding her gaze. The older woman finally sighed. "All right," she said at last. "But we talk to him my way."

I nodded eagerly. "Thank you. We couldn't do this without you."

She gave me a dry look. "We may not be able to do it *with* me." She puffed on her cigarette in thought. "We need to wait until dusk. Or near enough as makes no difference." She tapped the cigarette against the ashtray. "And you'll need to take me to his Territory. No arguments. I simply can't summon him from here."

My heart dropped. If we needed to wait until dusk *and* travel to Tarrytown, we would never beat Sabrina to Rikers Island in order to ambush her, as I had hoped. We'd be trailing her instead, trying desperately to catch up. With every minute we delayed, more people would die. I vacillated, but we had planned for this eventuality... well, okay, not this *exact* eventuality, but we had accounted for delays. I finally nodded to the two of them. With the cooperation—willing or otherwise—of the Genie, we could make it work.

More importantly, this course of action felt *right*. Like every event I'd experienced in New York was interconnected, leading me down a path of fateful coincidences to one inevitable conclusion. I just wished I knew what that was.

*A*s we waited to leave, my restlessness stretched minutes into hours. I counted the cracks in the ceiling, watching the nearly imperceptible march of the sun toward the horizon. Trish, other than a few quiet exchanges with Zelda, stood at the window and watched the rainfall. I wondered if she was counting something, too. Caden tried to distract me, to lure me into conversation, but my responses were terse and he eventually gave up, sitting on the couch and thumbing through his phone instead. Zelda smoked four more cigarettes and spent close to an hour choosing the perfect outfit for a summoning.

Finally, the four of us were packed into a little yellow taxicab, the rain pounding down as it cruised the nearly empty roads of Sleepy Hollow. We were stuffed in the Prius like sardines in a can; Madam Zerona occupied the front passenger seat and chatted amiably with our driver, while Trish, Caden, and I crammed on top of one another in the back seat. I envied the Genie his spacious locket.

I glanced at my phone for the millionth time.

5:05 p.m.

Our original plan had us arriving at the prison island no later than four. We'd assumed Sabrina would use her job to circumvent

Rikers' famed security. Instead of sneaking or killing her way in, she would give a live report from Rikers, drawing statewide attention to the island, making sure all eyes were pointed her way. Then she would seal her legend with an impossible feat: behead every living person in the prison.

Which meant she must have arrived by now. My hands fisted as I thought about it, but we weren't ready to spring our trap yet. We needed just a little more time.

5:06 p.m.

Thunder rumbled ominously above us, though I had missed the flash of light. Technically, dusk was still two hours away, but the weather had worked in our favor. The storm darkened the sky, muting the light, choking the day into an early submission to evening. Although the brewing storm right before our big altercation with Ahedrian seemed portentous, Madam Zerona treated it like a gift. According to her, the Headless Horseman could be seen on nights like this one, appearing during flashes of lightning, the whinnying cry of his phantom steed barely discernible beneath the sudden crack of thunder.

Which made the storm mighty convenient, especially on the heels of a stretch of good weather. That line of thinking reignited my consternation over my ever-increasing connection to coincidence. The certainty was growing in me that Caden was right: it was associated with my incarnation. I had always taken for granted the luck I seemed to possess, maybe even viewed it as my due for ridding the world of dangerous incarnates. In any case, I'd figured most—if not all—incarnates experienced the same link to fortune. We were born at the heart of legend, after all, and legends are not eternally retold because they're unexciting. Why, then, would we live our lives any differently?

But a different picture was emerging from the recesses of my memory. Coincidence, convenience, drama. My story was a hurricane, and I was the eye of the storm. Which, looking out at the sodden, rain-darkened street outside our cab, made me feel like it was *my* storm. A curious sense of ownership accompanied that thought and spurred another: could I *direct* this storm, this story? What if I could *use* my penchant for coincidence, instead of it just happening *to* me? A thrill ran through me. I thought back to the limousine and Morrigan's theatrical display with the map. She had been doing just that. Capitalizing on the randomness, the chaotic nature of coincidence.

Owning it.

"What is this?" I had asked her when she'd proffered the map with its many new pinpricks. "Proof," she had responded. "When you're ready for it."

5:08 p.m.

Two hours from sunset. Looking out the window past the back of Trish's head, it seemed like nighttime already. Had I somehow... *done* that? I could just picture Rachelle's rolling eyes. I hadn't even known we would need an early dusk. It seemed impossible. Arrogance on a scale that surpassed even my usual towering self-confidence. But...

As if on cue, I received a text from Rachelle: WATCHING 5PM EVENING NEWS, NOTHING YET. YOU GUYS CLOSE?

The cab continued down the street Caden and I had walked a few nights ago, as I texted a quick reply. Houses rolled by, the distances between them growing as nature reclaimed its place within the neighborhoods. Lights warmed the first several houses we passed, people visible in their comfortable living rooms or standing at their kitchen sinks.

5:10 p.m.

As we neared our destination, the houses were as silent and forlorn as they had been nearing midnight the other night. Perhaps the storm had knocked out a power line; I thought I caught the flickering of candles from inside one of the old residences we passed. It suddenly felt darker, later, and quieter as the taxi pulled over. The cab's headlights illuminated streaks of rain and the dark path I remembered so well, ambling beneath the skeletal limbs of the trees.

"This the place?" the driver asked dubiously.

Lightning flashed overhead, illuminating the tunnel of trees, highlighting their twisted forms in stark relief against the backdrop of the dark, rainy evening.

"Unfortunately," I confirmed, and we disembarked our safe little vehicle as thunder roared down at us reprovingly. Trish took two umbrellas we'd appropriated from Madam Zerona's shop, handed one of them to me, then unfolded hers and helped the Medium out of the taxi so she wouldn't be as exposed to the rain. Caden took the umbrella from me and unfurled it, holding it over our heads. It offered protection from the icy downpour, but the gusts of wind still slid through my clothes and provoked shivers.

Trish surveyed the area as the cab pulled away, her attention drawn to the muddy path ahead. The gaunt trees swaying in the breeze were as welcoming as a knife blade. "That way, I assume?"

"You know what they say about people who assume," I told her cheerfully, while Caden simply replied, "Yes."

Madam Zerona pulled a cigarette out of its pack and lit it beneath the umbrella. "This place is hallowed," she announced, blowing out a plume of smoke.

5:12 p.m.

I wanted to scream at her. We didn't have time for a smoke break.

Caden, surprisingly, nodded. "I feel that, too." They both spoke in hushed tones, like they were in a library.

I ground my teeth. "What does that mean, exactly? A lot of people have died here?"

Zelda gestured with her cigarette. "Not exactly. It *can* mean that, but it's more of a crossroads. A place to which the energies of the afterlife are drawn. Some would call those ghosts."

I responded automatically. "But... ghosts aren't real. Only *the* Ghost is real."

Madam Zerona scoffed. "The Ghost incarnate is the personification of every ghost *story*," she informed me. "What happens to mortals when their lives end? We don't know, kiddo. Whether you believe in an afterlife, ghosts, karmic reincarnation, or simply that our soul disperses into nature, the fact remains that death is one story to which we do not know the ending." She shrugged, the end of her cigarette lighting as she puffed on it. "Incarnates who are closer to the beyond, like me, we can sense *something* at hallowed places like these." She bent down and smothered the tip of her cigarette in the wet ground, then placed the butt in a plastic baggy and put that into her purse. "As the Medium, I have only ever interacted with ghost *incarnates*. Whether that proves or disproves the existence of real ghosts, I'll leave up to you."

My phone buzzed again, a text from Rachelle: GOING TO COMMER-CIAL BREAK. SABRINA REPORTING LIVE FROM RIKERS WHEN THEY RETURN. KEEP YOU POSTED.

"We should move," Trish said, obviously as impatient to get to Rikers as I was. "Emery, Caden, what should we expect?"

"We're approaching his Lair or Territory," I said. I pointed at the tunnel of trees down the path. "Those trees mark the edge of it. Last time, he appeared after lightning struck that tree."

Trish frowned. "Which one?"

A chill ran through me. The trees were all undamaged.

"One of those trees definitely exploded," Caden confirmed.

I slipped my backpack off but held it, not wanting to set it on the muddy ground. I partially unzipped it, then dug around for my Taser. Once I found it, I hesitated, then swallowed my pride and extended it, holster and all, to Trish.

She frowned at my offer. "What's this for?"

I stared at her. "Ghostly incarnates have a weakness to electricity."

Trish's frown deepened. "Huh. You're not a complete fool." Which meant I had impressed her. I was starting to understand Trish. She accepted the Taser and examined it.

I gave her a brittle grin. "Hunting monsters the hard way has taught me a thing or two."

"Please do not use that except as a last resort," the Medium said. "It will be challenging enough communicating with him if he's not peeved."

Trish nodded and strapped the Taser to her waist.

5:19 p.m. The evening news was only an hour long.

We began to pick our way down the path. Thunder rumbled in

the distance, and I idly wondered at the wisdom of holding umbrellas in the storm. As we neared the trees, my pulse quickened. I kept my eyes partially lidded, ready to squeeze shut if a bolt of lightning struck. It would not catch me completely off guard a second time.

The feeling of entering another incarnate's Territory, that undefinable, imperceptible chill that sent goose bumps up my arms, did not raise the hackles of my neck hairs to the extent it had when Caden and I first passed this way. I was beginning to think the correct term for the Headless Horseman's domain *was* Territory, not Lair. While certainly dangerous, if he was not responsible for the deaths in New York City, then he did not appear to present a threat to humans or society, thus downgrading him from Malevolent to Predator. Or upgrading him, I suppose.

The first barren trees stretched skeletal limbs above our heads, and I braced myself for the noise and light show. But we passed through the barrier without harm and emerged in the large clearing. It looked deserted and somehow dejected in the rain. The tree Caden had climbed was undamaged by our fight with the Headless Horseman, despite me clearly remembering the wood bursting into fragments as the incarnate ran Caden down at the top. There were, however, a few indications of our skirmish: the swath of displaced soil and leaves where I'd been dragged and then pile driven into the earth was the most obvious, but I also glimpsed some pulpy remains of a pumpkin kicked to one side of the path. Not to mention, if you looked carefully enough, you could almost make out hoofprints crisscrossing the play area.

I looked in the direction of the small farmyard Caden and I had spent the night in. It was difficult to see through the gloom, trees, and rain, but I didn't see any structure on the other side of the river. I smiled to myself. Not entirely unexpected. I wondered, briefly, if finding it had been another *convenience* of my incarnation.

We reached the center of the clearing with no trouble, and my heart sank. No Headless Horseman. If we had to wait until *actual* dusk to summon the incarnate, Sabrina would have *hours* on us. Even if we stopped her, many lives would be lost before we arrived. I imagined the halls of Rikers Island littered with headless corpses. We could use Iblis to wish safety for the people, but if we tipped Sabrina off, we would likely lose our opportunity to find and confront her. If she went into hiding, especially with Morrigan's resources, it could be years before I found her again. But how many lives would I sacrifice to put a stop to her tonight?

The answer had to be none. To willingly allow murder, even for a greater good, would be crossing a line I was unwilling to cross. *The greater good* could ironically be a path to evil; an excuse—albeit a persuasive one—to justify something wrong, something immoral. It was a cobbled path of good intentions just as candied as any of Morrigan's trails. And it headed to the same wretched destination. I would not walk that path today.

5:23 p.m.

The temptation to wait it out was strong; to allow even a few minutes, to just wait and see, hoping the Headless Horseman would appear at any time.

Even as I thought that, Rachelle texted: SHE'S ON. NO DEATHS YET. IT'S NOW OR NEVER, EM.

I opened my mouth to tell the others what I was thinking, that we needed to use our first Genie wish and act *now*, when Zelda's actions stopped me short. Head tilted to the dark sky, she stepped from beneath the umbrella's protection and closed her eyes, allowing the raindrops to splash on her face. She stood there, like a woman standing beneath the streaming jets of a shower, face lifted to the storm. Rain quickly soaked her clothes, her shawl, her hair. Her arms raised slowly, and, from my angle, I could just glimpse her lips curl into a smile. In that moment, I did not see a frail older woman standing in a downpour. I saw a powerful woman welcoming the storm, a mutual greeting, with the force of nature begrudgingly acknowledging her strength in return.

It became apparent to all in that clearing that the strength of the Medium incarnate resided not within the woman herself, but in her ability to connect. She stood before the storm, and *it broke first*. The deluge of rain lightened, becoming a fine mist. Lightning flashed no longer, and thunder, when it was heard at all, was distant. The clouds stayed heavy and dark, but all else lessened its intensity.

In the waning light, the shadows were long and muddled, difficult to discern from one another and the overarching pervasive dark. Movement near the tree line caught my attention. Shadows there sharpened, then resolved into the form of the Headless Horseman atop his steed.

I tensed, and I felt Trish do the same. Outwardly, very little had changed about her, but she seemed to come alive, ready to burst into action at a moment's notice.

The Headless Horseman guided his mount toward us at a walk. The horse approached Zelda and did not stop until it was near enough for her to touch its nose. The terrifying visage of the Headless Horseman towered over her, looming like the specter of death come to claim his reaping.

As before with Iris, the Headless Horseman appeared more solid, more *real* around the Medium. As if she pulled them from their realm and planted them firmly in ours. The Horseman's black armor gleamed in the low light, his trailing cape obeying the laws of physics rather than billowing out behind him as though he were perpetually moving through shades of night. Zelda reached up and patted the muzzle of the horse, muttering words of greeting too quietly for me to make out.

Then she turned to face the rest of us, keeping the Headless Horseman at her shoulder. When she spoke, the voice that emerged was deep and unfamiliar. It was still *her* vocal cords producing the sound, but the tone was warped beyond recognition. "You trespass once more upon my abode. Pray tell, for what reason should I stay my blade and refrain from exacting a toll for your intrusion?"

I glanced at the others, but they didn't immediately respond. *We don't have time for this.* At the risk of angering the incarnate further, I swallowed and took a half step forward. "We apologize for trespassing." I stumbled, not sure how to address him courteously. I decided to leave off an honorific altogether. "I am Emery Luple, a fellow incarnate. We have come to beg for your assistance."

The Headless Horseman did not move, but the Medium's head tilted to the side, inspecting me as if curious. "You trespass once with murderous intent, then dare to repeat your transgression imploring my assistance? What ails you, to elicit such audacity?"

I had a bit of trouble following his words, especially with his attention focused intently on me. Caden, however, spoke up. "A murderer in New York leaves behind headless bodies, Horseman," he said. "We came here the other night to talk, not to fight. We thought you might know something about it."

The eyes of the Medium slid to Caden while her head remained unnervingly still. The Headless Horseman seemed to be manipulating her body but was unfamiliar with the head's functions. He/they responded, "In what bold age do we reside, when weapons of war accompany discourse at the table of diplomacy?"

Caden shook his head, his expression—as always—earnest and open. "A misunderstanding, Horseman. With more beheadings occurring by the day, we feared you were involved. We brought those weapons with us not for war, but for protection. We did not mean to provoke you." To my eyes, Caden seemed to glow in the dark night. Standing opposite the imposing Horseman, his golden light was a contrasting match for the deep blackness of the other incarnate, reminding me of a hero standing in defiance of a black dragon.

The severe expression on the Medium's face softened, touched by Caden's angelic glamour. "Perhaps I reacted in haste," the Headless Horseman replied through her. His responses felt weighty, every syllable enunciated. "As atonement, permit me to entertain your request."

When it came to incarnates, I was accustomed to leading the conversations, comfortable in my experience with them. But as badly as I yearned to speak up, I had to admit Caden was doing an incredible job. I kept my mouth shut and allowed him to continue. Sometimes, leadership is about knowing when to step aside, when to rely on others.

"We have come begging for your help," Caden said, humble and direct. "We now know the identity of the murderer, but she still possesses the ability to harm us. Behead us, specifically." He took a few steps forward, almost close enough to touch the Medium. "You have no fear of decapitation. With your cooperation, we can more safely confront her."

"You entreat me to smite enemies not my own."

Caden nodded, then looked up at the incarnate with pleading eyes. "Murderers are enemies of us all. And to make matters worse, this murderer is trying to obtain immortality, to kill for eternity." He knelt, looking up at the mounted incarnate, his white frame seeming tiny beside the massive specter of horse and rider. "Please help us." I held my breath. Such an act from anyone else would seem overly theatrical and artificial... but not so from Caden, who exuded sincerity the way Trish exuded anger.

My phone buzzed in my pocket. I didn't dare look at it.

"Arise, little incarnate," the Medium's voice instructed, her tone showing no indication as to how the Headless Horseman felt about Caden's display. "I commend your integrity, and the mud ill-befits a man of your caliber." I blew out a breath as Caden clambered back to his feet. "Very well. I shall oblige and endeavor to inflict judgment upon this malfeasant, provided you aid me in recompense."

Caden frowned. "A favor?"

"Just so."

Caden, surprisingly, did not look to us for guidance, somehow understanding the negotiation was between the two of them. "I accept."

I nearly jumped at the low, unnatural laughter that clawed its way out of the Medium's throat. "You trust without hesitation, consigning yourself and your companions to the whims of a stranger."

"Not a stranger, Horseman," Caden replied smoothly. "I'm not the only one whose measure was taken during this conversation." *Holy hell.* He was even starting to *sound* like the Headless Horseman. "Make your request."

As the Headless Horseman paused to consider his words, I risked a glance at my phone. Rachelle had sent, *EM, SABRINA'S REPORT CUT*

OUT. IT ENDED WITH A SCREAM. PLEASE TELL ME U GUYS R THERE. GOOD LUCK.

Shit. Hurry up, Caden. At last, the Horseman said through the Medium, "Within the span of a year, fashion for me an imperishable head. Swear to this, and we have an accord."

Caden stepped forward, past the Medium, and raised his hand to the mounted, headless knight. The Headless Horseman leaned down and engulfed Caden's tiny hand in his armored one. They shook.

Madam Zerona blinked groggily a few times, then erupted in deep, racking coughs, her vocal cords protesting at being used to produce such a deep rasp. Trish darted forward and covered her with the umbrella. The timing was impeccable, as the drizzle surrendered to the return of heavier rainfall.

"We need to go *now*," I told the group. "Rachelle says there was a scream on Sabrina's live report, then the feed ended."

Trish and Caden both opened their mouths to speak, but a recovered Zelda cut them off. "The Headless Horseman will not be able to stray far from me at Rikers. His power wanes the further from his Territory we get, and outside of Sleepy Hollow his powers are rendered ineffectual without my support."

Trish nodded. "I will protect you, ma'am," she vowed. She turned to me, her usual sour disposition replaced with an almost eager gleam in her eyes. "Are we ready?"

Caden had returned to my side, and I gave him a you-were-amazing and good-luck-and-don't-die side hug. His subdued smile said he understood.

I hit Send on my text to Rachelle: *HEADING IN NOW. I WILL TEXT YOU WHEN IT'S OVER.* "Yeah," I said, "but we should be on Rikers already."

I recited again in my mind the wishes we had so carefully planned to make.

Wish #1: to evacuate the people of Rikers Island from harm, returning them only when it was safe to do so

Wish #2: for the Genie to aid us to the best of his abilities in the confrontation with Sabrina

Wish #3: to erase the word Ahedrian from the minds of everyone

I shook my head in frustration, looking between Trish and Caden. "We need to adjust our wishes."

Trish grimaced. "No helping it," she agreed.

"With the Headless Horseman's aid, maybe we won't need the Genie to fight with us," Caden said optimistically.

I rubbed the locket, and cinnamon clouds amassed before me.

I stood in a clearing with the Angel, the Monster Hunter, the Medium, the Headless Horseman, and the Genie. That is a sentence I never thought I'd say. My heart began to beat faster as I flashed them a thumbs-up and said, "For the last time: let's do this."

38

"I wish," I stated in a commanding, ringing tone, "for you to instantly teleport the group of incarnates in this clearing to a safe spot thirty feet away from Sabrina Miles on Rikers Island without alerting her to our arrival."

The Genie scowled and sniveled, "Your wish is my command, oh master."

We huddled together in the center of the clearing, red smoke blossoming around us and swirling into a scarlet wall of fog. It thickened, obscuring our view of the clearing, of our feet, of each other... and then it parted suddenly, revealing the creepiest plain, empty hallway I've ever seen. Scrawled on the white walls was the word "Ahedrian" repeated over and over again, spilling onto the ceiling, cascading down to the floors. It flowed in a multitude of scripts and fonts, etched into the walls as if carved there by a knife. We stood together, crammed in the narrow confines of the corridor, bright blue doors lining either side of the hallway. Sabrina was nowhere to be seen, but we heard raised voices filtering to us from down the hallway. It took me a moment to realize why that bothered me. *No alarm.* Rachelle said the feed had ended in a scream, but they hadn't had time to set off the alarms yet. It was unnaturally quiet here, the arguing voices muffled by a wall. The Headless Horseman did not fully fit within the tight space, his horse's rear haunches phasing through the wall to my left.

"That sounds like Gustav," I whispered after a moment, listening to the voices, blocking out the creepy word written everywhere.

"The asshole dropped us within thirty feet of Sabrina *on the other side of a wall*," Trish hissed.

Moving as quietly as I could, I began to half jog down the hallway toward the voices, which I realized were coming from ahead and to the right. The others followed me, moving stealthily. I still flinched at the scuffing of a shoe on the linoleum. I glimpsed a metal detector above a set of doors leading to my right, one of them slightly ajar. The voices were coming from there.

"*Ahedrian?*" I heard Gustav ask, his voice shrill. "This whole time?"

"Ready?" I whispered to the group. "When we go under these metal detectors, she'll know we're here."

They all nodded grimly.

"They were all criminals," Sabrina said, her voice cold and calm. "I thought you, of all people, would understand."

I unholstered my Taser, which I had reclaimed from Trish in the clearing, then burst through the doors. A white light blinked brightly, and an alarm rang out as we passed beneath the metal detector. It did not set off the facility's alarm, as I had expected, but rather sounded like one of those detectors at retail stores that blare locally for about thirty seconds when someone walks through them with security-tagged merchandise.

I held my Taser before me, my heart dropping as I took in the scene. The room we'd entered was large and multileveled, with stairs leading up to rows of cells on either side. The cells were not open-faced, but rather closed blue doors with bright white numbering and partially clouded viewing windows. Bars crisscrossed the upper level, however, producing an effect that *looked* like the cells were behind bars. Other than those metal bars as safety precautions, the expansive room —with its white-and-blue motif and sterile functionality—reminded me of a school more than anything, with plain mirrors at set intervals adorning the walls between the cells. There was even what looked like an inspirational quote written on the side of one of the upper floors.

Which made the two headless corpses beneath all the more jarring. "Ahedrian" was written on every blank space here, too, carved into the white walls and spray-painted like graffiti over the inspirational quote—which was so defaced I couldn't make out the original words. Maybe it wasn't inspiring at all.

We were twenty feet from the base of a set of four blue steps, Sabrina and Gustav arguing at the top of them, their argument making the corpses and scribbling seem even more surreal, more appalling. Two huge men stood a few feet behind Sabrina, garbed in practical civilian clothes that did nothing to downplay their clear purpose—to guard her. With a start, I realized I recognized one of them: Polite Ape, Morrigan's goon who had held the door to the limo for me. His presence was the final piece of unequivocal evidence that Sabrina and Morrigan were working together.

Sabrina Miles, red mane afire, stood poised at the top of the stairs like a Greek statue, fierce and bold and icily inhuman. And she was armed. With a sword.

The blade in her right hand was unlike any I had ever seen. Easily five feet long, it should have been too heavy for her to wield with just one hand, but she held it like a child might hold a foam sword. The hilt was spun silver, the grip hammered scales like the hide of a lizard, with each flake polished to a gleam. The pommel, at the base of the hilt, featured a roaring creature with fangs like crescent moons, eyes inlaid with sparkling rubies that gave the impression the hilt was alive. The cross guard was a mass of silvery, thorny stems spiraling outward, so that the blade seemed to protrude from a bristly bramble dipped in silver.

And that blade.

It was not forged of metal or alloy. It was a mirror. Not *polished* to a mirror, but an *actual* mirror. Perfectly reflective, from guard to point. Razor edged, about a handbreadth in width, it showcased detailed etching along its center all the way to its wicked tip, where the etching split into intricate floral patterns.

Even as I took in the horrific scene, Sabrina became aware of us. "I'm sorry, Gustav," she said in a tone that carried over the blaring alarm. Gustav, eyes wide, face drained of color, tried to scamper down the stairs toward us and out of reach of that terrible blade. Quicker than I could react, Sabrina swept the blade in an upward arc, a *whoosh* that caught Gustav across the back, flicking a thin line of blood into the air. The sound of the strike was a sickening crunch of metal on bone, followed by a scrape so low it seemed to come from the basement. I recognized it instantly from several days earlier, when I'd heard the attack in the parking garage. Gustav's wound was superficial, shallow, and he barely made so much as a grunt. But as he continued down the stairs and out of her reach, his head slumped forward and *slid off his neck.* His headless corpse faltered in its next step and collapsed, tumbling down the remaining stairs. His head bounced grotesquely before evaporating into nothing.

For a beat, I stood in stunned disbelief. Then I sprang into action before the others recovered enough to act.—or perhaps they were just more cautious than I. Either way, I bolted forward, squeezing the trigger of the Taser when I reached the base of the stairs. I didn't even use the red laser to aim, just fired with the instincts of an immortal. With a click, the coils snapped forward. It was the perfect shot, the spread of the conductive wires optimal, the aim precise. Even Sabrina's quick step backward would not be enough to save her... but she moved her magical blade in a blurring upward stroke, catching the Taser's coils before they bit into her and severing them as if they were made of cotton instead of copper. Decapitated, like the heads of twin snakes, the wires fell to the ground.

Damn. She was *fast*—and clearly proficient with the sword. Polite Ape and Goon #2 closed in around her, flanking her protectively.

"Emery," Sabrina said, a pained expression in her voice. "You keep turning up where you're not wanted." She held the blade in front of her in a wary stance.

I tossed the spent Taser aside, knowing I would not be able to

306 | JUSTIN SCHUELKE

reload it before she reached me with that magnificent blade. "You seem to have classed up your weaponry," I said, indicating her mirrored sword. "Much more elegant than a gun to the back of the head in a desert half the world away."

Her eyes gleamed. "You figured it out, did you?" She ran a hand lovingly down the flat of her sword's blade. "I'm so glad you approve. After I left your corpse behind in that desert, to be buried and forgotten in the sand, it still took me over two years to obtain the Vorpal Blade incarnate."

And there it was. One of those last two elusive pieces. The way Ahedrian murdered her victims, the answer to the clues with which the mirrors had tried to warn me. Not the Queen of Hearts or the Red Queen. There was no alliance between either queen and Sabrina. I wanted to howl in frustration. The answer was so much simpler. Even as I thought about it, the veils of my memory parted and the remainder of the verse about the vorpal blade from "Jabberwocky" came rushing back to me:

"One, two! One, two! And through and through
The vorpal blade went snicker-snack!
He left it dead, and with its head
He went galumphing back."

A SWORD whose sole legend was decapitating the wielder's "manx-ome" foe, the Jabberwock. It made perfect sense. Sabrina Miles *was* mortal, reaching for immortality by creating an incarnate, Ahedrian, through the use of a legendary weapon. The sound I'd heard was the *whoosh*ing of the weapon and its sound as it struck flesh: *snicker-snack*. It didn't matter where the edge of the blade bit, either; the result was instant death by decapitation. Which explained the confusing wounds found on the other victims: even a slice to the hand was fatal.

Sabrina saw the understanding dawn on my face, and she shook her head. "Honestly, after I ran into you in that parking garage, I feared that you'd come back from the grave vowing vengeance. My plan was in tatters, everything I'd worked for crumbling around me. Imagine my surprise when Rachelle called asking for my help. And I realized you *didn't know.*"

The alarm from the metal detectors cut off. Behind me, I heard Trish's voice—loud, in the sudden quiet—reciting, "I wish for you to instantly and safely relocate the people of Rikers Island to an empty location—"

I tried to respond to Sabrina, to draw her into conversation, but I saw her focus shift to Trish. Too late, I hoped. "Stop her!" she screamed at the two henchmen.

Polite Ape sprang forward in lockstep with Goon #2, the former wielding a hunting knife that looked anything but courteous, while the latter brandished a nightstick.

"—where they cannot cause harm or garner attention, returning them at dawn tomorrow," Trish finished.

The goons were almost on top of me when they suddenly veered off course and dove to the sides. *What?* Then the Headless Horseman thundered *through* me and up the stairs toward Sabrina. Sabrina, to her credit, did not panic. Watching the mounted incarnate approach, she waited in a fighter's stance, then wheeled out of the way at the last moment and scored a long slash down the horse's flank. With the Medium present, however, the Headless Horseman was in full possession of his powers, and the blade passed harmlessly through him as he went ghost on her.

"Your wish is my command, master."

Red flashes began to light up the windows of the cells, accompanied by loud bangs that sounded like fireworks. Scarlet tendrils of smoke curled out from beneath the cell doors. The Genie was teleporting the inmates away, one at a time.

My attention was suddenly riveted as my vision filled with the round, bald head of Goon #2. He swung his baton at my ribcage. I half turned, half retreated, and the nightstick slammed into my backpack, shielding me from the forceful strike. Unfortunately, that opened me up to Polite Ape, who had been closing in on me from behind.

That immortal corner of my brain flared awake, fully alert, and took over my body as I snapped my arm down, catching Polite Ape's wrist and sending the hunting knife skittering across the floor. At the same time, I kicked backward. With a meaty thud, it connected with Goon #2 and sent him staggering. My left hook caught Polite Ape across the cheek, and I followed through with a knee to his groin, driving him away from me.

The big grin on my face probably looked ridiculous, but memories were flooding in of lifetimes I'd spent as a fighter. My body responded instinctively.

Polite Ape and Goon #2 were big, though, and recovered quickly. As they did, Trish came flying in from the side, bringing up her knee to collide solidly with Goon #2, making him grunt. Despite her flawless form, Goon #2 used his enormous size to absorb the brunt of her attack and grabbed her, hurling her into the metal handrail behind him. She caught herself, barely, and the momentum flung her up and over the railing to land painfully on the other side. I realized with dismay that her superhuman strength and speed were absent while fighting humans. She was the Monster Hunter; against mortals, she was just an ordinary—angry—human.

I still wouldn't want her for an enemy, though. Trish regained her feet and flourished Goon #2's nightstick with a smirk. The man looked at her in confusion for a moment, then realized she'd pilfered his weapon. He roared back at her, but Trish was already tearing off toward where Sabrina and the Headless Horseman fought.

I had not been idle while Trish bought me time, of course. I was fumbling through my backpack of weapons, but Polite Ape did not give me opportunity to find what I sought. He grabbed me from behind, his arm locking across my throat, other hand gripping my head and pulling at a sharp angle. I flailed, my backpack straps falling down and entangling my arms. I bucked and jerked to pull out of the headlock, but my immortal memories slipped away through cracks rent by my youth. I knew I'd escaped this sleeper hold before, but I couldn't figure out how. The seconds ticked by, and I my vision tunneled as my arteries struggled to pump oxygen into my brain.

Then Caden appeared out of nowhere, colliding with my assailant using his now-signature shoulder bash. Polite Ape was ripped away from me, wrenching my neck before I popped free. Goon #2 rushed in to take advantage of my lightheadedness. I scrabbled to slip out of the backpack straps, then swung the bag and caught the man across the face. The bag exploded like a piñata, aerosol cans, spare batteries, and tranquilizer darts spilling out onto the linoleum. Unfortunately, despite all that, Goon #2 still managed to tackle me.

Goon #2 was not as civilized as Polite Ape. He pummeled me with his fists, his lower bulk trapping me in place. I sucked in shallow breaths, panting. A detached corner of my mind recognized that he was frantic, not taking the time to properly aim his blows or use his momentum to power his punches. Likely, his enormous size and surly disposition had caused him to rely on actual combat only rarely.

I reached out, my fingers groping the floor for something— anything—to help me. Even untrained, Goon #2's superior strength was noticeable, and his jabs battered at my head. I kept my chin tucked, trying to keep him from landing a solid hit on my face. I felt my fingers brush against something smooth, but I couldn't get a grip on it. *Dammit.* He grabbed my hair and wrenched my head toward him before slamming it back against the stairs. Pain sent dizzying white spots wriggling across my vision.

My hand slapped out again, and I strained, my fingers just barely able to touch the glass tube. I took a shot to the face, tasting blood as his closed fist caught my upper lip, raking it across my teeth. My fingers finally caught the edge of the cylinder and rolled it into my palm. A tranq. By some miracle, it was uncapped and hadn't broken on the linoleum. Another jab clipped my brow, close enough to my eye to send a bolt of pain lancing back into my head.

Goon #2 hauled me up for another skull-rattling slam, bringing me close to his ugly face, and I closed my eyes, held my breath, and jammed the tranquilizer dart into his shoulder.

My powers of convenience must have been in overdrive, because the effect was instantaneous. He sucked in a breath as his muscles went liquid, then his eyes rolled up into his head and he collapsed on top of me.

I squirmed out from under his bulk and examined him carefully. He was out cold.

That wasn't how tranqs worked, but I wasn't going to complain about my odd powers now, and I didn't have time to contemplate them further. Gasping to catch my breath, I took stock of the room.

Iblis stood off to one side, near where we'd entered, trying to look inconspicuous—undoubtedly hoping we wouldn't call on him to take action against his former allies. The Medium was crouching not far from me, her back against the blue door of a cell, between two spidery Ahedrian carvings. Her eyes were intent on the fight between Sabrina and the Headless Horseman. Trish was trying to skirt Sabrina to get around to her back, but Sabrina was too cautious. Moving with sure steps, Sabrina made a swift stab at Trish, who had lost the nightstick at some point. Trish backpedaled with a curse. Apparently the Vorpal Blade did not count as a monster, for Trish was moving at normal, human speeds.

That sword. The Vorpal Blade incarnate. It was not like ordinary weapons; Trish couldn't even get close to Sabrina, as the tiniest nick would decapitate her. And the ease with which Sabrina wielded it meant she had the extra reach of an enormous weapon without extra weight.

Sabrina spat at the Headless Horseman, clearly frustrated by the fact that her magical sword did not work nearly so well against a headless foe. With a weapon like the Vorpal Blade, she would have become accustomed to cutting down anyone who got in her way without much trouble, but the Headless Horseman was earning his imperishable head in spades. As I watched, he drove his steed forward and tried to spear Sabrina with the point of his sickle while she was distracted by a feint from Trish, but Sabrina rolled on her left shoulder and came up in a squat, the Vorpal Blade held at a defensive angle. She sprang forward, slashing at the horse, but the rider— unafraid of decapitation—took the slash across his own knee. Sabrina cursed and retreated, waving the sword to discourage Trish from following too closely.

The Headless Horseman followed, his sickle swinging down. He was going to score a hit! But his weapon phased through Sabrina's arm without effect, as though he were... well, a ghost. Both Sabrina and the Horseman froze, surprised. I heard Zelda swear, drawing my —and Sabrina's—attention, then the older woman took a few steps closer to the battle. I realized she needed to stay nearer the Headless Horseman for him to continue to be of use. Sabrina easily blocked his next sickle swing, sparing the Medium another calculating glance as she parried.

My attention was drawn to Polite Ape and Caden. Sabrina's henchman had a dominant reach and advantageous strength, but Caden was proving canny as he harried the larger man, then ducked out of range as Polite Ape countered. Caden, however, mistimed his next lunge, and the goon grabbed him, lifting him fully off of the ground, then slammed him into the metal railing. I growled and swept the other discarded tranq off the floor as I sprang forward, plunging the dart into the side of Polite Ape's neck. He dropped Caden in surprise, spinning to face me. Then, right on cue, he pitched forward and hit the ground, his lights out.

Caden rolled his shoulders and stepped over to me. We were both panting, sweaty and wincing in pain. "You okay?" we asked each other at the same time. He reached up to my face, and his touch stung, his fingers coming away bloody. He cringed, then put his hand on the side of my face, closing his eyes.

"What are you doing?" I asked, risking a glance at the goons. Polite Ape was squirming on the ground, while Goon #2 was clutching at his face, his heels drumming into the linoleum in pain. Pushovers.

"Shhh," Caden said. "I'm concentrating. I'm not really sure how this works."

Oh. He was trying to heal me.

"Don't force it," I told him. "Just let it flow. It will feel as natural as breathing. No, even more natural, like your heart beating. It's a piece of who you are."

I felt the difference immediately. The aches ebbed like a wave had washed through me and carried them away, taking the pain with it, exhaled out of my body. It didn't leave me wrung out or empty, either, my pain and wooziness replaced with energy. With a sense of clarity and purpose.

"Damn," I said when he opened his eyes. "I could get hooked on this stuff."

We sprang up the stairs. Trish and the Horseman were now between us and Sabrina, so we were looking at their backs, while Madam Zerona was ahead and off to our right, hugging the wall. We darted forward, not sure yet how we would be able to help but not willing to sit this out, either.

Sabrina suddenly unleashed a string of swings at Trish, driving her back and ignoring the Headless Horseman. Trish barely avoided the tip of the Vorpal Blade, cursing as she sprang away from the attack.

Sabrina then reversed direction and lunged with the Vorpal Blade, stabbing at the Horseman's steed. The Headless Horseman, caught off guard, phased... and Sabrina passed fully *through* him. Now on his other side, nearer to the Medium, she spun and delivered a backhanded slice toward the horse's flank, correctly anticipating the Headless Horseman would become tangible again immediately. The Horseman, however, caught the sword mid-arc in his giant, armored fist.

The Vorpal Blade froze, and Sabrina's eyes widened in fear and fury. She ripped the sword free, staggering backward from the force of the release. I couldn't help but be impressed with how quickly she regained her balance, the Vorpal Blade once again held defensively, separating her from her opponents. Her eyes roamed over the Headless Horseman, seeking a weakness to exploit. She glanced to the side and took in our approach, and then her eyes fell on the Medium.

I saw understanding dawn, and I rushed to intercept even as Sabrina sprang into action. *"No!"* I screamed, seeing the strike before she actually made it. I hurled the can of pepper spray, but it was a futile gesture. Behind Sabrina, chasing her like the specter of death itself, the Headless Horseman lunged forward, cape snapping out behind him, billowing as if someone had invited night inside. But Sabrina was faster than us both. With no one between her and the Medium, she closed the distance in a blink, the Vorpal Blade like an extension of her own body. It plunged down.

Snicker-snack.

Madam Zelda Zerona, the Medium incarnate, blinked once in surprise at the mirrored blade protruding from her chest. Then she smiled tremulously at Sabrina, a hint of confusion on her features. Her head began to loll to the side.

The Headless Horseman bore down on Sabrina with sickle in hand, but his vengeance was too late. Even as he clashed with her, his shape distorted, flattened, and he became nothing more than the wisp of a shadow. Then even less.

Zelda's head vanished, and her body toppled to the floor.

a hush fell across the room. Trish, Caden, and I were frozen, eyes wide in horror, staring at Madam Zerona's lifeless body. Sabrina swiveled in place, bringing up the Vorpal Blade warily.

"Her death, and Gustav's, is on *your* head," she declaimed in an icy, imperious tone. As though she dared to judge us. "Only criminals were meant to die this night."

"And a few dozen prison guards," I reminded her.

Her cold eyes met mine, and I saw something in them I did not expect: hatred. "Iblis was going to help me evacuate everyone not meant to die," she snarled. "But you had to play hero. Like some good deed could wipe your slate clean."

What?

I held up my hand placatingly. "Sabrina, this ends tonight. No one else needs to die here."

She licked her lips, eyes tracking our movements, not missing anything. "You are wrong, Emery Luple. By my count, at least three more need to die." She leveled the Vorpal Blade at me. "And do not call me Sabrina. After tonight, I am Ahedrian." The hundreds of scribbles above and around her seemed to grow as she said that, punctuating her threat.

She lunged toward me, and I scrambled over the handrail, keeping the metal bars between us. I now had the higher elevation, and she stabbed through the bars to try to pierce my shins. I grunted and dodged backward.

I glanced around. Caden was watching wide-eyed, trying to keep his distance from both the incapacitated men and Sabrina's wide reach. Trish was near me, now, but her stricken eyes were still riveted to Madam Zerona's body. She finally tore her gaze away in time to see Sabrina vault the handrail and chase after me with her deadly blade. I sprinted back toward the fallen henchmen, unsure how to counter Sabrina's assault.

I risked a glance over my shoulder. Sabrina shadowed me, sword held high. "For our final wish..." I yelled as I flew down the stairs. Sabrina skidded to a halt at the top, gauging the distance between me and Trish, then growled in frustration and rocketed back toward where Trish was standing. I realized that, since Sabrina had heard Trish make the wish earlier, she thought *Trish* held the Genie's lamp. Locket. Whatever. "I wish for you to give the Vorpal Blade incarnate to me!"

Sabrina closed the distance between her and Trish. Cinnamon-red clouds appeared near them, and the Genie, mouth stretched in a horrifying grin, said, "*Ohhh* master, your wish is my command." I flinched at the maniacal gleam in his eye. The locket at my throat disintegrated into fine, white ash.

The Vorpal Blade jerked out of Sabrina's hands even as she made an overhand swing at Trish, and she screamed in defiance as the blade levitated through the air to hang, suspended, above Iblis's upturned palm. "You want the blade, Emery?" The Genie howled in delight. "Then it is *yours!*" He gestured like he was throwing a fireball, and the Vorpal Blade flashed forward like a bullet, aimed precisely at my heart.

Time seemed to dilate. I saw the blade launch toward me with deadly accuracy. Even as my brain kicked into overdrive and demanded I dodge, dive, pivot, *anything—just move!*—I knew it was

too late. Even if it missed my heart, a surface scratch would be sufficient to kill me.

Then, in a blur, moving swifter than the blade, Caden was there.
He tackled me from the right, driving us both down to the linoleum
with bone-crunching force. We skidded in a tangle of limbs as the
Vorpal Blade shot through the space we had just occupied, clattering
across the floor and ricocheting across the room, like flat stone skipping along the surface of a lake.

It wasn't my imagination. Caden had not been close enough to
attempt that dive. Even the tackle itself had happened quicker than I
could have managed. He had moved... like Trish had when she
fought against the Genie. Maybe even faster.

We leapt to our feet in time to see Sabrina barreling toward us,
trying to retrieve the lost weapon. Trish was chasing her down. "Get
the sword!" she screamed at us.

Behind them, the Genie crowed in triumph. "I AM FREE!" A bolt
of fire seared through the air and exploded across Trish's back. She
cried out, dropping to the ground and rolling.

Caden sped to intercept Sabrina while I raced for the discarded
sword.

Across the room, the Genie dissolved into a veritable storm front
of roiling, red clouds. They churned across the floor, enshrouding the
other half of the room in a vermilion haze, flickers of orange lightning punctuating the clouds and giving the impression they were
alive.

Caden tried to tackle Sabrina, but she feinted in one direction,
then dashed in the other. I reached the fallen blade, and my fingers
closed around its hilt just as Sabrina slammed into me from behind.
She knocked us both to the ground, me on my stomach with her on
my back, but I managed to maintain my grip on the blade's hilt. She
clawed her way forward, fingernails raking my arm, scratching at me
to release the blade as she crawled ever nearer to it.

Suddenly, a wave of heat washed over me. A ring of fire sprang up
all around us, cutting us off from the others. *Dammit.* I had hoped
Iblis would accept his newfound freedom and leave, but apparently

his loyalty to Sabrina—or his hatred for us—ran deeper than I realized. Now freed, he willingly aided our enemy.

I heaved and managed to throw Sabrina off balance, then elbowed her in the chin. I'd been going for her nose, but the strike still stunned her for a moment, and I used that window of opportunity to buck her off me. The circle of fire, fueled by nothing more than the Genie's will, expanded to allow Sabrina space without singeing her. Within the flaming arena, there was only me, Sabrina, and a metal column supporting the upper-level walkway.

I hesitated, sweat dripping down my face. I couldn't use the Vorpal Blade, not even against a murderer like her. I would *not* sink to her level. The incarnates I had killed would reincarnate in a thousand and one days. Sabrina would just die.

I needed to shatter the Vorpal Blade. Even thinking about it made me wince. The blade was exquisite, a work of art so beautiful that contemplating its destruction made me sick to my stomach. It felt like I'd be shredding the *Mona Lisa.* But I hardened my resolve; it would reincarnate, in time. I risked too much if Sabrina managed to reclaim it.

She lunged at me, either knowing I wouldn't strike at her or not caring. It was an attack born of desperation, a last-ditch effort to retake control of the battle. I spun around, putting my back to her, using the spin to build momentum. I slammed the Vorpal Blade's flat, mirror-bladed surface against the metal column, expecting the glass to shatter into a thousand fragments. Too late I hoped those fragments couldn't decapitate me, or I had just doomed myself. The blade struck with devastating force... but it was far stronger than I'd estimated. It did not shatter but instead sent a vibrating numbness up my arms just as Sabrina plowed into me from behind. The blade slipped from my fingers, and we both went down, perilously near the flames.

The heat was searing, but Sabrina ignored it as she snatched the Vorpal Blade incarnate from where I'd dropped it. *No, no, no!* I ignored the tingling in my arms and grabbed her wrist, trying to wrestle the blade out of her hands. She fought savagely, trying to slash at me, to score even the tiniest of scratches with the Vorpal Blade's razor-sharp edge.

Across the room, several detonations sounded, accompanied by glaring flashes of light where the Monster Hunter and the Genie presumably battled.

Sabrina tried to use the sword's leverage to swing me around and into the edge of the flames, but I was at least as strong as she, probably stronger. Her foot flashed out as she tried to kick me, but the angle was wrong and her body wasn't centered enough to execute the move properly. I countered instinctively, pushing toward her with all my strength. Already off balance, she lost her footing and toppled backward. She tried to keep her grip on the sword, but I wrenched it from her hands as she fell.

I needed to get away, to *think*. So I did something foolish. I leapt through the wall of flames. I breathed in sharply before making the jump, knowing that inhaling at the wrong time would burn my lungs and probably kill me. Then I dove through, chin tucked down, trying to let my shoulders and right side take the brunt of the heat. I landed on the other side, my clothes smoldering, and rolled across the linoleum, beating out the flames. I sucked in a painful breath, my nerve endings afire. My shoulder felt like a hunk of meat that had hit a frying pan. I *just* managed to maintain my hold on the sword.

I needed to stand, to get the sword out of here and away from Sabrina, but I was finding it difficult to move through the pain, my entire right side in agony. The Vorpal Blade trembled in my shaking fingers.

I felt a hand on my forehead, and the pain snuffed out. Energy zipped through me, washing away my fatigue like a bucket of ice water to the face. I leapt to my feet, startling Caden, who had been kneeling over me. I searched wildly for somewhere to go, somewhere safe to keep the sword out of Sabrina's reach.

Not far away, Trish dodged bolts of red-orange lightning that flashed from the Genie's clouds, her superhuman speed barely able to keep up with the onslaught. Iblis was focused on her, oblivious to my escape from his ring of fire, unaware he had trapped Sabrina behind it. I had only moments until he realized this and helped her. I could stow the sword in a cell, but Sabrina—or Iblis—could retrieve it. I needed to put it somewhere they could not follow. But as I looked around, there were only metal bars, mirrors, cell doors, a metal detector, two goons, the ubiquitous scrawls of Ahedrian, and a wall of seething crimson clouds.

My attention was drawn back to the mirrors. They were connected to the Vorpal Blade incarnate; they'd tried to alert me of its involvement. But how were they connected, and why warn me? A suspicion began to gnaw at me.

A scorching ball of fire flew toward me, and I batted it aside with the Vorpal Blade. It caromed through the air and detonated at the feet of Polite Ape, sending him scampering backward in alarm. The ring of fire around Sabrina guttered out. *Shit.*

Sabrina, her face a twisted mask of rage, made to rush me once again. Caden stepped between us, but I knew he wouldn't delay her for long.

My eyes found the nearest mirror. It seemed to call to me, stirring the immortal corner of my mind. As Sabrina bowled Caden over and came at me, I made my decision.

I spun and reached the mirror just as Sabrina caught up to me. I raised the Vorpal Blade high as Sabrina's outstretched hand clawed at me, and then I plunged it forward.

Into the mirror.

I braced for the impact to run up my arm again, for the blade to crack the mirror and come to a sudden stop against the cement wall behind it. But the Vorpal Blade passed through the looking glass without resistance, like it was a pool of still water. Sabrina howled in rage, her wail of despair hardly human, as first the blade, then the hilt slid into the mirror and vanished from sight.

And just like that, the Vorpal Blade was gone. Home, I realized. The Vorpal Blade's resting place was through the looking glass. The mirrors had been trying to tell me that the Vorpal Blade incarnate was missing from its home.

Sabrina screamed and shoved me against the wall. Stunned from the impact, I pivoted in time to see her retreating, her red hair disappearing through the door where we'd entered, the metal detector once again blaring to life as she crossed its threshold and slipped around the corner. She was... *fleeing*?

Caden, closer than I, bolted after her.

Dammit.

"Go!" Trish screamed, dodging a stream of fire. Bolt after bolt of flame struck at her, but Trish sidestepped them as though she could see them coming. "Leave this asshole to me!" Even as she said it, thick orange tongues of fire ignited against her leather jacket... and she shrugged them off. *Hot damn!* She was right: there was little I could do against the firestorm that had once been the Genie, but I could catch Sabrina.

As I sped after Caden, the crimson clouds suddenly expanded, filling the area with the sharp scent of cinnamon and obscuring most of the room from view. I sped beneath the ringing metal detector, likely resetting its timed alarm, and the clouds chased after me. I saw Caden slip around the corner, turning right. As I ran, the hallways filled with thick scarlet clouds that obscured my view. I could no longer see the corner ahead. Even the walls to my left and right became hazy and difficult to make out, my feet pounding linoleum that disappeared in the flowing fog.

The intersection suddenly loomed before me, the word Ahedrian filling my vision, and I turned right, where Caden had vanished. But I couldn't see more than a few feet in any direction. I already felt lost in the sea of red mist. Orange lightning flickered, and the temperature spiked. I found a window and tried to look out, but the red mist was flowing outside, too, unhindered by the downpour. The crimson storm within met the natural storm without. Soon, all of Rikers Island would be engulfed.

I kept my right hand on the wall and started running forward, unable to see Caden or Sabrina. Footsteps sounded ahead, muted in the haze. I kept running. I came to another turn and took it, trusting my instincts. The corridor did not run at a ninety-degree angle, so I wasn't parallel to the first hallway but instead cut away from it.

I heard a low chuckle echo through the mist, like the Genie was somewhere nearby. An explosion sounded ahead, a detonation and a sizzle, accompanied by a shower of sparks that rained down ahead of me. Suddenly the lights in the building died, and I was plunged into near-total darkness. My eyes adjusted slowly to the gloom, the Genie's orange lightning making it—just barely—possible to see.

A bright flash illuminated the hallway, haunted with the Ahedrian etchings, filling my vision with bright red again. *That was a natural flash*, I realized, as booming thunder rattled the windows. I shot forward, my fingers flying over the wall as I pounded down the corridor. I couldn't leave Caden to face Sabrina alone.

I came to another turn, but I skipped this one, continuing forward. My intuition was like a compass in my head, prompting me onward. I skipped two more doors, then lightning from the storm outside illuminated the reddened hallway. On my left, an open doorway yawned in the brief flash, a darker shade of crimson against the scarlet mist. I blinked and the lightning faded, but I ground my teeth and, trusting my instincts, slipped through the open doorway.

Something felt right about what I was doing. I chose another hallway and turned again. I would be unable to find my way back now, but I felt a growing sense of certainty that I was trailing Sabrina's path. A bolt of orange lightning crackled to my left, revealing another doorway. I veered in that direction.

I could just picture Rachelle scolding me for my arrogance. I had skipped so many side corridors, turned down hallways on a whim, due solely to a *feeling*. She would berate me for my conceit, and if Caden was injured or worse while I was lost in a maze of red smoke, I would not forgive myself for lifetimes—maybe forever.

But each decision I made felt like a hole in Morrigan's map. Each choice coincidentally correct, lightning strikes conveniently timed to illuminate options I would have missed otherwise. I was taking control of my destiny, selecting which path to take, but doing so at random, guided by a gut instinct I could not explain.

I took control of the chaos. It was mine.

I needed to put a stop to Ahedrian. To end her story before she became a legend. This would *not* be Ahedrian's story, I vowed as I took another turn without conscious consideration. It was *mine*.

Red mist eddied around me as I proceeded down a left turn.

In my story, Ahedrian did not escape.

Right turn.

In my story, I found her and ended her killing spree.

I passed two more hallways without turning.

That's why I would find her: because I was the protagonist of my story, and the protagonist was meant to stop Ahedrian. It was as simple as that.

A gunshot sounded from ahead, and my heart leapt into my throat. *Caden.* I spurred myself forward, my fingers brushing the wall, when suddenly they encountered air—a slightly open door. I froze.

This was it, I knew. Sabrina was in that room.

$\mathcal{I}$ put gentle pressure on the door, easing it open. Slipped inside and ducked to the left, hugging the wall. Lightning flashed through several windows, illuminating the scarlet mist that hazed the room, the word Ahedrian looming out of the darkness like an omen. I scanned the space during the flash. I didn't see anyone, the swirling fog creating false movement to draw my eyes, but I caught a glimpse of exercise machines. I was in some sort of fitness center.

Orange lightning flickered through the mist, bright fountains of embers occasionally erupting as it struck equipment in the room. The pops and sizzles covered my soft tread, but even so I barely breathed for fear of giving away my position.

The room was large, filled with workout gear from treadmills and ellipticals to stationary bikes. No weight-lifting equipment, I noticed. My toe caught the edge of a yoga mat, and it slapped against the floor. Immediately, a gunshot rang out. I threw myself to the ground as glass shattered somewhere ahead of me. The bullet had found an enormous stand mirror braced against the back wall. Although it had not been a very close shot, it was remarkable given the fog obscuring the room.

Was Caden in here? I knew Sabrina was, the gunshot proved that —Caden wouldn't even hold a Taser, much less fire a gun. I continued down the wall perpendicular to the one I entered, watching my feet and straining my senses for any clue as to Sabrina's location. I came across a stationary bike and ducked behind it. It was the last in this row, I realized, before the gym opened onto a large area that looked like an indoor track.

Not that way, I thought. I didn't want to be caught in an open space when she had a gun. Much easier to hide and avoid getting shot among the equipment.

"Sabrina!" I shouted, pitching my voice in a sharp tone to encourage it to echo around the room.

There was no answer. I moved to another bike, heading back toward the corner of the room before trying again. "Morrigan lied to you," I shouted, careful not to say too much and make it easy for her to locate me by sound. I moved immediately this time, picking my way to another bike. "You won't become an incarnate." Another bike. "It doesn't work that way."

Silence.

Then, "You lie," came from the mist. It was quiet and certain, originating from across the room, I thought.

I advanced cautiously, picking my way closer to the center of the room. I could imagine her doing the same thing, imagine suddenly coming across her in the crimson fog. "You can't trust Morrigan," I said, putting a plea into the words. I had liked Sabrina when I first met her. She had reminded me of a previous Emery. If I could just get through to that person again...

A gunshot sounded and I ducked, but the bullet struck machinery quite a distance behind me. She was just trying to keep me guessing.

"And who can I trust, then?" came the mocking reply. "*You*, Emery Luple?"

I crept toward that voice, trying to keep the rows of fitness machines between me and where I estimated Sabrina hid.

"Why kill for immortality?" I asked instead of answering her. I slipped forward further before adding, "That makes you a monster, Sabrina."

"*Me?*" the response was immediate, shrill, disbelieving. And it seemed to echo from all around me. "You couldn't even save one little girl, and you call *me* a monster?"

I oriented myself in the direction of her aggrieved voice and continued to draw nearer to her, circling around, tightening my spiral further, with her at its center. I... *wait.* What was that about a little girl?

"Sabrina," I said gently, "I don't know what you're talking about."

Empty laughter sounded, wretched and heavy with despair. "You don't remember me?" She fired three shots in quick succession. I froze as one of the bullets careened past my hiding spot and pinged off the treadmill to my right. That had been close.

Her misery-laden words weighed on me, squeezing my heart. An ugly suspicion began to form. *No,* I thought, my hands beginning to tremble. *Impossible.*

"Mortals tend to forget your name when you die," she said bitterly, "but I didn't. I'm one of your precious loopholes."

I took a shuddering breath and neared her location, but every word she uttered pushed back against me, battered my soul like a slap to the face.

"I was only five years old." Sabrina's voice fluttered across the scarlet fog, which suddenly seemed to me to be a vapor of blood. "Morrigan spun tale after tale of how you'd arrive, a noble heroine, and save me from my torture." Her voice broke on the last word.

A flicker of orange lightning silhouetted Sabrina's profile ahead of me in the mist. She was on one knee, her body facing to my left, her head and gun arm aimed at an angle that would not hit me.

But I couldn't move. My mind was snared in a moment two decades past, when Huntington and I had arrived at the wharf to save a little girl.

"Oh, you came for me all right," she continued. "And I couldn't believe it. My heroine, in the flesh. Except you weren't heroic at all. You were *pathetic.*" She said the word contemptuously, firing the gun twice more in random directions. I saw the muzzle flash each time, briefly flaring the red fog between us. "You were too weak to save your partner, and you were too weak to save me. You wouldn't even *fight* against Morrigan. I was just a frightened child, goddamn you. And you didn't even *try* to save me."

She fired again, this time aiming rather close to me, and I heard her quiet footfalls as she slipped away from where I knew she was hiding. I'd missed my chance to sneak up on her, but I felt rooted to the ground, stunned. Anguish saddled me—I had never known what happened to that little girl, too cowardly to look into the consequences of my failure. And as the incarnations rolled by, I ran further and further from the memory of her wails. But my cowardice, my failures, had been engraved upon her soul. Because of me, she'd grown up to be a monster.

"There are no heroes," Sabrina said angrily. Her words echoed Caden's from the night before but twisted them into something ugly. "But that doesn't mean we shouldn't strive to make things better. After learning all about incarnates, I created Ahedrian to punish those who believe themselves above the law. To punish wickedness. I know I'm not a hero, but at least I'm not a victim." A gunshot.

I found my voice. "Sabrina, I'm sorry. I had no idea."

"I'm *Ahedrian!*" she screamed. A bullet exploded into the treadmill next to me, sending plastic slivers through the air.

I scurried from my hiding spot and ducked behind another piece of equipment. "You're *sorry?*" She barked a nasty laugh. "Is that supposed to make it all better?"

Enough. I could feel Caden's presence in the room, nourishing me with his soothing aura. Knowing he was listening to her accusations didn't fill me with the guilt and shame I anticipated. I had already told him about my failure that night, and... he had already accepted those shortcomings, even when I had not. I closed my eyes and pictured him listening to Sabrina, tried to imagine his response. I could feel his faith in me. What would he say to me right now?

This little girl had been counting on me to save her from Morrigan, and I had failed. I had to live with that knowledge. But that didn't make her actions my fault. I had not been the one to kidnap her, to torture her, to turn her into a monster, to unleash her on the unsuspecting people of New York. I was not responsible for Ahedrian.

It all goes back to Morrigan, I thought grimly.

But that wasn't fair, either. At some point, Sabrina became responsible for her own actions.

I couldn't wash my hands of her fate. But I could try to change it, as I had mine.

"Why would you work with Morrigan?" I asked. "She tortured you."

"She *taught* me," Sabrina retorted, her voice angled away from me. "About incarnates, about strength, about the evil in this world. She helped me to gain immortality. Ahedrian is the answer, Emery. I will never be a victim again." She spun and fired in my general direction. I flinched but didn't dive this time. As the lingering cobwebs of that tragedy were cast away from me, the sense of confidence I'd felt on my way to this room was slowly returning.

I was not in her story; I was in *mine*. And I would not die in my story.

"What I can't figure out," she growled, words rumbling through the crimson darkness, "is her fascination with you." Her voice was off to my left, now. "Everything always revolves around *you*. It's deplorable."

"I hate what happened to you," I said, projecting my wounded heart into my words. "I swear I tried to help you."

"Then you are as incompetent as you are weak," she spat back. After a moment, her voice took on a mocking cast, surprisingly near. "You left me for dead," she declared, "so I returned the favor in Saudi Arabia." She gave a low chuckle. I tracked her movements by her voice as she slipped silently through the red fog.

"I will haunt you for lifetimes, Emery Luple," she declared, not realizing she already had. "The Ahedrian incarnate will hunt you down every time you reincarnate. You will pay eternal penance for your failure."

Not six feet before me, a shadow resolved into Sabrina's back. She spun and aimed the pistol directly at my face. I raised my hands in a pacifying gesture. "Ahedrian—"

Several things happened at once. A howling gale ripped through the fitness room with enough force to stagger both of us. Sabrina's finger squeezed the trigger, but we'd been knocked askew and the bullet whizzed past my cheek. The crimson fog became a tide, the agitated, lightning-filled clouds sucked away by the wind. Fingers of scarlet mist streamed back out the door we had entered, tugging at my clothes, threatening to pull me off balance. Sabrina's wild mane fluttered around her face, obscuring her features from my view, but she leveled her handgun at me again.

The last of the crimson mist dissipated and the wind subsided, and I realized Trish must have defeated the Genie or forced him to flee. A strange realization to have while staring down the barrel of a gun. But I did not fear the bullet. It would not take me today.

This is my story. And I had finally figured out my incarnation.

Sabrina flicked the hair out of her face as the wind died. She smiled and said, "Goodbye, Emery. See you in a thousand and one days." Then she pulled the trigger.

From six feet away, it took two milliseconds for the bullet to travel from Sabrina's gun to my face. To comprehend how fast that is, the average blink is *four hundred* milliseconds. You can trust me on this. I did the math later.

Caden was already at my side, as I knew he would be. Light erupted from him, transforming his hair into a halo and flowing outward from his shoulders into two brilliant, expansive, angelic wings. One of those wings enfolded me, and the bullet cracked into it.

And stopped.

He was radiant, banishing the gloom. Like Trish against the Genie, this was an incarnate in his element. His seafoam gaze transferred from me to Sabrina, who gaped at us with undisguised shock... and loathing.

"I have heard you, Sabrina Miles," Caden said, and his soft words seemed a pronouncement that rang throughout the halls of the prison.

"I... am... *AHEDRIAN!*" she shrieked. She fired twice more, the bullets appearing, suspended, in the white glow.

Caden, the Angel incarnate, shook his head sadly. "You have so much pain. Your world is filled with it. Your choices corrupted by it. What you need," he lifted his hand, reaching toward her, "is to *heal*."

His luminous aura expanded, pushing the darkness back even further, and Sabrina scrambled back from it. She shied away from his light as if it were going to burn her.

I took a step forward, my hand outstretched for her to take. "You've suffered long enough," I told her, "Ahedrian dies tonight, but Sabrina Miles still has a life to live."

Her wide eyes showed whites all around, her chest heaving as she panicked. Then her upper lip curled in a snarl, and she slapped my offered hand away. She retreated a few more steps. "You have it backward, you fool." She raised the gun once again as Caden's light inched forward, and she repeated the same words she'd said a few long moments ago. "Goodbye, Emery. See you in a thousand and one days."

Sabrina put the gun to her own temple.

She pulled the trigger.

*W*ith the Genie gone, the generators finally kicked on, and dim lights flickered to life. After a moment to breathe, to think, the gravity of the evening crashed down on me. Caden, too, was quiet. We left the room wordlessly, the soft click of the door closing behind us sounding to me like the sealing of a tomb.

I replayed the final moments of the confrontation again and again, examining it from all angles, trying to figure out if there was anything I could have done differently.

I felt numb, shocked by more than her sudden death. She had been a specter of my past all along. Having spent years blocking out the traumatic events of that night, I was ashamed to realize I couldn't remember the name of the little girl from the wharf—but I knew it was not Sabrina Miles. At some point, she must have changed it, possibly in connection with her career as an investigative journalist. Or perhaps Morrigan renamed her to keep her hidden from me, until even Sabrina forgot the name to which she once answered.

Morrigan. I seethed at the thought of her. She had sculpted that little girl's future as surely as if she'd incarnated into the woman herself. Morrigan had molded Sabrina into a monster. It was heart-wrenching, though not surprising.

Caden took my hand as we walked the corridors of Rikers. While appropriately somber, he did not seem shaken. Sabrina's gruesome death, right in front of us, bothered me on an emotional level, but the physical violence was disturbing, too. Unlike Caden, however, I had seen my fair share of death and gun violence throughout my lifetimes. It was not something to which one wanted to become accustomed, but nor did it bother me to the extremes it once had. Then I realized his hand was trembling, and it took me out of my reverie. He had taken my hand, not just for my comfort, but for his, too. He was no stranger to death, working in a hospice, but the violence of Sabrina's death was a far cry from the peaceful or natural ends he'd witnessed before.

I squeezed his hand gently, letting him know I was there. Comforting him helped to soothe me, too. I remembered his words from—holy shit, was that just last night?—our walk through Central Park. He had told me that being a full-time hero was too much responsibility for anyone. The burden, I was finding, was in shouldering the blame alone. Always holding oneself to a higher standard of accountability, taking responsibility not only for your own shortcomings but also for those of others.

Speaking of accountability, I owed Morrigan a visit.

I turned my thoughts back to the boy walking down the hall with me, sharing my burdens. When the heaviness in my heart melted away at his touch, I had chalked it up to his healing powers. But maybe it was something more. His hand in mine banished the darkness within, just as his angelic aura had banished the darkness without. I felt safe, protected, nurtured. Since meeting Caden, I had often used his calming presence to soothe my own roiling thoughts. My mental scars from Huntington, too, had begun to heal the night we spent in Sleepy Hollow. But could his powers truly account for everything? No. They were a first step. *I* had confronted my demons—from Huntington's dead eyes to my fear of connection with mortals to the little girl on the wharf. I had healed my own scars through tears and grit. Sabrina, given the same choice by Caden, had fled from his angelic aura. I didn't entirely blame her. How could I, when I had chosen the same path for two incarnations?

Caden's angelic traits were not why I had survived the bullet, they were simply the *how*. I had known, before Sabrina fired that gun at me, that I would not die. I had felt safe. Protected. Invincible.

That feeling... it was not new. It was simply forgotten.

My Sanctum.

"You know what I love about you?" I said quietly.

Caden looked at me, his normally bright features noticeably dimmed. He gave me a small smile, but it seemed forced. "What's that?"

"After everything she did, you wanted to heal her. To forgive her." I shook my head in wonder, instilling my smile with as much sincerity as I could muster, hoping it wasn't my usual cocky grin. "You are truly the Angel incarnate."

As if *I* had healed *him*, I saw some of the pain in his eyes diminish. He quirked his lips into a more genuine, if self-deprecating, smile. "Actually, I think you're only half-correct."

I screwed up my face in exaggerated thought. "You are truly the Ang incar?" I teased, trying to alleviate the heartache with humor.

He rolled his eyes in a perfect imitation of Rachelle, and I knew, while he was not yet okay, he was getting better. "I realized something when I was protecting you back there. I'm not just the Angel." He paused, a blush creeping onto his cheeks. "I wasn't fully, um, *myself* until I made the decision to defend you. Like when the Vorpal Blade almost speared you, my instincts to protect you kicked into overdrive, and everything seemed to happen so quickly, but I knew I would be able to save you. And I simply... *did*." He shrugged self-consciously. "It's like you said. It isn't something I deliberately choose to do, but rather a piece of who I am. Natural. Like my pulse."

From ahead, I heard Trish's voice echoing down the hallways, calling out for us.

"Okay, so what does it all mean?" I asked.

He turned to me. "I'm the Guardian Angel incarnate," he

concluded. Then, still blushing but meeting my eyes, he added, "I like to think I'm *your* guardian angel, Emery."

I brought his hand, still in mine, to my lips and kissed it. "I could use one," I replied. I squeezed his hand again. "Does that mean you'll come back with me to Seattle?" I asked, my stomach doing a hopeful flip.

Before he could answer, Trish's voice cut down the hall again. I called back a reply, and she came barreling through a doorway up ahead. Her leather jacket was missing, revealing a gray tank top with one of the shoulder straps torn and hanging down limply, its end blackened. Several burn holes scorched her faux leather pants, and she wore only one boot. For all that, I think it was the least angry I'd ever seen her.

"You losers all right?"

I grinned. "All parts accounted for." I looked pointedly at her sock. "What happened to your other shoe?"

Trish gave me a flat look. "Threatened the Genie with it." She shrugged. "Only container I had on hand." At my widening grin, her expression darkened. "It worked. Never seen a red storm cloud flee before. It was... climactic."

"And well timed," I noted. "Sabrina shot at me from six feet away and missed because of you."

Trish frowned. "Is she..."

"She didn't make it," I said.

"She killed herself," Caden added softly. "She thinks she'll reincarnate as the Ahedrian."

An unreadable expression passed over Trish's face, but I thought I understood. So I did something foolish, again. I put my hand on her shoulder. Caden must have been rubbing off on me. "What happened to the Medium wasn't your fault," I told her.

She shrugged off my hand and said, "Of course it wasn't my fault. It was Sabrina's. I wish she *would* reincarnate just so I'd get a chance to kill her all over again."

Caden and I exchanged glances, and I forced a cheery smile.

"Well," I said brightly, "it's a good thing we don't have any wishes left, then."

Trish looked back and forth between us, expression softening a little. From glare to scowl. "Her body still there?"

Caden swallowed and nodded. "In the gym."

"I'll take care of it." The nonchalance with which she said that chilled me. "You two get out of here and leave the cleanup to me. I'll do what I can to minimize the damage, make sure people don't talk too much about Ahedrian from this point onward."

"You sure you don't want help?" I asked.

She gave me a pointed look. "Do I ever?" She hesitated, then extended a hand. "But good teamwork. Amateur." I shook her hand warmly.

Caden stepped forward and gave her the quickest side hug I'd ever witnessed. Trish could handle monsters and corpses, but even that hug clearly made her uncomfortable. But she returned it. Well, suffered it, at least.

I watched her jog down the hallway. "Come on," I said to him. "We have one more place to go."

"Where's that?"

I paused. "I'm not sure yet. Let's get our things, and I'll figure it out."

We made our way through the halls of Rikers, "Ahedrian" still scrawled on the walls and ceiling. Even in the brighter-lit corridors, it was eerie as hell.

I expected the metal detector to be silent this time when we passed under it, but something we wore set it off anew. All my gadgets and weapons were in this room, spilled around the backpack sitting at the foot of the stairs. I tried not to look at Gustav's headless body slumped across the bottom step. Disconcertingly, Polite Ape and Goon #2 were nowhere to be seen.

Caden collected the miscellaneous items strewn about the floor, tossing batteries, tranquilizer darts, and a blowgun into my backpack. I retrieved my Taser and popped off the front cartridge, reloading it with a fresh one before holstering it at my hip. Then I found the map

Morrigan had given me. I picked it up and smiled, unfurling it. "Can you come hold this?" I asked him.

He complied, holding it up for me to inspect. "What are you doing?" he asked me.

"Finishing this story."

I closed my eyes and stabbed my finger forward. "This," I said without opening my eyes, my finger touching a location on the map, "is where we'll find Morrigan."

Caden cocked his head. "And we *want* to visit her?" he asked skeptically.

"'Want' is not quite the word I would have chosen." I sighed, opening my eyes. "If I don't speak with her now, she'll hunt me down for a chat later, and I don't want it to be on her terms." I held my hand out for the backpack. "I could use a guardian angel," I said quietly.

He shouldered the backpack himself, then took my hand in his. "We'll do this the same way we've done everything else," he told me, eyes determined.

I felt it again, that sense of comfort washing over me. It wasn't pacifying, precisely—if anything, it seemed to sharpen my sense of purpose—but it was meditative, driving me to focus. I felt safe and invincible. I felt like I was home. Caden was my safe space. My Sanctum.

"Together."

*M*orrigan's New York Lair was, *of course,* a lavish villa. Even so, I wasted no time infiltrating it.

The overcast sky blotted out the moon's illumination and obscured our movements as we entered the manicured grounds, Caden matching my stride a step behind and to my right. The tempest was now exhausted, and the grounds were wet but the air was fresh, with the cleanness that accompanies a good storm. The wind still rustled the nearby trees, covering the sound of our footsteps as we made our way onto the property.

We'd found the manor less than an hour east of Rikers, in western Huntington on Long Island. The city's name was not lost on me, further evidence of Morrigan's cruel sense of humor. The Gothic-arched, black-metal gateway separating the residence from the populace was unlatched. For me, at least. Like Sabrina's apartment, when the door was locked for Caden but sprang open for me, I would not allow any impediment to keep me from my purpose. I could almost feel my incarnation urging me onward, coincidentally timing the rising wind with the opening gate, masking the sound of our intrusion. Mine were the powers of chance and happenstance and timing. And right now, at the height of my story, I was in my element.

Over the brick path we trod, unhurried yet unhesitating.

The building ahead of us had two staircases leading up to the front door. The manor was primarily white, with red accents that darkened to the color of blood in the night, despite the bright lights all around the grounds. The patio in front was as large as a small house, home to round glass tables crowned with extravagant canopies, and overlooked the grounds which were themselves ringed by a tall brick wall. As I ascended the left staircase, I caught movement in the yard: armed security. Despite their surveillance and the fact we made no overt effort to conceal our arrival, Caden and I proceeded undetected, my powers keeping the guards distracted with small contrivances and well-timed noises away from our route. But there was only so much coincidence and convenience could do; the security guard at the front door stiffened as he saw us approach.

"Hey! You ca—" he started. I pulled my Taser from its holster and fired the two probes into him without even slowing my stride. The darts bit into him, followed a clicking sound as electricity zapped into him. He seized up, his body spasming as the current ran through him. The Pulse+ would continue to deliver pulses of electricity for thirty seconds, so I dropped the device to keep him incapacitated and pushed open the front door. Caden winced and looked like he wanted to apologize to the guard, but he followed me through the door, staying near.

The interior of the manor was vintage colonial with a heavy-handed contemporary renovation. The foyer was dimly lit, with plush crimson—I was sick of red at this point—rugs over hardwood floor-ing, accent lights hidden in the walls' wooden paneling. Matching wooden stands held ornate lamps, most of which were off. The entryway opened into a ridiculous number of rooms: there were six mahogany doors, two stairways—one going up, the other down—and two hallways in the back. I didn't even scan my options, just turned and walked to the second door on my right. It was like I had been here before, as if I was visiting an old friend and was welcome to visit anytime.

I turned the beautifully wrought, golden-leaved door handle and pulled.

The room beyond was a luxurious lounge. Two bookshelves containing thick volumes and delicate trinkets flanked a fold-out desk with a mirror, a tray of brandy atop it. In the corner of the room was an ancient grandfather clock, its ticking audible from where I stood. Lush furniture circled a large cherrywood coffee table, the centerpiece of the collection a red velvet love seat. An enormous flat-screen TV dominated the right-hand wall. To the left of the TV, in the corner, was a marble bar counter with stools, a rack of hanging crystal, and a cabinet of liquors and wines.

Four people occupied the room. A stout White man with a combover and a chin that rivaled some peoples' foreheads waited attentively behind the bar counter. A scarecrow woman, all skinny limbs and straw-like hair, stood guard at the doorway on the far side of the room, armed with a rifle and a scowl that I'd give a seven out of ten—she really had nothing on Trish. A Black man whose barrel chest strained the seams of his dress shirt leaned against the wall in the corner to my right, a crooked nose complementing his bulging biceps and three—three!—gun holsters. And then there was Morrigan, reclining in the love seat with a book in one hand, a snifter of brandy in her other palm. Three pairs of eyes regarded me as I entered, narrowing as they realized I did not belong. Morrigan's eyes flickered to me over the top of her book, and she said, "Kill him," as if she were bored. Then she took a swig of her expensive brandy as a rifle and two handguns leveled at me. Damn, even the guy behind the counter was armed?

Gunshots cracked through the room and it took all of my willpower not to flinch, but I continued into the lounge unperturbed. I placed my faith in my incarnation to protect me. Here, at the heart of my story, I was untouchable. Fate, destiny, coincidence, my specialty... whatever you wanted to call it, it would shield me from death. And I was right. Behind me, Caden was radiating power and clean illumination again, his bluish-white light enfolding me like—appropriately enough—the wings of a guardian angel. Bullets crackled into the barrier of light and simply stopped, pattering to the thick rug. I sauntered to the desk and picked up the decanter of brandy. Caden remained no more than a step behind me, his brilliant aura warding off harm. The scarecrow lady, nearer to me and apparently smarter than the other two, dropped her useless rifle to hang from its strap around her neck and made to approach me. My hand tightened on the neck of the crystal decanter. It would be a shame to spill what was doubtless expensive brandy, but the weight of the decanter would knock her out cold.

"Enough," Morrigan commanded, her voice cutting through the sporadic reports of gunfire and rooting the other woman midstride.

I poured brandy into one of those two-sided measuring cups they use in bars, smiling cordially as the amber liquid streamed from the decanter. Like I had nowhere else in the world to be. Like I *belonged* here. After all—I was exactly where I was supposed to be. Then I rationed myself and Caden a snifter of brandy each.

I paused. Turned to the woman and asked, "I'm sorry, did you want one?" To her credit, she did not react to my flippant demeanor. She simply stared at me, waiting for Morrigan's follow-up instructions. I sighed. "Then you are dismissed," I said. I handed the second snifter to Caden, who accepted it with a quickly veiled expression of incredulity.

I joined Morrigan in the center of the room, sitting comfortably on a plump red—did I mention I was sick of that color?—chair. I leaned back, resting my right foot on my left knee. Caden remained standing, just to the left and behind me, his hands on the back of my chair.

I looked around at the people in the room, affecting a bewildered expression. "Did you not hear me? You're dismissed." I stressed the last word. I turned back to Morrigan. "Do you no longer train your... what do you call them again? Pets?"

The three mortal bodyguards exchanged glances, and the bartender's mouth popped open for a moment before he snapped it closed. Morrigan—unaware of the shock wave that passed through her goons—considered me for a moment, then placed her bookmark to save her place and set the book down on the table. "Leave us," she said quietly, not taking her eyes off mine.

The three of them exited quickly and quietly, a troubled frown on the bartender's face. I waved goodbye to the scarecrow lady, but she didn't acknowledge me.

Morrigan's scrutiny slid to Caden, and I took a sip of brandy to avoid fidgeting while she memorized his features. "You could make a lot of money with your talents," she told him, the hint of an offer in her remark.

Caden shook his head. "I'm flattered, but my loyalty is not for sale."

Morrigan arched a delicate eyebrow. "Oh, come now. You sound just like a mortal."

"Thank you." He smiled at her, sincere.

The spot above her left eye twitched. She returned her attention to me, saying, "I see why you like him." Her eyes widened as she looked between us. "But where is your mortal?"

"You know why I'm here, Morrigan," I told her, refusing to react to her obvious bait.

"Well, obviously. You found my little hideaway." She gestured at the extravagant surroundings with a distasteful turn of her lips, as if we were conversing in a cave. "Which means you have uncovered the truth about our incarnations." She leaned forward. "Moreover, you *believe* it."

I smiled at her, swirled the brandy warmed by my palm, and took another small sample of it. She was right: belief made it far easier to use an incarnation's powers or traits. It wasn't required—after all, Caden had been healing me subconsciously since I met him—but it made it easier and produced better results. This is true of most things, really; the first step to any action, especially a difficult one, is believing the goal is achievable. I think that even explains why I was so good at hunting monsters even though I was not the Monster Hunter. I believed I was, so I found myself capable of going toe to toe with them.

"Say it, Emery," Morrigan purred, her nonchalant façade easily identifiable for what it was.

I knew what she wanted, so I flipped it on her. "You," I said pointedly, "are the Antagonist incarnate."

I saw a spark of anger flare in her eyes before she masked it a blink later. "A matter of perspective," she murmured dismissively.

"And I am the good guy," I continued. "The personification of the main character. Every legend has one; every myth, every story relatable through the lens of a character. I am the Protagonist incarnate." The hero? Sometimes. Maybe even usually. I'd settle for the part-time version, though.

The path of coincidences and conveniences. Leading me to always be where I was meant to be, when I was meant to be there. Steered, driven by the hands of fate. Locked doors and guarded front lawns could not keep me from where I was expected to champion the story. *My* story.

I realized, too, why this was so problematic for Morrigan. If I was the Protagonist, then she too was assigned by destiny to a single, certain role.

Morrigan had striven to ensure I discover these truths. It was time to find out why. She downed her brandy and set the snifter on the small side table, her expression cool when she regarded me. "For the sake of argument, let us assume you have correctly allocated our incarnations and have not reversed our roles," she said, with an air of tolerating someone who was being unnecessarily stubborn. "Either way, we agree: the threads of our fate are entwined. This"—she spread her hands to indicate everything around us—"is *our* story to tell."

I considered her for a long moment as I tried to guess where this was going. Finally, I dropped the casual act and said, "What do you want, Morrigan?" I heard the exasperation in my voice, and I was certain she caught it, too.

Her eyes gleamed, like a cat's in the dark. "To rewrite our stories." Her feline smile raised the hairs on the back of my neck. "Think about it, Emery. Fate has shackled us together, all our accomplishments rendered meaningless if we don't also foil one another. Our very opposition is written in the ink of destiny, but neither of us flourishes in captivity." Her calm façade had crumbled, eagerness peeking through the cracks. "We can break this cycle of dependence upon each other."

I frowned. "I've never measured my successes based on whether or not I bested you," I said.

She shot me a flat look. "Then why are you here?" She chuckled, low and throaty. "Defeating Ahedrian was not sufficient. You needed to confront me."

My temper flared. "Because you ruined a woman's life," I snapped. "You fashioned a mass murderer and unleashed her on an unsuspecting city. The number of lives you destroyed to get me to sit right here"—I jabbed a finger at the chair—"to talk with you. It's appalling."

Morrigan reclined again, a monument to composure. Her smile was playful. "Then I would imagine you'd want to honor those lost mortals by hearing me out."

Hot anger scoured me. I wanted to walk out the door, but I could rise above my temper. I should stay, if only to keep her from engineering more heinous crimes to get my attention. I *would*. "I'm listening," I said, swigging the last of my brandy to keep from grinding my teeth together.

"You say you're the Protagonist." Morrigan waited for my nod, pleased at being in control of the conversation again. "Yet plenty of protagonists have fathers, do they not?"

"I suppose."

Her smile widened. "Come now, Emery, surely you've wondered." At my level stare, she asked, "Do you know who also never has a father?"

"Oedipus incarnate?"

She pursed her lips. "Me. Now, why do you suppose that is?" I glimpsed a frightening intensity in her eyes. This, I realized, was the culmination of years of work. She had guided me, nudge by murderous nudge, to this discussion. It was that important to her.

I shrugged, turning to Caden. "Did we come here for twenty questions?" I asked him.

He quirked his lips. "To 'have words with the devil' is the purpose you gave me."

"Cute," Morrigan said blandly, trying—and failing—to hide her irritation at being ignored. Then, her expression sharpening with undisguised interest, she dripped poison in my ear. "We share the same fate, Emery. Why not the same father?"

I went cold, despite the brandy warming my belly. "Morrigan." I leaned forward, infusing each of my words with certainty. "You and I are not related."

She waved away my statement. "Of course we are. We've already established our dependence on one another."

I shook my head, setting the empty snifter on the table next to me. "You are wrong," I told her quietly, borrowing Caden's calm energy to punctuate my words with simple confidence.

"You and I are archetype incarnates," Morrigan said, unmoved. "Antagonist and Protagonist, story unfolding before us, but the pages are our lives, Emery." She held up the book she had set to the side. "Who is responsible for plotting the course of our destinies?"

"We are," I answered firmly. "We may be the personifications of characters, but we are *people*."

Morrigan sniffed delicately. "People who are walking through someone else's story." She tapped the cover of the book with polished nails. "We are the children of the Storyteller incarnate. The Narrator. The Author. Fate." She set the book down again. "The label does not matter. The truth remains."

Something stirred in my chest, her poisonous argument gripping my heart with icy fingers. There was a twisted sort of logic to her argument. That made sense; she had spent years—decades, probably —constructing the pieces of this assertion. Morrigan was many terrible, evil things, but she was also intelligent and cunning. This led me to two conclusions: she had either spent all those years creating a labyrinth of lies and half truths to ensnare me in a scheme too obscure for me to identify, or she truly believed she and I belonged to destiny, kin by way of fate. I was not sure which one terrified me more.

The question, as ever, remained the same: what did Morrigan *want*?

I knew she was no less of a threat to me here than she had been in the limousine, gun pointed at my head. So why did I feel so invincible?

It was not her, I realized. It was me. She hadn't changed, become less. I had become *more*.

"Like any incarnate," I said quietly, feeling a current of confidence thrum through me, "we have specialties. But manipulating fate to our design does not mean we are in someone else's story. In fact, it implies the reverse: that we are masters of our own destiny."

Morrigan's dark eyes did not leave mine. Her gaze pierced me. "Except we *don't* control our fates, do we?" She slid her hand between the cushions of her couch. "We are swimming in a river, inexorably drawn by the current, and however we swim, we are pulled ever onward." She withdrew her hand and leveled a .22 at my head. "I could pull this trigger again and again... my choice... and you will"—*bang*—"not"—*bang*—"die!" *Bang.*

The gunfire was *loud*. She nearly shouted each word after she pulled the trigger, but the words sounded far away as my ears rang from the sharp reports. The bullets snapped into Caden's luminescence and sparked, rebuffed, rebounding harmlessly to the floor. Even so, I swallowed, trying to get my pulse under control.

Morrigan placed the gun on the table as casually as she had set the book. Her face was serene, her expression unperturbed, but her chest heaved slightly with emotion. "You see?" she asked pointedly.

"That proves nothing," I said, my voice—thankfully—firm. "Except that I am not foolish enough to come here without protection."

"It doesn't matter that you brought your guard puppy with you. If he weren't here, a different tool would protect you. If you want me to prove it, send him away and we'll try it again."

"I don't think so."

"It doesn't matter. One way or another, fate will not be denied." A haunted look slipped into her eyes before it was quickly extinguished. "Your current protection notwithstanding, I would think you would be just as eager as I to sever that connection."

"Sever it?" I repeated. "You think the Storyteller is our father, and you mean to *kill* him?" I shook my head, disgusted. And unsurprised, which bothered me more. "Is death the only solution you understand, Morrigan?"

Her nostrils flared, the only indication of her anger. "We are nothing but characters in his story. Think of our relation to him as merely metaphorical if it will ease your conscience. Either way, we both desire freedom, Emery. And we can attain it. We can unshackle ourselves from his story and reclaim it as ours." Intensity punched through her veneer of serenity.

Anger and revulsion threatened to overpower me again. That Morrigan honestly believed she knew me, believed we could ever want the same things, burned in my stomach. I felt the heat of it in my face. "This isn't *our* story, Morrigan. It is *mine*. You are my Antagonist, so maybe you feel your existence is meaningless without foiling me." I stood. "But I do not share your sense of fatalism, nor are my achievements dependent upon you." Morrigan sat forward, her mouth opening to stop me, but I cut her off. "I don't need you. I spent the last twenty-some years not even *thinking* about you." It was not entirely true, but the way she stiffened at my words felt savagely satisfying. "We are not kin, and you've wasted twenty-odd years deluding yourself."

Morrigan's countenance was brittle. "Twenty-one years, four months, three reincarnations, and six days. I know the exact *day*, Emery Luple." Her voice quavered with an emotion I couldn't quite place. "And you dare consider our destinies unbound?"

The intensity thrummed between us like a taut rubber band. "I do."

The tension in the air snapped. Morrigan stood, composure falling away to reveal a hatred that crossed the space between us like a living, writhing thing... tinged with a vein of desperation. "Fate will not permit us to walk out on one another. You'll see." Her words followed Caden and me as we left the room. "I will see you learn the truth, Emery. I'll strike you down again, and your despair will sate me for a thousand and one days, exactly." Her voice grew stronger, becoming almost a shriek. "And in that span, I will find our father and, with or without your help, sever my fate from yours."

No response could have pleased me more than the simple action of walking out of her Lair, unhindered and unharmed, leaving Morrigan behind to contemplate her own impotence in my story.

I couldn't help the grin that split my face as I took Caden's hand in mine and put Morrigan behind us.

43

Coming to terms with who you are is a fundamentally human concept. Self-discovery occurs often when we are young—our personalities, attitudes, likes, and dislikes all manifest during childhood—but the real secret is that we never stop growing. What do children, teenagers, adults, and seniors have in common? We're all people. We are in different stages of our lives, different chapters in our stories, but while we live, we never truly stop developing, advancing, progressing.

Becoming.

Incarnates are no different in this regard. Our chapters sometimes change perspectives, but we are still just turning pages. Like humans, our journey is in the reading, not the ending. The best stories don't end when the reading stops.

You may be wondering how I came to terms with my new identity so quickly, how I accepted the fact that I was not the Monster Hunter. In reality, I spent many nights reflecting on this—just ask Caden. He and I replayed the same conversations several times as I questioned my new identity.

But ultimately, it's like changing the title of your story. Important—

monumental, some would argue—but it doesn't change the pages within, the chapters of your life.

If there is one lesson I wish for you to take away from the first installment of my story, it isn't about classifications of incarnates or the difference between Lairs and Sanctums. I just hope you'll share your own story with others. Who knows? Maybe in the retelling, you'll become an incarnate too, someday.

～

A NONSTOP FLIGHT from JFK to Sea-Tac Airport is just over six hours. That's an uncomfortably long time to be crammed in the middle seat. Just this once, though, I didn't mind.

Rachelle sat to my right, her leg free of the cast, watching out the window as we neared the ground. One of Caden's moms had removed it to avoid too many questions at a big hospital; Rachelle hadn't even worn the cast for a week, but her leg was fully healed and bouncing happily for at least two hours of the flight. I know because it shook my seat too.

Caden occupied the space to my left, headphones hanging around his neck now that his things were stowed for landing. We had checked his huge duffel bag filled with his clothes and a few personal belongings, then spent the flight with our fingers entwined.

We took turns selecting movies, all three of our heads bent over Rachelle's tablet—in my lap—as we watched the in-flight entertainment.

I felt like I was bringing Caden home, which was strange. I had spent less time in Seattle this incarnation than I had in New York, but home is more of a feeling than a location. I could still hardly believe Caden had agreed to come with us. It felt like a dream, but his warm hand in mine kept me firmly rooted in reality. Besides, although my backstory memories made me feel like a Seattleite, the truest feeling of home was when we were together.

We had spent a few more days in New York City, wrapping up

loose ends. Rachelle and I spent hours filming and editing our newest video of *There's Always a Loophole*, in part to counter my rapidly depleting bank account but mostly to debunk some of the theories surrounding the Ahedrian murders. The incident was still under investigation, but the confirmed safety of every Rikers Island prisoner helped to discredit some of the story's more fantastical elements. The media reported the tragic deaths of two prison officers and two NYBC News employees: a cameraman and investigative journalist Sabrina Miles. Two days after the incident, a tabloid released a manufactured story that helped to explain the events: Sabrina had garnered the wrong kind of attention from her obsession with the murders and brought the wrath of the killer down on her and Gustav. The killer, however, had not escaped the prison guards and had been quietly detained by the warden of Rikers Island, two valiant guards losing their lives in the conflict. My video piggybacked on several of these hypotheses, further grounding the event. As no new murders occurred in the following days, the Ahedrian murders were mostly laid to rest as New York City residents found the next big thing to talk about.

It wasn't perfect. Although obscured by the storm hammering Manhattan, dozens of witnesses agreed they had seen a "blood-red storm" surrounding the prison island on the night of Sabrina's death. Although some meteorologic experts were able to explain the phenomenon as an unusual but natural event that occasionally occurred during certain types of harsh weather conditions, rumors persisted. Still, as long as Iblis did not reappear in some explosive act of revenge, I didn't foresee any issues with these rumors. The Rikers Island inmates had also apparently fallen victim to a mass hallucination during the storm. Several swore they traveled great distances in the night, only to end up back in their cells the next morning. However, it appeared the oh-so-sensible residents of New York were uninterested in the stories told by those once again behind bars, the truth be damned.

A few days passed, Rachelle and I downgraded hotels to something more affordable, a farewell tribute to Sabrina Miles and Gustav Falkenberg aired, and the Ahedrian murders became yesterday's news.

The death of Zelda Zerona, owner of Madam Zerona's Spirits and Seances for more than forty years, was quietly mentioned in the *New York Times* obituaries. While her body was hastily cremated by her "niece" (who I strongly suspected was Trish, the big softie), we attended a private funeral service for the old woman in a secluded graveyard not far from her shop. While I watched the ceremonial burial of her ashes, I felt a small hand slip into my own. Looking down, I saw the barest outline of Iris, the Ghost. While her childish face was somber, she shared with me a private smile, put her finger over her lips, and vanished. But I felt her hand in mine until the end of the ceremony. I did not see Trish among those who attended the funeral, but as we filed past the small headstone adorned with flowers and cards, I saw an old leather jacket folded neatly beneath some flowers and an unopened pack of cigarettes sitting on top.

As we touched down in Seattle and taxied to the gate, we passed a small private jet. For some reason, that made me think of Morrigan. The Antagonist incarnate. It felt satisfying, somehow, to identify her by nature. As if it somehow caused our relationship to make sense to me. Our confrontation at her manor would hardly be our final one, I knew. But after more than two decades, it felt incredible to have won an exchange with her, instead of just *surviving* one.

I contemplated her most recent plot for the hundredth time, a nugget of doubt creeping into my otherwise happy thoughts. Morrigan's aims concerned me, and despite being privy to her plans, I couldn't quite shake the feeling that I only saw the tip of the iceberg. Her schemes were like the Hydra incarnate: cut off one head and two more would appear. Case in point, her alliance with Sabrina. Somehow, in her experiment with transforming a mortal woman into an incarnate, Morrigan had managed to capture the Yeti, tame the Genie, *and* collect the Vorpal Blade. She had also willingly given them up to a mortal, which caused me no small concern. If she was so quick to surrender those incarnates, what greater treasures and surprises did she have at her disposal?

At least I thought I had determined how she had captured the Yeti—a feat I had once assumed impossible. As the Antagonist, her incarnation was an inversion of my own. If she was working to foil me, coincidences and conveniences would work in her favor. As demonstrated by the map she had poked holes in. Fate, destiny, the story... whatever you wanted to call it, things just *worked* for us within our roles. It raised as many questions as it answered, unfortunately. For example, did intent matter? Morrigan's map had ended up aiding me far more than it hindered me. Was that because it had started me down a road that would eventually lead to my undoing, the very thing the Antagonist desired? Or did it work because she *thought* it would foil me, but I had overcome her trap?

Trish's suggestion about me being a monster hunter during some of my previous incarnations also made sense now. Most monster hunters *were* the protagonists of their stories, so it was likely a fraction of my identity. It made me wonder what other experiences were buried in my immortal mind, unknowable to me until the right moment—or until I aged and the memories returned. It was daunting and thrilling at the same time.

The passengers began to disembark, and we patiently waited our turn. When it came, I was deep in thought about the consequences of being the Protagonist. Caden leaned in and said, "Are you coming, my beamish boy?" Rachelle rolled her eyes at our new nickname and gave me a little push to get me moving. I grabbed my bags and followed Caden down the narrow aisle. We had tested the mirrors every morning to ensure the Vorpal Blade remained safely tucked away in its looking-glass Sanctum. So far, the only reprise of "Jabberwocky" was Caden's new nickname for me.

We picked our way through the crowds to Baggage Claim. Rachelle kept pacing around us, happy to stretch her legs crutch-free. Caden stood next to me, both of us equally happy enjoying each other's proximity. We snagged his three bags from the carousel—the entirety of Caden's personal effects. The bag I shouldered was especially heavy, as it contained several chunks of metal he was planning on using to fashion the Headless Horseman's new head.

"You could have gotten these materials around here," I complained as I hefted it.

Caden grinned at me. "Nah," he said, "it needs to be authentically New York." Even though he had a year to complete the task, he planned to finish the head before his next trip. And he'd promised his moms that he'd visit in the summer.

We passed through the sliding doors leading out to the Arrivals curve. The curb was thronged with people, but I picked out Mom right away. She saw us at the same time and gave a wave, her face lighting up.

I jogged forward and wrapped her in a bear hug. "Welcome home, sweet pea," she murmured into my chest. It wasn't my Sanctum, but embracing her was a different kind of home.

I released her, and she gave Rachelle a quick hug, too.

I pulled Caden forward by the hand. "Mom," I said, "this is Caden." I blushed. "My boyfriend."

The Guardian Angel shuffled forward with a radiant smile, probably unaware of the soft light he shed. "Nice to meet you."

Mom wrapped him in a hug just as fierce, the two of them sharing quiet words. I loaded up her car with our bags, Rachelle jumping in the front passenger seat so Caden and I could sit together in the back. As Mom came around the car, she mouthed, "He's cute!" I flushed again, my silly smile still stretching my face as I slid into the back seat.

We told Mom stories from New York—all of them true, but very few related to the purpose of our visit—as she drove us home. I spoke the least, for once, content to listen to Rachelle, Caden, and Mom happily chat around me.

We arrived at Rachelle's house. She had a spare room, and since my apartment-slash-office was still out of commission, I would need to spend the next few days (or weeks, depending on my luck) at

Mom's. The three of us had decided it would be best for Caden to stay with Rachelle for the time being.

I helped them carry their belongings inside, Rachelle excitedly showing Caden his new room. It was small, which was the reason she'd never entertained the idea of a roommate before, but he said it was more than enough for him. I wanted to stay and help him unpack and settle in, but Caden gently encouraged me to spend the evening with my mom.

"Besides," he said, "I need to take stock of the kitchen. I want to make a special thank-you dinner for Rachelle."

I pulled him close. "I'll need to cook one of those special dinners for you, too," I said. "For coming all the way to Seattle with me."

"You can cook?"

I scoffed. "I can learn." In truth, I was fairly sure I'd been a chef in a previous incarnation.

Caden laughed softly. The late afternoon light filtered through the window and shimmered in his gold hair. "You were right when you said I never truly belonged until the day you came into my life, but you were wrong about the reason why, Emery." His seafoam eyes sparkled. "It wasn't because I'm the Guardian Angel." He tilted my head down and kissed me, his soft mouth molding to mine. When we parted, he said breathlessly, "it was because of you."

His words swelled my heart: the Protagonist and his Guardian Angel. I held him a little longer, then bid him goodnight.

I gave Rachelle a hug in the kitchen and thanked her again for letting Caden stay with her. She shooed me out the door when I let it slip he was going to make her dinner.

Mom and I got in the car to drive home, and she turned to me, a sly smile spreading over her features. "Now that it's just us, tell me *everything.*"

I laughed self-consciously but spoke about Caden the whole way home.

∽

MY NAME IS EMERY LUPLE, and I am the Protagonist incarnate. The main character. The best part about being an incarnate is the life. Multiple lives. I've had quite a few of them at this point. Sometimes when myths and legends come to life, it falls to me to care for them.

Who am I? What am I?

You think you have me figured out? This is not the end of my story.

ACKNOWLEDGMENTS

Starting a new adventure is always scary. I'm immensely grateful to everyone who helped me in this journey. Without the love, support, and technical skills of the following people, Emery never would have incarnated in the first place.

First, I would like to thank my husband, James, for his unending love and support. For listening to every chapter time and again, often the very second I finished writing it. You are my Muse incarnate. And thank you for celebrating every step of the journey along the way—we're in this together, which is my favorite place to be!

Thank you, Mom and Dad (sorry for Emery's whole "never has a dad" complex; it is plot relevant, I swear!). Thanks for nurturing my imagination while I was growing up, reading Dr. Seuss to me every night as a kid, and always being there for me. Your outpouring of support and love continues to mean the world to me.

To my #1 bro, Tyler, thanks for always pushing me—sometimes forcefully—to write. It took twenty years, but I finally wrote a novel! For all you readers still reading, if/when the Mermaid incarnate makes an appearance, you will have my brother to thank!

Also, I'd like to say a special thank-you to Todd Arntson, my best friend since childhood. I don't know anyone more devoted to ensuring this novel succeeded than you. Thank you for the encouragement, feedback, and countless reads of the manuscript in its various stages.

Speaking of multiple reads and manuscripts, I'd like to give a monumental thank-you to my editor, Alicia Z. Ramos. I could write an entire page singing your praises, but then you'd likely edit it down to a paragraph anyway, and it would be vastly improved to boot. I'm pretty sure you're some sort of wizard, because what you did to my manuscript was nothing short of magic. Thank you for pushing me to think about things I'd never considered before—mostly on the page, but I'm not going to lie: a little bit in life, too! Thank you for all your hard work, for your guidance and meticulous attention to detail, for so many hours spent getting to know Emery and the crew, and for making my work into something I'm incredibly proud of.

Thank you to Jeff Brown for the beautiful cover design. Jeff is incredibly talented and listened to all of my notes, then made my vision come to life in a way that looks better than it did even in my imagination!

In addition to the above friends and family, I'd like to thank my alpha readers Michelle Sasso, Linnea Mulvaney, Katie McDaniel, Sunshine Dunning, and Peter Brown for reading my first draft. It has come quite a long way since then, in part because of your feedback. Thank you to my proofreaders, too: Kevin Nolan, Todd Flatland, Heather Conti, Nick Rood, Teresa Schuelke, Terry Provonsha, and my family, the Wilson-Chang-Cordero-Steward-Butters clan—Nancy, Pop, Ang, Maddie, Cody, Steve, Colleen, and Lucy. I love you all!

A very special thank-you to Henry Behrens, Madeline and Cody Cordero, and Jamie Brooks for your help in articulating Emery's gender identity and expression journey in a way that celebrates everyone. #transpeoplecanhuntmonsterstoo! I hope I made you proud. Thank you so much.

That just about wraps it up! Oh, and a special thank-you to you, too, Class. Thank you for reading and supporting my story. Your contribution keeps my dreams alive. I can't wait to set out on the next adventure with you.

ABOUT THE AUTHOR

Justin Schuelke

I'm a Washingtonian living in the greater Seattle area with my husband, James, and our cat, Vincent. I graduated from the University of Washington with a degree in—wait for it—English. When I am not writing, I enjoy games of all kinds: board games, roleplaying games, video games, computer games, phone games... you name it, I'll play it!

Learn more about me at my website: https://jtschuelke. wixsite.com/incarnate.

Please subscribe to my mailing list for exclusive content, limited promotions, and more!

Made in the USA
Coppell, TX
22 December 2020